RIPTIDES
OF
LOVE

PART 1

By: Trish Collins

~ ~ ~ ~ ~ ~ ~ ~ ~ ~

Lucky Series

Lucky Day - Book 1

Lucky Charm - Book 2

Lucky Break - Book 3

Lucky Rescue - Book 4

Lucky Shot – Book 5

Lucky Honeymoon - Book 6

Lucky Me - Book 7

Lucky Number - Book 8

Lucky Guy - Book 9

Lucky Couple - Book 10

Lucky Bet - Book 11

Lucky O'Shea - Book 12

Jacobs Series

Riptides of Love

Parts 1 & 2

Loves Dangerous

Undercurrents

Parts 1 & 2

Breaking Waves of Love

Parts 1 & 2

Love's Storm Surge

Parts 1 & 2

Impact Zone of Love

Parts 1 & 2

Love's Sunset - tba

Daphne's Escape - TBA

Daphne's Revenge - TBA

Daphne's Oasis- TBA

Riptides
Of
Love

Book 1 - Part 1

A Jacobs Novel

~~~~~~~

Trish Collins

Riptides of Love Part 1 is a work of fiction. All of the characters, organizations, and incidents portrayed in this novel are either products of the author's imagination or used fictitiously. Any resemblance to actual persons, living or dead, business establishments, events, or locals is purely coincidental.

Copyright © 2016 by Trish Collins

ISBN-13: 978-0692793497

~ 1 ~

Ben Jacobs was attempting to finish the inventory. He had been working on it all week. Ben despised this part of owning a surf shop, but he knew that if he left it for anyone else, it would be done half-assed. He was the dependable and responsible one. The one that made sure the payroll was in, so everyone got their paychecks. He was the one who kept the store running behind the scenes. Ben was the oldest of three children, and at thirty-five, he took his responsibilities seriously. After his dad's death, Ben and his siblings took over managing the surf shop. Ben had always taken care of his brother and sister as they grew up. If either of them got into trouble, Ben was the one to get them out because he was the one everyone went to when a conflict occurred. He was trustworthy with all of their secrets.

"I have to be the one to make sure we have everything on this list in the store, and it's where it belongs," he said to himself as he moved the merchandise to where it belonged.

Ben thought about how Jeff, his brother and one-third owner of the shop, was out on a date. He always seemed to have a date or something more important to do instead of doing any kind of real work at the shop. Jeff was the partner who made an appearance when he wanted and took off when it suited him. He was irresponsible, easygoing, and didn't take anything too seriously. Jeff never had to because Ben always did. However, Jeff was excellent with the customers and could persuade anyone who came in to look at a surfboard to buy one. He was great with any and all of the females, and when they came in to try on a swimsuit, they wanted to know what he thought. They purchased it if he liked it, and he almost always adored the suit. It was more Jeff and Owen, their younger employee, which moved the merchandise. They just had that cool dude surfer look going for them, and they played the part well. It was something Ben wasn't sure he could pull off anymore, his appearance still that of a surfer, but he thought he was getting a little too old to be acting as if hanging at the beach, and surfing was the most important thing in life.

"I could have asked Mom to help, but then I would have to hear all about how I'm not getting any younger, that I'm not married with a bunch of kids," he said to himself, shaking his head. He knew his mother would lay the guilt trip on him as she always did about how she wanted him married with some grandkids, and since he was the oldest, it was his duty to be first.

Ben hadn't found the right woman, anyone he felt passionate about. His mother made it known that it was one more of his responsibilities, even though all of her children were of age to get married. Ben's mom didn't hold out much hope for Jeff, much less have kids. He never stayed with any girl long enough to learn their names, and as far as Dannie, his sister wasn't ready to make any commitments either. She was younger and having too much fun.

"Are you talking to yourself again?" A voice asked from the front of the store, and Ben looked up from the list in his hand and saw his young employee, Owen Fisher. Ben must have been so deep in thought that he hadn't heard the bell jingle on the door.

"I was just trying to finish up inventory I've been working on all week, and since no one is volunteering to help, I have to have a conversation with myself," talking to Owen over his shoulder. "Are you in here tonight because you have nothing better to do and want to help me, your great employer, on your night off?"

"Well, I would help," Owen moved toward the storage room.

"But?" Ben knew Owen wasn't there to help. He knew he had other plans.

"Yeah, but I have a date," Owen said with a goofy grin.

"Everyone has a date or something else to do that's more important," Ben needed to get a life.

"I have some time before I have to pick her up, so I can help." Ben wouldn't make Owen stay.

"Nah, that's okay. I'm almost done anyway, so what did you need?" Owen blushed as he looked away from Ben. "So," Ben wasn't sure what Owen wanted from the back storage room.

"So, I came in to get stuff from the back, the blanket, and the basket." Owen wanted to grab the stuff and go before Ben talked to him about being responsible and mature.

"Oh, I see, so you're going down to the beach," Ben was observing Owen's behavior, examining him a little closer now.

Owen's face got a little red, and Ben knew what that meant. It was code for sex on the beach. Ben looked Owen in the eye and said, "You have what you need to protect yourself, right?"

Owen didn't want to have this talk with Ben now, but he knew he was only looking out for him, so he said, "Yeah, I have everything I need, although not sure if I'll need it, but yeah, sure, I got it."

"Okay, then go have fun on your date, and don't get caught." Ben smiled at Owen.

"You know it. Hey, when's the last time you had a date?" Owen asked since Ben was no longer scrutinizing him.

"I have better things to do with my time," Ben laughed.

"Yeah, like what, inventory?" Owen shook his head at Ben as he went to get the basket and blanket out of the back room.

"I haven't found anybody that I want to take out on a date, okay," Ben said as he thought of how nice it would be to have someone and knew as the words came out of his mouth that it was lame but true. Even though many were interested, there hadn't been a woman to pique his interest in a very long time. Owning a surf shop attracted many it was one of the benefits, but he couldn't just take what they offered freely, not as Jeff did. That wasn't Ben's style because he needed more.

Maybe he was getting too mature and responsible for his own good. Ben was just considering how he needed to get out more when Owen pulled him out of his pity party.

"I know someone you can ask out. She's new in town," Owen said with a big smirk.

"Oh yeah, I'm not sure you're the one to pick a woman for me." Ben wasn't sure if he could choose someone either. "She'd have to be older than twenty-five," he said with a laugh.

"Oh, she is older, well not that old, you know, like your age, maybe younger. She came in earlier today when you were in your office. Her name is Liz. She wanted some surfing info. I think she said she's writing a book or something like that."

"And why should I consider asking her out?" Ben wasn't sure he wanted to know.

"Because she's hot. You do remember what a hot chick looks like, right?" That got Ben's attention.

"Oh, aren't you hilarious, and how would you know what is hot on an older chick?" Owen just smiled at Ben.

"Hey, just because she is too old for me doesn't mean I can't see what's in front of me."

Ben thought that maybe he should find out a little more about this older, hot-as-hell chick. "Okay, I'll bite. What does she look like?" Ben wondered just how old this older woman was.

Owen gave it some thought, and after a minute or two, he said, "She has fiery red wavy hair that goes to her shoulders and the greenest eyes you've ever seen. Her body is to die for, and even I could see how hot she was, big boobs, a small waist, and a sweet ass."

"Well, you seemed to get a really good look at all her assets. Did you get her age?" Ben shook his head, "So glad we pay you to keep extremely good track of all the customers." Ben was intrigued by the description of the woman. A redhead, the thought was appealing.

"Well, the hot ones, anyway. I always keep my eyes open," Owen was starting to walk away.

Ben started laughing and wanted to change the subject, "Hey, are you still going to be able to surf in the morning after your exhausting date tonight? The waves are going to be big, so I hear. I'm not sure if Jeff is going to grace us with his presence. I'm sure it'll depend on how late of a night he has. You know we'll hear all about it because he'll have no problem rubbing it in," Owen stopped walking and turned toward Ben.

"I'm not planning to be out that late. I'll be there at the crack of dawn," Owen said as he made a face at Ben. "I'm not old like you and Jeff. I can stay up all night and still be out there surfing for hours and blow you two away."

"You really do think you're a comedian? Hey, don't quit your day job. Oh yeah, you work for me." Ben called as Owen started to head for the door again.

"Maybe you need to go on that date with the redhead, then you can brag about how late your night was and give Jeff a run for his money," Owen said as he looked back at Ben.

Ben wasn't sure he could ever give Jeff any real competition because Jeff loved all females. Ben wanted to experience something with the person he was spending time with because, for him, it was quality, not quantity. However, quality hadn't come so easy for Ben, not lately, anyway. When he was younger, he thought he would end up married to Jenny, his high school sweetheart, and they would start a family together. However, she went off to college, met someone else, and wanted a career, not a surf shop in California. Ben and his brother Jeff had to stay behind to run the shop instead of going to college. Dannie didn't hang around for long after she got out of college, either. She wanted a life that didn't have anything to do with surfing, and now it was just Jeff, their mom, and him. Mom helped with the books and some of the office work, but most of the time, she was there to keep track of her boys and interfere in their lives. She wanted to make sure that she was right in the center of their lives.

"So, hello, are you going to ask her out or not? If you want some help, I can help you with some lines guaranteed to get you some action." Owen had a half smile on his face, knowing Ben's reaction.

"I don't know, maybe if she comes back in and is as hot as you say. I just might, you never know." Ben didn't want to give Owen the satisfaction of knowing he was interested.

"Ok, if you say so, because I just happen to know she's coming tomorrow afternoon because I'm going to teach her all about the surfboards. I guess you can kinda say I already have a date with her." Owen paused, then added, "Unless you want to do it."

"I think you need to get going on that date you have, and I need to finish up here so I can get some sleep if I'm going to keep up with you tomorrow," Ben blew out a breath.

When Ben woke the next morning, thoughts of getting to the beach to do some surfing came to mind. He wondered what the day ahead would bring. Would the waves be as challenging as the weather conditions were hinting, they might be? As Ben got his coffee going, he sat at the breakfast bar in his kitchen and started to think about what Owen had said about the redhead. He thought of all the women he'd socialized with in the last couple of years. He knew that none of them suited him, not that he had a commitment problem. The precise one just hadn't come along, at least, that's what he'd been telling himself.

Ben half put on his wetsuit, got his board, and set out for the beach. When he got to the spot where they enjoyed surfing, he found Owen waiting for him. Ben knew he was in for it because Owen would give him shit for being late. The kid seemed to have more energy than anyone he knew. Oh, to be young again, he thought as he leisurely walked toward him.

Owen was sitting on the beach, looking out at the waves. "It's about damn time you got here. I've been waiting thirty minutes for you."

"Yeah, yeah, so I'm old and slow. Give me a break," Ben blew out a breath.

Owen laughed and said, "Well, at least you know it, but I'm not giving you any breaks."

"Thanks, you're such a great kid, so remind me to dock your pay this week," Ben said jokingly. Now Ben was smiling as Owen stuck his tongue out at him.

"What, are you two now?" Ben grinned at Owen.

Ben sat beside Owen and asked, "How was your date?"

"It was ok." Owen looked out over the water even though it was still dark.

"Just ok, what? No bragging, not even about how late you were out?"

"I don't kiss and tell, you're going to have to get your own girl, or you can hear all about Jeff's social life if he shows up," Owen turned to look at Ben.

"Since when, you always have something to boast about. You're Jeff's best competition. I think sometimes he is a bad influence on you." Ben could see so much of Jeff in Owens's intentions toward his girlfriends.

"What am I responsible for now?" a voice came from behind as Jeff walked up.

"You're being a bad influence on Owen." Ben stood, pulled his wetsuit the rest of the way up, and grabbed his board.

"Hey, it's not my fault if he is a fast learner and that you have no knowledge to share with him on the subject. It's not like he's going around breaking hearts all over town. He's a decent kid."

"I didn't say he wasn't a great kid. He just has a different girl all the time, like someone else I know."

"Okay, just because you're not getting any doesn't mean the rest of us have to suffer. I, on the other hand, had a great time last night," Jeff said with a big lopsided smile.

"Hey, are you girls going to surf, or are you going to argue all day? The waves are waiting." As Owen got up and ran for the water, he called over his shoulder, "Are you coming, or are you too old and feeble?"

That got both Ben and Jeff's attention, "I think we should drown him and say a shark got him or cut his ripcord and make him have to swim in," Jeff said.

"Yeah, or we can make him work the next four weekends in a row," Ben replied.

"Boy, hit him where it hurts. Remind me not to piss you off," Jeff said as they paddled out.

The sun was coming up, and it was a beautiful sunrise. It was supposed to be a gorgeous day, and the waves were great. What more could anyone want? Ben thought while sitting on his board, waiting for the next wave, and contemplating the redhead, yet again. If she was as hot as Owen said, maybe he might actually get laid and break his very long dry spell. He knew he couldn't have meaningless sex because he wasn't about putting his dick in someone that was just a body and no soul. He was pulled from his thoughts when Jeff paddled by and caught a wave to the shore.

"I'm here to surf, not to feel sorry for myself. I just need to get it together," he said to himself.

"Talking to yourself again; maybe you are getting old. Thirty-five, and you're starting to lose it." Ben hadn't realized that Owen had paddled up next to him. "I thought you were here to surf, clear your mind, and enjoy the waves," Owen said.

"Yeah, I am. I'll get the next one," Ben paddled hard to catch the next wave.

Owen laughed, shook his head, as he said, "I don't want to end up like him talking to myself."

Ben caught the next few big waves, challenging Mother Nature and trying not to consider his life or the lack of one. After a couple good hours of surfing, things would look better, it always did. It was relaxing and mind-cleansing. It was just what Ben needed to get away from everything.

Ben listened as Owen expressed to Jeff how his ride was exceptionally better, and his skill surpassed and was superior to Jeff's. The way the banter flew back and forth, you would think the three of them were brothers. Owen was like a little brother in so many ways. He had been working for them for so long and was a part of the family. Ben could remember when Owen had gone through the surfing clinic when he was just thirteen. He was such a natural and got bit by the surfing bug. Owen started hanging around the shop and asking questions, and before they knew it, he was very knowledgeable with the surfboards. He was almost as knowledgeable as Jeff was.

When Owen was fifteen, he asked if he could work at the shop, and since he was already selling boards by talking with whoever would listen to him, it was a no brainier, and work kept him out of trouble. His home life wasn't the best, only having his mother. Before he started surfing and hanging around the shop, his mom had said he was a handful, but Owen had come a long way. He was going to community college in the fall, and Ben felt pride to know that they had some influence over how Owen conducted himself.

He was very proud of Owen because he really was turning into a very outstanding young adult. Ben thought about how he would do just about anything for him, even paying Owen's college tuition. He wanted him to have something he didn't get to have.

~ ~ ~ ~ ~ ~

Liz McGreary lay in the largest bed she had ever seen. The bed was one of those big four-poster beds with sheer white curtains that went all the way to the floor. It was four A.M., and she looked up at the vaulted ceiling, wondering what she was doing there. As a romance writer, she never got much sleep, as it was always when she started to write a new book, all those ideas running around in her head. However, this time it wasn't just the new book to keep her from her restful slumber. Just the fact that she was here all alone and her daughter Paige was on the other side of the country. She hadn't expected to feel so alone in this huge house, but she was used to always having Paige with her because it had been just the two of them for so long.

When Paige went into third grade, Liz started home-schooling her so that when she had to go out of town for book signings or go to meetings with her agent, she would just bring Paige with her. Paige would go off with friends and sometimes spend the night away. She even went on a few vacations with friends, but this was not the same empty feeling. Somehow, it felt so much more permanent. Liz knew she would have to deal with the loneliness, but she hadn't expected that it would feel similar to how she felt when her husband Michael died ten years ago. The loneliness was overwhelming. She told herself Paige was alive, just not with her every day.

Paige wasn't gone for good, but she had grown up and was starting her own life, and all Liz had to do was pick up the phone to talk to her. Liz overcame the emotional distress of her husband's death because she had to because she had to take care of her daughter. Paige became Liz's whole life, and everything revolved around what Paige wanted and needed.

Liz's daughter was going to come with her, spending the last summer with her before heading off to college in August, but Paige got an exceptionally good offer for an internship. This internship could land her a great job after graduation. So, as much as Liz wanted to try to accept the fact that Paige was growing up and had turned eighteen, Liz couldn't help feeling very alone. She knew she would have to overcome the empty nest feelings that would come when Paige left for school, but she didn't think she'd be working through them so soon. She thought she'd have this month with her in California, having fun on the beach while she did research for the new book.

Liz knew she wouldn't get any more sleep, so she threw off the covers and headed to the kitchen to start a pot of coffee. As the smell filtered through the air, the cobwebs from lack of sleep in Liz's head cleared. She sat on one of the brass bar stools at the breakfast nook, grabbed her pad from her purse, and started to write down some of the questions she wanted to ask the kid from the surf shop today. She needed to get her mind back on work and off missing Paige. She needed to learn all that she could while she was here. She had an appointment this afternoon to learn about the surfboards with the young man she had met yesterday. Liz thought about how cute the young man was and how Paige would be sorry that she didn't come after all. Owen was what he said his name was, and he seemed very nice and helpful.

"Well, I will just have to send a picture to Paige of Owen to rub it in," she said to herself.

After completing her list of questions for Owen and while finishing her first cup of coffee, Liz contemplated what she would do with her life and all her free time, time that she had always devoted to Paige. What was in the future for her now that her daughter was growing up and wouldn't need her so much anymore? After Michael's death, Liz had to be the breadwinner. She was a stay-at-home mom at the time and needed to figure out how to support herself and a child. Michael had a sizable life insurance policy, but Liz knew it wouldn't last forever. She had gone to night classes at the community college and got her English degree. Liz had always loved to write, so she tried writing while she was at home taking care of her daughter. As it turned out, she had done very well, and it worked out for both of them. Liz worked from home and was there for Paige. It was a struggle, in the beginning, to get her first books published, but once she found a good agent, things went well.

"Well, I made a life for myself before, and I guess I have no other choice. I'll have to do it again." Liz said to herself. She got up to pour herself another cup of coffee. "I need to take my coffee out to that huge deck and enjoy the sunrise."

Liz went through the large French doors to sit on one of the big lounge chairs with the cushions that were so soft and thick. She wrapped herself up in the blanket that was sitting on the back of the chair. It was chilly this time of morning. It was still a little dark, but the sun would be up soon. Liz could hear the waves crashing on the beach and smelled the salt in the air.

"Man, the waves sound so rough out there, but the air is so clean and refreshing," Liz said to herself as she took a big breath of the salty air and tried to relax.

"I have to stop talking to myself, or someone will think I'm going crazy. I'll be that lonely old lady all the kids talk about." Liz laughed at herself and closed her eyes to enjoy the sounds of being at the beach. As she lay there, she could hear people talking and laughing. Liz got up to check to see if it was people walking or running on the beach. She looked over the railing of the deck and squinted to see. She could barely see them, but there were surfers out there. *Oh, God, no way, there are people out there in the water. You could barely see.* "Are they crazy?"

Liz threw off the blanket and went back inside to her bedroom to change out of her nightshirt and shorts, grabbing a pair of jeans and a big sweatshirt. Liz pulled her top and jeans on as fast as she could and ran into the bathroom, washed her face, pulled her hair into a ponytail, and brushed her teeth. She went back into the kitchen to grab her notebook with her questions on it and her cell phone as she was heading out the door. If the crazy surfers don't kill themselves, then she wouldn't have to call 911. She could always try to ask them some questions.

Liz walked down the old, weathered staircase that led to the beach. As the sun was coming up, she could see that there were three guys out there. She walked to the part of the beach where the surfers were and sat down, getting comfortable. She watched everything they were doing out there with wonder and appreciation. It surprised her their commitment to capturing the massive waves. The turbulence of Mother Nature filled her with anxiety and anticipation, and she wondered whether they'd stay on top of their boards. At times, it was beautiful and physically passionate the way their muscles moved. Some rides were disappointing, but she found their single-minded determination impressive. It was unbelievably entertaining to see the skill they mastered, but at the same time, she was very aware of the danger. She could hear them yelling to each other after one had ridden a wave. They looked like they were having so much fun out there. But it still was crazy to want to stand on a board that you had to fight to stay on just for the thrill of it.

"I can't see how risking my life to stand on a board and ride a wave is worth it, as much as it may be fun, and the waves are so enormous that it just wouldn't be amusing to me, it would be insane. It wouldn't be worth my life. It must be the mother in me," she said quietly to herself.

Liz watched them take wave after wave, and it was cool to watch how they moved their body this way and that to stay on the board. There were a few bad wipe outs that made her grab her phone and hold her breath until a head popped back out of the water. They laughed at each other and yelled out how cool they thought the ride was. As Liz watched, she could see they were wearing wetsuits.

"I guess the water is cold this time of the morning. I wonder what they wear under their wetsuits."

That got Liz thinking oh yeah, what would it be like to watch them come out of the water and strip the wetsuit off right in front of her? The thought got Liz all hot, and she realized it could be a scene in her book, so she pulled her pad out and wrote it down. He would be tall and have broad shoulders with bulging muscles. Liz was writing on her pad exactly how she saw her surfer. He'd have long dark wavy hair, almost untamed looking, with dark eyes and a defined jaw line. Yeah, he was sounding good, really good. Liz could feel the tingle start down in between her legs.

"Okay, stop that, no one is going to come out of the water and strip for you. What are you thinking?" She laughed at herself when someone calling her name pulled her out of her fantasy. She looked up to see one of the surfers coming out of the water and heading her way. "Who can that be? I don't know anyone here," she said.

As the surfer got closer, she recognized the young blonde man who was coming up the beach. "Hey Liz, I thought that was you," Owen was smiling at her.

"Oh, Owen, I didn't know that was you out there. Are you crazy?"

Owen started to laugh, "Why do you say that?"

"Oh, I don't know, maybe because it looked like you were going to get killed out there. I had my phone ready a couple of times just in case I had to dial 911," Liz looked like a concerned mother.

"Are you staying around here?" Owen was looking over his shoulder at the other surfers. As she was talking to Owen, the other two guys were starting to come out of the water, and Owen waved to them to come over.

"Yeah, I'm staying right there," as Liz pointed to the house she was renting. "Are they your friends?" nodding her head in the direction of the other guys.

"Well, sort of, yeah, they are friends, but mostly they are my bosses they own the surf shop."

"Oh, okay"

"Hey Ben, come here. I want you to meet someone," Owen yelled over his shoulder.

As Liz watched two very large men walk over to them, she thought to herself oh God, here were two very big, tall, and hot guys standing in front of her.

"Ben, this is the lady I was telling you about last night, the one that is writing the book and wants my help," Owen grinned at Ben.

Ben's eyes stared down at her, and she couldn't help feeling very small. As she looked up at the two men, all she could think of was how strong and muscular they looked in their wetsuits. The thought of her surfer for the book came to life right before her eyes.

"Ben, Jeff, this is Liz. She's here doing research on surfing."

Liz stood wiping her butt, and she still didn't come up to their shoulders. She reached out to shake Jeff's hand and couldn't help but notice his golden-brown eyes and a great smile. Liz thought I bet that the girls just love him. He had light brown hair that was a little shaggy with that sun-kissed look to it from being outside.

"Nice to meet you," Liz noticed Jeff's hand was cold from the water.

When Liz turned to face Ben, she got this funny sensation inside. Here was the surfer she just described in her note pad. When she looked up into Ben's eyes, his very dark eyes, and reached out to shake his hand, something happened to her because she couldn't speak. A shock ran up her arm when his huge hand touched hers. She pulled back fast as if he had burned her. Liz's eyes widened as she stared at her hand. She was trying to figure out what just happened to her. She has never had that reaction to anyone before.

Oh my God, I need to breathe because I don't want to look as if I'm a high school girl trying to talk to the best-looking boy in school. Yet she knew that's exactly how she looked, that deer caught in the headlights look. Ben looked at her with his deep dark chocolate brown eyes, oh, and his dark hair.

"So," Ben said because she didn't say anything. "I hear you're coming in this afternoon to pick Owen's little brain, and I sense that shouldn't take too long. Maybe I could take you for lunch and show you around a bit." Ben couldn't help himself. He had to get to know her. As he looked deep into the most beautiful green eyes he had ever seen, he knew he had to touch her again. Would he feel that surge? He could feel the lust, undeniable chemistry between them.

"Oh, okay," Liz said so quietly. Ben almost missed it.

Liz was thinking, I'm a well-educated woman and a writer, and the best I could come up with was, "Oh okay," how weak. I have a bigger vocabulary than that. I could have said I'd love to, or that would really be nice. After a long-unspoken moment, the uncomfortableness stretched out.

Jeff looked at Liz and then to his brother. They were both staring at each other. "Well, we have to get back to open the store soon, it was nice to meet you, Liz, and when you get bored with my brother, you can come see me, and I'll show you the happening nightlife," Jeff said with one of those killer smiles.

Liz looked away from Ben to see Jeff's smile, the one she was sure he gave all the girls. Ben gave Jeff a big shove that almost knocked him off his feet. Then when Jeff recovered, he went after Ben. They started wrestling right there on the beach. Liz looked on, stunned at what was taking place. They looked more like two boys having a playground fight rather than two very large grown men.

Liz must have been frowning because when Owen looked at her, he said, "Oh, don't mind them. They're just idiots. I think maybe you should just skip going out with either one of them and stay with the mature one, and that would be me," Owen smiled.

As Liz looked at Owen, she could see he was learning some of those lady killer tricks. Oh, how that great smile could melt a young girl's heart. Maybe it was a good thing Paige hadn't come. Liz could see how Paige would fall hard for Owen because how could any girl not. He was tall and tan with his long wavy blonde hair and a nice young man's body.

Owen yelled, "Okay girls, we have to go to work. We have a surf shop to open." That pulled Liz out of her thoughts about Owen and Paige. She looked back toward Ben as they grabbed their surfboards and started to walk away. Ben turned as if he knew she was watching him and said, "See you later, Liz."

"Didn't I tell you she was hot?" Owen punched Ben in the arm.

As they left, Liz could hear Ben tell Jeff there was no way in hell he would let his brother date her. Liz stood there for a few minutes to get her bearings. She thought about how Ben's touch affected her. She had never felt anything like it, not even with her husband, and she wasn't sure what to make of it. Liz could feel the sensation of her breasts tightening, and her whole body was tingling on alert. Ben's sensual mouth tempted her with his grin. He had a toe-curling, totally hot body that her best fantasies couldn't match. The arousal hammered through her veins. How would it feel to have him hold and kiss her? All this anticipation and lust-induced excitement was overpowering her. She looked out over the water to try to breathe and calm her emotions.

"I just need to get back to work on my book, I can use all this sexual frustration for my characters, and it will make the erotic relationship between them more real. It's great when you're the one controlling fate when it's all fiction."

Liz decided to take a walk on the beach, there were no other people walking. She could use the exercise and the fresh air. The water was cold, so she walked where the waves had made the sand hard but not where it could get her wet. Liz thought it would be nice to walk every morning. Did Ben surf every morning? She started to consider what could be happening to her with Ben. She was going to have lunch with him, not sure how she would pull that one off, considering she couldn't even come up with a few words to say on the beach with other people around. She just stood there staring at him. What was she going to do when they were alone? Liz didn't have the smooth moves or the wit when it came to men, and when the man looked like Ben, there was no telling what would happen.

Liz decided to head back to the house because a nice hot shower sounded good. She was getting cold, and she hadn't realized it because she was so overheated trying to talk to Ben. How could she feel so hot on the inside yet be cold? Her fingers felt like ice, "Just what the hell is wrong with me? I don't have trouble talking to men, and I don't get all hot and bothered over them, either. But Ben, I just don't know what I'm doing or how to act around him."

Liz tried breathing, but she had to stop walking as she bent over, putting her hands on her knees, attempting to catch her breath while trying to avoid having an anxiety attack. The stress was getting to her; it must have something to do with Paige going off to college and the lack of sleep. Liz had forgotten all about the situation with Paige for a moment. Wow, she didn't think anything could make her forget that.

~ 2 ~

While Liz went up the stairs to the house she was renting, she just couldn't stop replaying what happened on the beach. Whoa, what exactly transpired down there? What was with the way she stared at Ben as if she couldn't get her fill? Could she really be looking forward to going to lunch with a man she didn't even know?

"I need to just stop because I'm not looking for any love affair, I'm here for research, and then I have to go home and send my only child off to school," she was talking to herself again.

Liz got into the shower that was big enough for three people to stand in easily. The hot water ran over her body, warming her skin as her tight muscles loosened, and she began to relax. She put her hands on the shower wall, closed her eyes, and started to think again. What if Ben had come out of the water and started to pull off his wetsuit. How hot was that? She let her mind go; Ben was so big, his shoulders were broad, and would he have chest hair? Would it go all the way down to his….? Oh God, I bet his legs were all tight hard muscle.

Liz's hands moved over her body, caressing her breasts, squeezing them together. Her breasts tightened and tingled with the thought of Ben touching her. She felt her engorged nipples. Liz pinched and pulled them hard, making her become aroused. She could feel it wouldn't take much with her fantasies of Ben. She reached down between her thighs, slipped her fingers into her sex, and found her clit, circling her finger hard on the nub, thinking about Ben kissing her, how his tongue would intertwine with hers, his mouth on her breasts sucking her nipples deep. Liz started shaking with the overwhelming sensation as her muscles clinched. Her orgasm hit powerfully. Oh yeah, that's what she needed to take the edge off.

Liz opened her eyes, "What if I didn't have a love affair, just some great sex?" She asked herself. "I could really use some downright hot sex. How long had it been? Do I even remember what it feels like to actually have sex?" Liz couldn't remember the last time she had sex with someone other than herself, and that didn't count.

"Well, I'm not really sure I can have an affair," she said to herself. "He may not want to have sex with you either; he might be a nice guy that wants to show you around town like he said." Liz started to feel insecure and was now talking herself right out of wanting to see if she'd go through with having sex. Even as she thought this, she knew it would never happen. That was crazy because she just met him, but deep down inside, she hoped he wanted more. Could she let herself get involved with a man again after Michael? She closed her eyes as Ben came to mind, remembering how his touch sent a shock through her. It had to mean something.

"I wonder if he felt it too, or was it just me? It's been so long since a man had made me feel anything, but his touch made everything tingle right down to my who-ha."

As she got the soap and lathered up her body, "I can't have a love affair. Just look at this body. Why would he want it? I have a child and stretch marks, for God's sake. I've been with one man," Liz had no real experience with men, which made the feelings of being inadequate seem overwhelming.

Liz wondered why she had gone so long without anyone. I had Paige and didn't want to bring a man into her life or into mine if she was being truthful. Paige is going off to school, and soon she will have her own life, and what will I have? Do I want to be alone for the rest of my life? Liz decided she needed to do something, but she wasn't sure what that was.

Liz tried to build up her self-confidence, "Come on, you're not that old, and you could use some great sex, as long as it's in the dark. Yeah, in the dark, you can do that." Liz said to the steamed-up shower as she let the water run over her body because she was tense again.

"I need to finish up in here and get out of this dream land and get back to work. You know what you came here for." Liz shook her head, trying to come back to her senses. Her head was spinning over wanting sex with Ben and being afraid to commit to anything new.

As Liz got out of the shower, she heard her cell phone ringing. Grabbing a towel, she ran to get her phone. Looking at the caller ID, she smiled to see it was her daughter. "Maybe she misses me as much as I miss her." As Liz answered her phone, she said, "Hello Honey, have you settled into your new apartment they set up for you?"

"Hey Mom," Paige didn't sound well.

"What's wrong? You sound sick, are you okay?" Liz knew that tone in her daughter's voice.

"I'm fine, just a little homesick. I miss you and being home. I thought that being on my own was going to be so great. You know, doing anything I want, when I want, but it's no fun when you have no one to share it with."

"Oh honey, you'll make some new friends soon, and it's not like I'm home anyway."

"I know. I guess I'm more Mommy sick then homesick." That made Liz a little happier to know Paige missed her, and she let out a small laugh.

"Paige, you'll be fine. You can call me or email me any time. You'll see, it'll go by fast, and then we'll be at home, and we'll do some shopping before you head to for school. If it helps, I miss you too, so much." Liz wasn't sure who she was trying to convince; it was going to be okay.

"I guess if you can do it, I can too. How is the house you rented? Is it really big?"

"Oh God, Paige, I'll have to take some pictures and send them to you because you will never believe it when I tell you it is gorgeous. This house has huge beds, I have a hot tub on the large surrounding deck overlooking the ocean, and the shower has three showerheads. I could have a party in there. That's how big it is."

"Okay, I see what you're doing. Make me jealous, you have that big, huge house to yourself and the beach out your door while I'm living with a shower head that doesn't put out enough water to get all the shampoo out of my hair." Paige said with no humor in her voice.

"I still really miss you even if I have the nice big house." Liz wanted to tell her daughter she would be on the next plane, but she knew Paige needed to work this out as much as she did.

"At least I know you're as lonely as I am. Have you got any work done? Find any cool hot surfer dudes?" Now Paige sounded more like her playful self.

Liz bit her lip and said, "I might have," thinking of Ben, his brother Jeff and Owen.

Paige wasn't sure she had ever heard that lighthearted tone in her mother's voice before, "So, what does that mean, you have? Is he cute, any my age?"

Liz thought about Owen and said, "I did meet a handsome young man, and he is oh so cute. He just happens to be around your age. His name is Owen, and he has long blond wavy hair, around six-foot-tall, has a tan to die for, and works for the surf shop I went in yesterday."

"Oh my God, you do want to rub it in, don't you? You will send me a picture of this Owen guy, right?" Paige sounded happier now.

"I might… I have a date with him at noon today," Liz was teasing.

"What! He's too young for you." Knowing Paige wasn't truly concerned about her going out with a teenage boy.

"When I say I have a date, I mean that I'm going to the surf shop. He's going to teach me all about surfboards." Liz was thinking more about the date she had with Ben.

"Oh, okay, but make sure that's all he wants to show you," Paige said, laughing. "Hey Mom, I have to go. I need to get ready for a safety meeting."

"Okay honey, I love you more than anything."

"I love you too, more than anything, and thanks for cheering me up."

"Anytime Sweetie, have fun at your meeting, bye honey," as the call ended, she was smiling. Liz relaxed on the end of her bed and considered how Paige had grown up, but not too much. She still needs my support, even if it's just moral support over the phone and across the county. It made Liz feel content to know that she could help steer Paige to be independent. That's what Liz had always wanted for Paige: to be a happy, independent, and responsible adult. Paige was getting there because she was all those things and more, but she still needed to be reassured every now and then. Liz's job of being a parent was not over, but it was definitely changing. That was a little sad, but knowing she'd done her job well gave Liz pride because of how Paige conducted herself. It had been hard at times to be a single parent, but Liz did it.

As Liz rationalized what she was about to do today, she thought about what to wear. What kind of outfit would attract a man? Did she want to attract a man? Liz thought for a minute and said aloud, "Yes, I think I do," but she hadn't brought anything to wear that was hot and sexy, so there wasn't much to choose from. She surely wasn't thinking in that direction when she packed for this trip.

Nevertheless, she would need something attractive to wear. She did have a pretty sundress, but would that be enough to turn Ben's head? The dress was snug across her breasts, and it was on the low side. It fit her waist well too, so maybe she could pull it off. Liz put the dress on her bed, decided on a pair of sandals, and then went into the bathroom to finish getting ready.

Liz was starting to get very nervous, so she told herself, "Hey, it's not like you're going on a real date. You're just working," so why did she feel so overheated? She determined it was all because of Ben. He did ask her to lunch after all. Not that it was a date or anything. Just a working lunch, that's all it was. Maybe if she kept repeating it to herself, she might believe it.

~ ~ ~ ~ ~ ~

Ben was at the shop trying to kill time all morning. He couldn't wait until noon and knew now she mesmerized him, making his life very interesting. When she reached out and took his hand with her tiny fingers, it was as if he had grabbed ahold of a live 220-volt electrical wire. How could something so little have such residual power? Ben walked into his office, hoping that maybe he could find something to occupy him. As he sat at his desk, he leaned back in his chair and closed his eyes. All he could think about was Liz and her stunning golden-green eyes. How they were what drew him in first. He thought about how he could fall right into those shimmering eyes. Her red hair, he could see how she attempted to tie it back, but with the wind blowing so strong, some of the traitorous pieces got loose, leaving locks twisting in the wind. He wondered what that hair would feel like, twisted in his fingers or maybe sliding down his chest, oh God, going down to his... He was becoming aroused and had to swallow hard. To think all he saw of her was eyes and hair. Just thinking about her appearance not only appealed to him but also excited him. She had worn that huge sweatshirt that covered most of her body and jeans. Ben snapped out of his daydream when Jeff came in.

"So, what yah thinking so hard about with that big shit-eating grin on your face? It wouldn't be a certain redhead, would it?" Jeff said with a teasing expression.

"Go to hell." Ben didn't want to talk about Liz after his childish behavior on the beach.

"Oh, is that any way to treat your baby brother," Jeff still had that stupid grin on his face.

"Baby Brother, my ass, you pulled that shit this morning just to get under my skin," Ben knew how Jeff just loved to do that.

"Hey, it's not often I get to ride ya about a girl. I was just having a little fun with ya." Jeff sat down in the chair across from Ben.

"Well, I'm sure we both appeared to be two idiots fighting over a girl, as if we were back in middle school," Ben was now frowning at Jeff.

"I don't think Liz minded. She looked as if she enjoyed it," Jeff just smirked at his brother.

"Hey, you aren't interested in taking her out, are you?" Ben hoped Jeff would be hands-off.

"No, I'm not unless you aren't interested. Then I could definitely see myself going out with her. She might have a few years on me, but she's one hot number, and I didn't get a really good look at her body. But I think she's more interested in you than me," Jeff lifted his brows up and down.

"And you won't see any part of her body if I have anything to say about it." Ben sent a stern message to let Jeff know to leave it alone.

Ben hadn't been this interested in anyone in a long time, so Jeff thought as much fun as it'd be to get under his brother's cool, controlled skin, he decided not to push his luck. "Hey, I have an early lunch date, but I will be back before you want to leave for lunch. Liz will be here around noon right, and Owen is going to go over the different boards with her. That should only take what thirty minutes or so." Ben wasn't surprised that Jeff had lunch plans.

"Yeah, that sounds about right, so who is the lucky lady today?" Ben was relieved that Jeff didn't seem interested in Liz.

Jeff just smiled and said, "I'm going to lunch with Tara today. She has to take her lunch before the café gets too busy."

"Okay, have fun. Tell her I said hi," Ben was smiling now.

"Boy, you're more pleasant when I'm not talking about your girl."

"She's not my girl yet, but if she felt the same jolt that I experienced when we touched, it won't be long."

"It's about time you found yourself, someone," Jeff just got up and walked out.

After Jeff vacated his office, Ben glanced at the clock on the wall. It was eleven-thirty, only thirty more minutes to go. Ben's thoughts returned to what he thought Liz might be hiding under that enormous sweatshirt. Owen had said she had large boobs. "Hmm... that would be just fine with me, with a small waist and an ass to die for. Oh man, I don't need to get myself all hard again because sporting a huge boner won't do."

~ ~ ~ ~ ~ ~

Liz made her way down the beach to the surf shop. As she got closer, she looked up at the large oval sign. It had a nasty-looking jaw on it with what looked like shark's teeth around the edges. The sign had the words Jacob's Surf Shop in the mouth of the shark. "Hey, don't they want to stay away from the sharks while surfing?" As she got closer, she could see the new window display of bikinis. They looked like three small triangles and a bunch of strings, something you used to play with your cat, not beachwear.

"I don't care how great my body looked when I was younger. I would not be caught dead in something like that. All the fabric together wouldn't even come close to covering one of my boobs, much less my essentials," Liz whispered to herself. It looked like having that string up the crack of your ass would hurt. She tried to keep things from going up her butt. Why would she purposely wear something like that? As Liz started to come to the doorway, she thought about what would happen once she entered, and her heart started to race out of her chest, and she kept telling herself to take deep breaths. Just as Liz was ready to go in, Owen and Jeff came out, almost knocking her to the ground. They were carrying surfboards to some girl's car. Jeff grabbed Liz around the waist and heaved her into him before she could fall.

"Oh, sorry about that. I didn't see you there, you, okay?" He held her close, smiled down at her, and started to release her.

Liz was startled as she began to get her balance back, and she looked up to see Ben standing right behind Jeff in the doorway with his brows in a frown. Jeff let her go just a little more as he heard a growl from behind. He knew who was standing there.

Jeff said in a very low voice over his shoulder so only Ben could hear, "You wouldn't want me to let her hit the sidewalk, would you?" Ben just growled again to let Jeff know he didn't like it, and Jeff laughed aloud.

Liz looked up at Jeff with confusion on her face and said, "Are you laughing at me?"

Ben told Jeff to go finish helping the customers and go to lunch. Ben reached down, grabbed her hand, and pulled her out of the doorway into the store. Liz almost couldn't breathe once the realization set in that Ben was holding her hand. She pulled her hand away and noticed he was staring down at her. He was looking at her chest as it was heaving in and out. Ben's eyes said so much, he was attracted and turned on, and Liz looked away. She was trying to catch her breath. Owen came into the store just then, and he looked at Ben, then at Liz, and asked, "Everything okay here?"

Liz recovered faster than Ben did, so she said, "Yes, why wouldn't it be? Are you ready to get this lesson started?" Liz walked away from Ben, knowing he would be watching her back.

Liz walked with Owen over to the area of the store designated for the surfboards. They had all different kinds and colors leaning up against the wall. She looked them over as she pulled her pad out of her purse. She dropped her pen and leaned over to pick it up, as she was still trying to calm her shaking hands. She needed to relax and breathe. Liz didn't know what was happening to her emotions because they were all over the place.

Ben got his first look at Liz's body in that sundress. Oh, my God, she was so hot, and as he came to the door, and saw his brother had his paws all over her. Jeff knew that would drive him crazy seeing his hands around her waist, even if it was to stop her from falling. Ben couldn't believe how strong his immediate attraction and possessiveness of her was. She tempted him more than he could imagine. He realized how his touch had affected her and had enjoyed watching her chest nearly bust the seams of her dress when she tried to settle herself.

He needed to look busy but also needed to be able to see her. He moved over to the jewelry counter to look like he was assisting customers. Ben was so intrigued with her. Liz could grab a man's attention in that dress. She was so vibrant and gorgeous. Her dress was white with green flowers, and it made her extremely emerald eyes stand out. She was so incredibly sexy, with locks of red curls falling over her neck. The dress fit snugly across her large beasts, and he could see the top of her round mounds. There was more than enough for him. How would they feel in his large hands? He lowered his gaze to see her tiny waist and then to her very nicely shaped legs with her little sandals and painted toes. Good Lord, she just bent down to retrieve her pen from the floor. Liz had a nice, shapely ass. How would it feel in his hands or pressed up to his thighs? She was every man's wet dream and would be his wet dream if he had anything to say about it. It had been so long since any woman had affected him on this level, maybe not ever. He didn't even know anything about her, like where did Liz live.

Liz was looking at all the boards and listening to Owen, she shyly glanced over toward Ben, and he was intensely staring right at her. Liz experienced a jolt to find him watching her with an alluring smile on his lips. She smiled coyly back, lowing her lashes, and brought her attention back to her pad and asked Owen, "How come you have so many different shaped boards?"

He answered, "The tall boards are for the less experienced rider, more surface to stand on and easier to keep your balance, and more of the board sits on the water, but harder to do much more than ride the wave in. They are for the beginner. The small tight boards are for surfers who want to do tricks. The smaller the board, less surfaces on the water, making it easier to maneuver." Liz thought about it for a minute, writing on her pad. Owen added, "Also, the boards can go by the weight."

Owen answered all her questions. Liz didn't realize there were so many different boards. She felt a little overwhelmed. She was now looking over her notes to see if she needed any more info on the boards. Liz had some more questions but didn't think it was appropriate to ask Owen about the wetsuit thing or if it was possible to have sex on a surfboard. Those would have to wait for some other time, and someone that she would feel comfortable asking those things. She glanced up to see Ben still looking at her from across the store. Liz looked away to ask Owen one more question.

"So, if I were going to start to learn how to surf, which board should I buy?"

"Well, I would say you can use the tall red one or blue one. We also have foam boards for the beginner. Do you want to learn? You would do really well, you're so…." Owen didn't finish.

"What am I?" Liz wasn't sure what Owen was getting at.

"You're so petite and compact you have a lower center of gravity. You'd probably do great. I could teach you if you wanted to learn, or maybe Ben can teach you."

Liz just pretended she didn't hear the remark about Ben. "I like blue. It's my favorite color. But I don't think I want to try to stand on that thing after watching you guys this morning. I'd kill myself, but thanks anyway," Liz smiled. "Hey, can I ask one more question? It's a little crazy and has nothing to do with surfing, but…?"

Owen smiled at her and said, "Yeah, shoot."

"I want to know…" Liz bit her lip, then took a breath and asked, "Can I take your picture?"

Still smiling, "Will it be for the book, like a character or something?"

"Or something, I have a daughter that's your age, and she was supposed to be with me on this trip before heading to college, but she couldn't come. I told her all about you and how you're helping me, and I might have told her how cute you are and that she's missing out on a great time."

Owen thought about it a minute and leaned in to say, "Just so you know, I have a girlfriend, if you were thinking about setting me up with her. Does your daughter have red hair like yours?"

"No, she has strawberry blonde hair, and it's really long and blue eyes. It's okay that you have a girlfriend because I would have expected a good-looking young man like yourself to have many of them, and you're safe. I wasn't trying to set you up," Owen gave her one of his biggest smiles, and Liz said, "Hold that right there, and don't move." Liz pulled out her cell phone and snapped the picture.

"So, maybe when your book comes out, I could find a good-looking younger man in it that looks and sounds like me?"

Ben was still across the store observing them, and she could see him out of the corner of her eyes. She wrapped things up with Owen and told him she may have more questions for him later. Liz strode toward Ben, who was now trying to look busy as if he hadn't been watching them the entire time.

"Hey Ben, I think I'm all done with Owen for now. Are you too busy to go for lunch? If you are, we can do it some other time." It sounded as if she was trying to get out of going for lunch.

Ben looked at Liz from top to bottom, and when his eyes were on hers, he said, "We are definitely going to lunch. We just have to wait until Jeff gets back. He should be here any minute."

Owen could tell Ben wanted Jeff to get his ass back, so he gave him the I'll call him sign by putting his fingers to his ear like he was on the phone. Ben caught Owen's meaning and gave him a nod. Owen went into the office to call Jeff so Liz wouldn't overhear. Out of the other office, Owen could hear the big loud voice of Linda Jacobs, Ben's mother, and she was yelling for Ben.

"BENJAMIN, where are those invoices from the shipment that came in yesterday?"

You always heard Linda before you saw her coming.

"BENJAMIN, where are you? I need those invoices."

Both Liz and Ben turned toward the booming voice. A woman appeared from around the T-shirt racks. She was as big as her voice. Her brown hair had a little ribbon of silver running through it, with a round face. The woman was taller and had about sixty pounds on her. Liz had decided this must be Ben and Jeff's mother. As she caught sight of Liz, she came to an abrupt stop.

"Oh, I didn't realize we had anyone in the store. Sorry for my yelling." The woman looked Liz up and down, this wasn't their normal customer, and for starters, this woman had clothes on, a very nice little sundress, and was older than the usual twenty-somethings that came to their shop.

"Mom, this is Liz. Liz, this is my mother, Linda Jacobs," Ben introduced the two women.

Liz moved over to where Linda was standing and put out her hand to shake his mother's. "Nice to meet you. You have a great place here," Liz said with a smile.

Linda was still taking Liz in, and Ben wanted to break the weird vibes his mother was giving off, so he said, "Liz is a writer doing research for a book she's writing. Owen showed her the surfboards this afternoon."

Linda said, "Nice to meet you. What kind of books do you write? I love to read mysteries."

Liz bit her bottom lip and replied, "Oh, I write romance novels."

Linda just looked over at Ben and moved her eyebrows up and down. "Is there all that hot and heavy sex in them?" Ben just rolled his eyes and needed to get Liz out of the store soon.

"Some," Liz said with pink in her cheeks.

Ben noticed it right away because Liz's skin was so fair that when she blushed, it showed. Ben wanted to get his mother back to the office and Liz out of the store before his mom could get too much into their business.

"Mom, what are you yelling about this time?" Ben asked, hoping it would bring her attention to what she wanted, and then she could go back to her office.

"Oh yeah, I needed the invoice from yesterday." It brought her back to what she had wanted and away from Liz.

"Well, you're going to have to ask Jeff when he gets back from lunch. He signed for it."

"Oh great, you know what that means? I'll ask what he did with it, and he won't remember. However, ask him what girl he went out with a month ago, and he can tell you her name, size, and what they did.

That's how he gets away with dating so many women at the same time. I don't ask for names anymore," she said with a chuckle.

The door chimed to say someone was entering the store, and Ben hoped to God that it was Jeff, so his mom could go off on him, and he could sneak out with Liz.

"JEFFREY."

"Oh great, what did I do now, or what didn't I do that I was supposed to?"

"I need that invoice from yesterday, the one you signed for," she started to get loud again.

"I gave it to you yesterday, Mom. I think I put it on your desk." He looked in Ben's direction.

"Where, you come show me," Linda left in a rush to find the invoice.

Jeff just smiled and pointed at Ben and said, "You owe me big time for this."

Ben knew his brother had no idea where that invoice was, but it got his mother to go back to the office without giving him or Liz a backward glance, and Ben was thankful for that.

As Ben was just about to get Liz out the door, the door jingled again, and the shop had about ten teenage girls looking at the bathing suits. Ben thought he would never get out of there. Owen came from the back and said, "I'll help them, you go to lunch."

Ben took Liz's hand and went out the door.

~ 3 ~

As Ben walked her down the sidewalk, Liz couldn't talk because her mouth was too dry to ask where they were going. All she was aware of was that he was touching her. They walked for a minute while Liz observed the appealing muscles in Ben's back as they shifted under his tight t-shirt, and then she let her observation slide further down to his tight butt. She wondered, before today, if she ever had the slightest interest in looking at a man's ass. Ben twisted to glance down at her and caught her staring at his backside, and she immediately looked away.

Ben smiled as her face colored a reddish-blush again. He liked it and asked her, "What would you like for lunch? We can have burgers at the diner or sandwiches at the café." Liz glanced up at him, and her eyes were so big and bright. They were the most beautiful color he had ever seen. As her cheeks got even redder, he knew she was embarrassed getting caught checking him out. Ben said, "By the way, you look great today. Your dress brings out the amazing color of your eyes," and it didn't hurt that he could view the top of her breasts from his vantage point.

"Thank you, I… I think the café; do they have a decent salad?" Now she was stuttering, what the hell, what's next?

"Are you one of those who only eat salad?" Ben said jokingly.

"Hey, what's wrong with eating healthy. I eat more than just salad. I just happen to want a salad if that's okay with you," she said with self-satisfaction. She wasn't even sure if she would be able to eat anything because her stomach was churning all over the place.

"That's fine because I can go for one of their big triple-decker turkey club sandwiches; it's the best in town." Ben liked how she was a little feisty and stood up for herself.

They walked one more block and came to a beautiful little brick building with a white awning that covered the tables out front with red and white tablecloths. The café looked so peaceful, a place where you could have a nice conversation. Liz was looking forward to getting to know Ben. They came to a stop, and he asked, "Do you want to take a table out here, or we can go inside if it's too hot?" She was aware of him watching her.

Liz was already hot and overheated, but it didn't have anything to do with the weather. She thought a minute and said, "I think outside, it's a nice day, and there's a little breeze. This is such a cute place." Liz really liked the looks of this café and needed to write a note in her notebook about how it might be suitable for one of her books.

"Yeah, I like their food, and it's not far from the shop. If we're really busy, they'll deliver." Sometimes he became so busy in the office that he forgot to eat and ordered takeout to keep working.

"Oh, I imagine that would be very convenient for you," Liz just smiled at him. She realized he was easy to talk to. Once she started talking, the conversation was nice.

The waitress came up to their table with a big smile. "Hey Ben, how's things going at the shop?" She briefly glanced over at Liz and looked back at Ben.

"Hey Tara, I'm fine, keeping busy, you know. Has it been hectic here today?" Ben smiled.

"It's been busy, not too crazy that I'm going insane, but active enough that I'm not bored to death. You know how it is. Do you need to see menus," she asked.

Ben turned his attention to Liz, she wasn't smiling anymore, and Ben said, "Yeah, I think Liz is going to need one."

The waitress asked, "What would you like to drink," she just looked at Ben.

"I'll have a Coke, and what do you want, Liz?" Ben asked.

"I'll have water with lemon, thank you," Liz said softly and looked away. She knew they knew each other because he had said he came to the café often. So why did she get the feeling as if she was interrupting something that was going on between them? The way the waitress glanced at her made Liz think she had a relationship with Ben. Wondering if it's more than just the food and how convenient the café is to the surf shop. Somewhere in the back of her mind, she knew it was most likely her own feelings of being insecure and self-doubting that made her feel this way. She was aware she had no right to Ben or to be jealous of anyone he chose to spend his time with, but she was feeling a little annoyed and very resentful just the same. Why did she want to go out to lunch with Ben so badly? She knew nothing about him. Just as Liz went to get up and bolt, the waitress said, "I'll be right back with your drinks."

Ben looked at Liz with concern on his face and asked her, "What's wrong?"

Liz wasn't sure she wanted to confide in Ben. "I guess you know her well because you come here all the time, but I get the feeling there's more to it, like I'm intruding on something."

"What, you think there's something going on between us?" Ben's wide smile spread across his face, and could she be a little jealous.

Liz started to think how unconformable this was making her feel and that maybe this lunch was a mistake. How can she manage to get out of this situation? "I'm sorry, it's really none of my business. Maybe I should go," Liz went to grab her purse.

Ben wasn't smiling anymore because he didn't want her to leave. "NO," he said a little harsher than he intended to, as he put his hand over hers to stop her movement. "I mean, I want you to stay," he said softer. "The waitress is one of Jeff's girlfriends, she's the one he went to lunch with today, and she knows all about how Jeff can be. So, we talk about him sometimes when I come in, and she's never seen me in here with a lunch date before."

"Oh, is that why she was looking at me so funny?" Liz laughed in an attempt to hide her embarrassment. "I thought maybe you had dated her, or she wanted to date you," Liz noted. Ben called their lunch, a date, which surprised her by how much she liked it.

"Hah— that would be a BIG NO. Tara has always had a thing for Jeff. Her hopes are that one day he'll settle down, and she will be the lucky one, and she isn't my type."

"Now I feel foolish," blushing again, she looked down at the table.

"Don't beat yourself up over it. One, you don't truly know me, which I want to change, and I'm a little delighted to see you just a bit green-eyed with envy," Ben was tickled.

"I am not envious," she exclaimed. "I just didn't want to step on anyone's toes." Liz was attempting to backpedal. She didn't want Ben to know she had been partially jealous.

"So now that's cleared up, I want to get to know you better. Tell me about yourself." Ben wanted to know everything. He just couldn't help how she made him feel. He leaned closer.

Tara returned with the drinks and a menu for Liz. "I'll give you a few minutes to look it over and be back to take your order."

"Tara, this is Liz. She's here doing research for her new book. She writes romance novels," he motioned in Liz's direction.

"Nice to meet you," she reached out to shake Liz's hand. "Jeff mentioned that you were in the shop learning about surfboards at lunch today."

"Nice to meet you, too," Liz felt so trivial after what she thought about Tara and Ben.

"I'll be right back. I need to refill some drinks," Tara said.

"So, what did you want to know about me?" She said, looking over the menu. Liz thought about what she could tell him that wouldn't bore him to death.

"I want to know everything. What's your last name, for starters? Where are you from? Did you always want to be an author?" He could sit across from her and listen to her all day and didn't think it had anything to do with her different accent, either.

"Okay, my last name is McGreary. I live in New Jersey. I didn't always want to be a writer; I started writing as a necessity." Liz wasn't sure how much she wanted to get into her marriage and her daughter. "I've been writing for a while." Liz was looking at Ben's deep brown eyes.

"Really, when did you decide to become a writer, and why did you say it was a necessity?" This woman intrigued Ben.

"Well, I have been writing for roughly ten years now, and it was a necessity because when my husband died, I was a stay-at-home mom, and I needed to support my daughter and myself." Liz wasn't sure how Ben would handle the news that she had been married before and had a daughter.

"Oh, I'm sorry to hear about your husband. It must be hard for you." He paused and then added, "How old is your daughter?" Ben hadn't even given it a thought that she might be married and had any kids, holy shit, he didn't want the surprise to show on his face.

"My husband has been gone over ten years but thank you." Liz wanted to get off that subject, so she moved on to her daughter. "Paige just turned eighteen, she was going to come, but she won this really big internship. She's working for them for part of the summer before she heads off to college in August."

"Wow, you must be proud of her. Where is she going to school?"

"I'm so proud," she smiled. "Paige has always been an excellent student. She was accepted into the Marine Program at Boston University. She wants to become a marine biologist." Aware she was bragging but couldn't help it. "I know she'd have loved to be here."

"That's really cool. You can do so much around here if you're into all that. I think she would get along with Owen. He loves that kind of stuff too." Ben moved closer, and he hoped she didn't notice his need to be closer to her.

"I told her all about Owen, just how cute he is, and how he was assisting me. I even took a picture of him today that I sent her. I just had to gloat a bit to show her what she is missing, even though I realize she would have liked to be here." She looked down at the menu on the table.

"I bet Owen just loved that you were talking about him with your daughter and took his picture. You know I could help you if you want." Ben wanted to help her with her research and a whole lot more. The idea that he was sitting so close and could smell her aroused him.

Tara moved back to their table and asked, "Are you ready to order?"

As Liz looked at the menu, and decided, "I'll have the grilled chicken salad with ranch dressing on the side. Thank you."

"I'll have the turkey club on rye with fries," Ben added.

"Okay, got it, I'll go put your order in, and your food should be right out."

As she was walking away, Ben said, "No rush, thanks, Tara." He wanted this lunch to last so he could find out more about her. Ben was so eager to help Liz with anything she needed just to get closer to her. "So, is there anything I can assist you with? I have been surfing for as long as I've been able to stand and swim." He watched as she bit her lip and debated what she was going to say, and he found himself wanting to bite her luscious lips.

Liz considered how she could ask what she sought to know and said, "I do have some questions that I didn't feel were quite appropriate to ask Owen."

Ben was looking at her mouth, how her teeth pressed into her lip. He was smiling big when he said, "Something you couldn't ask Owen, now you have my full attention, you can ask me anything," he wanted to get ahold of that lip. Watching her was achingly arousing.

Liz wasn't positive that she wanted to ask Ben. "So, what I want to ask…" she paused, "The questions have to do with some of the sex in the book. Do you have a problem with that?"

"I… You want to know about my sex life? Wow, I didn't see that coming?" Boy, he really didn't see that coming. Liz looked away.

"Well, not yours particularly, and you don't have to answer if you don't want to." Liz leaned over to pull out her notepad from her purse and hoped it would hide how she was blushing.

Now Ben was truly interested in the kind of questions she had for him. "Okay, so ask, and I'll do my best to help if I can."

"First, I want to know… what you wear under your wetsuits," and Ben just had to grin.

"I wear compression shorts. They're like tight bikers' shorts. Why would you want to know that?" He leaned onto the table to get even closer to her.

"Just in case my surfer strips off his wetsuit, I want to know what to say he's wearing under it," Liz stated as a matter of fact and tried not to sound embarrassed about questioning Ben.

"What do you mean when you said your surfer?" He wanted to know. "Oh, were you thinking about that this morning, is that where you got this idea from?" Could she have been thinking about him in his wetsuit? Oh God, he hoped so.

Liz's face turned redder as she said, "It's where I got the idea from yes, but I just thought it would be a sexy scene for the surfer in my book. That's what I meant when I said, my surfer."

"I can show you what I…" Ben corrected himself, "I mean what they look like."

The thought of Ben taking off his wetsuit and showing her how he looked in those tight shorts and his bare chest, with hair that went down across his tight abs and his long muscular legs, went through her mind again. The thought made her not only blush inflame more but her neck and chest were getting hot and tingly too. Oh yeah, the thought of him looked so good and hot. Liz had to close her eyes just to let the remarkable image of him go through her mind. Her whole body was burning up; it felt like it was on fire. As they sat across from each other, the awareness between them spiraled to crazy heights in such a short time.

Ben was observing her as she closed her eyes and felt her fantasizing about him, he couldn't help but revel in it, and he let his eye roam down over her red, darkened neck and the top of her breasts. He could see the outline of her nipples getting hard. He saw how this was affecting her, and the thought of how it might be turning her on was making him hard. He wanted her so badly, and every nerve in his body was on high alert.

When Liz opened her eyes to look at Ben, she could feel the undeniable overwhelming sexual tension between them. His brown eyes looked so dark they were almost black. Ben was breathing a little harder. They were just staring at each other when the waitress stepped up to their table and reached across them to put their food down. As she asked if they needed anything, both of them just shook their heads. Liz was relieved because it broke the intensely strong pull, they were both feeling.

Ben just said, "Thanks."

Liz was the first to look away. She stared down at her food, trying to regain her composure because she didn't know what in the hell was going on with her? This was so unlike her. She was obsessing about taking his clothes off, and he was sitting right in front of her watching. She cleared her throat and said, "This salad looks really good." She had to change the subject.

"Yeah," Ben was still staring, and Liz could feel it because her face and chest were still burning up. She knew she'd have to look at him again but wondered how long she could avoid it.

"Liz?"

"Yeah?"

"Look at me," she could hear the raw emotion in his voice.

As Liz brought her gaze up to his, she strained to steady her breathing. She wasn't sure what she should do or say under the circumstances. She'd never been in this situation before. She chose to say nothing and instead took a big sip of her water.

"I'm sorry," he knew she was very embarrassed.

Now confused, Liz asked, "Why are you sorry?" What did he have to be sorry for? It was all her, and she was the one undressing him.

"I didn't mean to embarrass you, although the color in your cheeks is very pleasant. I'm very aroused by you. If that helps, you appear to have this effect on me, and I can't seem to explain it." He put his hand on hers.

"I'm sorry too because I got carried away. I could just see it, you know, you..." She stopped talking.

"Don't be sorry, it's certainly alright with me. Actually, I enjoyed it a lot, and I haven't felt like this in a long time." At that moment, he wanted to be able to fulfill her every fantasy.

"Oh," Liz's mouth rounded. It had been a long time for her too, but she wasn't going to confess that to Ben.

Ben stared at her mouth yep, he was a goner. He hoped their delicious lunch would take forever to eat, so he had time to get his full-out boner to go down. Although the way she was looking at him, there wasn't a ball-breaking chance of that happening any time soon. "So, do you have any more questions? Though, I'm not sure I can handle too much more." Again, he watched how she thought about what she was going to say.

Liz debated with herself for a minute and said, "Well, there is one more... and again, you don't have to answer, but I was wondering...

if you can have sex on a surfboard. Well, if it's possible." Liz paused, then added, "I wasn't asking if you had... you know."

Wow, now didn't that just put a picture in his head about sex on his surfboard with her. He wasn't sure he could go out on his board ever again without having a hard-on. The thought of sex with Liz on his board, oh hell yeah. Ben had an amazingly big smile on his face when he said, "I guess it can be done. I've never tried, but now that you mention it..." Ben didn't add any more. He liked the way she thought. It would be exciting to discover what she'd conjure up in bed or anywhere else. All Ben knew was that he was painfully hard, probably the hardest he had ever been. God, he wanted her.

Liz continued making notations in her pad because she wanted to make sure she got everything. So, when she had to come up with the hot sex scenes, she could recall all of what Ben had said and how he made her feel, the sensation of lust, and this way she could avoid looking at him. This was just too good not to use in her book. It's better than what she'd come up with.

After they had finished their lunch, Ben didn't want to let Liz walk away, so he asked, "Can I walk you home?"

"I don't live... Well, the house that I'm renting isn't far, but sure if you want to."

Ben paid the bill, stood, and reached for her hand as if they had known each other forever. Liz gazed up at him and took his out-reached hand. They walked on the beach back to her house, and Ben asked some more questions about what it was like to write a book.

As Liz was talking about herself, she realized she didn't know anything about him. She could see her house in the distance, so if she was going to discover anything about him, she had to divert the conversation back around to him. "What about you, Ben? How long have you owned the surf shop?"

They stopped walking, and Ben turned to look down at her. He noticed how tiny she was compared to him. "In one way or another, we've always owned the shop. My dad opened it when we were little, and when he died, my mom didn't want to sell it, but it was too much for her to run, so Jeff and my sister Dannie and I took over. We worked there as kids growing up. When I was a teenager, it was certainly a great job to have with all the girls coming and going." Ben smiled down at her and continued. "I've always loved the shop, but lately, I feel like I'm getting too old to be a surfer beach bum."

Liz looked into Ben's eyes, "You own a business that is geared toward the youth, but you are not too old. I was on the beach this morning watching you surf, so I know. You looked totally hot out there," the words were out before she realized what she'd said.

Ben was studying her face as he was staring at her lips. "I want to kiss you, Liz, can I?" He whispered, "I want to so badly," and his head lowered as he peered into her eyes, trying to gauge if she would withdraw from him. Ben wanted to give her a moment, but her green eyes just stared at him. When his lips touched hers, his hands came around her waist, and he pulled her in close. Her hands came up and went around his neck. The kiss was soft at first, just a brush of their lips. He could feel her chest pressed tight against him as she breathed.

He proceeded to take more, to taste her. He ran his tongue along her bottom lip, and she parted hers for him. That first slide of her tongue sent a jolt down his body. When their tongues twisted around each other, they both moaned. He pulled her into him tighter as his hands slid down over her ass. He knew she could feel how his body reacted to her because he was so aroused. He pressed his hardness into her stomach. She didn't pull away, but she did break the kiss. There was a flickering light flashing in her eyes as she fought for breath.

Breathlessly, Liz said, "Oh My God," she considered her surroundings and remembered that they were on a public beach out in the open in the middle of the afternoon. Kids and their parents were playing in the water not far from them. Liz dropped her arms from his neck and immediately took a step back. She touched her lips with her fingers as if they were on fire. That kiss had overloaded all her circuits, as current went from her head to her toes.

Ben was breathing hard as he said, "I'm so sorry. I didn't mean to get carried away like that. That was just… I don't know… I'm not usually like that." Ben wasn't sure he made any sense.

Liz just stared at her feet and took a deep breath, and without a word, she started walking right past him. She looked toward her house and realized she needed to get home fast. What was she thinking? What was she doing? That was just it. She wasn't thinking. Her brain went blank.

Ben just stared at her as she passed him and was stunned for a few seconds before he'd come to his senses. He ran after her and had to make this right. Ben had to make her understand that this wasn't how he regarded a lady. How had he lost control? What had happened to him? As he yelled after her, "Liz, wait," she continued walking as Ben caught up to her. "Please Liz, wait, let me explain."

"I need to get home." Liz hadn't stopped walking, and she wouldn't look at him either.

He said again, "Please stop, Liz please," because he needed to make this right.

Liz stopped but continued to look straight ahead at the house. Ben stepped in front of her as he put up his hands. "I'm so sorry. I don't know what came over me. I don't normally act like this… not since I was sixteen, anyway. When I kissed you, everything just went into overdrive. I wasn't thinking that we were in public. Please forgive me." She wasn't saying anything, so he said, "Say something because the fact that you're so quiet is driving me crazy. Just yell at me, tell me to go to hell," he trailed off as he noticed her mouth curved into a small smile.

"How can I forgive you when I was right there with you? I kissed you too. It's just that I'm amazed more by my own actions and how I lost control. I don't lose it, you just seem to do something to me too, and right now, I'm not sure that's a good thing. Ben, I don't know what I'm doing. I don't live here, and I don't have affairs. I haven't been with a man since my husband died, and I don't know why I just told you that. I'm not mad, but I have to go," Liz started walking again.

"Liz, can I see you again?" As Ben came to her side, "Tomorrow, I'm helping some underprivileged kids learn to surf. I will be out here around three, and I was hoping you'd join me. You might get something that will help with your book." He hoped she wasn't going to refuse.

"I'll have to see. I'm not sure what I have going on tomorrow." She was well aware she didn't have anything that was important, but it was necessary to put him off because she needed time to think. Now they arrived at the bottom of her steps that led to the house. As Liz started up, Ben reached out and grabbed her arm.

"Liz," she turned and was now eye level with him. He leaned in and put a light kiss on her lips, and whispered, "I enjoyed lunch," as he looked into her eyes.

"I did, too," she couldn't help herself because she wanted another kiss, knowing it was a bad idea.

"I'll see you tomorrow," he smiled at her and watched as she turned away from him and disappeared up the stairs. When she didn't say anything, he couldn't help the emotions that overtook him. The feeling of regret, that maybe he just fucked up with the first woman that had made him feel anything. Ben turned away and headed back to the shop. As he strolled down the beach, he replayed that explosive kiss. She just felt so right in his arms. That's what was always missing, the feeling of how those puzzle pieces just clicked perfectly together. Liz got him hot and hard in ten seconds flat, and something told him she would be it for him.

He had never believed in love at first sight, but if she wasn't the one for him, then he wasn't sure there was one out there. "Now, how do I get her to realize that I'm the one for her?" He said to himself. Liz had said that she didn't have affairs and hadn't been with anyone since her husband, and he had been gone a long time. Ben wondered why Liz had been alone for so long. Did she love her husband so much that there would never be anyone else?

~ ~ ~ ~ ~ ~

Liz made her way inside the house, shut the door behind her, leaned against it, and took her first deep breath. She was safe now. It was just her and her thoughts of Ben. Liz had to figure out exactly what she was doing and what she was feeling. Could it all be because Paige was leaving? She didn't want to be alone, and that's why her reaction to Ben was so strong. She didn't really want to be alone, did she? That kiss had made her forget everything, where she was, that she had a child to get off to college. She hadn't been with a man in over ten years.

"Oh my God, I told that to Ben." That only proved how crazy she was. "Why did I say that?" Liz shook her head as if she was trying to get her brain to refocus. She was tired and not thinking straight. That was the best she could come up with, unable to quell the churning in her stomach, it had twisted into a knot, and she was so overwhelmed.

Liz went to lie on her bed, knowing she wouldn't be able to sleep, but she had to try to rest. Liz shut her eyes, and everything ran through her mind repeatedly. The image of him kissing her, touching her, his body pressed hard up against hers, it had been so long since she'd been in a man's arms, feeling that massive thick length of his erection pressed against her belly. She shivered at the thought of what it might feel like to be with him.

She shifted impatiently on the bed, her body electrically charged and the ache down between her thighs from her neglected libido. The sexual tension that was between them could burn her body to ashes. What was she to do about Ben and their undeniable chemistry?

She must have dozed off because her phone rang. It roused her. As she went to grab it, she noticed it was nighttime. Wow, how long had she been snoozing? The phone rang again, and she glanced at the caller ID, and it was her agent, Katherine Jackson. Liz knew that Kat was calling to check in on her as she automatically did whenever Liz was off on a research excursion. Kat liked to keep tabs on her. Not only was she her agent, but also her very best friend.

"Hey, how's the book coming? Pick out any big hunky, masculine guys to make your hero?" The sweet voice of her agent asked as she was trying to get information because Kat was anything but sweet.

"Hi, Kat," Liz tried to clear the sleep from her voice.

"What's wrong? You sound funny," Liz could hear the concern in Kat's voice.

"I was taking a nap. You know how I don't sleep well when I start a new book. The ideas just whirl around in my head until I start to situate them on paper." Liz was rubbing her eyes and, with a big yawn, said, "I've learned a lot about surfboards today. There are so many different kinds."

"You have to take care of yourself, Liz. You know no one is going to do it for you, right? Have you been eating correctly? You know, if you exercised on a regular basis, you would sleep better." Kat was always the best friend if you wanted her to be or not. She was the kind of person that found time to work a full-time job, exercise, eat the healthiest foods, and get eight hours of sleep every night. Liz swore she had a clone out there somewhere because she was the most rested person Liz knew, which made her look young, and she had one of those killer bodies with all lean muscle. Kat was the kind of friend you couldn't help but love.

"So, how's the gigantic house? It's wonderful, right? You're right on the ocean. Find any hot surfer dudes outside your door?"

Liz closed her eyes, and the image of Ben and his very hot kiss appeared. "This is California, all the dudes are hot, and most of them are too young, so don't get any ideas."

"Most?" Kat didn't miss a trick. "You met someone, didn't you? With this being the first time away from Paige, you could have a hot affair and some real sex," Kat sounded excited.

"What are you talking about? I've been here three days, and all I had time to do is search out a surf shop and meet a young man that has agreed to help me." Liz would not get into what happened today because Kat had been trying to set her up for years. The minute she mentioned Ben and what happened at lunch, the kiss, it would be all over. Kat would never leave it alone. Needing to figure out what was going on first before she shared anything, but Kat knew her all too well.

"Sorry, but there's something in your attitude that's saying something is going on, and I don't want to discuss it. Am I right? It's ok if you don't want to tell your best friend in the entire world. I won't pressure you about it," and Liz could hear Kat's frustration.

"Really, since when, besides there's nothing to tell for now anyway," Liz wanted to bounce what was happening to her off Kat but not just yet.

"Okay, so we're dropping that topic. How about, have you heard from Paige?"

"I talked to her this morning. Liz told Kat about how lonely Paige was feeling. "I told her that she'd be making friends and going out having a good time, not that I want her to go out with a bunch of strangers. I just hope she'll be making the right choices, you know?"

"Paige is the best kid you could ever ask for, and she'll be fine. She'll be at school making her own decision about who to hang with and have sex with, and you won't be there to help her. You have done your job nurturing her, but you let her fly at some point."

Liz was so not prepared to have this conversation with Kat about Paige's sex life, even if she knew Kat was right. Right now, she was so confused about her own sex life and didn't even want to think of Paige having one. "Kat, you are so straightforward about all this because you don't have children of your own. You have to know I want Paige to spread her wings and soar, but parents don't want to think of their child having a sex life, and that's all I want to say on that subject."

"You'd have to have a sex life for it to be a subject matter up for discussion, or we could discuss the fact that yours is nonexistent," Kat said with a laugh.

"I don't want to go over the same old thing." Liz could hear the irritation in her own voice.

"Well, if you just let me set you up with someone, I think we could quickly fix the problem. I know a million guys that would love to help your situation," she said mockingly.

"Kat, we've talked about you not fixing me up. If I'm supposed to meet someone, I will do it all on my own. You know how I feel about all of this, and I have Paige to think about." Liz hated to argue with her friend and knew Kat was only trying to help.

"Liz, Paige is off to school, and you are just using her as an excuse to not find someone new. You're afraid because it's been so long. Michael has been gone a long time Liz, ten years. I don't know anyone who could survive ten years without sex."

"Kat, I'm well aware of how long it's been for me, believe me. I just want to meet someone and feel something. I can't have sex with some stranger. There just hasn't been anyone that I've wanted to bring into my own life, much less into Paige's." Not until Ben, because she definitely felt something for him, and she really might want to have sex with him too, and that was a very significant change.

~ 4 ~

Ben had walked into the surf shop with a smile on his face because he now had some ideas on how to win Liz over. He didn't realize that everyone at the store was waiting for him. As he looked at them, they all scattered like cockroaches when you turn on the lights. He knew they wanted to know how lunch went. Ben never took long lunches, if he even took one at all, but he just went to his office and closed the door. He would give it ten minutes before one of his family members would be knocking.

As he sat in his chair, he proceeded to go over every little detail that happened and what Liz had said. He knew how she felt when he had her close and the smell of her skin. The shocking feeling when he touched her, how he lost all control, and that was the first thing he needed to work on. He couldn't lose it like that again. That would be the fastest way to make Liz run as she had today. Ben needed to get himself in check because he knew he wanted to get to know Liz better and maybe even for a deeper commitment.

Ben closed his eyes, reflecting on that kiss. How fast he'd gone from a soft press to wanting to take Liz there on the beach, not caring who watched. The sound of a knock pulled Ben out of his daydream.

Not sure. He wanted to know which family member was at the door. He said, "Who is it?"

"Your mother, can I come in?"

With a groan, he said, "Can I stop you?"

The door opened, and Linda stepped in, "You took a long lunch. Anything I need to know about?" She said as she sat in the chair across from Ben.

"I'm guessing you already know why my lunch was longer than usual. That's why you're here." Ben knew the minute his mother sat she wasn't leaving without what she wanted.

"Is there any information I should be informed about?" Linda gave Ben the look. The one she used when they were kids when she wanted to know the truth.

Ben broke, "What exactly is it that you want to know?"

"You took Liz to lunch? Do you like her?" Linda hammered the questions one after another.

Shaking his head at how his mom looked excited, "Yes, and yes."

"You're not going to give me one-word answers?" Linda frowned.

"You wanted information? Yes, I took Liz for lunch, and yes, I like her."

Linda squinted at her son, "I guess what I want is details."

Ben started to laugh because he knew his mother wasn't going to let up. "I like her a lot and asked to see her again."

"Oh, that's good, Honey. What are you doing for your date?" Linda was now sitting on the edge of her seat.

"I'm not sure there will be a next date, but I asked her to come to the surfing clinic tomorrow. I told her she might be able to learn something for her book. I need to take it slow with her mom."

"Why?" Ben could tell his mother didn't want to talk about going slow.

"Liz has some issues, and I don't want to get into them right now. You have to trust me on this. If I push her, she'll bolt back to Jersey faster than a blink of an eye."

"Okay, then, what's your plan? I know you just met her, but I like her. She's so cute and petite, with red hair and greener-than-green eyes."

"Mom, before you have us married with kids running around, Liz is only here for the month, and she'll be going home," Ben didn't want his mom to get her hopes up, although he was going to do everything in his power to keep her here.

"You want to keep her here?"

Ben closed his eyes with a soft breath. "Yeah, I do," Ben paused a minute and then looked at his mother and added, "I need some time to think."

"Okay, Benjamin, I will leave you to it. If you need anything, let me know."

"Thanks, Mom. I may need to take some time off from the shop. I want to spend it with Liz, to get to know her better, help her drop her defenses, and trust me. I haven't felt this way about anybody, and I just met her. I have to slow down as much for her welfare as for my own."

"You know I love you, and I'll do anything for you." With a smile, Ben's mom got up and left the room, closing the door behind her.

Ben reclined a little in his chair and thought about what he was going to do tomorrow if Liz came to the beach. He got out a piece of paper and made a list.

1. Need to pull back, not come on too strong. 2. Talk more, less touching, and find out more about her. 3. Try not to look at her as if I want to eat or jump her bones. 4. Try to have fun and enjoy being with her. Laugh more, smile, and joke around with her. 5. Keep it light and try to allow her control of the relationship.

"I can do that… I think." Ben needed to relieve himself of some of the sexual tension if he was going to have any chance of control with Liz. He left his office and went straight up the back stairs to his apartment on the third floor. Ben headed straight for the bedroom and lay on his bed on top of his bedspread. Ben hadn't jerked off in a long time but knew he needed to if he would have any restraint.

Closing his eyes, there she was, Liz in that dress she wore. What did her body look like under that tight dress? Ben pulled the button of his jeans open and unzipped. He pulled them off, throwing them to the floor, and he was hard again. Just the thought of her, did that to him. Thinking about taking her dress off, seeing her big tits, what would her nipples look like? He took hold of himself and started to stroke up and down the length of his cock. *Oh God, how would they feel in my palms as I squeeze her firm breasts and bring her stiff nipples to my mouth to suck them hard?*

Ben was moving faster now and harder as he could feel his balls pulling up tight. It felt so good. If only it were Liz's hands on him or her wet mouth sucking him deep, coming hard, that thought pushed him over the edge. Ben came with a yelling moan as the hot semen sprayed over his stomach as he worked to slow his breath. He grabbed tissues from his nightstand to clean up.

He got up and went into the bathroom to wash up, looking at himself in the mirror. He thought how right it felt being with Liz. Ben pulled his jeans back on and zipped up as he thought, wow, it had been a long time since he had to do that, but it felt so good to fantasize about her. He never remembered it being so good. It was always so lame to have to jerk off. Just the thought of having Liz naked in his bed was a hot fantasy. He just may have to revisit that one later, and he hadn't even thought about how it would be to be inside her.

"Ok, I'm going to get hard again if I don't stop, and I need to get back to the store." Ben went back downstairs, feeling more confident that he wouldn't screw up tomorrow. Smiling, Ben turned the corner that led out of the stairwell. He almost ran smack into his brother.

"Where were you? I was looking for you." Jeff was staring at Ben as if he knew something was up with him.

"I was upstairs. I just had to take care of something. What do you need?" Oh yeah, he took care of something, all right.

Jeff was still looking Ben up and down. "How did lunch go with Liz?"

"I like her more than I have anyone in a long time. We had a great time at lunch." Just thinking about lunch made his lips curve up. "I asked her to come to the beach for the clinic tomorrow with the kids. I told her I'd help her with her book and teach her all about surfing, maybe even get her to try it."

"Wow, I'm glad lunch went well, but don't you think she'd like a night out on the town, you know, dinner and drinks, maybe dancing?

"I don't want to rush her. I want her to feel comfortable with me before I make any kind of real moves on her. She was married, her husband died, and she has a daughter that is Owens's age. I don't trust myself to be alone with her right now. As I was walking to her home, I kissed her right on the beach, and I lost control. It started out as a nice soft kiss, and very quickly, it turned so hot, I just couldn't help myself, and I don't want to do that again. The losing control thing because I definitely want to kiss her again."

"I don't think I've ever seen you so into someone like this before. So, you think she could be the one to capture your heart and settle you down?" Jeff's voice filled with sarcasm, but he could see how serious Ben's feelings were for Liz.

"I don't know, but I want to try and find out. I just have to take it slow I don't want to scare her off." Ben really didn't want that. "I might be taking some time off work, so you're going to have to run the shop while I'm gone. Please try to be the owner, not the employee. That means when I'm not here, you'll have to open on time." Ben knew it would be a growing experience for both of them. With Jeff taking on more responsibility and himself letting some go.

~ ~ ~ ~ ~ ~

Liz was wide-awake after taking such a long nap earlier. She opened her computer and started on her book. The first thing she did was start her character list, starting with their names. Liz pulled out her pad, the one that went just about everywhere with her. It had names and places that had intrigued her over the years. She looked over her list of names and out came the name Jonny Richardson as her surfer. The name wasn't one of her favorites, but it had to sound laid back. A surfer dude shouldn't have a name that makes him sound smug or snotty. Although it could also be Jonathan Richardson the Third, if she wanted this to be a rich guy slumming, hanging around a surf shop, but not wanting anyone to know he's rich.

So now that she had a name, what would he look like? The image that she had down on her pad was of one surfer, Ben. He was big...

all the guys are big with impressive lean muscles and broad shoulders. Liz wanted him to have dark brown, almost black eyes with a little gleam of danger in them. He had shaggy brown, tousled, and untamed hair kissed by the sun. Jonny was going to have a chiseled jaw, and he was tall, like six — something, his height just like Ben's.

"Okay, now that I have him on paper, I need his love interest. What could her name be? Hmm... let's see something fun and sassy, maybe Samantha Kneece. I'll call her Sam, so Jonny thinks at first that Sam is a man by her name. It'll be a rude awakening for him. I want her to have long blonde hair that she wears up in a baseball cap all the time. Now how tall do I want to make her? Maybe five-seven, not too tall, but could still pass for a guy's height."

Liz spent the next three hours going over the list of characters. It was now twelve-thirty, and she worked right through dinner. Her tummy growled to let her know she hadn't eaten. This was what Kat always gave her crap about, not taking care of herself. Liz got up and stretched her back since it was hurting from sitting so long. She moved over to the fridge, pulled out the milk, and then went to the cabinet to grab a bowl and cereal. It wasn't the most nutritional dinner, but it would satisfy her stomach.

As she was eating, Liz took one more look over her list of characters and made some notes. She closed her computer, happy with the work she had accomplished. The book was starting to shape up. Liz thought about Jonny, the surfer in her book, and how his appearance mirrored Ben. Liz knew she would fall in love with Jonny's character. She always did. So, did she make them so much alike because she wanted to fall in love with Ben?

Liz knew she was deeply afraid to give so much of herself to anyone. She loved Michael with all that she had, even though their marriage wasn't the best. When he died, it was all she could do to hold it together. If it wasn't for Paige, Liz wasn't sure how she would have made it.

On an emotional level, she was skeptical about whether or not she was capable of giving anyone a long-term relationship. It had been so long since having anyone she could depend on for emotional support. Liz had her best friend Kat, but it wasn't the same as having a partner to share all your accomplishments, all your hopes and dreams, or the overwhelming sorrow with.

Liz definitely had regrets about how she hadn't allowed anyone into her life, although it wasn't her intention. It started out with her needing to take care of Paige and herself. That's how Liz had become so fiercely independent, and she didn't know if she could change that about herself. Knowing something was changing in her body because physically, she was sexually charged. That was very significant because she hadn't felt the need for a man's touch as she did now. The anticipation of seeing Ben again excited her. Their physical chemistry was overpowering.

As Liz was thinking all this through, she went to get ready for bed. She went to the bathroom to wash her face and brush her teeth. Looking at her reflection, Liz asked herself why she didn't allow a man into her life before now. She knew it wasn't a conscious decision, just something she couldn't handle before. Then it just became how she lived her life, telling herself it was for Paige. She didn't need to bring a man into her daughter's life after losing her father. Liz never thought about how she was depriving herself of her own emotional and physical needs.

Liz knew this was what Kat had been saying for years, why she tried so hard to fix her up. It was funny that Kat could see her needs better than she could. It was never important what her needs were because it was always about Paige's needs. Liz went to her bedroom and put on a big T-shirt for bed. She pulled back the covers and climbed in, with her thoughts on tomorrow. Turning off the light, she stretched out, thinking over what she wanted to do about Ben.

"I think I'll just see how I feel tomorrow and if Ben is interested in me, and then I'll see where it goes from there, even if it scares the shit out of me. I owe it to myself."

Liz rolled over, trying to get comfortable, but when she closed her eyes to sleep, the image of Ben in his wetsuit on the beach appeared. She smiled and just allowed the fantasy to roll through her mind and over her body. Liz definitely wanted Ben to be interested because she absolutely felt consumed by him, and if the kiss was any indication, Ben was definitely interested.

"I need to go shopping, I don't own anything sexy, and I'm going to need all the help I can get."

Liz got up the next morning feeling refreshed. It was the best night's sleep. That she had in a long time. She went to the kitchen to start the coffee and to search for a telephone book, because she had some shopping to do, but didn't know where to start.

"I know I could stop by the café. I bet Tara would know the best places to get what I need." Liz poured her coffee, taking the phonebook and her phone with her out onto the deck. It was going to be a great day, there were surfers out on the water, and Liz wondered if Ben was one of them. She pulled her thoughts back to what she needed to do, looking up the number for the café. She asked for Tara, but she was off. Surprisingly they gave Liz her cell number.

Liz was feeling a little unsure, but she took a big breath and dialed Tara. "Hello, is Tara there?"

"This is Tara. Who's this?"

"Tara, it's Liz from yesterday, Ben and I had lunch at the café."

"Oh, hey Liz, what's up?"

"I need some help. I was hoping you could help me. I want to go shopping, but I'm not sure where to go. I've only been here four days and don't know my way around. I was just wondering if you could tell me the best places to shop."

"I can do better, I'm off today and need to do some shopping myself. If you want, we can go together."

"That would be great. I could use another woman's opinion. I'll buy lunch. Just tell me what time, and I'll be ready." Liz had told Tara what she needed to buy.

"How about I pick you up in an hour? Just give me directions to your place, and I'll see you then." Giving Tara the directions to the house she rented. Finishing her coffee, Liz watched the surfers. Then she went in to shower to get ready to buy something sexy.

~ ~ ~ ~ ~ ~

Ben woke up thinking about Liz. He went to bed thinking of her, too, and realized that she was all he'd been thinking about. Ben got up and went into the bathroom. He needed coffee and went to start a pot. The aroma filled his small kitchen. Leaning against the counter, he looked out the window at the ocean. The waves looked good, and Ben wondered what the day would bring. The kids should have a good time. It would be a great learning experience for them.

Ben loved working with the underprivileged kids, they didn't have much, so when they had the chance to have fun, they just soaked up the encounter. The kids tried so hard and never complained when they got frustrated or defeated. It just made them more passionate about surfing and determined to master the skills. The kids were used to things being hard for them, so when the waves thrashed them around physically, it didn't even come close to what some of the kids had to deal with in their own lives. It gave the kids the feeling of accomplishment and built self-esteem and character. Ben loved to see the kids having fun and bitten by the surfing bug.

Ben was drinking his coffee when the phone rang. He looked at the caller ID and grabbed it on the second ring. "Good morning, Jeff. What can I do for you?"

"Hey, I heard something I thought you should know. I just got off the phone with Tara."

"And I should know this why?" Ben wasn't sure where Jeff was going with this.

"Tara and Liz are going shopping this afternoon," Jeff added.

"Okay, that's nice of Tara to do. So again, I ask why I need to know this," Ben was puzzled.

"Because it's what they're going shopping for, I think you'll want to know," Jeff said smugly.

"Okay, I'll bite. What are they shopping for?"

"Sexy things."

"How would you know that?" Ben wanted to know what Tara told Jeff.

"I called Tara this morning to see if she had plans for lunch because she's off today, and she told me she already had a lunch date with Liz. I didn't even know they knew each other. Tara told me about you bringing Liz in yesterday, and Liz called her this morning and wanted to know where she could buy sexy stuff, wanting another woman's opinion."

Ben closed his eyes, letting out a big breath, "I'm having a hard enough time thinking straight now without thinking about her in something sexy. And I do mean HARD — it's how I've been since I met her on the beach."

"Just thought you should know, if she's buying something sexy, I'm sure she'll want someone to see it." You could hear the pleasure in Jeff's voice.

"I have to go, I need to get downstairs and get the stuff ready for the surf clinic today, and I need to concentrate. I have to be ready by three o'clock to take six kids out to teach them to surf. I don't need a distraction. It's going to be tough enough if she comes out to watch, and now I'm going to be thinking about her in something sexy." Ben hung up on Jeff because he didn't want to hear anymore. He could feel himself getting semi-hard with just the picture of Liz in a lace bra and panties in his head. Now, how was he going to control himself when he saw her again?

~ ~ ~ ~ ~ ~

Tara picked Liz up right on time, and they headed inland. Liz wasn't sure where they were going, but she figured Tara knew the best place to shop. When they pulled into the mall parking lot, she took a big breath and told herself repeatedly that she could do this. Tara parked the car, and as they got out, she said, "So, where do you want to start. What exactly are we shopping for?"

Liz could feel the anxiety and apprehension creeping in. "I need everything, but we can start with the under part and work our way out," she said and blushed.

Tara laughed at Liz, "You mean lingerie. You're so funny, Liz. You can't even say the word without blushing. When was the last time you bought yourself something sexy?"

"It's been a very long time. I won't say how long, but to be honest, I haven't needed it." Liz couldn't help feeling pathetic.

"Ok, I'm not going to pry. I can't imagine why you haven't needed anything sexy, because I just like to buy it for myself. Even if no one will see it, I know it's there, and it makes me feel sexy."

"Well, when I was married, I had nice things, but after my husband died, I just didn't buy anything like that. Money was tight, and any bra and panties off the sales rack would do because no one saw it anyway. Here I am ten years later, now I have the money to spend, yet I never do." It felt good to say it.

"Wow, ten years, that's a long time," Tara said as they walked into Victoria's Secret.

Liz looked around, not knowing where to start. She went by a big table of panties. Tara was looking through the pile, pulling out the ones she liked. Liz pulled out panties, looking at them. "These are interesting. They don't look very comfortable."

"Just look through, see if there are any you like, and we can try them on later. Most of the time, they have matching bras, so it makes choosing easier." Tara had a pile put aside for herself.

Liz was looking for a little bit more coverage because most of them were thongs, and she didn't think they were right for her. Liz asked, "Do they have anything in a brief? I don't think I will look or feel good in those."

"Liz, you may not want a thong, but you don't need briefs. What you need to look for is a bikini cut, you get the comfort, and it still looks sexy."

Liz found a few she thought might work, but there wasn't much to them. Then they moved to the bras, and they were very interesting because Liz had more boobs than the bra would cover. They went to the dressing room. Liz tried on the panties, and they weren't that bad, but the bras, she would need a bigger size. If only she could get one without all the padding, that would be so much better. She was already big enough without the help.

Tara said, "Okay, let's see what you picked out."

"Oh God, tell me you're not going to make me come out there," Liz sounded horrified.

"Oh, come on, Liz, no one's here, and you did say you needed another woman's opinion."

"Okay, just keep in mind I've had a child, and I have more boobs than this bra will hold." Trying to breathe, she sucked in and opened the curtain. Closing her eyes, she stepped out. Knowing her face and neck were red because she felt it.

"Liz, you look great. What are you talking about? You had a kid? If you didn't tell me, I would never have known. Okay, the bra needs to be more like the lace ones without the padding, but let me tell you, if I had the boobs you have, I would be showing them off, not covering them up.

Liz opened her eyes and looked at Tara, "I had a good bit before I got pregnant, but when the titty fairy came, he never left, and I have stretch marks that didn't go away either."

"Well then, there is hope for me yet on the boob front, and your stretch marks aren't that bad. I have a friend that has them a lot worse than yours." Tara said, laughing and playfully teasing Liz.

Liz and Tara spent the next three hours picking out clothes and laughing at each other. Tara helped her find things that Liz was comfortable in and had some sex appeal. Liz got some flirty dresses and a few skirts with lower-cut tops and shorts that were much shorter than Liz had ever worn before. They also hit the shoe store, which was Liz's downfall. By the time they stopped for lunch, they both were carrying more bags than their arms could hold.

Liz's feet hurt so bad. It felt good to sit down and put the bags down and rest her arms because they hurt, too. As they ate their lunch, they talked about their shopping trip. Tara was looking straight at Liz, so Liz said, "What? You're looking at me like you want to ask me something, but you're not sure you should."

"Well yeah, I… you don't have to answer, but I was just wondering, is this all for Ben?"

"Okay, it's for me, I really needed to do this a long time ago, but it's also because of Ben. I haven't found anyone that makes me feel the way I do when I'm with him. I know it sounds crazy since I just met him yesterday, but there is just this thing between us. I can't explain it. For the first time in ten years, I want to have a man in every way." Liz could see Tara's amazement over her confession.

"So let me get this straight, you haven't had sex since your husband died?" Now the total surprise on Tara's face said it all.

Liz just said, "Yes, it's been that long."

"Wow, it's like you're a virgin all over again. Why…, well, it's none of my business."

"It's ok, I just never wanted to bring a man into my daughter's life after her father's death, and my life was all about her. I guess there was never any one man that tempted me before now. There's something with Ben. I get all tingly, I can't think, and when he kissed me yesterday on the beach, I lost all control. And I never do that, at least not until Ben, so believe me, it scares me."

"If it makes you feel any better, Ben is a great guy. I would love it if Jeff was a little bit more like his brother because I'd be married by now," Tara smiled at Liz.

"I have a confession to make. Yesterday I thought you had dated Ben, or you wanted to."

"Nah, Ben and I are just friends because of his brother."

Liz looked at her watch and realized she only had an hour until Ben would be out on the beach teaching the kids to surf. "I just realized I need to get going, Ben is teaching some kids to surf at three today, and I still have to figure out what I'm going to wear."

"Okay, no problem, you want my opinion on what you should wear. My choice would be your new jeans, the blue-green top, with the electric blue lace bra and panties and your new sandals. I had a great time shopping with you. It was fun."

Liz and Tara cleared the table, picking up all their bags, as they walked to Tara's car. "I want you to know I had a great time, too. I really appreciate all your help today. I don't think I could have done it all on my own. Now where did you park? Because I think I bought out the mall, these bags are getting heavier by the minute."

~ **5** ~

Ben went into the shop to get the foam boards, longboards, and helmets the kids would use. He had Owen put the boards on the rack on top of his Jeep, then gathered the wax, the blocks for the boards, some bottled water, and a hand full of protein bars. He pulled out six kids' medium t-shirts with the surf shop logo on them. The kids should be there in thirty minutes.

Ben went out the door and onto the beach to check the waves. They were waist-high and choppy, a swell coming in from the northwest. The wind was strong, but the surf was definitely rideable. Ben stood there a minute as he looked down the beach. He could just make out Liz's house and wondered if she would be out here today.

What would he do if she didn't come today? Would he go and knock on her door? He told himself control was the key, and he absolutely wasn't going to be thinking anymore about her shopping trip. Ben went back to the shop to get his wetsuit on and go over all the rules to make sure the kids stayed safe.

~ ~ ~ ~ ~ ~

Liz made it home just in time to throw the bags on her bed and pull out the outfit she wanted to wear. She jumped into the shower, brushed her teeth, tied her hair into a loose ponytail, and put just a little makeup on. She got dressed and grabbed her shoes and her pad. With no time to overthink seeing Ben or to change her mind, she left the house.

Liz went out onto the deck and looked down the beach for Ben. She could see him in the distance with the kids. Liz ran down the steps and went to them. He was instructing them on the finer points of the sport and the importance of stretching and safety as some of the kids waxed their boards in a counterclockwise motion. He turned to see her standing behind him. Ben smiled, putting his hand up to motion for her to come to him. Liz walked to his outstretched hand.

"Hey, I want you to meet Liz, she is a writer and is here to learn about surfing too, so she is going to watch us and ask questions. She's a friend of mine, so be nice to her, ok?"

A blonde-headed girl asked, "Is she your girlfriend?"

Ben answered in an even tone, "That's none of your business, Kate. I did say be nice, didn't I?"

The girl just looked at Liz and said, "Sorry."

"Okay, let's get started." Ben drew a wave in the sand with a shell and explained that the surfer nearest to the peak of the wave gets to ride it and told them about the riptides and how to swim safely out of them. Ben had everyone lay on their tummies on the sand and practice popping up and getting into the stance with one leg out front, balancing most of their weight on their back leg. It looked easy enough on the sand. As the kids seemed to get the hang of that, Ben put blocks under one of the boards on the sand and he had them do the same on top of all the boards rotating turns. Each kid got a turn on the one with the board and with the blocks. That didn't prove to be so easy. As the kids popped up on the board, it would move under them. It was fun to watch. They seemed to like it, even though you could tell they were trying hard to master the stance. As she watched the kids writing on her pad, Liz could see Ben watching her.

"Okay, time to get in the water and remember, I will be working with each and every one of you, but when I'm with someone else, I want you to ride the waves in, feel the peak on your tummy, and practice paddling. This way, you'll know when to pop up when it's your turn."

Ben took them out past the breakers into hip-deep water, and everyone got on their boards, lying on their tummies like Ben said, and he took one kid and waited for the next wave to get close.

Ben yelled, "Paddle hard! Paddle harder, as hard as you can!" A second later, he yelled, "Pop up," and the kid did just as they did on the beach. It was exciting to watch, even if the ride only lasted one or two seconds and sometimes not at all. Ben went through one child after another, and she couldn't help herself cheering them on. By the end of the surfing lesson, Liz knew all their names.

As they gathered on the beach, Ben handed out bottled water and protein bars and told them to practice and make sure they stayed hydrated. He told them surfing takes a lot out of you. As the kids finished the water and their bars, Ben handed out a t-shirt to each of them, told them they may be sore tomorrow, and said how hard surfing works the core muscles.

Ben asked, "So, who had fun today, and who's coming back? Come into the shop, so you can tell me how you're doing," all the kids raised their hands. Ben's smile was as big as the kids.' You could see how he loved teaching the sport. They all seemed to have a great time and looked up to Ben. As the parents came to pick up the kids, Ben spoke to each one.

Ben didn't say anything to Liz when he was teaching, but he did look over at her and smile. He seemed to do that a lot. After all the kids left, Ben walked over to her and sat down.

"Hey, you learn anything? Looked like you had as much fun as they did," Ben liked the fact that Liz did seem to enjoy the kids. He knew how much he loved doing the clinic, and it was nice to see she shared his feelings.

"It was so cool to watch the kids work so hard to get it, even when they wiped out. It's a great thing you do for these kids. I can see they really like you, too." Liz was impressed with Ben's passion for the kids and the sport.

"I love to do these clinics for the kids. They don't have much, so when you give them an opportunity, they just soak it up. When I have the kids here, I teach them the sport I love, and if I can pass the surfing bug around, it's good for business. That's how Owen ended up at the shop. He went through the clinic and started hanging around. He sold surfboards before we even paid him."

"Well, you did look like you were having just as much fun as they were, and you certainly seem to be a very capable teacher. You know just what to say to them to build their self-confidence. Your knowledge comes across with understanding, and the result is an exceptional achievement." Ben was just watching her mouth move.

"Wow, you like using them big words. I'm just a surfer bum, ya know," Ben said jokingly.

"Oh, I see you are going to give me a hard time because I'm a writer. I use them there big words all the time, and I work so hard to not allow my vocabulary to show." Liz gave Ben's arm a hard shove. She felt his tight bicep through his wetsuit, which reminded her he was wearing it, and her face blushed red again.

"Hey, I don't hit girls, unless…" He rolled so fast Liz didn't even know what he was doing until he was right on top of her, looking down at her.

"No, I won't hit a girl, but I will restrain them from hitting me."

Liz's green eyes were so big with disbelief. "I… I didn't hit you, I shoved you, and that's not the same thing."

"Liz, I want to kiss you, but I don't want to push you into anything you don't want. I don't want to make you bolt like yesterday. So please, tell me what to do, I like you, and I want to get to know you." Liz wanted Ben to kiss her again, so Liz just reached up and put her hand on the side of Ben's face. "I'd like you to kiss me too, but I need… I need to go slow. I don't do this, and I'm not sure how." Ben released some of his weight off her.

"I want to do whatever you need to feel comfortable with me, but you do something to the inside of me. It's crazy, I'm afraid, because when I kiss you, I don't know how to explain it. I just go wild."

"I do understand because I feel the same. I'm sure you have more experience than I do," Liz just stopped talking because she didn't want to embarrass herself any more than she already had.

Ben sat up and pulled her with him. "I think we should talk and get to know each other. We know how physically attracted we are to one another, but we really don't know that much more. I'd like to take you to dinner and spend some time together. What do you think?"

"I think I'd like that a lot, but why don't I make you dinner? That way, we can talk and maybe do some kissing because even though I ran or bolted as you say, I really do like kissing you."

Ben's amusement said it all. He liked kissing her, too, and if she wanted him to, well, hell yeah, "I'd like that too. Can we get together tonight, or is that too soon?" Ben wanted to spend as much time as he could with her, but alone. He wasn't sure if that was a good idea.

"I think I could pull together dinner and wine. How about around seven? Is that good for you?" Liz thought, okay, dinner, I can do. If things went nice and easy, she could do this, just talking and getting to know him. Liz knew she had an obligation to herself to attempt to have a mature relationship. She wasn't sure if she was capable of serious involvement, but with the understanding that she was a responsible adult, why not. Surprised by the fact that she really wanted to trust the strong, overwhelming feelings she had for Ben and that they surpassed the anxiety and embarrassment. Emotionally and physically, she owed it to herself to have a life. Liz's body wanted and needed the physical contact, and all she could think of was getting Ben alone and out of that wetsuit.

"Are you sure you want to make dinner? I'm not sure being alone with you is such a good idea. I don't know if I trust myself." Was he afraid to be alone with her?

"I need to get to know you, Ben, and I don't want to have to deal with people in a restaurant. I want to know how it will feel to be alone with you because so far, you've kissed me in a very public place. I need to have time with you without anyone else."

"Okay Liz, I just really don't want to scare you off because I'm telling you right now, I want you, and if we are alone, I'll be trying very hard to restrain myself. I'm not sure I could go the whole night without touching you and wanting more. It's been a while for me."

"Ben, I want that too, but I'm not sure of myself or how to do this. I need to try to see my way. Am I making any sense?"

"Yes, I know you said you haven't been with anyone in a long time, and as far as not knowing how to do this, you just let it happen. I'll go as slow as you need me to go, and I don't want you to do anything that makes you feel uncomfortable. As long as you tell me, we can stop or change anything because I'm willing to do whatever it takes to make you feel more comfortable with me. Liz, I really like you." Ben placed his hand on the side of her face, ran his thumb over her jaw, and looked into her eyes. "Liz, can I kiss you?"

"Yes," she absently licked her bottom lip.

Ben pressed his lips very slowly to hers as he continued to look deep into her eyes. His hand slid to the back of her neck and into her hair to pull as to get closer, and he could feel his control slipping, so he ended the kiss, pulling back just a little. "Are you ok?"

"I'm good, that was nice... really nice," looking into his dark, chocolate eyes.

"I need to let you go so I don't push things again on the public beach, and I need to get out of this wetsuit." The mention of taking off his wetsuit made her blush as her face, neck, and chest turned a deep red. His mouth turned up, looking down at her, he knew what she was thinking. "I just love it when you blush like that. It's like I can tell what you're thinking."

As Ben looked down at her neck and chest, he could see the cleavage of her breasts and just a little bit of the blue lace bra from the low-cut top she was wearing. Ok, he really needed to go, he was getting hard, and he couldn't hide it in his wetsuit.

Liz pulled him from his thoughts, "Is there anything special you'd like to eat for dinner? I make amazing lasagna if you like Italian?"

"I'm not hard to please, because when I get a home-cooked meal, I eat everything." He couldn't help himself, thinking there was definitely something special he wanted to eat, and that would be her. What would she taste like? Ben's muscles clenched. He seriously needed to leave before he couldn't hold himself responsible for his own actions. It was essential for him to practice restraint, but it was extremely hard. He knew he was going to embarrass himself when he got up to leave, so maybe he could get her to leave first, and she wouldn't see how seriously aroused he was.

"I need to stop by the store and pick up what's necessary for dinner. So, I will see you later." Liz went to stand, and Ben stood to help her up as she reached for his hand. Liz didn't miss his hard, massive bulge, and the corners of her mouth turned up.

"What?" Ben was wondering what made Liz smile so sinisterly.

"I just love it when you react like that. It's like I can tell what you're thinking." Liz looked directly at Ben's crotch.

Ben knew she hadn't missed his erection as she threw his words back at him. Okay, so he responds to her being near him. He would not be embarrassed. He was seduced and mesmerized by her luscious scent, fascinating eyes, tousled red hair, totally hot body, and she should be flattered by the way she absolutely stimulated him.

"I told you I wanted you. I can't help what you do to me. You seriously create a physical frenzy in me, and if I don't go, I just might embarrass myself." Ben smirked, letting her know he wasn't sorry she made him hot.

"Ok, see you later." Liz reached up, kissed Ben on the cheek, turned, and walked away.

Ben just watched her hips as she put an extra swing in them, as they swayed back and forth. He needed a minute to get himself back in check, so he loaded up the boards on the Jeep and headed to the shop. Ben was very pleased with the way the day had begun. They had talked some about her fears. He tried to reassure her that he would do whatever she needed. Ben would like to talk more about what she wanted. As long as he knew where he stood, he could handle anything. The more he found out, the more irresistible she became. She just totally intrigued him emotionally. She needed nurturing. Mentally, she gave him a run for his money, and physically he was incredibly attracted. She fit as no other ever had. He liked it a lot. Ben put the boards away and headed up to his apartment for a shower. He wanted to pick up something special for Liz before dinner. As he headed up the stairs, Jeff was on the way down.

"Hey, how did the clinic go?"

"It went great, the kids really did well, and Liz came out to watch. I'm having dinner with her. Actually, she's making me lasagna." Ben had the biggest smile on his face.

"Wow, I'm happy for you, so things between you two are going well then. Man, how'd you score a home-cooked meal? Maybe you'll get to see the sexy things she bought today. You can tell me all about it tomorrow" Jeff moved his brows up and down.

"I managed to see a bit of a sexy blue lace bra. I bet she got that today. I wonder if there are matching panties. I so want to find out, but I have to keep reminding myself to go slow and stay in control. We talked some after the kids left, and I reassured her that I would do whatever it took to make her feel comfortable with me." Ben was serious about keeping himself contained. "Are you heading out?" Ben noticed Jeff was all dressed up.

"Yeah, I'm taking Josie out, we're having dinner, and I'm taking her to the new nightclub for some dancing. Are you still planning to go surfing in the morning?"

"I'm not sure about the surfing. I'll have to see how things go, I'd like to, but right now, I want to spend time with Liz. So, you think you'll be out there, or you plan to be out late tonight?" Ben's lips curved up.

"I'm not sure if I'll make it either, you know, if neither of us show up, Owens's going to give us shit, you more than me. He's used to me not showing up, but you're always out there."

"Yeah, I know, but he'll just have to get over it, I have a month to try to get Liz to stay, and I'm going to need all that time to convince her. I have to get going. Hey, do you know where I can go to pick up something special for Liz?"

"Like, what are you looking for, flowers or jewelry?" Ben knew if anyone knew where to get a girl a gift, it would be Jeff.

"I'm thinking of a bracelet with a small key on it or a charm bracelet that I can buy a key charm. I want it to be nice, but I don't want her to think I'm trying to buy her. Do you know what I mean?"

"Yeah, go see Mac at Julie's Gifts. They have sterling silver bracelets and are very nice without looking like you spent a ton of money. Is that what you are looking for?" Jeff liked it when Ben came to him for help or advice because it didn't happen often.

"That's great, just what I was looking for. Thanks, Jeff. I have to go. I'm meeting Liz at seven and don't want to be late. I'll talk to you later," Ben took the steps two at a time. He was eager to get ready and pick a bracelet for her. His anxiety had taken over his heart. It was pounding out of his chest. Tonight, would be so critical to any future. He was thinking long-term relationship. Knowing she was skeptical about getting involved, it was essential that she trusted him with not just her body but with her heart.

~ ~ ~ ~ ~ ~

As Liz started dinner, she tried to convince herself everything would be fine, and those insecure feelings were just nerves. She couldn't relax the overwhelming anticipation. Liz knew she was going to need her backup. It was time to call Kat and fill her in on what was happening. Kat would know how to do this because she had the experience. Liz went to get her phone while she finished getting ready. As the phone rang, she could feel her stomach twisting.

"Hey Kat, do you have some time to talk?" Liz was nervous telling Kat about Ben.

"Hi Liz, what's up? You sound upset?"

"You know there was something I didn't want to talk about the other day? Well, I need to tell you because I need your help. I don't think I can do this on my own." Liz was just rambling on.

"Okay, calm down. Tell me what you're talking about so I can help. Just breathe," Kat never heard such desperation in Liz's voice before.

Liz took a big breath, "I've met someone. I like him a lot. I invited him to dinner. What do I do now?" Liz was beside herself.

"Oh wow, this is big. Okay, first thing to remember is that you are a very intelligent woman. Second, you're a very beautiful, sexual woman. Third, it's about damn time you started taking care of your own needs. Now tell me what's going on." Kat was so calm and practical that Liz could feel some of the stress easing up.

"I met Ben yesterday on the beach. He is one of the owners of the surf shop that I'm using to do my research. When I went to shake his hand, we touched. It was as if he burned me, so I pulled away. I have never felt anything like it. Then I couldn't speak. I got all tongue-tied, and my whole body went all tingly in parts that haven't ever. I just don't know what to do or, better yet, how to do it. Kat, I need your help before I have an anxiety attack." Liz knew she was rambling again, but she couldn't help it. She was so nervous.

"Okay, you know he's interested?" Kat wanted to make sure Liz, and this guy were on the same page.

"Yes, he is very interested. He has made that very clear and wants me, at least sexually. Ben wants to get to know me. He's very pleasant to talk to and look at. It's just when he kisses me, I lose all control, and you know I don't like to lose control."

"Does he know you're a successful writer and have money?" Kat sounded concerned.

This made Liz angry that Kat would think Ben was only after her money. "I don't know if he knows I'm a successful writer, he knows I'm a writer, but as far as the money, I don't like what you're implying." Liz wasn't so sure it was a good idea to call Kat after all.

"Liz, you know that's not what I mean, I'm sure he wants you sexually, but I just want you to be careful, that's all. Some guys can be very deceiving, and what do you know about him?" Liz thought, okay, maybe Kat has a point. Some caution wouldn't be a bad thing.

"Okay, I'll keep that in mind, but the surf shop does very well, just so you know, and he may have a ton of his own money that I don't know about. Now let's get back to what I'm going to do tonight." Liz paused, "I need help. Tell me how to do this. I haven't been alone with a man in such a long time, much less naked in front of one. I don't even know if I could have sex. I might get so nervous I pass out. I'm not sure I can even have dinner with him. Okay, I'm officially insane, crazy." Breathing hard, she was going to hyperventilate, pass out, and that's how he would find her.

"Liz, slow down and listen to me. I can only help you so much. At some point, you have to decide if this is something you really want. I think you can do this and need to do it for yourself. If your body is reacting to Ben this way, it's a sign you're ready to get involved with this man. Just take it slow, and don't let him rush you into anything you're not ready for."

"He has already said he doesn't want to rush or do anything to make me feel uncomfortable. I told him it had been a long time for me, and I wasn't sure about him."

"Wow, you talked to him about how long it's been for you, and that you haven't had sex in over ten years." Kat was surprised Liz had confided in Ben because she didn't share that with anybody. So, Ben must have made her really feel comfortable.

"I just kinda blurted it out, I told him I didn't do affairs and that I haven't been with any other man except for my husband, and I had already told him earlier that Michael had been dead for a long time, so I'm sure he figured it out. When he kissed me for the first time, it was so… I lost control and bolted. He knows I'm skittish, he's afraid he'll scare me off, so when we talked today, he reassured me he would do whatever it took to make me relaxed with him."

"I like this Ben guy more and more. What is the name of the surf shop? Can you send me a picture of him?" Kat was going to have him checked out just to be safe.

"Ben is a very nice guy, and I heard that from an outside source. The name of the shop is Jacobs Surf Shop. Why do you want to know that? I'm not sure about the picture." Liz wasn't sure what Kat was up to, but she definitely had an agenda.

"I'm going to see if they have a website. Maybe there will be a picture of him. I want to see what he looks like."

"You're going to check him out, alright, in more ways than just his looks, aren't you? I don't want you to credit-check him. Are you listening to me, Kat?"

"Yeah, I hear you. Can I look him up so I can see what he looks like?" Kat was still going to have him investigated, she just didn't have to tell Liz unless she found something, and if she did, she would have to deal with Liz being mad.

"So, about tonight, what am I supposed to do? I even stopped by the drugstore just in case. I have an hour before he gets here." Liz decided they would have dinner on the deck. This way, they were alone but still in the public eye. She started to get everything to bring outside to set the table.

"Wow, you actually bought condoms."

"Yes, and I'm not sure if I got the right stuff because I have never in my life bought condoms."

Kat laughed and said, "I'm sure you got what you needed, but he'll probably have his own anyway. So, which of your amazing dishes are you making him? Tell me it's your lasagna?" Kat made a yum sound as if she could just taste it.

"I am making my lasagna, and I was thinking we would have dinner out on the deck. This way, we're alone to talk without anyone overhearing, but not really totally alone. What do you think?"

"I think that is a really good idea and keep things as simple as you can. You don't need to feel pressured or pushed into anything. As long as you feel in control, it should be a very pleasant evening, and remember you want to do this. It's the unknown, that has you feeling nervous and not that you're undesirable. You said it yourself he wants you, and you want him. So, have fun and enjoy his company. Liz, you need to talk and get to know each other, find out what he likes, and let him know what you like. Maybe take a long walk on the beach."

"Okay, I think I can do that. I just have to remind myself to breathe. I have to go. I still have to make the salad and set the table, thanks Kat, and have I told you lately I love you, and you're the best?"

"You know it, and back at you, you're the best anyone can ask for. You remember that."

After hanging up with Kat, Liz felt more confident, knowing she'd be fine. Her best friend would never let her fall flat on her face. Now, if she could just maintain control, that was the key. For the next hour, she tried to keep busy with getting ready for dinner.

She had ten minutes before Ben would arrive and had everything just the way she wanted it. All she needed was for him to get there. She decided that because she was so nervous, she couldn't keep walking to the window. Liz would try to rest her eyes on the couch and breathe. This was it, she was doing it, starting a life for herself, even if things didn't work out with Ben. Even though she hoped it would, she knew she was going to need more in her life. Just what the more was, she didn't know. As she lay there and tried to rest, she heard the roar of a vehicle. She scrambled up and ran to the door and could see Ben coming up the walkway.

~ 6 ~

Ben had found exactly the bracelet he wanted but wasn't sure how he could present it to her. He didn't want her to think he was coming on too intense, but he wanted her to have it. On his way to her place, he also picked up some flowers. Although he knew it was overkill, he just couldn't help himself. He could feel the anxiety building inside him and wanted tonight to be perfect. It would be vital to any future relationship. He needed to heed his own warnings to remember to keep in control and let her run the show.

Ben made it to her house, and as he parked his old beat-up Jeep in her driveway, he couldn't help but notice the black Beamer next to him. Wow, nice ride. Sure, it was a rental, but still… and this house, it was huge, and she rented it for a month. As Ben made his way up the walkway, he thought, man, she must have some money. So why would she want to get involved with a beach bum, surf shop owner? She was probably going to laugh at the stupid little trivial sterling silver bracelet he bought for her. Ben wanted to take both the bracelet and flowers back to his Jeep. He was uncertain what to do, but before he could decide, Liz opened the door.

"Ben, you made it."

"Hey Liz, I was just admiring the BMW in your driveway." He stepped up into the doorway and now noticed what Liz was wearing, a blue top that crisscrossed her breasts, and there was a lot of cleavage showing. His eyes surveyed farther down past her chest and took in her cute denim skirt. Wow, she looked great, and keeping control would be harder than he first anticipated.

"Liz, you look great." He stepped closer as she stepped back from the doorway to let him inside.

"Thanks, come on in. Dinner will be ready shortly. Do you want something to drink? I have wine, beer, and soda." Liz led him into the kitchen and went to the refrigerator to get the drinks.

"I'll have a beer, and by the way, dinner smells fabulous. This is a really nice house. How many bedrooms does it have?" Ben took the beer Liz handed him as he scanned around the kitchen. Walking to the French doors, he saw she had set the table on the deck.

"I see we're having dinner outside. You have a great view." Ben spun around to find Liz watching him. "By the way, you look fantastic. Oh, I have something for you," he handed her the flowers he had forgotten he was holding.

"Oh, Ben, that is so sweet of you. I love them. I haven't gotten flowers from anyone in a long time if it's not my birthday or Mother's Day. I buy them for myself sometimes because I love fresh flowers. Now when I smell their fragrance, I'll be thinking of you, not that you haven't been on my mind anyway." Liz gave him an aroused grin.

Ben strolled toward her. His eyes were very dark and aroused. When he handed her the flowers, he made sure they touched. Both of them felt the sexual tension the minute their hands touched. Ben stepped in, putting his hand to her face to make her look up at him.

"Just so you know, you drive me absolutely crazy, but I promised myself I'd stay in total control. Can I kiss you?" Ben was gazing so deep into her eyes, and she could feel herself melting. Liz put the flowers on the counter behind her, reached up, pulled him in, and kissed him. He moved his hands around her waist but didn't draw her into him. He let her incline into him as her hands went around his neck. The kiss was soft and sweet, he could smell her, and she was intoxicating. Ben was getting hard and could feel the need to deepen the kiss, so he pulled back just enough to disrupt the kiss but didn't pull all the way back.

"You smell so good, Liz. I'm not sure dinner can compare." Ben was just staring down at her.

Liz had to break the overcharged moment, "Oh, dinner is ready. Why don't you grab the salad and the bread. I need to put these flowers in some water, then I'll grab the lasagna." With shaky hands, Liz managed to succeed in getting the flowers into a vase and the dinner out of the oven. They both sat down, and Liz served the salad and the lasagna.

"Boy, this looks so good. It's been a while since someone cooked for me. My mom loves to cook, but if you want the home-cooked meal, then you have to listen to her go on about your life. She wants grandkids, and she's not shy about it." Ben dug in, letting his eyes close, as the sensation in his mouth was overwhelming. "Oh God, this is wonderful. Oh, Jeff is going to be so jealous. Do you cook like this all the time?" Ben appeared to be enjoying her cooking.

"I do cook like this, I love cooking, and this is one of my favorite meals. When I spoke to Kat today, she asked if I was making my lasagna." Liz was enjoying watching Ben devour his food.

"Can I keep you? I would be a very happy man." The words were out before he thought them through. "I'm sorry, I mean…," his fork stopped halfway to his mouth.

"That's fine, I realize what you mean, and I do enjoy feeding people. It's just the caregiver in me. I take care of everyone."

"Who takes care of you, Liz?" Ben stopped eating to look at her.

"I have my daughter and my best friend and agent, Kat." Liz understood what Ben was insinuating.

"Do you have any siblings, and what about your parents?" Ben was certain she was the one who attended to everyone's needs, and she didn't ask anything in return.

"I have an older brother that I don't actually keep in touch with, and my parents, I haven't spoken to in nineteen years. I don't even know if they're still alive." Liz just said it, so matter of fact. Ben contemplated asking why she hadn't talked to her parents.

"That's a long time. Do you mind if I ask you what happened?" Liz didn't say anything, and he doubted she was going to answer.

"I got pregnant at the end of my senior year. My parents were very disappointed because they had plans for me to go to college. They didn't really like Michael, and they wanted me to have an abortion. I refused. My parents told me, don't come to them when things don't work out. I never spoke to them again. Even when Michael died, my parents didn't reach out. They have never seen Paige, and it is their loss. I can't even imagine my life without Paige."

"Liz, I'm sorry you had to go through all that. I can't even envision life without my mom as much as she can be a pain in the ass, and the loss of my dad was hard. But I can see why you're as tough as you are and why you take care of everyone else."

Liz was so surprised that Ben would get that. She hadn't realized it herself. "I just do what I have to and take care of Paige. She is everything to me. It has been just the two of us for so long." Liz looked down at her plate and realized she hadn't touched her food. She picked up her fork and noticed Ben's plate was empty.

"Ben, would you like more? I make so much when I make it at home, I give some to Kat, and I freeze the rest. Do you want to take some to Jeff? I can put it in a container for you?"

"I'll have a little more even though my stomach is full. My mouth wants more. I'll take some home, but not for Jeff. I might let him watch me eat it or might even let my mother try it. She always likes to find a cook as good as she is. This way, she can steal your recipes." Liz scooped out a little more and put it on his plate.

"Hey, you need to save room for dessert. I made that, too. Perhaps we may need time to digest dinner. Maybe when we finish, we could take a walk on the beach." Liz started stacking the plates to clear the table. Ben put his hand on hers to stop her.

"I'll do that. You made a wonderful dinner. You go sit and enjoy your view." Ben was smiling at Liz because he knew no one did this for her, and his mother taught him manners.

"I can't let you do that. You're my guest. What kind of hostess would I be if I made my guests clean up? How about I let you help me?" Liz teased.

"You'll let me, well thank you so much, but you have that backwards. I think it would be me letting you help." As they started picking up dishes, he bumped her with his hip. She almost lost her balance as she recovered. She pushed him in the back.

"Hey," he said, and she laughed at how he acted as if she hurt him.

Ben and Liz loaded the dishwasher, she put some of the leftovers in containers for him, and he went out to wipe off the table. They worked effectively together, and the ribbing and banter flying back and forth made the clean-up so much fun it didn't feel like work.

When they finished, Ben took Liz's hand, leading her out the door and down the deck stairs. Liz just allowed him to lead her, as she appreciated his backside. When they made it down to the sand, Ben turned slightly to face her.

"I have to say, I think that was the best dinner I have ever had."

"Stop sucking up. No one likes a suck-up," she liked teasing him.

"What are you talking about? I'm not sucking up. You just can't accept when someone gives you a compliment."

"Yes, I can, but I know a suck-up when I see one."

"Oh yeah," Ben reached down, grabbing her around the legs and whipped her over his shoulder, and started toward the water. As Liz screamed and pounded on his back, he just laughed at her.

"Suck up, huh? You're going to get wet if you're not nice to me. I don't care if I get wet, Lizzie. Say you're sorry, or you're getting wet." Ben was running all over the beach, just barely coming to the water's edge.

"Okay…okay, I'm sorry you're a suck-up. Now put me down, or I won't make you any more home-cooked meals." That stopped Ben in his tracks, but he didn't put her down. As he realized her butt was sticking out of her skirt. When he went to reach for her skirt to pull it back into place, his fingertips skimmed her lace panties. He felt Liz tense as she realized what he was doing.

"Oh, I'm sorry. I was just trying to tug your skirt down. I kinda forgot you had it on when I heaved you over my shoulder. I didn't intend to get fresh with you." Ben started to lower her to her feet, but her skirt continued to ride up.

Liz was trying to hold it down, and she felt embarrassed over her ass sticking up in the air, well aware she was blushing again. The laughter of the moment was gone. They had just been enjoying each other, but now it was all serious. Liz wanted the fun back. She never had someone do that to her, even if her ass was in the air. She knew Ben couldn't see it, and she just wanted to let go.

"Liz, I'm so sorry for putting you on my shoulder and for touching you." Ben was worried that she was ready to bolt but wasn't sure if he could blame her if she did.

"It's okay, I'm fine, no harm done," she put her hands on his shoulders. "I couldn't see my ass in the air, and you didn't see it either. You just showed everyone else your girlfriend's ass." Liz smiled up at Ben as she wanted to express to him she was all right.

Ben didn't miss the fact that she called herself his girlfriend. "So, you're really, okay? I think if anyone is going to get to see it, it should be me," he pointed to himself.

Ben was now being playful again, trying to lighten the mood. He took her hand again as he rubbed his thumb over the back of hers. They walked silently for a while. It was content silence. The sun had almost settled in the sky, and it had gotten darker.

"Liz"

"Yeah," Liz looked up at him.

"Do you want to head back? It's starting to get dark." Liz was a little disappointed, she didn't want the evening to end, and Ben wanted to go back.

"Yeah, I guess we should. It's getting late." Ben could hear the sadness in her voice.

"Hey, I'm not ready to go home yet, unless you want me to. I just think we should get back to your house before it gets too dark." Ben leaned down close to her ear as he said softly, "I don't think were done with each other." That sent a chill down Liz's back. He turned and leaned down and said, "Get on. I'll give you a piggyback ride." Liz wasn't going to over think this, so she just hopped on. She wrapped her legs around his waist and crossed her feet in front of him. She put her arms around his neck as Ben grabbed her legs.

Ben could feel her snuggled up to his back and her breasts pressed to him, and he knew her sex was pressing against him, too. Oh God, he was getting hard again. Every time they moved, her tits moved, too. Ben started to run down the beach, Liz just thought it was for fun, but he needed to get her home where he could be alone with her. Control, he was supposed to be practicing control.

"What are you doing? I'm too heavy for you. I don't want you to hurt yourself."

"I need to get you home, so I can be alone with you. You did offer dessert, right, and you're not even close to being heavy. I could run at least a mile with you up there." Liz didn't miss the double meaning about dessert.

"You know, I'm not the dessert, right? Although I did make a sweet dessert." Liz said into Ben's ear. She still wanted to keep the playful mood as she started to play with his ear.

Ben could feel her breathing on his neck, and it wasn't helping with his control thing. He readjusted her and slid his hands farther up her thighs. He could feel how tight and slender her legs were. As they reached the house, he slowed down. He wanted to enjoy touching her just a little longer.

"I have something else for you." Ben wanted to give her the bracelet he had bought her.

"I just bet you do, but…." Liz still liked the playing mood, but she wasn't sure she was ready to have sex with Ben, not yet anyway.

"No, I don't mean that, don't get me wrong, I would love that, but I bought you something today. It was just you, and I wanted you to have it."

They were at the stairs as Ben turned around so he could put her down on the step. Then he turned so they were face to face. He couldn't help himself. He kissed her, and as their lips touched, he could feel himself getting even harder. He pulled her into him, and the kiss deepened. As their tongues touched, he could feel her getting aroused. He knew he needed to pull back but didn't want to. Liz broke the kiss, she was breathing hard, but she didn't pull away from him. She was just scanning his eyes.

"Do you know what you do to me when you do that? I know what I do to you because I can feel it, but I don't think you know how you affect me." Liz wanted Ben to know she did want him.

"Why don't you tell me? Because if I affect you the way you do me, we wouldn't be just standing here." Ben knew he was pushing her into something she might not be ready for, and her body language said he needed to pull back.

"Ben, I want to be with you, I do, but I can't, not just yet. You make me feel things that I have never felt with anyone else. I'm not sure how to deal with that, and I don't want you to think I'm just stringing you along. I love when you kiss me and the way you pull me close. I just go blank, and I can't think. All I feel is how close you are, and I have no idea where to go from there."

"Liz, I don't think you are manipulating me. I know you need to go slow," as he smiled and continued, "I know this in my big head, but the little one sometimes doesn't care. I don't want to push you, and tonight has been better than I hoped, so let's go up and have that dessert you made." Ben took Liz's hand and went up the stairs.

"You relax, and I'll go get dessert," Liz walked away, and he needed time to pull himself together.

"Control," he said to himself.

Liz came out with a peach pie, ice cream, and whipped cream. Okay, controlling himself was going to be harder than he thought. Liz put the tray on the table and leaned over to cut the pie. Ben almost lost it. He could see a large amount of her chest and her bra. It was almost too much for him. He was so aroused it hurt. Liz looked up and then glanced at where he was staring. Her face turned red. He didn't think she was very comfortable with showing that much of herself.

"Liz, please don't be embarrassed. I know you may not wear things like this. I do like the way you look, but I also liked the way you looked on the beach that first time I saw you in that big sweatshirt and jeans." Ben tried to reassure her. "I just can't help myself when you came out here with pie, ice-cream, whipped cream, and the way you look. My imagination went crazy."

"Okay, I can definitely see where that would have an effect on you, and maybe we'll get there to fulfill your fantasies at some point." Liz put the pie on a plate and handed it to him with a smile.

With a huge grin, he said, "You will be the death of me," and Liz stopped. Type equation here.

"Don't say that—do you want ice-cream or whipped cream?" Ben didn't realize what he said until Liz got serious on him.

"Liz, I didn't mean it like that. I'm sorry."

"It's ok. It's just that, they were my husband's last words to me. You didn't know that, so let's just drop it." Liz didn't really want to get into that with Ben.

"Oh Liz, I'm so sorry. I really feel bad that I brought up such bad memories for you."

"Can we just let it go for now? I will share that with you if you want some other time, but I just want tonight to be about my future and not about my past."

Ben understood and wanted to ease past the emotional moment, so he pulled the box from his pocket and handed it to her. "I told you I have something for you, and I want you to open it now."

Liz took the small square box from him and just looked at it. "Ben, you know you didn't have to do this." Ben could tell she was still having a hard time getting over the emotional feeling.

"I know I didn't have to; it just had your name on it. Liz, look at me." As she did, he said, "I got it for you because I wanted to."

Liz opened the box and was so surprised to see a very delicate silver bracelet with the cutest little key on it. She took it from the box and just gazed at it. It was so beautiful. Liz hadn't ever seen anything so exquisite.

Ben was happy he decided to give it to her, especially because it put that gleam in her eyes. She didn't look like she would laugh in his face now. She looked with amazement at the small gift as if it was the best thing anyone had ever given her.

"Oh Ben, it's so beautiful. I can't believe you got this for me. I love it." Liz got up from the table and went to kiss Ben as she leaned in. He pulled her into his lap. She freely and passionately kissed him, she could feel his erection press against her ass, and she couldn't help but squirm a bit.

The dessert and bracelet were forgotten, Ben stood, taking her with him, and he went to the huge lounge chair and laid her down on his side, so they wouldn't go too far. He didn't break the kiss as she pushed her tongue into his mouth. He just let her take the lead, and he would go where she wanted. Liz moved so she was now on her side, which lined them up, and Ben wanted to press himself to her so badly.

Liz just let herself go and tried not to consider where this might be going. Just let her body lead her. She wanted to feel Ben against her. His arousal was intoxicating. She pushed harder against him, he moved to his back, and she moved on top of him.

Ben's hands moved to the side of her waist, just below her breasts. She didn't pull away, so he went father up her body until he reached the bottom of her breasts and could feel how heavy they were. He wanted to cup them but didn't want to press her, but when she pushed into his hands, he almost lost it. He caressed her breast on the outside of her clothes, and her tits were so big, his hands didn't even cover them. He would have to stop this because he was going too far for sure, and Ben broke the kiss.

"Liz, if we keep doing this, I will go crazy. I want you so badly, and I'm going to lose it. I need to know what you want because I don't want to push." Ben hated to stop, but he knew she would withdraw from him if he pushed her too hard.

"I just want to feel you up against me. I haven't had anyone so close in so long. I didn't realize how much I missed the contact, and you make me want to go crazy, and there's never been anyone to do that. I want more, and that's a first for me, but I think we should move inside." Liz didn't want to stop because she wanted to feel Ben inside her.

"Is this what you really want? You need to be sure." Ben's little head was saying, "YES, PLEASE!"

"I know I don't want to stop. I want to feel you against me."

Liz went to get up, and Ben stopped her. "Liz, I think we need to talk some more because I want that too, but I'm afraid if we move too fast, you'll regret it later, and I don't want that."

"Please, Ben, can we just see where this will go? I'm not sure about being intimate, but I want to try." Ben let her go, there was no way he wanted to tell her no, but he had to slow her down.

"Liz, I don't have any protection with me, and I'm pretty sure you're not on the pill, so this can only go so far."

"What if I told you I went to the drug store today?" Just the fact she went in and picked up condoms was a sign to Liz that she just might be ready for a sexual relationship.

Ben was very surprised that Liz was going to go through with this. "Liz, I still think we need to slow down and get to know each other first."

"So, you don't want to have sex with me?" Liz started to get up and pull away from him.

Oh shit, "Don't think I don't want to because…" he grabbed her hand, pressing it hard on his erection. "I definitely want," God, her hand on him made his dick jump. Liz didn't pull away from him.

"Oh my God, you're so big. I'm not sure you're going to fit. So, you see, I just may not be able to satisfy you." Liz's self-doubts were back, all her bravery gone. She was thinking again, and that wasn't a good thing for having sex with Ben. Liz pulled away, and Ben let her go. She went to the table and started to clear the dessert dishes. Ben came up behind her and put his arms around her.

"Liz, I don't want you to think I wouldn't be satisfied because that couldn't happen." Ben now had his mouth close to her ear.

Liz just stopped, "I'm thinking it's not going to happen tonight. We both know you're going to go home very unsatisfied, and I'm going to go to bed wondering what I did wrong." Liz could feel the tears welling up, and she tried to swallow them back. She really didn't want Ben to see her like this. She pulled away from him as she gathered the forgotten dessert back on the tray. Liz took everything inside and started to put it away. When Ben came in, he just stood there watching her.

Ben was thinking about how things had gone so wrong and wondering what he should do now. Maybe he should have given things a chance to play out, let her stop things when it was too much for her. He was afraid if it went too far, he wouldn't be able to stop himself. He could see she was very upset, and that was definitely not, what he wanted. He needed to talk to her, so he pulled her away from what she was doing.

"Liz, please stop and talk to me. I didn't mean to hurt your feelings or make you feel like you're not good enough to satisfy me. I want you to know that's not how I feel. Just the fact that you haven't been with anyone is a huge turn-on for me. I know that when the timing is right, I will be a very happy man, but I want something more than just my satisfaction. I want you to be ready and satisfied, if not more because it's been so long for you."

Liz wouldn't look at him. She stared straight at his chest. She knew if she looked into his face, she would cry. "I just needed the feeling of human contact. I really wanted to feel loved in a way that I've deprived myself for far too long." The tears started down her face as she fought hard against them.

Ben put his fingers under her chin, making her look up at him. As she closed her eyes, he moved his hand to her jaw and wiped the tears with his thumb. His heart was breaking for her.

"Liz, please don't cry. It will happen when you're ready. I want it to be perfect for you." Ben took her hand and asked, "Where is your room?"

That brought Liz out of her stupor. She couldn't have heard him right because he couldn't want to have sex now. She didn't want to have sex, everything was wrong. "What?"

"I asked where your bedroom is."

"Why?"

"Liz, I need you to just show me where it is, please." Liz went around him, going down the hallway into the master suite. She had no idea why he wanted to see her bedroom. Liz turned on the light, walked halfway in, and turned to look at him. She just waited for him to say or do something.

"I want to hold you, Liz, on your bed and feel you next to me," Liz looked unsure. Ben went to the bed, turned on the lamp, and turned out the big overhead light leaving a dimly lit room. He sat on the edge of the bed, pulled off his shoes, laid on his back on top of the coverlet, and patted the bed where he wanted her to join him. "Come here, Liz."

Liz walked over, slipped off her shoes, and lay down beside him, he put his arm around her shoulders, and his hand rested on her back. He pulled her in close and kissed her forehead.

"I'm sorry, I should have handled that differently, I didn't want to rush, and instead, I cut you off. I wanted to let you lead and go with what you were comfortable with. When it started to get to where I wasn't going to be able to stop, I panicked because I really don't want you to regret being with me."

"I'm sorry too. I was moving so fast and didn't want to over think it. When I do that, I'll talk myself right out of what I need. It's pretty much how I've survived all these years without sex."

"As long as you're interested, and I know I am, we will have sex. I want to make you feel so incredible, to see you come for the first time by my hands, lips, and cock. You just don't know how much I want that," Ben was hard again.

"I want to experience that. I want to lose myself in the feeling of you. To come by someone else hand, I have taken care of my own needs for so long. I can't even imagine what it would be like."

"Liz, I could do that for you, if you'll let me. I would love to feel your body as you come. We don't have to do anymore. Just let me take care of you for once."

Liz wanted to say yes to Ben's request, but she was thinking now.

Ben felt her tension next to him, so he just took it upon himself to try. If she didn't want it, she'd stop it. He reached down, brought her face to his, and kissed her. He deepened the kiss by running his tongue along her bottom lip, and she opened for him. Ben took that as a good sign, so he started running his hand along her back. Each time he went farther down until he was at the top of her ass. Liz was getting aroused. He could tell by the way she was breathing, and she moved her leg over his. Ben now kissed her neck, moving down over her collarbone. His hand moved to her ass. She was pushing herself against him, passed being aroused as her leg pressed on his dick.

Ben kissed his way down her chest. He felt the top of her breasts and moved her top aside to expose a little more to him. Liz made a small sound as if she was losing herself in the amazing feeling. So, Ben knew it was time to make her come. If he waited much longer, he would lose control. His hand reached inside her skirt, and he could feel she was very wet as he rubbed over her panties. Ben found her clit and made little circles with his finger. She was thrusting herself against him. He knew she was close, so he pressed harder and faster as he sucked on the top of her breast.

"Oh yeah, come for me, Liz." His voice was raspy with his own need. She started to shudder and moan as she came hard. Ben watched her face tighten up, as she dug her nails into his arm. Ben closed his eyes because he was coming just as hard. The hot semen coated his underwear. Just watching her come was too much for him. She was so beautiful. As Ben opened his eyes to see Liz watching him, she must have known what happened because she had an amazingly big smile on her face.

"Oh my God, Ben, you couldn't know how that was for me. I don't think I have ever had a release that strong before. I can't believe you did it without taking off my clothes. I've been nervous about taking my clothes off in front of you."

"Liz, I plan to look at you. I want to get my fill because you're a beautiful woman. I want to see what's under your clothes, what color your nipples are. I want to look at your pussy and taste you. I want it all, Liz. Can you handle that?" He paused, "But, this was enough for tonight. I'm going to have to clean up because, in case you didn't realize it, I came in my pants. Which hasn't ever happened before, but I just lost it when you came."

Ben got up and went into the bathroom. She just watched him go. When he shut the door, she let out a huge breath. "Oh my God, I can't believe I did that." Ben made her feel so good. She didn't know how she managed to live without a man in her life. Could she go all the way and have sex? As Ben said, he expected to see her naked. That would mean all of her imperfections would be on display. Ok, don't think, just let it happen and remember this is something you want and need. Liz got up and pulled out clothes to wear to bed. She went to the bathroom in the hall, putting on a big T-shirt and boxers she liked to wear. Liz went back into the bedroom and climbed in bed.

Ben went into the bathroom. The first thing he noticed was the huge shower. As he pulled off his jeans and his soaked boxers, he thought about how it would be to shower with Liz. Her naked body pressed up against the wall, while he buried himself deep inside her. He'd pump so hard into her and could feel his body reacting to the thought, and he just came. Ben pulled himself out of the fantasy and looked for a washcloth. He would get Liz into that shower soon.

Ben came out of the bathroom in his jeans and walked to the bed as he noticed that she had changed clothes. She was ready for bed, and it was time for him to leave, even though he didn't want to. Liz patted the bed for him to join her, so he got in next to her as she snuggled into his arms.

"I have sweats or shorts that will fit you if you want to get out of your jeans.

"I should go."

"You don't have to go. If you don't want to, you could stay. I'd really like that."

"I'd like to stay and hold you, Liz."

Ben changed into the sweats she offered him and got comfortable under the covers as he spooned her. He wrapped his arm around her waist, so the bottom of her breasts rested on his arm. He could get used to having her in his arms every night. Ben listened to Liz's breathing slowly, so he knew she was asleep. He closed his eyes and fell fast asleep.

~ 7 ~

Liz cleared the sleep-induced fog from her head as she realized Ben was sleeping next to her. She didn't think he was awake yet because his breathing was still slow and steady. He had one hand on her breast and his leg over her hip as he still spooned her. She could feel he had an erection that snuggled against her ass. Liz didn't want to move and wake him. She closed her eyes and began to go over last night. How wonderful it felt to have Ben touching her as he gave her the best orgasm she could remember. He didn't even take her clothes off. How crazy was that! Liz wanted him to touch her more, and maybe she would actually have sex with him. She was getting wet thinking about Ben. She wiggled her butt against his erection.

"Good morning to you, too. I thought you were awake. So, you can feel what you do to me even in my sleep?"

Liz giggled, "I guess I can, and it wouldn't have anything to do with the fact that you're fondling my boob, would it?"

"I'm quite fond of your boobs, as a matter of fact," Ben whispered into her ear as he kissed her neck. "What do you want to do today? I was hoping we could spend the day together."

"I'd like that, but I'm not sure what I want to do." Liz couldn't think with him kissing her like that. "If you keep kissing me like that, you're going to drive me crazy, and then I won't be responsible if I attack you." She turned to face him, and she looked into his smiling eyes.

"So, you're going to attack me? I don't think I'd press charges." Ben was kissing her cheek and moving his way down her neck. He gave her neck a little love bite as he sucked.

"Oh my God…. Hey, you're going to give me a hickey!" As Liz struggled to get free, Ben sucked harder. "Hey, stop. I'm not a kid. I can't walk around with a hickey on my neck."

"Sure, you can. This way, all the dudes around here will know you're taken." There was so much truth to that, wanting to mark her as his own. Ben realized it felt so right for him, and it had from the first time he laid eyes on her. Staying the night and sleeping with Liz was one of the best nights, and they kept their clothes on.

"Ben, I can't. I'm thirty-seven. It will look ridiculous." Ben stopped and rolled her over and just looked down at Liz. "What? Why are you looking at me like that?" Liz wasn't sure what happened to stop the fun play, but Ben got all serious looking.

"You're thirty-seven?" He asked it as if he didn't believe her.

"Yes, I have an eighteen-year-old daughter. Remember, why, how old are you?" Liz hoped he wasn't going to say something like twenty-nine or less. She hadn't given much thought about how old Ben was, but now, the way he still just stared at her, Liz wasn't sure she wanted to know any more. A big smile came across Ben's face as Liz just waited for him to say something.

"I don't think I'm going to tell you how old I am." As his playful tone was back, Ben rolled on top of Liz.

"Is it that bad? You're not jailbait, are you? Good thing we haven't had sex yet." Liz figured if he was going to have fun with this, then so would she.

"No, I'm not jailbait, smart ass, and I'm plenty old enough to be on top of you."

He started to run his hands down her sides to see if she was ticklish, and she started squirming and laughing. Ben's face was in the crock of her neck, kissing and snorting in Liz's ear. She was screaming and thrashing to get out of his hold.

"Stop, I'm going to wet my pants…Please." Liz almost couldn't breathe when Ben stopped.

"So, your ticklish, good to know for future reference, so do you want me to teach you to surf today?" Ben wanted to get Liz out in the water with him, and the thought of them on the surfboard together was hot. The image of Liz in a wetsuit came to mind, *oh yeah*. He could get close to her, which would help her feel comfortable with him, and that was what he wanted more than anything, for her to be completely relaxed.

"Good subject change, you know. I could just ask Jeff or Owen how old you are."

"They won't tell you because I'll tell them not to, and that was a good subject change yourself. What about the surfing lesson?" Boy, Liz didn't miss a thing. He thought after tickling her, she would have forgotten about his age. Ben didn't want to give her any other reason to get uptight. The age difference wasn't that much, and her age wasn't a big deal to him, but he needed to call his brother and Owen.

"I don't think that's a good idea. I could break my neck."

"I won't let you break your neck."

"Okay, I'll try, that's the best I can do, but remember, no laughing, you hear me. I need to take a shower and make some coffee. Do you want me to make you some breakfast before we go?"

"You don't need a shower to go surfing, you'll want one after, and I think I should take you out for breakfast after that dinner you cooked for me last night. If we were at my place, I'd cook you breakfast because I make a mean omelet."

"Okay, but I still need to use the bathroom. I at least need to wash my face and brush my teeth and hair." Ben let her up and watched her as she went into the bathroom. He noticed she didn't shut the door. He got up and started to collect his clothes and shoes. Ben went to the bathroom door and looked at her.

"Can I get my boxers? They should be dry by now."

Liz turned to retrieve his boxers from the shower door. She blushed as she gave them to him. Liz had forgotten he wasn't wearing any underwear. Ben just smiled, turned, and walked out.

Liz looked at herself in the mirror. She could see in her reflection the happiness she felt. She saw the very small changes, like the light in her eyes and the color in her cheeks. She knew it was all because of Ben. Just having him stay last night and hold her, he made her feel like this. People take for granted the closeness that comes when you have someone special in your life. The feeling of having someone embrace you, just listening to him breathe, and the weight of his body, made her feel safer than she would have ever thought.

Liz realized how much she was just a shell of a person before and knew that she was changing because of Ben. He made her feel more confident. Liz knew becoming attached to Ben wasn't a good idea because she was here for the month, and then she had to go back to her old life. They couldn't be any farther apart, with her in Jersey and him living here. She would have to enjoy the time she had with him.

When Liz got home, she knew she would have to make some changes, and after being with Ben, it should be easier to start dating. She finished getting ready and went into her bedroom. The room was empty, and Liz noticed Ben had made the bed. She went to her dresser, pulling out a new pair of shorts and a fitted t-shirt to wear for the day. Then she made her way to the kitchen to find Ben.

Ben was leaning against the counter, drinking a mug of coffee. There was a mug of coffee on the counter behind him.

"Wow, you made the bed, and coffee, too." Liz reached for the cup that Ben was handing her.

"I just left it black. I wasn't sure how you took it. You might like it sweet."

"I do, two spoons full of sugar with a little cream. Thanks for making it." Liz took her first sip of coffee and let the hot liquid glide down her throat. "Mmm… this is really good. It hits the spot."

They got into Ben's beat-up jeep and headed to the diner. Liz looked at the pretty houses and the beach as they went by. As they pulled into the parking lot, she noticed how crowded it was. Liz saw the diner. It was a long, narrow building with picture windows along the front. You could see the people eating inside. The food must have been good because, by the looks of the outside, it didn't look like they should be serving anything. It looked like the building was condemned. As Liz got out of the Jeep, she looked at Ben. "Do they have good food here?" Liz looked skeptical.

Ben just took her hand, pulling her inside. Liz was surprised to see the inside was very nice, clean, and how many people the place held. A young, pretty waitress came up to them and smiled big at Ben. "Hi, Ben. I'll have a booth ready. Just give me a minute to clean one off for you."

Liz could feel her insecurities again, even more now that she knew Ben was younger than she was. He must have felt her tense up because he squeezed her hand. Liz looked up at him. He smiled, leaned down, and kissed her right there in the diner. She blushed right down to her chest, and he whispered into her ear so no one could hear. "By the way, nice hickey. I like it."

Liz grabbed her neck where Ben had sucked on it. She knew she was now even redder than before. She turned into him to hide her face in his chest. As the waitress came back to the front, she grabbed menus and silverware and nodded her head for them to follow her to their table. Liz noticed Jeff and Owen were having breakfast a few tables down as they walked. Ben sat down in the booth and watched her walk right past him. Liz walked up to Jeff's table, as they both looked up at her. "Hey guys, can you do me a big favor and tell me Ben's age?"

Jeff just turned to see if Ben was in the restaurant, and Ben was nodding his head in a no motion, but Owen couldn't see Ben and just answered, "Thirty-five, why?"

"I just wanted to know, and he didn't want to tell me. Thanks," Liz turned and walked back to the table where Ben sat. She had a huge smile on her face as she saw Ben shaking his head.

Ben knew she got what she wanted by the look on her face. He would have to remember that she didn't forget about anything and that she'd get what she wanted in the end. He watched as Liz approached the table, and when she sat down, he said, "Remind me that you don't play fair and that you will always get what you want."

"Hey buddy, you snooze, you lose. Them there are the breaks." Ben noticed Liz didn't seem too affected by what she had just found out. She was still in a playful mood.

"So, are you ok with me being younger than you?"

Just as Liz was about to answer him, the waitress was back to take their order. "Can I get you some coffee?" She looked at her and back to Ben.

"I'll have coffee, and we'll have two of the specials. Liz, do you want more coffee?"

"I'll also have coffee, thanks," the waitress took their menus and left to put in their order. "So, as I was about to say, I don't really have a problem with your age besides the fact I hate it."

"It's no big deal, not to me anyway, I like you just the way you are, and it's going to be so much fun to teach you to surf. Just remember now, it's my turn." With a devilish grin, he was looking forward to getting Liz into a wetsuit and out in the water.

Ben noticed Jeff and Owen leaving as they walked to their table.

"Thanks dudes. If I wanted her to know, I would have told her."

"Sorry 'bout that, I didn't know. So, what's the big deal anyway? Liz should know she's dating a man way older." Owen just looked from Liz's smiling face back to Ben. "What?"

"Thanks Owen, you are my new favorite guy," Liz couldn't help but feel a little better about the age difference, and besides, this was just about having fun and hot sex. They were both adults, and she could enjoy a younger man. She wasn't looking to get married or anything. She would have fun and go home, back to her life in New Jersey.

Liz now knew she could get a life when she went home because of how Ben made her feel. He wanted to have sex with her that made her feel desirable, she wanted Ben too, and no one had ever had that effect on her. Maybe tonight would be the night for them, caught up in her thoughts, her phone rang, pulling her back to the present. She pulled it out and looked at the caller ID.

"I have to take this, it's my agent. Excuse me," Liz scooted out of the booth and went out the door. She knew Kat wanted all the details from last night, and she couldn't talk with the guys around. Liz answered and said, "Hey Kat, I have so much to tell you."

"So, tell me, I'm dying to hear what happened. Are you still a virgin?" Kat was snickering.

"Yes, in the way you mean, but I did have the best orgasm of my life by a man." Liz went on to tell Kat everything that happened. How great Ben was without even taking any of her clothes off. She could only wonder how great things would be if they were naked.

Ben watched Liz walk away and couldn't wait until they were alone again so he could get his hands on her. Jeff and Owen slid into the booth as Jeff cleared his throat. That brought Ben's attention back to his brother.

"So, I guess things are going well. You didn't come home, and you can't miss the hickey on Liz's neck." Jeff said with a smirk, knowing Ben didn't do things like that.

"Yes, things are going very well, and the rest is none of your business. I don't want you to say anything to Liz about the hickey." Ben didn't want Jeff teasing Liz and making her withdraw from him, so he changed the subject. "Owen, can you get a long board and a wetsuit ready for Liz when you get back to the shop? I'm going to teach her to surf this morning, and I don't want to spend too much time getting everything ready."

"Yeah, I can do that. Man, I wish I could be there to watch. I bet she does great."

"Thanks, and goodbye. Liz is on her way back, and I want you dudes gone before she gets here." Both Jeff and Owen got up and walked by as Liz came back to the table.

"See you later, Liz," Owen was grinning from ear to ear.

"What was that about?" Liz wondered why Owen looked like he knew some great secret.

"I just asked Owen to get a board and a wetsuit ready for you." Liz's face started to turn red as she looked at her hands.

"Oh great, everyone's going to know how much of a spaz I am, and I didn't even think about the fact that I will have to get into a wetsuit. What am I going to wear under it? I didn't bring my suit." A huge smile invaded his face, and she just looked at him. "I am going to wear something under it, right?" Ben had to let her off the hook and told her she would just pick out a suit, and it would all be ok. Even though he wanted to continue the playful banter, he didn't want to make Liz feel any more anxious about learning to surf because he wanted her to be as open and comfortable as possible. Their food came, and he reassured her it would all be fine.

They went into the surf shop, Owen had the blue board at the door, and he said, "I have a wetsuit in the dressing room waiting for you."

"Thanks Owen, Liz, you pick out a suit, I'm going upstairs to get my stuff, and I'll meet you back here." He leaned into her ear and said, "I want to see the suit before you put on the wetsuit, and it has to be a bikini." The hot air from his breath made her skin break out in goosebumps and her nipples harden to a point. She shivered, and he didn't miss her reaction. As he leaned into her, she could feel just how he reacted to her by the hard rod pressed against her ass.

Liz whispered, "I can't wear a bikini. I don't have the body."

"The hell you don't. I think your body is hot as hell, and you will do as I asked. I will be the only one that will get to see it." Ben hated being so aggressive with her, but he knew she didn't think of herself as being attractive, and he had to make her see that she was a very beautiful woman. He also knew he was a selfish bastard and wanted to see her in a bikini. That thought made him even harder. "I promise you. It will be sexy. It's making me hard thinking about you in a bikini just for me." He nudged his erection harder up against her.

"Ok, but just for your eyes only, and it's not going to be a string bikini. I have to be able to hide the fact that I've had a child." Liz was trying to think of how she was going to pull this off.

"I told you before, Liz, I want to see it all, and I will love licking and tasting every inch of you. I want to feel every part of your body in my hands, and I want to know how it feels to be inside of you. This is how I feel about your body. You make me crazy, and I can't stand it. You are the most beautiful woman I have ever seen, and I want you. I'm going to get my stuff and hope my hard-on goes down, but I know the minute I see you in your suit, it will be back, and it's going to be very hard to surf knowing what's under your wetsuit." Ben walked straight to the stairs and disappeared.

Liz started to look through the bathing suits, not sure what she was going to find if anything she could wear. Everything Ben just said was going through her mind. What he wanted to do to her, it made her insides melt, and she was wet and horny. She wanted to feel Ben inside of her, too. It made her want to pick out a suit that would drive him crazy. It gave her such power and the confidence to pick a much more daring suit than she would ever have before.

She found a couple of suits and took them into the dressing room. Liz took a big breath and tried them on, she did find one she liked, and she didn't even think it looked half-bad. She stood in the mirror looking very pretty in a hot pink and black two-piece bathing suit. The top of the suit was black with small hot pink flowers and little green vines with a gold accent between her very full breasts. The cups had underwire, so it felt just like a bra. The bottoms were hot pink and had the same accents on each side, holding the back and front together, and they were more like a brief cut, so it didn't show any signs of the few stretch marks she had. Liz just turned around to look at her ass when she heard Ben.

"Can I come in and see Liz?" The want in Ben's voice let Liz know just how much he wanted her.

"Yes, I found a suit I can handle wearing and one I think you'll like." Liz walked out from behind the curtain, enjoying the look in Ben's eyes as she turned around to give him a full view. It made her feel sexy and wanted. It was a feeling she hadn't felt before. She didn't even remember Michael looking at her like this.

She heard him say her name so softly, "So, do you like it?" She asked, even though she knew he did, she wanted to hear him say it.

Ben walked closer, putting his hands around her waist, and pulled her close to him. "I love it Liz, you're so beautiful, I don't want to put you in a wetsuit, and I don't want to keep you all to myself either. I want to show you off. It's crazy, you make me crazy."

He bent down and kissed her as he pulled her hard against him. Her breasts pressed flat against his chest, his hands ran up her back, and his fingers spread wide as he moved them to her sides. He touched the side of her breasts, she gasped, and she broke the kiss. They were in the dressing room area but still in the hallway, and people could see them if they walked by. Ben pulled her behind the curtain as if he could read her mind and turned her to face the mirror as he kissed the side of her neck, his hands went around her waist.

"I want you Liz, so bad I almost can't control myself. I want to feel you. Can I touch you?" His hands moved up her stomach to just below her breasts, waiting for her answer.

She moaned and hissed, "Yes, please touch me, Ben," Ben's hands moved up to cover her breasts, and he squeezed and pushed them together as he kissed her neck, he looked into the mirror, and he watched her watching him. Her tits were so big, they spilled over his big hands, he pulled the top of her suit down a bit, and he waited for her to stop him. She didn't, so he slid the strap on one side down and could see her hard nipple. It was a dark rose and so big he had to pinch and pull it. As she closed her eyes, a loud moan escaped her mouth, and she pressed up against him as if she needed him to hold her up. His dick was so hard, he thrust it against her ass as he pulled down the other strap. Now he could see both of her tits, and he wanted a taste.

"Excuse me, but you might want to take that upstairs. This is a place of business, and we can hear you out here." Jeff snickered because he wanted to give Ben a hard time about having what sounded like sex in the changing room. It was something Jeff never would have believed his brother was capable of, much less actually doing. It was more his style, and it was good to see his brother having a bit of fun for a change and losing that steel control of his.

The sound of Jeff's voice pulled them back to where they were. Liz's face and neck quickly turned beet red as she wrapped her arms around herself. Ben knew she was embarrassed. He turned her in his arms and whispered in her ear, "I'm so sorry I got carried away. Are you ok?" He pulled her suit straps back into place as Liz buried her face into his chest. He wanted her to look at him. "Liz, look at me," she didn't move, so he put his hand under her chin, pulling it up.

She just closed her eyes. There was no way she was going to look at him. All she wanted to do was shrivel up and die. She needed to get out of there, go home, and never try to be with a man again. Even though it felt oh-so-good, and she wanted to do so much more. Being with him made her lose her mind and her control. She didn't do things like this. She was a respected author and a mother, after all, and a person that was as straight as they come. Liz didn't break rules or do anything that could be perceived as irresponsible, and this was as irresponsible as it got. If anyone recognized her and sold the story to a gossip mag, it would ruin her. She just might die from the embarrassment, and then she wouldn't have to deal with it.

"Open your eyes. I need to know you're ok. I need you to look at me. Please, don't pull away and withdraw from me. Talk to me, please." Ben was so afraid she would bolt, and that would be the end of it. There was no way in hell he wanted that, so he had to get her to talk to him. "If it makes you feel better, this is not something I do. I should have better self-control." Liz opened her eyes. He looked deep into her green eyes, holding her so she couldn't pull away.

"I have never ever done anything like this, and I can't ever do it again." Ben wasn't sure if she was talking about him touching her or the fact that they weren't alone. He hoped it was the latter of the two. Because he wasn't done touching her, he wanted so much more.

"What can't you do again?" Ben wasn't sure he wanted to know.

"I can't be in this situation where I'm in public and engaging in irresponsible behavior. I am a well-known author. If something like this made its way out into the public, I would lose my reputation. When I'm with you, I forget everything and everyone around me. I lose control, and I don't like that, ever. I need to get out of here. I'm not sure I can do this." Liz stepped back from him. Ben was not going to let her pull away. He was starting to have strong feelings for her, and he had sensed he could fall hard if they had the time to get to know each other. He wasn't going to let her cut their time short.

"I understand that you have a reputation to protect, and I don't like losing control either. But please don't pull away from me, Liz." Ben moved close again, "I will control any public display of affection and try not to make you lose control in public, but when I get you back to your place, I will make you lose more than control." Ben kissed her forehead, "I'll make sure there isn't anyone out there, okay, and I'll be right back." Ben turned and left, looking at herself in the mirror again. She could see the arousal and happiness in her face that was disturbing and thrilling all at the same time. Liz pulled her clothes and the wetsuit to her chest and waited for Ben.

Ben made sure no one was around as he pulled her out of the changing room and through the door. When they were in his jeep, she was so glad she didn't have to face any of them in the store, even though she knew she would have to eventually.

As Ben drove along the beach, he stole looks at Liz. He noticed she hadn't yet put on her wetsuit. Liz was looking out her side door, and Ben was wondering what she was thinking. "Liz, are we ok? Please tell me this is not going to send you packing."

Liz didn't say anything at first. "I just think we should start the surfing lessons and move past what just happened, even though I won't be able to show my face in the shop ever again."

"I'm sorry, Jeff's an ass, he was just trying to get a rise out of me, but he was right. I shouldn't have started anything in the dressing room. Maybe we should slow things down because I don't want you to think this," he motioned his hand between them, "is just about sex because it's not."

"Ben, you know I'm only here for a short time, and then I have to go home. I'm not sure what is going on between us, and I'd like to find out, but how much more can there be? I wanted you to touch me, I needed you to, but this needs to be about us having fun together. I can't do more than that. I need to be able to take care of myself and know what I want. Being with you is what my body is craving, but my mind, on the other hand, is not sure of anything."

"Okay, let's just have fun and see where things go after we get to know each other better. Are you ready to have fun and learn how to surf?" Ben got the surfboards and put them on the sand. He could see that Liz was nervous by the way she was just standing with her wetsuit to her chest. Ben knew he needed to get her relaxed, so he went to her and took the wetsuit from her.

"I'll help you. Then we'll get started," he said with a grin.

"Do I really need your help, or do you just want to put your hands on me? Now, no PDA," Liz said with a more relaxed tone.

"I will be good, I promise," Ben said as he held out the wetsuit for Liz to step into. He helped get her arms in and turned her, so she faced him. Liz watched him as he pulled the zipper up. Ben stopped just as it was pulling her breasts together. He couldn't help himself as he let out a big breath and pulled it the rest of the way up.

"You remember how the kids started the other day? I want you to start the same way."

"You want me to start in the sand on my stomach?" Liz wasn't sure how all this would work out, but she decided to just have fun with it. Trying new things was how she would grow, hoping she didn't break her neck in the meantime.

Ben was trying to treat Liz just like any other student that he would teach surfing to. However, he knew she wasn't like any other. She was special. How was he going to get her to understand how he felt about her? Just the thought scared him. How would she take it because he wanted it all with her? One month was not going to be nearly enough to make her want marriage, maybe even a child with him. How would Liz feel about more children? She would be so beautiful with his child in her round stomach. Ben's thoughts drifted as he and Liz went into the water.

"Ben, are you really sure about this? I don't want to kill myself," Liz looked a little fearful.

"It will be okay, just lie on your board, and feel the wave as it lifts the board and try to relax. Close your eyes and just feel." Ben watched her climb on her stomach, which left her ass in the air, and the thought of sex on the surfboard came back to mind.

"Oh man, this control thing isn't easy," Ben said under his breath.

"Did you say something?" Liz could hear Ben mumbling something but couldn't understand what he said.

"I was just thinking aloud. Can you feel the wave as it lifts you?"

"Yes, and you're right. It's so nice to be out here on the board, and my eyes closed just listening and feeling." Liz did look so peaceful, but it was time to mix things up.

"Okay, now you're going to try to stand when you feel the rise and do the stands you practiced on the beach. Remember to paddle as hard as you can to get on top of the wave. I'll tell you when." Ben watched her as she waited for the next wave.

Liz was having a good time, and she was going to give it her all. When the next wave came, she started to paddle as Ben yelled for her to paddle harder. She could feel the rise in the board, so she tried to pop up as Ben had taught her to do. As she popped, the board went flying out from under her, and she realized she was going to wipe out. Liz went one way, and her board went the other, but the cord wrapped around her ankle yanked her leg where the board wanted to go. She popped up out of the water to take the biggest breath she could, spitting out the water that went rushing in when she tried to breathe under the water. Choking and trying to get her bearing. She was looking for Ben as he rushed to get to her.

"You, okay? That was a good start. You'll get the hang of it next time." Ben said with a smile.

"Next time, you mean I have to try again? Can't I just say I wasn't very good and leave it at that?" As she pulled the surfboard back to her, she knew he would make her try again.

"What, you think you're special, that you would be the one to get it the first time?" He said as he was laughing at her.

"Well, yes, I did. I figured with the teacher I have. I would be great right off the bat." She was laughing now, too, as he told her, "So next time, make sure you center yourself on the board, okay?"

Liz got back on her board and paddled back out so she would be ready for the next wave. After many attempts, Liz was starting to get the hang of it. She did get to ride one wave for a few seconds, and Ben told her how great she was doing.

"I think we should call it a day. You're going to be sore, and you won't feel it until tomorrow." Ben helped her get the board off her ankle, carrying it to the jeep. Liz heard clapping as she came out of the water and looked to see Owen standing there on the beach.

"I knew you'd do great. Didn't I tell yah?" Owen came to her side.

Liz asked, "How long have you been here? Because if you saw my first tries, you wouldn't be saying that," and they walked to the jeep.

Owen put his arm around Liz's shoulder, "We all have to start somewhere. I think you did great the first time. Right, Ben? She's a natural."

Ben looked at Owen's arm and said, "I told her how great she did. I think you might want to remove your arm, or I can do it for you."

"Oh right," Owen slid his hand off Liz. "Did you like it? Maybe you can see now why we were out here just before dawn surfing in some rough water. How you could clear your head or just think things through or not think at all." Liz could see now how easy it would be to enjoy this every morning. She could look out over the ocean every day and never get tired of it. Just that thought of staying here in California with Ben was too much. Wow, where did that come from? That kind of thought could get her in trouble, big trouble.

~ **8** ~

Ben and Liz said their goodbyes to Owen, so they could return to her house. She was anticipating what was next, would Ben follow through on his promise of making her lose control. God, she hoped so, and her thoughts returned to what transpired in the dressing room. Liz thought about how his hands roamed over her breasts, how it would feel to have his tongue on her, or him sucking her nipples, which made her legs clench together and her eyes shudder closed. The sensation of his hands everywhere on her, she shivered, and her breath hitched with the thought.

She hadn't had a man's touch in so long, it astonished her just how much she was craving Ben's touch, and removing her clothes didn't appear to be such a big problem anymore. The realization of how she was changing, growing, made her smile slightly to herself. It felt so appropriate to have some control over her own life, for once, it was about her desires and not what was best for everyone else.

Ben glanced over at her as she sat motionless, even a little tense. Her head rested against her seat, looking exhausted. Maybe he should just take her home and let her get some sleep. Ben was experienced enough to know how surfing could drain you, especially when you were a beginner. He was profoundly disappointed that they wouldn't experience that emotional and physical bond. Ben decided this time, he would allow Liz to make that decision, and if she was too worn out, then he would just go. He might have to jack off. Ben pulled into her driveway and wondered if she had fallen asleep. "Hey Liz, we're home, you awake?" He watched her eyes pop open as she smiled.

"I'm wide awake. I was just thinking about my day and the amazing new things I've experienced. Things I would, under no circumstances, have done before, and how considerably more I plan to experience," she said with a grin.

"So, you had a decent time, even though you wiped-out and the other surfer called you a Kook?" Ben started to feel the anticipation growing that this wouldn't be the conclusion to their time.

"What is that supposed to mean anyway? Should I be insulted?"

"It just means that you're a newbie and you obstructed a more experienced surfer, but I think everyone does that until they get how it works." Ben got out of the jeep and came around to her side to assist her down.

"I wasn't intentionally obstructing anyone because I went where the board commanded me to. I was struggling to stay on the darn thing and didn't even realize there were other riders nearby." Liz pulled out her keys and unlocked the door.

Ben remained in the entryway as she went inside, twisting to see him standing in the doorway, she said, "You are coming in, right?"

"Do you want me to come inside? Because if I do, Liz, things might happen after what transpired in the shop this morning. I'm not certain I can control myself, especially since I'm painfully aware of what you're hiding under that wetsuit." Ben tilted his head in her direction and held his breath.

Liz sauntered over to where his feet seemed planted to the floor and put her arms around his neck. "I definitely want you to come in, and I'm well aware of what could transpire. Actually, I'm counting on it." Liz pressed her mouth up against his and dangerously dragged her tongue over his lower lip. Ben groaned as he advanced her through the entryway kicking the door closed. He spun her so fast and pressed her against the door as their kissing became frantic with their insatiable appetite for each other. He quickly took over the kiss as their tongues intertwined, and his hands roamed over her body, still encased in the wetsuit. Ben broke the kiss, pulling her with him.

"Where are we going?" She asked as he went into the master bathroom and turned to face her.

"Liz, please tell me you trust that I would never hurt you because I want to cherish you." He had so many things he wanted to do to her in his head, and he didn't know where to begin. He had to get her out of that wetsuit first. He needed to know, unquestionably, that she was all right with what they were about to do.

"Ben, I trust you. I need you so much. I truly want to feel your body against mine." That must have been all the reassurance from her he needed because he went to her and stood directly in front of her. He studied her eyes so intensely, she thought he could see deep down into her soul, and slowly he slipped the zipper downward. She closed her eyes and inhaled shallow breaths to overcome the overwhelming sensitivity of her body.

"Liz, open your eyes. I want to know you're with me. Just tell me to stop if you don't like it or if you change your mind." The zipper now hit the bottom, and he was slipping it down her arms.

She opened her eyes and said, "I will not change my mind. I...." She didn't finish because Ben was now kissing down her neck and moving downward over her collarbone. As he loved her body, he took the wetsuit with him. Ben wanted the wetsuit gone, going to his knees, and having her step out of it. He stood as he pulled off and grabbed her hand to pull her into the shower and closed the door. He started the water to allow it to get hot, and he turned to her.

"You still okay, Liz. I want to take your suit off. I can shower you with it on, if you'll be more comfortable," he said as the water ran over his shoulders and down his chest.

Liz was just watching him, he was only wearing the tight white shorts, and they were getting wet and see-through. She could see his chest with short brown hair that dusted its way down his perfect abdomen and into his shorts and the outline of his very large penis. Wanting to touch his tight abs and feel the soft trail of hair.

"So, that's what the shorts look like under your wetsuit." Ben realized, as he glanced down at himself, that while he had been watching her, she had been beholding him. He looked back at her and could see she was enthralled with his body.

"Do you want me to remove them?" Ben thought it might encourage her, to feel more confident about her own body, but Liz didn't answer. She just nodded her head. Ben stuck his thumbs in the waistband, dropped them down, and stood before her. Her eyes studied him from top to bottom.

"Ben, I want to touch you… can I?" She heard herself say as she stepped into him and spread her hands across his chest. As she slid her hands over the soft hair there, she took a deep breath.

Ben closed his eyes, tried to absorb her touch, and kept his hands in tight fists by his side, letting her explore his body. When her fingernail scraped his flat nipple, he let out a hiss. He was so hard if she touched him any lower, he would lose it for sure.

He opened his eyes and said, "Liz, please, I can't take much more, and if you keep that up or move any farther south, I'll lose it, and that's not what I wanted for…" Ben didn't finish what he was saying because Liz had gone to her knees, took him into her hands, stroked his hard length, and looked up at him.

"Ben, I don't know what I'm doing, but I want to taste you. Will you tell me what to do?"

Liz was just looking up at him with her beautiful emerald-green eyes. He wanted her to suck him so badly, but he was subconsciously fighting with himself not to get off and come.

"Liz, I really want you to give me a blow job, I do, but I can't come before your needs are taken care of," Ben fought for control as he tried to pull her to her feet.

"Who said that's how it has to be, this is what I want, and if I get you off, you'll feel so much better," Liz said with a smile. Seeing him so worked up gave her the confidence she needed. Liz's tongue swept out past her lips, as she ran it along the head of his penis, licking the bead of pre-come that gathered there, drawing him into her mouth, and sucking him as deep as she could. He was so big it made her gag as she pulled back and tried it again.

Ben let out a growl through his clenched teeth as Liz used one hand to stroke him and the other to run down over his balls. He opened his hands and tangled them into her hair to hold her to him. Ben couldn't stop her, so he just allowed her to do what he had fantasized about her doing.

"Tell me what to do and what you like? Do you like it when I suck you deep, or do you want me to lick your balls?" She needed to know what he liked because she wanted to please him.

"Liz, anything you do right about now is going to make me come because just you speaking about doing those things are enough. I'm too damn close… Liz, I need to pull out." Liz started to protest when he pulled out and quickly untied her top and pulled her up, so she was kneeling in front of him. He slipped his dick in between her tits as his hands squeezed her huge tits tight, surrounding him as he slid in and out. Oh, hell yeah, that was the last rational thought he had.

"Holy Shit, Liz," Ben threw his head back, letting out a roar as the thick hot white cream erupted from him, as he was trying to catch his ragged breath, and he saw stars. He thought he might faint, so he slid down the wall, and when he managed to reopen his eyes, she was sitting blissfully pleased with herself, with her chest and neck full of his come. Ben knew he was a sick son of bitch, but he selfishly liked it, his mark on her. He stood and drew her with him beneath the water spray to cleanse her, and he moved his hands over her breasts to wash away his seed. Liz looked mesmerized by him. Her eyes were bright and wide open.

"That was so hot," Liz stated in amazement, "Oh my God, Ben, to see you come so intensely like that was the most incredible thing I have ever witnessed.

"Liz, I need to apologize because I should never have selfishly allowed it to go that far," Ben had the soap and was now washing her.

"Ben, I'm not sorry, and you shouldn't be apologizing because I wanted to do this, and as for you wanting to satisfy me first, you thoroughly cared for my needs last night, and we didn't do anymore. I have never felt more powerful than I did just a minute ago. Although I wasn't sure what I was doing, nevertheless, it must have been satisfying because you... so don't ruin it for me," Liz couldn't talk anymore because Ben was now kissing her, and that's when she realized her bathing suit top was on the floor. She wasn't sure when it happened but was relieved, she didn't have to contemplate him removing her clothes. Her body was now hard-pressed against his, and it felt so incredibly good.

Ben's mouth moved down her neck as he whispered in her ear, "Your turn, you know turnaround is fair play. Now I'm going to taste you, and you're going to come on my tongue."

"But," he could feel how her anxiety made her tense as he went to his knees. Ben pulled the bottoms of her suit downward and didn't look up because he knew if he did, she might reconsider what he was about to do to her and stop him.

"Just close your eyes and take in the sensation of what I'm doing," Ben said as he spread his hands over her hips. He could smell her arousal and knew she wanted this as much as he did, but he was still afraid she might pull back.

Ben kissed down her stomach and felt her suck in as he moved to her hip where his hand was, and his mouth was watering with wanting to taste her, but he didn't want to move too fast, so he encouraged her to open her legs more by moving his hands up and down her inner thigh.

"Liz, you're so beautiful. God, you're wet, and I can't tell you how much I want to satisfy you." Ben looked up at her, and her eyes were closed, and the pleasure that was on her face. It made him smile against her skin, it was time to move south, and he loved that she was a true redhead.

"Spread your legs a little more for me, baby," she did as he asked, and Ben spread her folds with his fingers. He put his face so close that he rubbed his stubble on her and heard her intake of air.

"Oh my God, I'm not certain I can stay standing" Liz leaned against the shower wall for support. She felt his hot breath on her skin as he opened her. She knew she should be embarrassed, but it felt amazing. She couldn't have stopped him even if she wanted to, and she didn't. The moment he put his mouth on her clit, she couldn't control the sound that escaped her lips, even as she tried to press them together.

Ben sucked her clit, flicked his tongue over the little nub, and could tell this was not going to last long, so he added his finger to her pussy. She was wet and so tight. Ben let out a groan of his own and turned his hand, so his finger reached the spot that he thought she'd love. Then he added a second finger as she got close and wanted her to come in his mouth, so he pulled his fingers away, and she let out a sound of protest. When his mouth replaced his fingers, her legs started to shake. Ben grabbed the back of them to steady her as he could feel the sensation of her muscles starting to contract around his tongue. He closed his eyes to take in the endearing sounds she made.

"I'm going to…"

Liz let out a scream, and he pushed his face even deeper into her as she was holding onto his head and pulling his hair so hard, Ben wasn't sure if she even knew she was. He didn't want to let go of her, he moved his mouth back to her clit to ride out her climax, and when her muscles slowed, Ben allowed her to slide down the wall, so she was sitting as he watched her. He was hard again and knew he'd give anything to be able to put that look on her face every day.

Liz melted down the wall because she had never felt anything like that. She tried to slow her breathing as she gathered her wits while thinking about what just happened and realizing that she was stark naked, sitting on the tile floor.

Ben watched her and knew the minute she started thinking because her face had changed from pleasure to embarrassment. He reached for her, pulling her into the warmth of his embrace, and whispered into her ear, "That was so amazing, and I would be an extremely happy man if I could do that every day. To watch you come is the most incredible thing I have ever witnessed."

Liz just snuggled into his chest, breathed in his skin, and asked, "What happens now? The water is getting cold, should we?"

"I think we should dry off," Ben drew her to her feet and grabbed a towel off the rack and wrapped her in it, then got one for himself. He reached for her, hugged her close, caressed her face in his palm, and made her look at him. "You, okay? I want to make love to you now, and I need to know that's what you want, too."

Liz was thinking once more, and she knew she wanted Ben to make love to her, but she didn't want to think about it. She liked it when he just took charge, and she didn't have to contemplate what would happen next. She wanted this for herself, wanted his closeness. As Liz looked into Ben's eyes, she said what she was thinking. "I want you to make love to me, but I don't want to have to think. I want you to take over the control of what happens next." Liz could see the intense look on Ben's face, how he seemed to be struggling with her words.

Ben closed in on her and took her mouth. The kiss had so many emotions. She could taste herself and could feel his passion and lust. The kisses became more urgent, and his desire grew to an ache as his hands came around her, this was what she needed. The heat that came off Ben's body turned her on and gave her a deep craving for him. She sensed her need for him was developing into something so much stronger than them just having fun. She put that thought out of her mind when Ben moved them to the bedroom without breaking the kiss. She backed up against the bottom edge of the bed, picking her up, he placed her very gently in the middle with the towel still wrapped around her, and she knew what was to come next.

Liz tried taking a calming breath, attempting to relax, as she kept reminding herself this was what she needed. After what happened in the shower, she shouldn't be self-conscious. He had seen all of her, but for some reason, when he tried to pull the towel free, she held it. Ben leaned over her, his body next to hers, and kissed her as her mind went back to his tongue intertwining with hers.

Ben slowly removed the towel from between them and pressed his bulky body onto her much smaller frame. He could feel the impression of her hard nipples pressed against his chest. There were so many things he wanted, his mind was reeling. Breaking the kiss, Ben pushed his mouth over her ear and said, "I want to look at you and touch you."

His body glided down hers, kissing her neck and her shoulder. That gave her time to stop him if she was going to change her mind. God, he hoped like hell that she didn't stop him as he moved lower over the top of her breasts. He was encouraged to go further and covered one of her nipples with his lips running his tongue softly over it, Liz shivered, and he knew she was intensely aroused.

Ben pushed back so his body was no longer on top of hers. He had her naked in the shower but tried not to stare at her body. He didn't want her to halt their foreplay, but he couldn't hold back any longer. He sat back on his heels and gazed over her stunning form. Liz went to cover herself, wrapping her arm around her body.

Ben stopped her as he grasped her wrists "Don't, Liz. You are the most beautiful woman I have ever seen, and you have to know what seeing you does to me. I want to please you in so many ways. I almost don't know where to start. Please don't hide from me. Your body is so hot. It turns me on, it's driving me crazy."

Liz closed her eyes as she said, "I haven't had this kind of attention in a long time, and it makes me feel uncertain of myself. No one has ever looked at me as you are right now."

"I know it's hard for you because it's been so long, but there isn't a thing I would change about you, not one thing."

"Really?" She didn't sound like she believed him.

"Do you want me to tell you all the things I love about your body? Because I will, you have the fullest breasts, and your nipples are standing tall for me. They call to me, wanting me to suck on them," Ben's large hands covered them, and he rubbed his thumbs over her nipples and watched as they sprang back to attention. Oh yeah, he was infatuated with her tits, "I could just play here all night." Ben bent and ran his tongue over her nipple, and it tightened even more. Her nipples had to be the largest he'd ever seen.

"I do not have a perfect body, by no means," Liz watched him move over her chest.

"Well, I say you do, at least for me."

"I have stretch marks and a baby belly."

"So, you're a mother, and I love that about you, so if these marks are because you had a child, then I like them, too." Ben said as he ran his hand over her tummy, "If I was so lucky to have my wife carry a child, a few stretch marks would be worth it, besides who has the perfect body anyway?" Ben kissed the marks.

"You have the perfect body, Ben. You want children?" Liz could hear the want in Ben's voice, and she just watched his face and couldn't believe she asked him that question.

"I'm not perfect, not by a long shot. I have scars from surfing and stuff." Ben looked serious as he lay on top of her again. "I hoped one day to have children, but to have them, I needed a wife or at least a steady girlfriend. Someone I cared enough to want to have a child with. I dated a girl in high school and thought we'd get married at some point, but she wanted different things." The thought of Liz pregnant with his child. Ben contemplated the image as he ran his hand over the marks that he wished were from his child.

"What did she want differently?" Liz again couldn't believe they were having this conversation, as they were in bed naked.

"I had to take over the shop, and she didn't want to run a surf shop because she wanted to go to school, and I had to stay. The long-distance relationship didn't work out, she met someone, and that was that. I don't want to talk about this." Ben went back to kissing her.

Liz was no longer thinking about children, only the sensation of Ben's body on top of hers. This was going to happen, and oh, how she needed it. Ben kissed down her neck as his hard-pressed body stroked hers. She ran her hands down his back and drew him to her. "Ben, I need…" she started to say.

"Shhh, I know, I will take it slow," she didn't want it slow.

"No, I want you now. I need you now, Ben," she said as she ran her hands over his ass and pulled him into her harder. Ben took her mouth and kissed her hard as his tongue tangled with hers. He could feel her need, and his need to have her was overwhelming.

"NOW! BEN PLEASE!" Ben reached between them and positioned two fingers to her opening, and slowly he pushed them into her and found she was so wet and ready. Liz broke as she bucked his fingers, and he started to move them faster in and out.

"I need you… in me" Liz reached for him, covering his penis. Ben removed his fingers as Liz tried to position him to enter her.

"Liz wait, I need a condom," but her need was overpowering. God, he wanted her with nothing between them, he knew this wasn't good, but he couldn't think straight as she inserted the head of his dick inside her wetness. Ben lost it, pushing slowly into her because she was so tight. He pulled back, and she groaned.

"Don't you stop, oh my God, don't stop!" Ben slid into her as Liz squeezed his ass, trying to pull him more into her.

"Move faster. I need more," that was all Ben could take because his restraint was gone. He was enthused as he started thrusting harder into her, and Liz wrapped her arms and legs around him.

Ben knew at this pace he wasn't going to last long and reached down in between them and stroked her engorged clit in little round circles. He could feel her tighten around him as she was going to come. Ben watched her as her face pulled tight, she was so close.

"Liz, open your eyes. I want to see you come," just as she opened her eyes, her orgasm smashed into him, and her muscles clamped down on him hard. Ben tried to ride it out, but he needed to pull out as his spine started tingling and his balls pulled up tight, Liz let out a scream, and Ben knew he was a goner.

"I have to pull out, I'm coming," Ben threw back his head and yelled as his hot come spurted over her stomach and chest.

Liz closed her eyes and savored how amazing she felt. How had she lived without this? Ben had been wonderful, and at that moment, she had overwhelming feelings for him but wasn't sure what to do about it. Ben was holding his body just above hers, so he didn't put all his weight on her. He had his head in the crest of her neck, and she could feel him breathing against her skin. She thought to herself just how simply perfect he was. How they both lost control being around each other. These thoughts were dangerous, but she couldn't help herself. So far, she loved every minute she spent with him and had to remember that this was a fling and nothing more.

Ben raised his head to look down at her, and his face was so serious, "Liz, I want you to know I have never had sex without a condom before. I know I'm clean, and I know you're clean, but I have a feeling you're not on any kind of birth control."

"Oh yeah, I'm not," she said calmly, "but you don't have to worry, there is a slim-to-no chance that I'll get pregnant. A couple of years after Paige was born, I tried to get pregnant, and when it didn't happen, my doctor said I have scar tissue around my ovaries. It's not impossible, but we tried for six years and nothing, so I really don't think you have anything to worry about."

"Um okay, I…"

Liz could see the sadness on Ben's face and wasn't sure if he was sad for what she had gone through or if it was disappointment. "It's okay Ben, really I have come to terms with it a long time ago, but if you feel better using a condom from now on, I understand."

Ben didn't know what to say to that, so he said, "We need to get cleaned up. I'll be right back." He left the bed, went into the bathroom, then came back with a washcloth, wiping her stomach and chest, and threw it on the floor. Ben pulled the covers down, helped her climb under, and drew her close to his side. He ran his hand down her back and up as he was trying to soothe her.

All he could think about was how disappointed he was that Liz would never carry his child. As crazy as that thought was, he had seen her image of her with a big round tummy with his child. He took a big breath and tried to put it out of his mind because the most important thing to him was if he had her, that's all he really needed.

Liz could feel how Ben was struggling with what she told him. They had just made love, and it was the best thing she had ever felt, and she didn't want him thinking about all that other stuff now.

"Ben, I know the conversation got a little heavy, but it really is okay. I'm truly glad I waited so long because you are the person, I was supposed to share this with. I have to say you were great. I don't ever remember feeling so wonderful." Ben leaned his head down to kiss her, and she could sense his strong emotions.

"Liz, I feel it too, so much. I'm willing to do whatever you want to do about the condoms. I'll wear them just in case, but it was amazing to have you skin-to-skin. I think I'm getting hard again just thinking about it," Ben rolled on top of her, kissing her once more.

Liz didn't want to put a damper on things, but maybe they should use condoms from now on. Having a baby was not really in her plan at her age, and she broke the kiss and said, "Ben, I think maybe we should use the condoms from here on out. I know there is a very slim chance, but I don't think we should push our luck."

"Ok, do you have any? Because I wasn't thinking, my wallet is out in the jeep."

"I told you the other night I picked some up. They're in the nightstand," she smiled at him.

"Boy, I'm glad you did. Now that I've had you, I'm not sure I'm going to be able to get enough of you. I hope you're ready for that."

"I think now that the first time is over, and I know how wonderful it was, I just might enjoy that," she stopped laughing when Ben reached into the bedside table, grabbing a hand full of condoms. "Well, I guess you weren't kidding," she heard him say, "Nope."

Ben made love to her again, and this time he went slow and looked deep into her eyes, and they both knew there was so much more going on here than just two people having sex. They had only known each other for days, but they had a bond that was strong already. After they both came together, the exhaustion set in, and Ben hauled her on top of him. She laid her head on his chest, and he wrapped his arms around her. She listened to his heart beating. The sound was so soothing, and she closed her eyes, and Ben's slow intake of air told her he was asleep.

Liz was thinking through all that had happened, not using a condom that first time, how reckless that was, and how she was doing so many things she would never, ever do. She always considers her actions and the repercussions.

Ben had made her feel so good. All she could say was it was temporary insanity, and knew it was not really taking any big chances because if she did end up pregnant, it would be a miracle. Not that she wanted a child at this point in her life. Although Ben would make a great father and he deserved to have children, but she also knew it wouldn't be her to give them to him. That thought saddened her more than she could imagine.

The feelings she was starting to have for Ben were overwhelming, but would she consider trying again to have more children if Ben asked her to? What would it be like to carry Ben's child? She must be crazy because she was really contemplating another child when she was sending her child off to college in less than a month.

Liz picked up her head to look at Ben, he was so handsome. He looked so peaceful, and as she observed him, he smiled, and she thought at first glance he was awake, but then she heard a little snore. God, she could so get used to this, and that wasn't good for her to be thinking. She was gone within thirty days and had to go home because Paige needed her. However, didn't she deserve to have someone special in her life? Liz knew she couldn't stay and wondered if she would ever find someone like Ben when she went home. All of this was just too overpowering for her. and Liz felt her eyes grow heavy and exhaustion taking her over, so she just let it.

Ben woke with a start, dreaming of children running through a field as he called for them. They just kept running, and he saw a huge wave coming toward them, and he couldn't get to them in time. The wave crashed over them, and they were gone. Ben was gasping for breath when he realized where he was. He was alone in Liz's bed and looked to see the time. The sun was going down outside, so he had slept a long time. The clock said it was eight-thirty and had slept for hours. Ben laid his head back and thought about his dream because it was crazy. He almost never dreamt. Where did those kids come from? They were in a field, then a huge wave came. None of it made any sense, maybe the kids had to do with the talk he had with Liz about children and the wave had him realizing he would never have a child with her.

"Wow, that was really rough." Ben sat on the side of the bed and rubbed his hands over his face. Then he went in search of some clothes to go find Liz.

~ 9 ~

Liz lay on the lounge chair out on the deck after she woke. She knew she needed to do some serious thinking, so she slipped away from Ben not to wake him. So many thoughts went through her mind all at once, and it was hard to consider everything thoroughly. First, she needed to figure out her feelings for Ben. Only knowing the man for days, how could she possibly think that there was so much between them? If she were home, she'd never have jumped into a relationship with a man, much less a sexual one. Not that she was remorseful for having sex with Ben because she wasn't. Why now? Could it be her fear of losing Paige? That she was going to be alone to live, a life she didn't really have without her daughter? It could also be because Paige wasn't there. She never had this kind of freedom before to do what she wanted. Without anyone knowing, she was having an affair. It was crazy because, after her marriage, she didn't think she could give that much of herself to anyone ever again. With Ben, things felt easy and uncomplicated, they just seemed to fit.

What was even crazier, that she'd ever consider trying to have another baby at this late stage in her life. That was extremely insane, even though she wasn't really too old to have a child. Why would she even contemplate it? Did she want another child to keep from being alone? She didn't think it was possible to have any more children, so why was this pulling so hard at her heartstrings. All of this was running through her mind, the affair, if you could call it that, and the idea of another child, it just overpowered her. Liz was getting a headache and closed her eyes to try to get all her thoughts to stop swarming in her head. "I'm going to have fun and hot sex, that's all, and nothing else," she said to herself and then heard Ben calling her name, so she yelled, "I'm out here, Ben."

Ben opened the door, stepped out, and saw her on the lounge chair. As he sat on the edge, "I didn't realize how long I slept. Why didn't you wake me?" Ben leaned down and kissed her, "Are you hungry? We can get something to eat if you want?"

The sun was starting to set, and the colors in the sky were brilliant. "We can stay in, order a pizza, or I can make something. This way we can watch the sunset. You were sleeping so soundly, I didn't want to wake you," Liz pulled him down to lay with her.

"I don't want you to have to cook for me again. I should be wining and dining you."

"Ben, I love to cook, it makes me happy to take care of people, and food, at least good food. I know how to do."

"And that's the reason I should be taking you out. You're always taking care of everyone else, and I want to take care of you tonight. So why don't you go and put on that pretty little sun dress you had on the other day. The one you looked so sizzling hot in, that drives me crazy, and I need to go home and change. I could be back in one hour to pick you up, and I'm not taking no for an answer."

"Okay, we can go out, but let's watch the sunset first," she said as he wrapped his arms around her and just relaxed into her. He could do this every night for the rest of his life. But there was no way he could tell her that because she'd consider him crazy after only a few days. Man, he had it bad, he could smell her strawberry shampoo, and he rested his head on top of hers. Ben wasn't watching the sunset. He was looking down at her.

"It's so beautiful, isn't it?" She sighed.

"Yes, you are that," Liz looked up at him. He wasn't looking at the sky, just staring at her. She blushed, and Ben said, "I didn't think I'd be able to put that color on your face anymore."

"I hoped it would go away eventually because I hate when it happens."

"Well, I, for one, hope it never goes away because I love it. You're so cute when your cheeks and chest are all pink."

"Well, don't get used to it Mister, because I want it to go away." Liz lifted her chin in defiance as if she could control it.

Ben just laughed aloud at her, she tried to be just so tough, but he knew better. She smiled up at him because she knew she had no control over how she blushed. Liz looked back to the sunset, the beautiful color was fading, and dusk was settling in.

"You know Liz, I had the greatest day today. I don't think it could have been any better."

"Yeah, well, you got laid twice, so how bad could it have been? Not that I'm complaining."

Ben rolled her beneath him and looked into her eyes, "I wasn't talking about making love to you, although that was amazing. But spending the day with you, teaching you to surf, and finding out you were pretty damn good your first time out."

"I don't know about me being any good because all I know is I didn't kill myself out there. I had fun trying to stay on the board, and now I can see why you guys were out in that rough water the other morning when the waves were so big. The limited times I actually stayed on the board for more than a second, I could feel the adrenaline high. I can see how you get hooked."

"As they call it, you get bitten by the surfing bug. Could you see yourself trying it again?"

"You know Ben, I would never have thought I'd be saying this, but yes, I think I would try it again. I wasn't really the athletic type growing up. I was a cheerleader, but nothing that required having any real physical strength. It felt so good to use my body in ways I never did before." Liz smiled up at him because after her words were out, she realized how he would interpret them.

"Yes, you did in more ways than one, and as far as the surfing, let's see how sore you are tomorrow, now I think I had better go and get changed because if we get on the subject of all the other ways your body moved today, we'll never get anything to eat." Ben leaned down, kissed her, and started to get up.

Liz pulled him back down and said, "Ben, I want you to know I had an incredible day, too. I can't remember a day that I spent with someone that has meant more to me than being with you. To have someone to hold me and make love to me, it's something most take for granted, and I wanted you to know how special it was to me."

Ben pushed aside a hair that was blowing across her face, "I know you haven't had anyone in your life in a long time, and we've only known each other days, but I have feelings for you. I can't explain it but today meant more to me than you'll ever know."

Ben pulled her up with him, and she knew she had to lighten the mood because it was getting serious, and she essentially needed to figure out how she felt about him before she could have this conversation. She regarded what he was wearing and began to laugh, "What in the hell do you have on?" Liz backed up a step so she could get a better look at him.

Ben looked down at himself and said, "It was a t-shirt that was sitting on your dresser. I didn't think about needing clothes after we were done surfing. It's a big shirt you must sleep in, and I didn't really look to see what was on it. I just checked to see if it would fit me." Ben was smiling now because he could see a half-naked man and woman on it.

"I do wear it to bed, but it's a left-over promo shirt from one of my books. That's why it's so big." She pointed to the shirt, "That's the cover of my last book, but it looks so much better on you because it fits you. I like where the half-naked woman sits on your chest." She ran her hand over his chest. The shirt was tight and showed off Ben's chest and biceps.

"I happen to like it too, and I think I'm going to keep it. Especially if you wore it to bed, it's been next to your body. Plus, it has your name on it. I can tell people I know a famous writer," Ben pulled the shirt out so he could see her name across his chest, and it amazed him just how he liked the sight of it there.

"One, you can have the shirt if you really want it. Besides, it fits you. Two, I'm not that famous, that you should go around bragging that you know me because people might just say, "Who is that?" and it won't look good for you. Three, if you want to walk around with a romance novel on your chest, who am I to question your manhood? So, if you're okay with it, so am I." Liz just shook her head.

"I would be proud to show my support for you," Ben smiled.

"I think you might want to read something I've written before you go showing all that support. You may be very surprised and not like it, plus you might need to know what you're talking about if they start talking about one of my books."

"Just how many books have you written anyway?" Ben looked alarmed.

"Published I have sixteen and two not, so I have eighteen altogether." Liz just grinned because she could see what Ben was thinking, "I don't expect you to read my books Ben, and I was just teasing you. I think we need to go get dressed so we can get something to eat, or I will need to cook something here."

"No, we're going out, but it is getting late, so I need to move. I can be back in forty minutes. Will that give you enough time to get ready?" Ben kissed her and ran to his jeep. He had put the bottom of his wetsuit back on and wore Liz's t-shirt home. He pulled into the back parking lot because he didn't want any of his crazy family to see him. He didn't have time to go into any details about what was happening with Liz, plus he wasn't sure himself. Ben silently went up the stairs and went into his apartment. He stripped out of his wetsuit, laid Liz's shirt on his bed, and ran to get a quick shower.

As Ben stepped under the hot spray, he took a deep breath and allowed the hot water to run over his back. He closed his eyes and leaned his head against the wall because the image of Liz's shower came to mind. "God, that was so damn good. I could definitely get used to that. Don't go there, or you're going to get hard again, and you don't have time for that because Liz is waiting for you." Ben reached for the soap to finish his shower and got dressed. The entire time he was thinking about how the day went, how great he felt when he was with her. How she just fit with him, like two puzzle pieces, and knew realistically, there was no way he could fall in love with her in two days. But if he only went by the way he was feeling, he couldn't deny he wanted more with her. Ben wanted more time to see if what he felt for her was real or did it have more to do with the way he felt lately. How he didn't want to be alone anymore and what it could be like to have a wife and family, a life more than what he had now. Ben grabbed his keys and headed back to Liz.

Liz had watched Ben sprint away, and the first thing she did when she went inside was check her phone. She knew there would be a hundred calls from Kat and Paige. She started to listen to her messages. They started out with Kat saying, "Call me," then went to, "What the hell is going on? You better call me, or I'm getting on a plane to make sure he hasn't killed you." Liz figured it was best to just call Kat and get it over.

Kat answered on the first ring, "Okay, so you're not dead, better start talking and tell me what's kept you from answering my calls."

"Well, hello to you, too. I have been busy trying to have the life you said was necessary to have."

"So, tell me everything," Kat sounded breathless.

"I don't have a whole lot of time because Ben is going to be picking me up, we're going for dinner, so it has to be the short version. Ben and I had sex twice, and it was amazing. I came so many times, I couldn't count anymore. I have no idea why I waited so long to have sex, and I know I won't be able to do without it anymore. I like him a lot, and he taught me to surf today, and I was good at it." Now Liz was the one out of breath.

"Oh my God, Liz. That's great. All I've been able to think about is you. So, you like Ben? It must be electrifying when you first start a relationship, and everything is fresh and new."

"Hold on, Kat, no one said anything about a relationship. Remember, it's just a summer fling. I can't go crazy. Ben is the first man that I've had sex with, in a long time, and I'm not about to fall off the deep end." Liz wasn't sure if she was trying to convince Kat or herself. Although, she didn't want Kat to start making more out of all this until she could figure out where she stood.

"Liz, I just don't see you having an affair with this man and not caring about him. You haven't allowed yourself to get involved with anyone for whatever the reason. I think you have to feel some emotional connection to him. Otherwise, you would have never permitted him to get close to you."

"How do you know me so well? Okay, I do feel something for him, I'm just not sure what that is, and it's only been two days. I don't want to make more out of this than I should. I need to be careful because I can't make a mistake and fall for him. Besides, I don't have the experience to be making any decisions. The last time I started a relationship, I was seventeen. I'm not sure I would have chosen Michael as my spouse if I were older, more mature, and if I didn't get pregnant, the first-time having sex with a boy. Kat, I can't do this right now, Ben will be back any minute, and I'm not ready. I'll call you tomorrow. Okay, I love you. You know you're the best."

"Okay yeah, love you too. Tomorrow, you better call me!" Liz hung up and ran to get ready.

When Ben picked Liz up, he could tell something was different. For one, Liz was quiet and withdrawn. He wasn't sure what happened and why she looked deep in thought. He hoped she wasn't regretting getting involved with him. What would he do if she pulled away? Would he just let her walk away? He started thinking of ways he could try to keep her with him. Man, he was sounding like a stalker. He needed to get a hold of himself. What was wrong with him?

"Liz, is everything okay? You're quiet?" Ben held his breath and waited for her answer.

"Everything is fine. I was just thinking about my day. I told Kat about how I learned to surf. She wanted all the details. I didn't really have time to talk, so I told her I would call her tomorrow."

"All the details, is that going to include what happened after you're surfing lesson?" Ben could feel the pressure on his chest starting to ease. He had been making too much out of her silences.

"Well, you have to know, she is the closest thing I have to family, and Kat is my very best friend. I won't share any of the particulars, if you prefer me not to, but I have to warn you, it will be very difficult to hold her off. She might even show up here, so it really may be in your best interest if I tell her everything. She can be a little overprotective where I'm concerned, even though I'm older. She thinks she's wiser." Liz gave him a grin because she knew he really didn't have much of a choice.

Ben looked over at her and said, "I guess you can tell her if you want, but you have to make sure I get credit where credit is due," smiling, he added, "By the way, you look great." Ben pulled in front of an Italian restaurant, "They have the best pizza. I hope this is okay."

"This is great, I love pizza. and just so you know, I promise all credit will be where it belongs." Ben helped Liz from the jeep with his body so close, her body slid down his. He kissed her, took her hand, and pulled her into the restaurant.

As the waitress cleaned tables, she looked up and said, "Hi Ben, you can sit anywhere."

"Thanks, I'm sorry it's so late. I know you want to go home," Ben said to her as they sat.

"That's okay, we're open until eleven, so you're fine," she said as she gave them their menus and took their drink order.

"So, what kind of pizza do you like? We can order anything you want?" Ben didn't need to look at his menu because he knew how he wanted it with everything on it. This was his favorite pizza joint, the place where he and his friend hung out as kids, where he took Jenny on their first date and kissed her for the first time. Why was he thinking of her now? He shook his head and looked at Liz. She was so beautiful with her red hair and her dark green eyes. He could stare at her all night.

Liz looked up when she felt his stare, "What?" She smiled at him. "I think I want everything." Liz paused and added, "On my pizza, if that's okay with you?"

Ben smiled back at her, "Hell yeah, that's the way I like it, with everything." He took her hand in his. As they waited for their pizza, Ben wanted to know more about Liz and how she got into writing. He knew she started writing because she needed to make a living, to support her daughter and herself after her husband died, but he wanted more, like how she came up with topics for her books. How she went about starting to write the story and where she came up with so many ideas to write eighteen books. He realized he wanted to know everything about her.

"You're staring at me? Is everything alright?"

"Yeah, I was just thinking about what you said about writing eighteen books. I want to know more about you, how you manage to go about writing a book, like where do your ideas come from?"

"Well, sometimes I start with a character. I may see someone and like how they look or how they act, and I see a storyline."

"So, can you make me into a character?" Ben liked the thought of her wanting to put him in one of her books.

"I have already," she smiled at him.

Ben looked surprised at her statement. "You're writing this book about me?"

"Well, the book isn't about you, but I am using how you look as my male surfer character."

Ben had a huge grin, and he said, "I like the sound of that, so did you use my name or give him a different one."

"I didn't use your name. I picked the name from a list of names I keep in my notebook. When I come across a name or a place I like, I'll write it down, so I can use them another time. I also do the same when I like how someone looks. I carry this notebook everywhere with me. I never know when I might see a place or a person I like. The café we went to the other day, for instance, I liked how it looked, so it may end up in this book. I also have a surf shop in the book, so when I describe it, it may sound a lot like yours. So, you see, if I have an actual person or place, then when I describe it in detail, the readers will believe it really exists."

"Wow, there is so much more to writing than I thought. Is it hard to come up with ideas? Do you ever experience writer's block?" Ben looked over to see the waitress coming with their pizza. He waited until she set it on the table, and she asked if they needed anything else. Ben was thinking how there was so much more to this woman than he first thought. Not only was she hot as hell, but she was intelligent. He wasn't sure it would be possible to learn everything about this woman in a lifetime, much less a month.

Liz glanced over at him, and he appeared to be deep in thought. She said, "I don't experience writer's block all that often, but when I do. I just walk away for a bit, and when I go back to it, it all seems to work out. As far as coming up with new storylines, I'm a people watcher." Liz pulled a slice onto her plate and went on talking. "I came up with the surfing book one day when I was driving and talking to my daughter. I said it would make a good story to have four or five guys who own a surf shop that swear they'll be bachelor's forever, and have them fall in love one by one. Paige said if anyone could make it into a book series, I could, but as I got started, I changed my mind and made the owner a woman, and her name is Sam. She wears big baggy clothes, so her love interest, at first, thinks she is a man." Liz looked up from her pizza, and Ben was still staring at her again. "I'm talking too much."

Ben was shaking his head, "No, you're not. Really, I was just thinking, I'm not sure I will ever be able to fully understand how you do that."

"Do what?" she asked.

"I just can't believe how you can come up with a whole book by one small idea, much less a series of books." Ben was taking his next piece of pizza.

Liz laughed, "It's what I do, and it seems people enjoy it." She took her next slice.

They talked as Ben took the last piece, and the bill came. Every minute he spent with her, the more intrigued he was. How could he keep her here? Would she want to stay and live in California? She could write anywhere but her daughter, would Liz stay in New Jersey because of her? All these questions went through Ben's mind as Liz went on telling him how she wrote so many books.

"If you don't mind me asking, how is it to write the love scenes? I… maybe I shouldn't ask, never mind." Ben shook his head and put his credit card on the table.

"I don't mind you asking questions, and when you write romance novels, love scenes are part of it. I wouldn't have anyone buying my books if there was no sex in them. I have to admit, it was hard at first because I didn't have much to go on, but Kat helped with that. She is really great. My first two books didn't have enough sex in them, so no publisher wanted them, but one day I'll rewrite them. As far as the sex, I sometimes have to make stuff up, and other times I write what I might fantasize…. It can be hard to see it from the man's point of view." Liz was now looking down at the table as she started to clear it. She could feel her face start to heat.

"So, what you're saying is, all I need to do is read your books, and I'll know all there is to know about what you like. I could give you a man's opinion if you want when we get back to your place." Ben said with a huge grin as he moved his brows up and down.

They got up from the table, and Ben grabbed her hand, drawing her out the door. He helped her into the Jeep and hopped into the driver's seat. He held her hand all the way home. He wanted to get her back to the house so they could be alone, and he could show her how much she was starting to mean to him. Maybe he couldn't tell her just yet, but he could express his feelings by making love to her and making her understand how he was feeling about her. The closer they got to the house; he could tell she was getting anxious. Ben knew she was over thinking what was going to happen once they got home. Ben was hoping that after this afternoon, she would feel comfortable with him and not so nervous about them being together. He wanted to kiss her, underdress her slowly, and love every inch of her body. Ben could feel himself getting hard just thinking about how he wanted to love her. He would just have to make her stop thinking so hard.

Liz was beginning to get apprehensive about what was going to happen once she and Ben were alone. Why was she feeling reluctant? He had seen every part of her, and she really enjoyed being with Ben. Didn't she want more time with Ben? She knew the answer was yes. She just needed to relax, inhale and exhale. Liz closed her eyes and remembered how it felt to have Ben's touch. As she relived how having Ben's hands on her breasts and how he sucked her nipples. She could feel herself getting very aroused.

Ben looked over at her to see she had her eyes closed and said, "Liz, you okay? I know you might be a little apprehensive, but it's going to be fine. I want you, but if you're not into it, it's fine. I'll just hold you." Ben was pulling into the driveway.

"I know it's going to be wonderful, but I can't help obsessing. I just want you to take over again. You make me forget I'm nervous and just make me feel so appreciated." She really needed the body-to-body contact, and Ben could make her nerve endings go wild. He just seemed to know what sent her off the deep end in no time.

He came around again to help her out, and this time when her body slid down his, he held her close to him. He pressed his hardness against her and reached up as he slipped his hands just behind her ears to hold her face up to his and pressed his lips very softly to hers. His kisses were slow and undemanding. She pressed herself against him, and his kisses moved to her ear. He whispered, "I'm not only going to take over, but I'll drive you mad. I want to love every inch of you, and once may not be enough," he felt her shiver in response to his words. "But we'll need to move this inside. Remember, no PDA," he smiled down at her.

At that point, she couldn't remember her own name, much less where they were and what she was doing. or who could see them. She shook her head to clear it some and agreed as he pulled her to the door. Once inside the door, he pulled her close again and said, "Now I get to take this dress off of you, like I wanted to the other day. I wanted so badly to see what you were hiding underneath it. I was so damn hard throughout lunch, and after I left you, I had to take care of myself. The entire time, I thought about taking this dress off of you."

Ben drew her to the couch and pulled her down. She straddled his lap as he drew her dress from underneath her so he could reach beneath and cup her ass. Ben's kisses were getting out of control, as he squeezed her ass and dragged her across his rigid cock. Liz was now rocking her hips in sync with his movements, with only the thin layer of her panties and his jeans between them. Ben slid his hand further beneath her until he felt her wetness, Liz moaned, and he knew she was aroused and ready. Ben pulled the zipper of her dress down and then the strap to free her breast. It was just in line with his mouth, he reached down, drawing her nipple into his mouth. He sucked softly at first, then tugged a bit harder. Liz pressed herself into him, as her hand went into his hair, to hold him there. Ben slid her panties aside and pressed two fingers into her folds.

She started to ride his fingers hard, which tugged her breast away as he sucked harder. Liz threw her head back and screamed as her orgasm hit her hard. Ben could feel her inner vaginal walls clamping down on his fingers as he kept sliding them in and out of her.

"God Liz, that is so amazing to watch."

Liz was trying to catch her breath and not blackout because she could see little twinkling of flashing lights behind her eyes as her heart raced, and rested her head on his shoulder, trying to relax. Her orgasm had been so incredibly strong. Ben just knew how to make every thought she had disappear. Her mind went blank the minute he started touching her. All the things she worried about in the car were gone the moment his lips touched hers. The key was to not overthink things, and as long as Ben took charge, she could lose control. This thought surprised her because she always liked being in control of herself and, if she could, everything else around her.

Ben pulled her out of her thoughts when he stood up with her still holding onto him. She wrapped her legs around his waist as he cupped her ass and walked them to the bedroom. Putting her down next to the bed, Ben rested his hands on her collarbones and let one hand slide down her shoulder taking the one strap that held her dress in place with it, letting the dress fall to the floor.

"I'll give you my point of view now if you'd like," as Ben stepped back and took in his fill of her standing there in just her lace panties. "I think you are the most beautiful woman I've ever seen, and when I touch you, I lose all intelligent, coherent thoughts." Liz started to cover herself as her face and chest turned red. "Don't do that. Don't shy away from me when you have to know how stunning you are. A man could die after being with you and not care if he went to heaven," Ben knew by the look on her face that was the wrong thing to say.

"I'm sorry, Liz. I didn't mean to say it like that. You'll have to forgive me because, as I told you, I may not have any intelligent thoughts with you standing before me." To distract from his words, Ben slowly unbuttoned his shirt as he watched her. and the shirt slipped off his arms to the floor. He then undid his jeans and slipped off his shoes and socks, while never looking away from her because he just loved to look at her. His pants and boxers hit the floor next, and he stepped out of them. He stood naked before her and allowed her to see what she did to him.

"Now, I want you to remove your panties and climb onto the bed because I want to appreciate every inch of your luscious,' sweet body." Ben watched as she did what he asked, climbing onto bed and laid her head on the pillows. "Do you trust me, Liz?" he asked as he went to her closet to pull the sash from her robe and a silk scarf.

Her beautiful green eyes opened wide as she said, "Yes, of course, why?"

"Because Liz, I want to cover your eyes and tie your wrists to the bed. Are you going to be okay with that?" He said as he moved closer.

"I don't know because I've never done anything like that. Michael was very traditional when it came to sex. The biggest thing for him was doing it doggie style," she said with some concern in her voice as she watched him.

"I won't tie you tight, and you'll be able to get loose if you really want to, it's not to hold you hostage, just to make you use your other senses, and I'll untie you if you don't like it."

It took Liz a minute to think about it, but then said, "Okay, I'll give it a try, but I just want you to know I'm not sure about this."

Ben started with her wrists as he took the sash, looped it through the headboard, and told her to put her hands over her head. She did as he asked, and he placed one hand in a loop he made and slid the knot down, then he did her other hand. Ben asked, "Is it too tight?"

"No, it's fine, but I won't be able to touch you."

"Know you'll have your time to touch me after. Now, I'm going to cover your eyes. I hate to do that because I love to watch you as you come." Ben reached around her as he tied the scarf to cover her eyes, "I'm going to leave for a minute. I'll be right back. I won't be long."

"Ben, where are you going, don't leave me," Liz could feel the knot in her stomach tighten. Panic was setting in, she trusted Ben, but why was he leaving her tied to the bed. She was pulling at her restraints just as a soft whisper brushed her ear. She stopped tugging as Ben told her it was going to be all right. "You're going to like it, I promise, and if for some reason you don't, we'll stop, you still have all the control, Liz."

Liz didn't feel as if she had any control, but she settled down and took in steady breaths. She felt the bed move, and she knew Ben was gone. Now she was thinking, *I'm naked, laid out for the world to see, and can't even cover myself. Was Ben standing at the end of the bed, gawking at her?* She squeezed her legs together, drew them up, and tried to roll to her side.

Ben went into the kitchen and pulled open the fridge, he took the whipped cream and chocolate sauce. He looked in the cabinets and found honey. That was a good start. Ben knew he was taking her out of her comfort zone, but she needed to experience how things could be with him. She would never get bored in bed, he liked doing it doggie style as much as the next guy, but that wasn't the best he could do in the pleasure department. He took all his ingredients and headed back into the bedroom. The first thing he noticed, she turned onto her side and pulled her legs up into a tight ball. Ben knew she was feeling insecure, and he didn't want her distressed. He walked over to the bed and said, "Did you miss me?" He put the food on the nightstand, went into the bathroom, and grabbed some towels. He noticed she hadn't said anything. "Liz, are you ok?"

She said in a very small voice, "Where did you go?" and the site of her was pulling at him, maybe it wasn't going to go the way he thought it would.

"I went to the kitchen. Do you want to know what I brought back with me? Lift up your bottom so I can slide this towel under you," Ben was checking out how her tits moved as she moved to her back and lifted her butt. After he had the towels in place, he said. "I like how you look like this." He put one finger on her neck and ran it down her collarbone, and she sucked in hard, her back arched up. Ben then went in between and under her huge tits but didn't touch her nipples. He was teasing her and knew he might pay for it later when he untied her.

Liz just wanted to be untied, as she waited for him to come back, but now that he was touching her, her body was on fire. His finger was going to burn a path in her skin, and she wanted him to run it over her nipples. She tried to move to make his finger go where she wanted it most.

"What do you want me to do, Liz?" Ben took the whipped cream and put some on his finger because he knew she wanted him to touch her nipples. When she asked him to touch her, he would put it on her tip and suck it off.

"I want you to touch me," she said.

"I am touching you," smiling down at her because she was trying to get out of saying what she wanted.

"You know what I want."

"You have to tell me Liz, just say it, and I'll do it."

"I want you to touch my nipples, please," her pleading was what broke him. He smeared the cream over one of her very tight nipples as the cold made her suck in deep. He leaned over and sucked it off.

"Oh my God, that was cold, but then your hot mouth was wonderful. What was that anyway?"

"So, you liked it? It was whipped cream," he took some more and put it on the other nipple, and again she gasped, but this time he just ran his tongue around the tight bud and flicked it back and forth. She made the most pleasant noises of her delight, and he said as his breath brushed her skin, "I could play here all night." He stuck his finger in one more time, and this time he ran it over her lips, and her tongue came out and licked it off.

"Mmm, that's so good," she said, and Ben put some on his own lips and kissed her. Ben rubbed his stiff cock on her to let her know she wasn't the only one excited, and she broke the kiss and said, "I want to taste some on your dick."

Oh God, he was going to blow before he ever got inside her. Taking some of the cream he smeared it on the tip of his cock and drew in a breath. Dammit, that was cold, but he climbed up her and rubbed the tip on her lips. She opened her mouth as her tongue licked the cream. Ben watched and almost lost it. He closed his eyes because if he watched her, he knew he would lose it. She ran her tongue around the ridge of his head and then sucked him deep into her mouth, a hiss escaped his lips, and he had to pull out. If he let this go much longer, he would be coming, and this was about pleasing her, pulling free from her warm, wet mouth.

"I wasn't done with you," Liz made a sound of displeasure, and her bottom lip made a pout.

"I know, but this is about you, and I have other things in mind." He heard Liz suck in air with anticipation of what was to come. Ben smiled, taking the chocolate sauce, and swirling it on her abdomen. His fingers trailed over the chocolate, and he brought them to her lips. She opened her mouth, and he let her suck off the sweet treat.

"Oh, I get it now. I'm your dessert, is there going to be ice cream next, maybe a cherry on top. I have to tell you that this will most definitely be going into my next book." She grinned up at him.

"Really, you'd put this in your book?" He asked her, "I wished I had thought of the ice cream. I could if I bought it, maybe I should get it and put the honey back." Ben said as he was licking the sweet sauce off the trail he left on her body. "You know where I'll put the ice cream and the cherry, don't you?" Just the thought had him pulling back. "I'll be right back," he liked the idea more than he should. Ben was back in no time with the ice cream and the cherries. This was going to be the sweetest dessert ever. He couldn't believe Liz was letting him do this to her and that she would write about their sexual experience in her book.

How did he feel about being able to read all about their expose? He realized she was becoming more comfortable with not only him but with her own sexuality. It was beginning to register she trusted him, and he enjoyed that thought a lot. Ben took the bowl of ice cream, stuck his tongue into it, lapped some up, and kissed her. As their tongues intertwined each other's, the ice cream melted.

"Humm, that's good strawberry is my favorite," she said.

"It's my new favorite, too," he said as he lapped up more and went down in between her legs and spread her. "Now I'm going to eat it at my favorite place." He heard her gasp as he swirled his tongue around her clit. She almost leaped off the bed as his cold tongue did crazy things to her.

"Oh my God, I can't believe you just did that."

He was smiling at her unexpected pleasure. She was breathing hard. He liked how her chest was shifting up and down. Now for the cherry, he wasn't sure how she would take what he had in mind. He took it into his mouth and went down on her. He used his tongue first, which was cold, but then he pushed the cherry inside her and sucked it out again. He did it again and again, and she started to come, and he sucked her juices as her legs jerked.

All she said was, "Oh God, oh God," over and over again.

He took the cherry into his mouth one last time, and when he kissed her, he slipped it into her mouth. Ben pulled the blindfold away from her eyes because he wanted to see how she responded to what had just happened. He was hoping he didn't go too far, as alarm and panic ran through him when she didn't say anything.

Liz felt so taken back by how much she enjoyed what Ben had done to her. She didn't know what to say, so she said nothing. She had never experimented with sex like this before. As her eyes readjusted to the light, she just lay there. Until she looked into Ben's eyes, and she could see the fear as he looked at her. He immediately went to untie her. She didn't want Ben to misread her reaction, so she smiled up at him.

"That was…" Liz trailed off when Ben interrupted her.

"Liz, I'm sorry I shouldn't have gone so far. Please forgive me."

"I will forgive you, but you have to tell me for what?" Liz looked confused.

"I… wait, you aren't mad or upset? I know I was pushing you out of your comfort zone, and I wanted to show you how things could be…" Ben stopped himself from saying anything else. He was lying on top of her, looking down into her beautiful eyes, and he could see she wasn't uneasy about what he had done to her. He relaxed just a bit and released the breath he didn't realize he was holding. "I was worried that I may have pushed you a bit."

"Ben, you have to stop worrying that I'm going to bolt every time you show me something new. I wanted to do this," she put both hands on the sides of his face to make sure he looked at her. "I want to experience things that I have never had the courage to ask for, or to even know I wanted, until you showed me. Okay, I wasn't sure at first about you tying me up, but as you revealed how sexually stimulating it could be. I just don't think I could have asked, and I did tell you I wanted you to take over. I have been so out of the sexual loop that I don't even know what I want. I do know that I like what you did to me more than I want to think about it right now."

Ben looked pleased as he said, "So, I didn't scare you?"

"I may not have the experience with this, but I am a romance writer. I do make this stuff up, though I never thought in a million years that I would have firsthand knowledge. I'm not sure I would have ever experienced this without you. I guess I felt you were safe and controlled. Now I see you have a crazy and erotic side to you, and I have to say. I like it."

Ben liked the sound of that as he pushed his hardness against her to show her just how much. He kissed her, and the talking was done, he wanted to make love to her and express how he felt about her, and that's exactly what he did.

~ 10 ~

Ben awakened to the sound of his cell phone buzzing and planned to let it go to voicemail. When it buzzed again, he let a sound escape his lips. He was holding Liz's warm naked body close, and he didn't particularly want to let go, but he also knew his family hadn't called or interrupted him the entire weekend. He was aware he needed to return to work if there was still a surf shop. Ben had never left Jeff in charge for a whole weekend. Jeff didn't do many weekends at all, much less by himself.

His phone went off again, and this time Liz nudged him, "I think someone is requesting you. You might need to answer it."

Ben slipped from her body as he cursed, grabbing his phone from his pants on the floor. He looked at the caller ID. It was Owen. He called his voicemail to discover what was up. As Ben listened, he looked outside and could see it was still dark.

"Is everything ok?" Liz asked in a gurgled, sleepy voice.

"I'm sorry it woke you, it's just Owen. He wants to do some surfing. He isn't used to me having anything going on, so I'm really surprised he hasn't called before now."

"You should go, Owen depends on you, and he needs you," Liz rolled to her side to look at him.

"I know he does. My brother and I are the only real male influences he has. I just don't want to leave. Surfing isn't what I want to do right now," he smiled at her. "I have an idea, maybe you can come with me."

"I don't think Owen would appreciate me being there, besides I think he might be feeling a bit neglected, and I'm tired because someone kept me up half the night. I have to do some writing today, but you should definitely go have fun." She rolled over and pulled her pillow in to burrow her face in it.

The sight of her snuggling her pillow didn't compel him into wanting to leave, but he knew she was right about Owen. He could use some thinking time, and surfing was a great place to do that. "I have to go to work today, too. Will I see you later for dinner?" He stepped to the edge of the bed as he pushed a stray hair away from her face. Her hair was wild from sleeping and so soft. He ran his fingers through it as she opened her eyes to look up at him. God, she was gorgeous, her stunning green eyes staring up at him. He didn't want to leave her, ever.

"Dinner sounds great. I'll make anything you want?" She beamed at the look that came into his eyes and could tell just what he was thinking. "Call me later and tell me what you'd like for dinner."

"I don't even have your number." That made him think just how much he didn't really know about her. She recited her cell number, and he kissed her, leaving her in the big warm bed.

Ben texted Owen that he was on his way, and he just had to stop home to get his stuff and would meet him. Owen was waiting for him just as he always did. When Ben walked up to him, he asked, "You miss me?"

Owen didn't say anything, and it hit Ben immediately that something was wrong. He sat next to Owen and looked at him. "What's wrong?" When he still didn't say anything, Ben had a sinking feeling it wasn't going to be good. "Are you in trouble? Has something happened that I need to know about? You know you can tell me anything, right?"

Owen didn't look at Ben, "There isn't anything bad. I'm not in trouble. I was just thinking… I want you to be happy, I do, but… if you end up with Liz, you're not going to want to be responsible for me. I can't pay for school, and if you do get married to her, you're not going to have the money for my school. I'll understand if you changed your mind, and you want to back out."

Ben let out the breath he was holding and said, "Owen, you have to know, you have been way more than an employee to me, you're like my kid brother, and there isn't anything in the world that will change that. Although, I do hope things work out with Liz, and even if I married her, I have made a commitment. Have you ever known me to back out of anything I said I'd do? You don't need to worry about money because I have more than enough to send you to school. So, you need to stop worrying. Is that the only thing on your mind?" Ben reassured Owen that he would always be there for him.

"It's just, I have to register for classes this week, and I wasn't sure if something changed. I don't know what I'm doing. I can't sleep, my stomach is in knots. I feel sick all the time. This is so lame. I should be able to handle going to school. I didn't have any problems in high school. I don't know why I'm so uptight about this. I don't know what I should bring to registration." Owen had his head in his hands and ran his hands through his hair.

Ben reached over, put his hand on his shoulder, and gave it a little squeeze, now understanding Owen's apprehension. Ben said, "When you come in today, bring in all your paperwork for school, and I'll go over it with you. What day is registration? I'll go with you, and I'm sorry I haven't been thinking about how you might be feeling, but I can tell you that your emotions are normal. Every kid that's starting college is feeling the same way. Take a deep breath, and we'll handle it. It can't be hard to get you in school, many people do it." Ben could feel the relief in Owen's shoulders. "I think you need to do some surfing and stop thinking. I got your back and always will."

Owen smiled at Ben and said, "So, how are things going with Liz anyway? She looked like she did really well on her first surfing lesson. Did she like it? You should have had her come, so I could give her the finer points." Ben just shook his head as he slapped Owen up the back of his head. "Hey, what was that for?"

"You're going to give her finer points, who the hell do you think taught you? And Liz didn't think you'd want her here." Ben grabbed his board and started for the water. He was glad to see that Owen was back to his easygoing, happy-go-lucky attitude.

"I just… never mind. Why wouldn't I want her to come?" He grabbed his own board and headed for the water. "So, did you spend the whole weekend with her? You know, you didn't miss much, just Jeff being a pain in the ass, complaining how he shouldn't have to work. I told him to quit whining like a baby. I don't think he realized how many weekends you worked, so he could have a social life." Owen got on his board to paddle out over the break of the wave. The ocean was a bit rough with the tide coming in.

Ben was sitting on his board, waiting for the next wave as he looked over at Owen, also sitting waiting, "So far, things are going great with Liz. She is a very fascinating woman, and I like her more than I want to admit, it scares me. I want to convince her to stay longer, so we can really get to know each other. I feel like I'm speed dating. I guess what I'm trying to say is I want more of everything."

"I like her if I get a vote. I think she will give you a run for your money. You'll never get bored with her around, and you can't complain because she's totally hot. I'm gonna take this one." Owen laid on his board and started paddling to catch a big wave.

Ben smiled and thought, if this all worked out for him, he would be the happiest man alive. What if it doesn't work out? Where did that leave him? That was a thought he really didn't want to think about. It was time to surf and stop thinking in that direction. Ben paddled and rode the next big wave.

~ ~ ~ ~ ~ ~

Liz woke and rolled over to look for Ben, finding the bed empty. "Oh yeah, he went surfing with Owen," she said to no one. Liz tried to get her hair under control, it was a mass of bed head. She must have been tossing and turning after Ben left. As she lay there, she thought how so much had happened in the last three days, and she smiled. She thought about how these days with Ben have been some of the best days she had had in a very long time. The sex was so good, it was crazy. Ben was such a great lover, and he tied her up.

She would never have thought in a million years that kind of stuff would turn her on, but it was the best thing she had ever experienced. Knowing she didn't have the sexual experience. What could Ben teach her about herself, what she might like when it came to sex, and just how much fun it could be finding out?

When Liz moved to get out of bed, her stomach pulled tight, and her back hurt. "What the hell? Oh God, that hurts. Oh, I'm sore from surfing. Shit, maybe a hot shower will help. Damn, I'm so out of shape. If Kat was here, she would whip me into shape." That thought also made her think, thank God she wasn't because she would be giving me a lecture. "If I exercised regularly, I wouldn't feel like this now." Liz went to take her shower. As she climbed in and the hot water ran over her, the memory of her and Ben showering together washed over her. She definitely wanted to experience everything Ben wanted to show her. Liz trusted him to take care of her and knew he wouldn't hurt her. She would have a discussion with him tonight at dinner about helping her to learn what she would like when it came to sex. Just the thought of talking to Ben about this was getting her hot with want.

~ ~ ~ ~ ~ ~

Ben went home to shower after they finished surfing. The waves were great, and surfing was just what he needed to clear his head. He knew when he got into his office, there would be plenty of paperwork to do, and he would have to deal with his family. His mother was going to want a play-by-play of how his weekend went. If he could just get in the door to his office without her finding out, he could put off the interrogation for an hour or so. He needed time to consider the information he wanted to share. Ben would rather not have this conversation with his mother at all, but he knew better. He was fully aware how she would want to know how this weekend had been, the best he had in a long time, and if he could stretch it into a lifetime, that would be totally fine with him. That would be the million-dollar question, could he pull it off.

Ben went to the shop early, hoping he could get to his office without someone noticing him and have time to clear some work off his desk. He felt like he was sneaking in after curfew as a teenager, not that he ever had. As he made it into his office and let out a big sigh, he had made it. Now he closed his door, turned, and got the first look at his desk. Shit, it was loaded with paperwork. It was going to take a good hour to clear it just so he could see the top. He needed to consider what to tell his mom, but he couldn't do it with his desk looking like this. Ben got lost in the paperwork when a knock on his door pulled him out of his work haze.

Ben took a big breath, let it out slowly, and said, "Come in." He waited to see which family member it would be. When Owen walked in, Ben relaxed a bit. "You're here early. You have your paperwork?"

"Yeah, I thought it would be better to go over it before we opened, and then I might not feel like I'm goin' to upchuck." He sat in the chair on the other side of Ben's desk. Owen handed the papers to Ben and looked at his desk. "Man, you were only gone a weekend, and the shit piles up. You'd think nobody does anything around here."

"I know, it looks like that, but everyone around here pulls some of their own weight. I just happen to keep everything running on paper."

"I think some do more than others, like one brother who likes to come and go as he pleases." Ben knew Owen had been around long enough to know how things worked around here. In Jeff's defense, he did his part by selling the merchandise, and without that, there would be no surf shop. How things ran now might have to change with Owen going to school and him wanting a life besides work. He put in sixty hours a week, while Jeff hardly worked forty, and he liked to come and go as he pleased. Ben was going to have a conversation with his mother about how it was going to have to change.

Owen pulled him back to his college paperwork when he said, "I know I shouldn't complain about Jeff, but he's an ass. He acted as if he worked weekends all the time. I have worked my share, but not as many as you. Listening to him made me mad. I just had to tell him to shut up. Even your mom got tired of hearing him complain."

"I'll take care of it. Now, let's see what you're going to need for registration. What day do I need to be there?" Ben looked up from the paper in his hand.

"Wednesday, anytime between 9-6 p.m., and I would like to go as early as possible, so I can ease the anxiety that I can't seem to shake. It helps to know you'll be helping me. I want you to know how I appreciate everything you've done for me. I'm not just talking about school, but everything." Ben could feel the swell of pride for the kid that showed up in their life needing a family. Owen had become such a big part of his family.

"Owen, you have conducted yourself in a manner that I am very proud of. You deserve to have a college education. It was something I couldn't do when I was younger with my dad's death, my mom needed me here. I want more for you Owen, than just this surf shop."

"I have always loved being a part of the store and a small part of your family. I think of Linda as my other mother and you guys as my big brothers, even though you guys can be a pain in the ass." Owen was smiling, and it eased the heavy mood.

Ben made sure Owen knew what he needed for Wednesday and reassured him it was going to be alright. After Owen left, Ben went back to work now that he could see some of his desk. He had almost caught up when Ben heard the next knock on his door.

"Come in." Ben was hoping it wasn't his mother because he hadn't decided what to say. It was Jeff. He came in, sitting in the chair Owen vacated. "What can I do for you?" Ben asked with an amusing tone because he knew Jeff hadn't come in out of concern for him.

"So, how are things? Did she dump you yet, so I can have my life back?" Ben realized how selfish his brother was and how he was the enabler. He let his brother get away with everything. Well, it was time for Jeff to grow up and pull his share of the load. He was as much of a partner as Ben, so it was about time he started to act it.

"I'm good, and no, she hasn't dumped me. I think we need to have a talk about how things might need to change around here." Ben allowed Jeff to absorb what he was saying.

"What? I don't want anything to change, I want it to go back to the way it was."

"I understand you like how it is now because you work when you want. You come and go as you please. While everyone else holds down the fort, and you don't have to worry about it. As I took this weekend off, the first in many years, I realized you have not ever worked the entire weekend alone. Where I worked a lot of them so Owen could have some time off. While you might assist sometimes, it's only when you want to. I have to say, you're spoiled, and it's about time you start pulling your weight around here. It's not just the work schedule, but you need to take on more responsibility, too."

"Wait a minute, this is all because you have a girlfriend, so I haven't been pulling my weight. I sell almost everything that's in this place, and I work hard enough. I can't believe you're going to pull this shit."

"I know you think this is just because I want to have more than just this place, and it does have something to do with it, but it's not all that's going on here. Mom works her twenty hours a week, and she can't work more than that and keep getting Dad's social security. Owen is working almost forty now, but he's going to be going to school in September and won't be able to keep up with school and be here as much. School is going to come first for him. So that leaves you and me. I already work sixty hours, so what do you think is going to happen? I can hire someone else, but if I have to do that, you will receive hourly pay because I'm not going to be paying you salary when you work maybe twenty or thirty hours. You will still share in the profits at the end of the year. Either start acting as if you give a shit about this place, or you live with the consequences. I'll be discussing this with Mom later."

"Well, thanks for nothing. I don't know where you get off thinking you get to make these decisions. We all own this place, and if you think you are the only reason this place is still open, you better think again." Jeff got up and left his office, slamming the door.

Well, that didn't go over very well. Not that Ben thought it would. Jeff liked how things were because he didn't have any real responsibility. He knew his mother would come to him and would be next to come through his door. Especially after Jeff went to her complaining about him, Ben knew he had thirty minutes before she would show up. He didn't have time to get his thoughts together before the next knock. Ok, so this had to be his mother. "Come in," Ben was sitting back in his chair, prepared for this conversation.

"Hi honey, I just left Jeffrey, and boy, did you get him in a way. I knew it was coming with you wanting to take time off. You do so much around here. The way Jeffrey had complained about having to work this weekend when he had plans, even I had all I could take of him. But did you have to be so hard on him?" Linda rested her hands on the edge of Ben's desk, that still had work Ben needed to finish. Ben knew she wanted to keep the peace, but things had to change.

No one likes change, it makes us grow, and it makes us feel like we don't have control. That thought made him think of Liz. Funny, he hadn't thought about her almost all morning because he had to take care of everything else. He wished he could call her right now. Was she writing as she said she was going to? Ben found that he didn't want to be here for the first time, he wanted to be with her.

His mother brought him back to the situation at hand when she said, "I told Jeffrey we were all going to sit down and talk about how things are going to change. I know we need to stand together on this because Jeffrey does need to take on more responsibility. I just don't think he sees just how much everyone else picks up the slack. He has always taken the easy way out, where you have always taken on more than your share of the responsibility. I think it's time we called Danielle, too, so she's in on where this place is going from here. She has been doing her own thing long enough and not taking on any responsibility, either. I need to know where she stands."

Ben's mother smiled at him, and he knew where she was heading, so he said, "What do you want to know? I won't get away with anything, even though we have so much going on here."

"Don't be like that. I just wanted to know how your weekend was, is that so bad?" Linda smiled sweetly at him.

"I have a feeling it's going to be more painful than you make it."

"How are things going with Liz? I was thinking about you all weekend when I didn't have to listen to Jeffrey."

"I have to tell you that this weekend was one of the best that I've had in a really long time. Mom, I know it's crazy, but I like her. I feel like she just fits. I know that's just insane because how can I feel so much for a woman in just three days? She's smart, funny, and has a sharp wit. Liz is just amazing." Ben realized his mother hadn't said anything. Once he started talking about her, it all came pouring out. "Mom, tell me I'm being ridiculous, tell me I shouldn't be impulsive." His mother didn't say any of those things.

"Benjamin, do you love her?" That's all she asked. Well hell, he didn't know if it was love, but what he did know was that he wanted her to stay here in California. He wanted the time to find out just how he felt about her. He also knew he wanted to be with her right now and not talking with his mother, but he had responsibilities here, and he couldn't leave just because he wanted to. Maybe he held a little hostility where Jeff was concerned because Jeff would just leave with no thought of anyone else. Ben knew he couldn't do that without considering how it would affect everyone.

"I don't know about love, but I do know I want more of everything with her. More time with her. I know I don't really want to be here, and that says a lot." His mother shook her head up and down as if she understood how he felt.

"I think you deserve to be happy, Benjamin, and if she makes you happy, go after her. I fell for your father very fast. I just knew somewhere deep inside I wanted to be with him, and I can tell you my parents weren't happy about it. A beach bum with a dream of opening a surf shop was not what they saw for me. He made his dream a reality and made me very happy, with three beautiful children. Now thanks to you, it is a very big, successful business. That has supported us all very comfortably, I might add. I know you are the glue here. Even though we all work together, I don't think Jeffrey realizes that if you didn't pay the bills, make out payroll, and order the stock, there would be no shop to sell the merchandise in."

"Ok, so when do you want to have this meeting? I think the sooner we do this, the better." Ben wanted this settled.

"I think we should give Jeffrey a day or two because it will give him a little time to think about things and to calm down. I will call Danielle and see when she can do a conference call. I want her to know what's going on. If she doesn't want to take any responsibility in the store, then the end-of-the-year profit checks will change, divided by participation. I know in the past we divided it up equally, but I don't think it's fair. I also want to include Owen this year. I think he deserves it, he works hard, and he cares about this place. I see now dividing it equally doesn't make everyone take an active part in the store." Ben's mother had said her peace and smiled at him. "I know this is not going to go over well, but I want my family together again, and I'm not above bribing them," she stood, turned, and walked out.

Linda was a tough woman, and Ben knew the checks were yet another problem that was going to be hard to take, but it was coming from her, not him. Although, it could be the solution to his problems if Dannie comes back, then he could pass some of the paperwork onto her, and she could work the floor to pick up the slack with Owen being at school. Jeff was still going to have to do more. Maybe he could take over ordering. Ben was rubbing the back of his neck. What a morning, it wasn't even noon yet, and all Ben wanted to do right now was talk to Liz. So, he picked up the phone, and she answered on the second ring as if she was waiting for him to call.

~ ~ ~ ~ ~ ~

Liz had dressed and made her coffee. While it was brewing, she pulled out her computer and her notebook. She grabbed her cell phone and put some music on, it worked as background noise, otherwise, it was way too quiet. She made sure she had everything she was going to need to write because when she got started, she didn't like to have to stop to get something. Her coffee was ready, so she got the biggest mug she could find and sat at the breakfast bar and read what she wrote to get her back into the book. Liz was getting a lot done when her cell rang. She looked at the call ID, it was Kat, so she had to get it. "Hello."

"Hello, what the hell? You were supposed to call me this morning." Liz could hear how irritated Kat was with her.

"I just got up, and I was trying to get some writing in. Ben went to work today, so I was working. You know why I'm here."

"Okay, it's good that you're getting some work done, but right now, I want to know what's happening between you and Ben." Kat wasn't going to let this go, so Liz just took a deep breath and started telling her about last night when Ben tied her up.

"I can't believe you let him do that. You are so not the type."

"That's just it, Kat. I don't know what type I am, and I've never experimented with sex. Michael was very plain when it came to sex. I'm sure it's because we were so young and didn't know any better, or he didn't think I would go for it. Although I'm not sure, I would have at that point, either. All I know is that last night was the most amazing experience I have ever felt, and it makes me want to attempt more. I plan on talking to Ben tonight after he comes for dinner about trying new things."

"Liz, you need to be very cautious. What do you know about him? If you open that door, he might consider you are up for anything, and the situation can get out of control very quickly. You need to make sure you have a safe word. This is so that if he does anything you don't want, you say the word, and things stop immediately." Liz could hear the concern in Kat's voice.

"I have confidence in Ben, he hasn't done anything without my permission first, and he has given me every opportunity to refuse. I believe I have to experience this now with him, while I don't have anyone judging me, and after I leave, I don't have to see him again. I have this opportunity to be anything or try anything, without anybody knowing, and it's justified research. If I was home, I could possibly run into the guy, and that would be very embarrassing." Liz wanted this for herself more than she had wanted anything before.

"I may just have to come out there and introduce myself to Ben and let him know if he mistreats you in any way, I will kick his ass." Liz loved Kat so much and was well aware she could not only materialize at a moment's notice but also kick Ben's ass, big time. Liz had to smile at the thought of Kat putting Ben down.

"You make certain you call me every day. I know you're alright because I will be there if I don't hear from you. I'm not kidding."

"I know you love me, and you will always be there for me. Through the years, you have been my very best friend, but you need to let me spread my wings, as you said, I needed to do for Paige. I need to grow. The only way to do that is to learn more about myself. Ben's teaching me my likes and dislikes. Don't worry, I'll be fine." As Liz mentioned Paige's name, she realized she hadn't talked to her in days and needed to call her daughter today.

Liz hung up with Kat, trying to get back to work. Just the thought of speaking to Ben about this was making those uncertainties creep back in. What would happen if Ben questioned what she wanted to try? How would she know what to request? What would she refuse to try? Her love scenes in her books didn't really help either because they didn't get overly crazy, so she couldn't even go with something she had written. She could drive herself insane all day if she gave it too much consideration. Liz decided she would just speak with Ben and see what he thought about her wanting to experiment.

Liz went back to work, and she was getting into her character of Sam. Liz was at the point where Sam saw Johnny for the first time. She was so into her story and didn't hear her phone at first. When it rang a second time, she picked it up without looking at who it was.

"Hello," Liz said into her phone, thinking it was probably Paige.

"Whatcha doin'?" a deep male voice said on the other end. It surprised Liz at first, but then she knew who it was.

"I'm writing, what are you doing?" She asked him.

"Thinking about you… because I had a shitty morning once I got to work, and I didn't want to think about that anymore. So, I decided to think of something that makes me happy, and there you were in my head." She smiled at how he could make her feel so special.

"So, is there anything I can do to make your day any better?" She said in a playful tone.

He let out a sigh and said, "Just hearing your voice makes me feel better, but I can think of a few things that will make it even better."

"Yeah, like what?" She asked.

"I could have you here naked on my desk, now that I can see the damn thing."

"I don't think you're going to get the naked part, but I can meet you for lunch. Maybe a picnic on the beach, would that help? I could meet you at the bottom of my stairs, and if you have enough time and you're really good, I could give you a treat," she said with a laugh.

"I would love that, but I'm not sure I can get away. The shit hit the fan this morning with Jeff because I took the entire weekend off. I talked with Mom, and we're having this big meeting about how things are going around here. There's going to be some changes, and I know how that's going to go over." Ben let out a frustrated breath.

Liz now understood why his morning had not gone well, so she suggested, "Okay, you can't leave, but you do need to eat. I'll just bring the picnic to you, and maybe, I just might get you naked on your desk. You got a lock on that door?" Ben let out a giant laugh.

"I can't see you doing that, with the way you feel about no PDA." Ben had some challenge in his voice.

"What time do you want me there? I want to discuss something with you."

"What do you want to talk about? Is it something bad or something good?" he asked.

"All I'm going to disclose, is it has to do with last night and you tying me up."

"Now, I have to know, good or bad?" He said with a little hesitation. He wasn't sure he really wanted to know.

"You'll just have to wait and see." Liz liked the fact that she had the upper hand for once. "What time?" She asked.

"Would now be too soon?"

Liz got ready to meet with Ben. She fried up some chicken with her special recipe and made macaroni salad. She got together everything they would need. She even put some wine and glasses in the basket she found. She had a plan to get Ben good and relaxed by getting him naked and blowing his mind.

Liz showed up at the shop at twelve-thirty, and when she walked in, she saw Jeff first. He didn't look very happy, and his usual playfulness was gone. He was helping a customer, but what she noticed was he wasn't smiling as she had seen all the other times. Jeff saw her, she smiled and waved, but he just looked away without even acknowledging her.

Owen came up next to her and said in her ear. "Don't worry bout' him. He's just being an ass today, to everyone."

"Oh, so I shouldn't take it personally. He's having a bad day, too?" Liz leaned into Owen just a bit so no one would hear her.

"You here to see Ben?" he pointed to the basket in her hand.

"Yes," she looked in the direction that Linda had come from the other day.

"His office is right down the hallway, first door on your right," Owen said as he walked her to the hallway.

She thanked him and knocked on Ben's door. She could hear him moving around inside. The door opened, and he pulled her into the office, shutting the door and locking it. He bent and kissed her as if he never had before. She could feel his need as his tongue pushed into her mouth and intertwined with hers. He removed the basket from her hand and dropped it on the chair next to them without breaking the kiss. She reached up and entangled her arms around his neck and ran her fingers through his long strands. He pushed her up against the door and pressed his hardness against her. Okay, she needed to put a halt to this. Otherwise, they would be having sex on his door. She drew back some to break the kiss.

Liz observed Ben's eyes and saw how his pupils dilated. How he pressed against her, and she couldn't mistake his hard-on. She pulled away from his embrace and put her hand up to give him a little shove, so she could step around him.

"I came on too strong?" Ben asked as he looked her over.

"I… If I didn't move away, we would be going at it against your door." She took a much-needed breath, "I brought lunch, fried chicken, and macaroni salad."

"All I need is you naked," he said as he stepped closer.

"All in good time, first we eat, then I want to talk, and if we have time," she left it at that.

"Woman, are you trying to drive me crazy?" Ben stepped even closer, and she put up her hand to stop him.

"I have a plan, and you're going to just have to comply. I promise you won't be disappointed." She said with a smile, and all she heard from him was a grunt. She made him sit in his chair and then set up their lunch and poured some wine into the glasses. "Now I want us to eat, and you can tell me why your morning was so shitty."

Ben reached for some chicken but kept his eyes on her until he took his first bite. Ben's eyes closed as he made a sound of such delight. "Damn Liz, this is the best thing I have ever tasted. Man, you could spoil me forever." Ben was now eating as if he was a starving man. Liz was just watching him, and it made her feel good because this was a way, she liked to take care of the people that were important to her. That thought caught her off guard because was Ben becoming important to her? She shook off the thought.

Ben told her all about what had transpired that morning at work. How his mom wanted to make changes in how they divided the end-of-the-year checks. How she wanted Danielle, his sister, to take a bigger part in the shop, and most of all, how Jeff's role in the store was going to change. They finished their lunch as Ben filled her in.

"When I came in, I waved at him, and he just ignored me. I could tell he wasn't happy. He didn't have that sparkle in his eyes the way I've seen before." Liz came around the desk and began to massage the muscles in his shoulders. Ben leaned back into her as he moaned, and she could feel how tight he was.

As she was working on loosening the knots, she said, "I wanted to talk to you about last night." Ben stopped moaning, and she could feel him stiffen up again. "It's not bad, as a matter of fact, I think you are going to enjoy it a lot." She kept working his shoulders, "First, I want to say I thoroughly enjoyed what you did to me, but…."

Ben interrupted her as he said, "But, is never good."

"Let me finish, I just never experienced anything like that, and I wouldn't have known I liked that if you hadn't shown me. I trust that you would never hurt me or do anything that I didn't really want. What I'm getting at is, I want to experiment with what I might not know that I like. I don't even know what to ask for, so before you ask, I don't know. I want to try more."

Ben turned his chair around as she stood in between his legs. He looked into her eyes as her cheeks reddened. He knew this wasn't easy for her, asking for what she wanted. He smiled and said, "I see." His eyes ran over her body, and he was hard and could take her right here.

"But I also want to explore how to give pleasure, not just receive it." She knelt down, keeping her eyes on him as she undid his pants. Ben just watched as she opened his pants and freed him. "This time, I want you to tell me what you like and how you want me to do it."

Oh shit, she was going to give him a blowjob right here in his office. He couldn't respond at this moment, as he just watched her. Liz wrapped her small hand around him and started to work it up and down the length of him. He found his voice, "I love what you're doing," he said, as he wrapped his hand around hers and showed her how hard to squeeze and how fast.

When she had it, he let go and told her in a whisper to suck his head. Rewarded when she did, he groaned as he closed his eyes to take in the pleasure. She sucked him hard and deep as she still ran her hand where her mouth just was. Oh, God, he has died and gone to heaven. She was now running her hot tongue along the ridge of his dick and then down the length of him. Liz sucked the spot between his dick and his balls. He could feel the tightening in his groin, and he knew. "Liz, I'm going to come…baby…oh God, that feels so good." She moved lower, and he leaned back to give her better access to his balls. He could feel them pulling up tight. "Suck my dick, suck me hard, ohhh fuck…I'm coming." His hands wrapped in her hair tightly, and he threw his head back and tried not to yell out. After, Liz rested her head on his stomach when Ben was finished coming to catch her breath. Ben relaxed his hands and let her go as he pulled her up into his lap.

She looked at him, "Now, didn't I say you'd like my plan?"

~ 11 ~

After Liz left, Ben attempted to get his mind back to his work. If he could forget how she touched him, how his brain just abandoned every other thought. He knew he'd have to suppress his thoughts if he had any chance to get any work done, but knowing it and doing it, were two entirely different things. He gave himself a minute to relive the movements. He closed his eyes, relaxing his head on the back of his chair. How her petite hands stroked him and how she sought his command to do what would pleasure him. He had to fight the urge not to take control, stripping and taking her on his desk. His mind was in extreme fantasy mode. Ben's thoughts conjured up what he wanted to do tonight. Payback would be so enticing. She hadn't allowed him to touch her earlier. He just hoped she could take as good as she gave. That thought made Ben smile a wicked smile. He would have to stop at the adult store before heading to her place.

For now, he had to get back to work. He had cleared his desk and was working on the employee schedule so to make it fair for everyone, so all would work their share of weekends and evenings, and if Dannie was to return, then he'd put her into the rotation, and she could help with payroll. He also didn't have Owen's school schedule yet, either. Ben knew there were many what-ifs, but he liked to have a plan. Something he could have ready for the meeting.

His mind kept wandering back to Liz and how she wanted to experiment with sex and what she may like. Ben's mind started to go through things he wanted to explore with her. Liz had shown him that she could be very adventurous, also spontaneous. It took him by complete and utter surprise because he never would have thought she would have done anything like what she did today. It certainly made getting back to work virtually impossible. God, he wanted to keep her and said a little prayer that this relationship would become a permanent part of his life. He glanced at his calendar and knew she'd already been in California almost a week, only three weeks left. Ben knew there wasn't an overabundance amount of time left. The last week had flown by so quickly. He wondered if he had enough time to express to her what it would be like if she stayed.

~ ~ ~ ~ ~ ~

After Liz went home, she attempted to get into her writing, but her mind kept returning to what had happened in Ben's office. That was so far out of character for her, and she could never imagine herself doing something so irrational before. There was just something unrestricted about being with Ben that gave her the courage to be extremely daring in ways she couldn't ever envision. She wondered what the future held for her.

Liz knew her nights would be the most amazing she'd ever had, but could she just go home in a few weeks and not think about him? Just walk away from him and not look back. A small part of her wanted to do just that, the part that wanted to discover her wild side and not take responsibility for her own actions. *A wild side I didn't even realize I had before now.*

Now that she wanted it, what if she enjoyed it too much? Would she feel as comfortable with any other man? She didn't think she would ever again discover someone like Ben. There was just something so comforting about him. She thought of the reaction her body had to him and the sensation he could evoke. For a moment, she considered if she had true feelings for him. That was a crazy thought, and she shouldn't become attached to him. This was just a summer fling, nothing more. Maybe if she kept repeating it, she would believe it.

Liz's cell phone rang, and she was anticipating it would be Paige. It had been days since she had last spoken to her. "Hello,"

"Hey Mom, you must be really hard at work because I haven't heard from you. Are you so into your new book that you didn't realize that several days had gone by?" Paige asked.

"I have been writing, but you must have also been busy." She did not want to mention what other things had taken up her time.

"Oh, I have been. There's so much I have to tell you, I met some people here, and we've been hanging out and having fun." Paige sounded so much better than the last time they had spoken. She was discovering her own direction, and in a way, Liz was doing the same. Finding her own path to a new life was making her very happy, but Liz wondered if it would?

"What have you been doing, and who are these friends?" Liz could feel her mother's instincts kicking in, and it amazed her how quickly she could be pulled right back into being Paige's mother. Being a mother never ends, even when your child becomes an adult.

"Relax Mom, we all work for the company, and they are all around my age. We've been going out in a group, like going bowling and to the movie's things like that, nothing to get you all concerned about me, so breathe, Mom." Liz could tell she was trying to reassure and ease her mind, letting her know that she was doing fine.

"Okay, I'm not worrying. You sound really good, and I'm so glad you're settling in. I had faith in you because you always made friends so easily before. I knew it was just a matter of time."

"So, what else have you been doing besides writing? Tell me you're not closed up in that house when you have that great view and the sunshine outside your door because I hate that you're there all alone." Liz didn't want Paige to be concerned about her.

"I've unexpectedly made friends, too. I had a surfing lesson yesterday. I've been having fun and attempting new things."

"No way, you're surfing. I would have paid big money to see that," Paige laughed, "You need to have someone videotape it the next time and send it to me. Tell me the guy that gave you the lesson wasn't that cute guy you sent the picture of."

Liz was laughing when she said, "Why, what if it was? Would you be jealous?"

"Yes, I want a surfing lesson from that guy and a little Hubba-bubba."

"Paige, I can't believe you said that, Owen is a very nice young man."

"Oh yeah, he's nice all right, young, and hot, so tell me, was it him? How hot is he on a surfboard?"

"I hate to burst your bubble, but no, it wasn't him, but I've seen him on a surfboard, and I can tell you, it's definitely something great to watch," She could just mention Ben's name and hope Paige wouldn't notice anything else. "Ben, the owner of the surf shop, gives lessons, and he talked me into it."

"Oh, is he cute too? I want pictures, Mom. I have to see what he looks like because all the guys out there are so hot. As much fun as I'm having being here, I still wish I were there with you. I can't believe my mother's surfing. Who are you? Because the mother I know was always one that would never allow me to do anything that even hinted of being dangerous, much less getting on a surfboard herself. Wow, I can't wait to see you. I've been counting down the days. Oh yeah, I registered for my classes, and I need the credit card number to get my books. I can't believe that once I get home, we'll only have a few weeks before I head off to school. I can't wait to go shopping for the stuff for my dorm room."

As Paige went on, Liz knew if Paige had been there, there would be no way in hell she would have ever gotten involved with Ben. She would have declined his offer for lunch, and everything preceding, would not have happened. She wouldn't have been approachable for Ben. Liz knew once she was home, she'd be busy getting Paige ready for school. She'd have to rent a U-Haul to get all of Paige's stuff up to school, and then Liz would fly home once Paige settled into her dorm. She didn't want to think how lonely the house would be once she got back. Wow, that was a depressing thought.

"Mom, are you even listening to me?" Paige said with a laugh.

"Sorry Honey, I was just thinking about all that we have to do once we get home. Shop, rent a U-Haul, get you ready for school."

Paige must have heard the sadness in her voice because she said, "Mom, I know how tough this is on you. With me going off to school, but you have to remember, this is where you've always wanted me to be. You, unquestionably made me do everything I needed to do to get into a great university. I studied hard and got good grades because you expected it from me. Now, you need to relax and try to appreciate all the benefits of the fruits of your labor. I won't be far away, I can drive home on long weekends, and you can just come whenever you want. You can work while I'm in class. It will be great, you'll see." Paige appeared to have everything under control. She sounded like the adult, and Liz felt like the kid that was so unsure of themselves. Most kids that were going off to a big college felt insecure and unsure, but not Paige, she was strong and confident. It made Liz feel so much pride for her daughter.

"Knowing this, what I've always wanted for you and it happening is two entirely different things. I've never lived completely alone, I always had so much going on at home, and now it will be so quiet. I think that's going to be the hardest part. But you're right, you won't be far, and we will talk every day. I might have Kat set up some book signings for when I get back."

"Mom, you know that's just putting off the inevitable. What you need is to have a life. Go out with Aunt Kat and meet some guys. I'm sure she could hook you up. She's only been trying for years. You deserve to be happy, Mom."

"Wow, where did that come from? I have a life, thank you very much, and I don't need a man." This conversation was getting too close to the truth for her liking. "But if I ever did find someone, you would be okay with that?" Liz held her breath for a beat as she waited for Paige's answer.

"Of course, Mom, I want you happy. Dad has been gone a long time. You've always put me first, and I'm grown. Now you need to start thinking about yourself for a change." Liz couldn't believe what she was hearing because her daughter wanted her to date.

~ ~ ~ ~ ~ ~

Ben was watching the clock as he planned to get out on time today, come hell or high water. He needed to see what was happening out on the floor. Would Jeff still be pissed off? He also needed to find out who was covering the evening hours. Most likely, it would be Owen, but they were only open until eight tonight.

When Ben walked out on the floor, he didn't see Jeff and hoped to God he hadn't left yet. Jeff was supposed to be working until five like him. When he saw Owen, he asked, "Where's Jeff?"

"He went to load a board onto somebody's car," Owen said as he was helping some girls at the jewelry counter.

"Is he still in a pissy mood?" Ben asked as Jeff came back through the door.

"If you want to know if I'm still sulking, the answer is no. I had some time to think, and Mom reaming me up and down about how self-centered I was. I guess I hadn't given it much thought about who was covering the shop. I can see now that you were the one to do most of the evenings and weekends. I should do my share, even though I'd rather not. Mom said when we have this meeting, she wants Dannie to do her share, too. So, if she comes back, that will be one more person to help around here."

"I made out a tentative schedule, it will rotate, and everyone will have to do some nights and weekends. Owen has registration on Wednesday, and I'm going with him. He wants to do it early, so it'll relieve some of his concerns about school. I need you to be here early, and then I'll be better aware of his schedule. The number of hours Owen will work is going to depend on his workload at school. What I'd like to see happen, is for you to for to take over the ordering. That's what I'm going to propose for you to have more responsibility. If Dannie is going to come home, then I'd like her to take over some office duties and work the floor. That would mean I could work the floor more, too. I think if we work together, it could be easier for everyone, and if something comes up and you need time off, then whoever is doing the scheduling will have to clear it. You won't be able to just leave." A customer came in, and Jeff shook his head as if he understood and went to help the lady.

It made Ben feel better that Jeff got how a few changes could make everything run much smoother and more efficiently. Ben turned to go to his mother's office because he needed to find out when this meeting could take place. The sooner, the better. She was on the phone, so he sat in the chair across from her desk to wait.

"Honey, I know I'm springing this on you, but we need your help." Linda listened to the person on the other end. Then she said, "We're having a meeting on how things are going to be around here. Because I'm making changes, and I want you to be a part of it." She listened again and then said, "It will affect you. Do you have time tomorrow morning to do a conference call around ten?" She listened once more, then said, "Okay, I'll talk to you tomorrow, I love you, bye." Linda hung up and looked over at Ben.

Ben asked, "I'm guessing that was Dannie?"

"I guess you heard we're having the conference call tomorrow. Will that work for you?" Linda asked.

"That'll work, I talked to Jeff, and he's calmed down and now sees that some changes will make everything easier. We talked about him taking on more responsibility, so I suggested that he could take over the ordering. He will have a better understanding of how the store operates, and if Dannie comes back, she could help with some of the office work and the floor. This should free me up to help on the floor and have a life."

Linda smiled at him, "If we can get everyone on the same page, I will love having the family back together."

"I made out a tentative work schedule that will put everyone working nights and weekends in a rotation, so it's fair for everyone. I have to go with Owen on Wednesday morning to get him registered for school. When I know his schedule, I'll include him, but I want school to come first. I have plans tonight, and I'm not supposed to come in until later tomorrow, but I'll be here for the meeting."

Linda asked as if she didn't really care, "Plans with Liz?" Ben knew better.

"Yes, she's making me dinner. I'm getting out of here in," Ben looked at his watch and said, "Ten minutes," Ben smiled with the thought of being with her.

"Okay, have a nice night," Linda smiled back at him.

Ben went to his office, turned off his computer, and cleared his desk. He was on his way out the door and made sure nobody spotted him. He was free at last, and all he wanted right now was to get to Liz. Ben knew what he wanted to introduce her to tonight and hoped she was going to go along with what he had in mind. He needed to feel her, to be close to her. Although his day was busy as hell, she still managed to come to his office and give him the best blowjob. Now, it was time to blow her mind. He just hoped he could control his needs until after dinner and not rip her clothes off the minute he walked through the door. He made his stop and picked up what he thought he would need for the night, along with a few other things.

~ ~ ~ ~ ~ ~

Liz wrote all day and lost track of time as the book was moving right along. She couldn't remember the last time the words just flew out as they did today. The relationship between her characters sounded very familiar, she was aware of the similarities between her and Ben's relationship, but it just was too good not to use. Her thoughts turned to the afternoon in Ben's office and liked him telling her what he wanted her to do to him. Pleasing Ben was very satisfying because he did so many things that she relished in and wanted to do so much more with him.

The thought of what he might have in store for her tonight made warmth spread throughout her body. Liz wanted Ben more than she wanted to admit. She looked up at the clock to see how much longer until Ben got out of work. He had said he was leaving work at five that afternoon. She had made an easy roast in the crock-pot for dinner, so all she needed to do was make the potatoes and veggies. If Ben left on time as he said he would, he should be here in thirty minutes. Liz saved her work and closed her computer, picked everything up, and put it in her bedroom. She changed her clothes, pulled out the ponytail in her hair, and shook it. Her red curls went everywhere, so maybe she needed to do something with it. She pulled out her curling iron and put a little makeup on. Even though Ben had seen her that afternoon just the way she had been when she was writing, now she wanted to feel sexy for him.

Ben pulled up next to her car, and when he looked at her BMW, he wasn't intimidated by it anymore. He knew she didn't really care about material things. Liz was more down to earth than anyone he knew. Ben would never have guessed she was some big writer. At some point, he should Google her, just to see how big. But right now, he needed her touch and grabbed the bag he bought and headed for her door. Ben felt funny ringing the doorbell when they were so intimate, but he didn't want to just walk in like, "Honey, I'm home," so he knocked and opened the door, and went inside.

"Liz, it's Ben," he said loudly, so she could hear him because he didn't want to scare her. The first thing that hit him when he walked to the kitchen was the smell, and damn, it was so good, it made his stomach grumble aloud. He didn't know what she made for dinner, but if the smell was any indication, he was going to thoroughly enjoy it. She wasn't in the kitchen, so he went down the hallway in search of her.

He yelled again, "Liz, are you down here?"

"Hey Ben, I'm in the bathroom. I'll be out in a minute," so he stopped when he entered the bedroom and put his bag on the nightstand, as the door to the bathroom opened just when he looked up to see her come out. As he took her in, his eyes roamed over her face and then down over her breasts, and he could feel his body heat and his nostril flare as his jeans tightened. Liz wore makeup that made her amazing green eyes sparkle, and her hair curled around her face as she had changed into a cute sundress with no shoes, her little red painted toes curled into the carpet. He just stood there for a few seconds, just staring at her before he went to her.

"Liz, you look amazing. I'm not sure I'm going to make it through dinner," he pulled her close to him. Wrapping his arms tight around her waist, he leaned down to kiss her because she was so petite compared to him, and he towed over her. She went up on her tippy toes, and he had to get her closer, so he slipped his hand down over her ass and picked her up to him. She wrapped her arms around his neck and held him tight to her.

He had to break the kiss because if he didn't, they would be on the bed in no time, looking deeply into her eyes, "If we keep this up, we won't eat or anything else because I missed you today and I want you so bad…" he trailed off.

Liz smiled a wicked smile and asked, "What's in the bag?"

"That's for later. You'll have to wait and see," he lowered her back to the floor.

"I bet I could get you to show me what's in there," she stepped back with a little side-to-side sway.

"I bet you could, too, but you're not going to if you know what's good for you. After what you did to me this afternoon," he smiled a wicked smile back at her.

"Okay, you win this time. I'll wait," she leaned into him.

"I like the sound of that, I win, but when it's time, I'll make your wait worth it." He pulled her back to his side and kissed her on the cheek as he gave her backside a little smack.

"Hey, what was that for?" she asked and looked up at him.

"That was for trying to derail my plans for tonight, and now what is that delicious smell?" He took her hand to pull her from the bedroom because he had to get her out of there. It was too tempting to rip her clothes off and take what he wanted all day. They made their way to the kitchen, and Liz asked him if he wanted a beer or like some wine. As he watched her walk to the fridge and lean in, she looked over her shoulder at him, he had been looking at her ass, and she grinned, "Are you going to have wine?" he asked.

"I was thinking of having a beer myself," she said.

"Ok, me too. After the day, I had a cold beer sounds great. How did your day go? Did you get a lot of writing done?" Liz handed him his beer and started getting the rest of dinner ready.

"Actually, I got a lot done. I love when it just comes and fills the pages," she looked up at him, and he smirked at her. "What?"

"You're a romance writer, so I bet it just, "COMES," he said.

Liz's face started heating, so she knew it was turning red and turned away from him. She didn't want him to see how he embarrassed her when he talked so openly about sex. He came up behind her, wrapped his arms around her waist, pressed his lips against her neck, and whispered into her ear. "Was there any mention of any cherries?" He pressed his body against hers.

Oh God, she was getting really hot and tingling down between her legs as he spread his hands over her abdomen, and she sucked in. "I… I didn't get that far," and just the memory of what he did to her with that cherry made her legs weak. What did he have in store for her tonight? She wondered and found herself really wanting to know because he had her wound so tight. "If you keep that up, we will not be eating dinner, and I think you need to go back to sitting on the other side of the bar, so I can finish this." He made a grumbling noise and moved away. "You can set the table. Do you want to eat inside or out?" He smiled again, and she knew what he was thinking, "Stop that, and set the table." Pulling out the salad and bread, Liz asked, "How was surfing this morning? Was everything okay with Owen?"

"Yeah, he's just a little anxious about school, and he just needed some reassurance. I need to get him registered on Wednesday morning. He's just feeling so unsure of himself, and I told him I would be there for him, financially and for emotional support." Ben was now putting the salad and bread on the table.

"So, you're paying for school for him, that's great. I like Owen, he's a great kid from what I can tell." Liz was now bringing the rest of dinner to the table. They sat, and Liz dished out the food.

"He is a great kid, and he deserves a chance to do something with his life. I'm at a place in my life where I can help him out. I didn't get that chance to go to school because of my dad's death. I know I would have probably ended up here working at the shop anyway, but to have the experience of going to college and maybe doing something else with my life, it's like wanting what you knew you couldn't have. I'm not sorry I didn't go. I just wanted to go because all my friends went, and I had to stay behind." Ben realized for the first time; he was trying to give Owen the chance he didn't get to have. He needed to make sure this was what Owen wanted to do and not something he was pushing on him.

Ben knew he would have been working for the family business college or not, but to have his business degree, he might have been able to do so much more for the surf shop. Even though the shop was doing very well, he always wondered if he had his degree would it have made a difference. He had to learn the ins and outs of the business really fast, how to do payroll, and the taxes. If he had made a major mistake when he took over all the responsibility, there would be no shop left. It definitely would have made things easier for him.

Liz pulled him from his thought when she said, "You know, it's never too late to go to school."

"Me. That ship has sailed." It never really occurred to him to go to school now.

"I didn't get to do the college thing after high school either, I got pregnant with Paige, but after Michael was done, I did do some night classes. It took a while, but I did earn my English degree. I wanted to teach, so when I ended up home-schooling Paige, it worked out well. Even though I never taught in a school like I had hoped to do." He didn't know that about her and respected her for trying to better herself. Maybe he could take a class or two sometime when his life wasn't so crazy.

They finished eating, and he realized they had talked all through dinner. The conversation was so easy with her. He talked, and she listened, and when she was talking, he found himself very interested in what she had to say. This was so much more than the best sex he's ever had because she was perfect for him. As they cleared the table, he said, "By the way, dinner was delicious, we got into the college conversation, and I forgot to tell you."

"I'm glad you enjoyed it, so if you had gone to college, what would you have wanted to get your degree in?" She asked him.

"Well, most likely business. It would have helped out so much when I took over the surf shop."

"You still can. I know you're busy with trying to work and all. Now they have courses you can take online these days. You go at your own pace, and you already know so much about all that. It would be a breeze for you, and in the end, you would have your degree. Not that you'd get the full college experience, you know, no co-eds," she smiled at him.

"Who needs co-eds when I have you," he took her into his arms. "We need to move this into the bedroom. We can play school, I'm your professor, and you're my student." He liked the sound of that and took her hand to guide her down the hallway.

Liz had to control her breathing, or she would hyperventilate. This was it, she would find out what he was going to expose her to because the pleasure she felt last night, was crazy. Could he surpass that? She didn't know, but she sure wanted to find out.

Ben stopped at the end of the bed and let go of her hand, which she had realized was starting to sweat. She just stood there watching him move the chair to the side of the bed and then went for the bag he had left on the nightstand.

"Come here and sit. I want to talk to you first before we get started," he patted the bed where he wanted her. She sat and looked down at him in the chair. "What I want to teach you tonight is about your own sexuality. You know, you don't have to do anything you don't want to, that's first. I know in the past, you haven't felt sexy. I totally disagree. I also know this might, at first, make you uncomfortable, but if you want to go through with what I have planned, I think you'll find out something about yourself."

Okay, now she was intrigued and wanted to learn more about herself, find out what she liked. She took a big breath to steady herself and then said, "I want to know. I trust you."

"Then let's get started. I know you have been alone for a very long time, so I'm pretty sure you have a vibrator. Did you bring it with you?" She shook her head yes. "I want you to get it out and any other toys you may have." He knew this was not what she had expected him to say, so when she hesitated, he looked into her eyes and asked, "Liz did you hear me?"

She answered, "Yes, I just don't know why you want me to take it out?"

"You'll see. Now do what I asked." She reached for the bottom drawer, opened it, and pulled out two things. She laid them on the bed next to her, where Ben could inspect them. The embarrassment she felt made her turn her head. She didn't want to see Ben regarding her private things and didn't want him to see her shame. Liz had been alone for so long, she had taken care of her own needs, but now that Ben was looking at her stuff, she felt dirty. If only the bed would open up and swallow her whole.

"Liz, I know you feel like I'm intruding on your personal things, and I do get it, look at me, Liz. Don't be embarrassed because we have needs. We all do, this is what I want to teach you. One, you never need to feel embarrassed with me." She looked at him now. "What I want you to do is pleasure yourself, while I watch as I will be doing the same. I want you to watch me. What my intentions are, is for you to feel comfortable with your own body, not to be afraid to touch yourself, or to ask for what you want, and to tell me what you like and how you like it. In a way, the same thing you did to me today, but you will be touching yourself." Liz hadn't said anything, so he asked, "Are you up for this lesson on your sexuality?" He'd let her decide what she wanted to do.

Liz needed a moment to think. She wasn't sure she could go through with it, pleasing herself in front of Ben while he was watching, but he said he would be pleasing himself, too. Now to watch him might be hot. Finally, she said, "Okay I'm in, but…"

Ben cut her off when he said, "I'll start if you'll undress, and I will show you how I take care of my needs, which I have to say. I've done more now that I met you. You can drive me crazy and send my body into freakin frenzy." He stood and started to remove his shirt and then his pants. She was just watching him, and he knew it wouldn't be long until she would be into this. He sat back into the chair with his long legs stretched out open, so she could see everything he was doing, pulling open the bag, he took a tube of lube and put some into his hand. He took hold of his dick, which was hard already from just talking about what he wanted her to do.

He started to move up and down, "I like it how I showed you today, a tight grip. Can I have something to look at?" He asked, and he could see when she realized what he wanted, she stood and started to undo the zipper on her dress. Keeping her eyes on his hand moving up and down, she allowed the top of her dress to fall, and her breasts were on display for his eyes. She moved to pull the rest of the zipper down, and her tits moved. "I love your tits. I like to suck them and how they spill out over my big hands when I hold them." He was now moving a little faster, but he didn't want to climax too soon. He wanted to watch her masturbate, wanted to see her come by her own hands.

He could see the more he talked to her, the more encouragement she got, and her dress dropped to the floor between them. "I want to see you Liz, your hot pussy lay on the edge of the bed with your legs spread wide for me," and she pulled pillows to the middle of the bed and laid down so her legs hung off the bed, so she could still see him. Yes, this was going to be better than he thought, and she started to move her hands over her body. "Oh God, Liz, that is so hot. Talk to me. Tell me what you like. What's your fantasy when you touch yourself?"

She took a big breath and started telling him, "Before I met you, I would think about the men in my books touching me, but now, it's all about you touching me." Her hand moved over her tits, and she put one finger into her mouth and sucked on it, then moved it to pinch her nipples. "I like it when you play with my nipples, pinch them, suck them," she could see he was moving faster as he watched her. Liz moved one hand down over her stomach.

"I want to see you touch your pussy," Ben said with a groan, and she ran her fingers down her slit. "Put them inside, two fingers, yes, just like that." She did as he asked and moved them in and out, then she reached for the vibrator with her other hand and turned it on. It was making a little buzzy noise as she ran it over her nipples too.

"God, that feels so good. I'm so wet Ben, and I'm thinking of your hands on me."

"I want to see how wet. Spread yourself for me," She did and ran the toy over her abs and down further until it was over her clit. "Yes, I want to see it inside you," his voice had a harsh tone to it, and his hand was moving so fast.

She could tell he was close, "It won't take long once I put it in, so enjoy," and pressed it to her opening, trying to prolong her own orgasm and could see the anticipation on his face.

"I'm so close, Liz. I need you to come for me," and she plunged it deep inside as her orgasm collided with what she knew to be the truth, it was all for him. The hum of it almost couldn't be heard because it was deep inside of her, and Liz closed her eyes and let out the sound of pure satisfaction and heard him say, "Liz, watch me. I'm coming." She opened her eyes just as he pulled his dick so hard, and he came looking at her. "Yes, how I love to watch you come," he said as he stroked up and down.

When he was done, he joined her on the bed and lay next to her, his body pressed against hers. He kissed her hard because the passion he felt for her was more than he could stand and wanted her to know how he felt about her without telling her. He could feel the wetness of his come between them, and yet he didn't care because all he wanted was all of her. He reached to get a condom and was ready in no time, as he rolled on top and looked into her eyes, "I have to say that was the hottest thing I have ever seen. You are the sexiest woman I ever want to see." He entered her and couldn't control himself. He pounded into her as she was moving just as hard, but he didn't take his eyes off hers.

As he looked down at her, he could see her emotions, soul-deep, and knew then, he was not alone in how he felt. He knew they were going to need to have a talk soon about where this was going, but she wouldn't take it well if he told her that he loved her because he already knew he did. They both came hard again, and he rolled off but didn't let go. He pulled her on top of him, "We need a shower when we can move again," Ben said to the top of her head as hers rested on his chest, and her hands tangled in the hair there.

"I... it might be a while before I can move again because I was a little sore from surfing and now."

"Oh God, Liz, why didn't you tell me you were sore? I wasn't even thinking, I'm so sorry. I forgot all about you surfing yesterday," he pulled her up so he could look at her face.

"I didn't think it was a big deal. I woke up sore, but as the day went on, it eased up, so I didn't give it any more thought. But now, my stomach and my lower back are really hurting again after that workout," she smiled at him.

"I will make it up to you. I have just the thing," he rolled her off him and went into the bathroom to depose of the condom, and when he returned, he went for the bag on the floor.

She had forgotten all about the bag because they hadn't used anything he had brought earlier except for the lube. So, when he pulled the contents out, she watched with anticipation. The first thing she saw was massaging oil, and she thought, okay she could get into that, no one had ever rubbed her sore muscles. Next came a small black thing, but covered by his big hands, she didn't get a good look at it, "What is that?" she pointed to his hand.

"It's something I want to use another time," he said as he put it back into the bag and rolled the top down so she couldn't see in. "Roll over onto your stomach, and I'll massage your back, and then I'll do your front," she did as he asked.

"I still want to know what that was," but the minute his hands started to move over her skin, she didn't care anymore. He spread his hands over her lower back, working muscles that hurt so good. Now as a moan escaped her lips, he worked higher on her back. Oh God, his hands felt almost as good as when he was inside her. Ben now massaged her shoulders, and she couldn't hold it in any longer as she groaned and said, "I will give you ten years to stop that."

"Oh yeah, what would you say if I said I'd give you more than ten years?" He knew he shouldn't have said it, but he couldn't help himself. He worked his way back down to the lower part of her back again and was working the muscles hard where he knew they hurt. She moaned again, and this time it was much louder. The sound was getting Ben hard again, and he moved his hands lower to her ass. He squeezed her checks, letting his fingers drift a bit too close to her center. He wanted her again, but she was hurting, and he was such an asshole. It wasn't going to be easy not to want her bad, when he still had to do her front with her tits staring him in the face. Ok, he needed to control himself, and this was going to be so hard, literally speaking.

"Oh, I have to tell you your hands are like Gods. You're going to spoil me. I've never had anyone massage me before."

"I want to take care of you for a change." Here we go, he thought, "Roll over, and I'll do your stomach." She did, and he had the most spectacular view of her chest. "I need to close my eyes for this because I can't look at your tits staring at me like that. I know I'm an asshole, but I want you again. And if I keep looking at the great view, I'm sure I won't be able to control myself." Ben put more oil on his hands and rubbed it in before he closed his eyes as he moved his hands over her stomach.

Liz watched Ben's face, he was so handsome, with a five o'clock shadow on his jaw. He was so gentle and kind. Ben loved and cared deeply for his family. You could see how he was the one to take care of everyone like she did. When she loved someone, she'd give him or her all she had to give and ask nothing in return. She'd bet all her money that he was the same way. What would it be like to have Ben love her? She knew physically they were a great match, but love. Earlier, when she was looking into his eyes, she thought she saw deep feelings for her, but could it be love. He did make that comment about giving her more than ten years. She wondered how serious he truly was. She had to stop thinking like this, knowing she'd only get hurt when it was time to go home, and she did have to go.

"I think we need to shower. I'm starting to fall asleep." She lied, but if she told the truth, she was falling deep, and she didn't want to think about it anymore. Ben lifted her off the bed and carried her to the bathroom. "I could walk, you know," she said into his neck.

Ben loved the feeling of her breath on his skin and with her pressed against him. "I'm sure you can, but I don't want you to fall after my incredible massage. I might have weakened your knees." He held her as he opened the shower door and started the water. He was holding her as if she weighed nothing at all because to him, she was so small. He stepped into the shower and closed the door behind him, still holding her tight to his body. He let the water spray over them. Liz seized the moment he closed his eyes and brushed her lips against his. Just the lightest touch, and he wanted to deepen it but let her control it. She bit his bottom lip and then licked it with her tongue. He let a moan escape, and she deepened the kiss. Her tongue was deep into his mouth, and he still let her have the control. It took everything he had, but he didn't want to push, though his body had other ideas. He didn't have a condom and didn't want to push Liz into any more sex tonight. He could feel his control slipping fast. "Liz," he said, "I don't have any protection."

"We won't need it for what I have in mind," she said.

He closed his eyes, letting her have her way with him. If this kept up, he could wear out all his working parts.

After their shower, they climbed into bed. Liz was exhausted, she could hardly keep her eyes open, and Ben spooned up against her back. All she wanted right now was sleep to take her. Ben wanted to talk, and she could barely understand him as she said, "I can't talk, I'm sooo tired I need sleep. Tomorrow," she said.

Ben lay next to her and could hear her breathing had slowed. He knew she was asleep in two minutes flat. He wanted to have that talk about where this relationship was going and wanted to tell her he was falling in love with her. Well, not falling, because he already knew he loved her. As he lay there next to her, he knew he didn't want to be anywhere else, and maybe it was too soon to talk about forever, but he needed to know she wanted more than the month they had.

He also knew she would return to New Jersey at the end of the month because she had to. Liz took her responsibilities very seriously, and her daughter would always come first, as it should be. Would Liz return to be with him? Was he important to her? Or was she just using him for the great sex because she had said how alone she felt before they met? Could she just leave and not look back, not even think about him? Ben knew that by the way he was thinking, he was tired because that wasn't Liz at all. He needed sleep. Tomorrow, he'd talk to her, and he snuggled against Liz as he tried to rest his mind.

~ 12 ~

The next morning, Liz woke in a subconscious dream state and knew that she was awake, yet she found herself fantasizing about the man next to her. Ben had rolled onto his back, and she snuggled to his side and had one hand on his chest, with her leg thrown over his. Ben had his thigh pressed between her legs, and she thought about rubbing herself on him, like a cat in heat. She could feel the warmth spread through her core. Last night, Ben had shown her that not only was it okay to self-serve, but he encouraged it. It was so hot to watch Ben's hand stroking over his penis, fondling himself. He hadn't felt self-conscious about what he was doing at all. Ben was very comfortable in his own skin, and that was one of the things she most admired about him. He was so unprotected and open when it came to sex, he talked about it, and it never left him embarrassed. She was getting better when it came to that. Just a week ago, she was terrified to be naked in front of any man. She hadn't thought she was sexy in the least bit, and now with the way Ben looked at her, he made her feel not only sexy but also more confident in how she was.

So, if he was educating her in becoming more sexual, then what could she possibly teach him? Did she have anything she could present to him in return? Maybe today, she would do some research on how she could please him. Just maybe she could surprise him with some sex act or even a sexy outfit. As that thought went through her head, Ben started to stir, and she could tell he was awake. So now, she did press herself against his leg and moved her hand over his nipple. He groaned in response, and she moved her hand farther down his washboard abs. She loved his abs and the light dusting of hair that was a straight line to his hard-on, she noticed, and he put his hand over hers to stop her from moving any farther, and now she groaned.

"I need a little break because if we keep this up, I will wear out all my working parts. I have to use the bathroom, and I'll be right back," Ben detangled himself from her and went into the bathroom.

Okay, she hadn't seen that coming. He needed a break from her, and right away, all her confidence she had just felt disappeared, and her insecurities were back. Maybe he had had enough of her, which that thought made her stomach do a somersault. Before Liz could obsess any further over Ben's dismissal, he came back into the room and climbed back into her bed.

Ben said, "I want to talk," as he tried to pull Liz back up close to him, she pulled away and started to get out of the bed. Ben snagged her arm before she could get too far, "Hey, where are you going?" He could tell something was wrong.

"I…I have to…," she didn't finish what she was going to say because she couldn't think of any excuse but didn't want him to see the disappointment she knew was in her face.

Ben could see something was bothering her, "Come here, what's wrong?" He pulled her down on the bed to sit next to him, "What did I do? Because, not three minutes ago, you had yourself all pressed up next to me, and now you can't get away from me fast enough." Liz stood but didn't say anything, and she wouldn't look at him. "Liz, talk to me."

"I don't know. You said you need a break from me, and I just thought I'd give it to you," she tried again to pull away.

Okay, now he knew what upset her, he started to pull her back into the bed. She tried to fight him, but she was so tiny he just scooped her up and pulled her in close, "I did say I needed a break, but I didn't mean it like that. What I need is some recovery time because men need time to rebuild. We aren't like women. I don't want a break from you, per se. We just need to slow down a bit, that's all." Ben could feel her relax a bit, "As a matter of fact, I wanted to talk to you about our relationship."

Ben's phone rang as he sighed and closed his eyes. Liz couldn't help knowing his phone would save her from the conversion he wanted to have. She didn't want to take a break from him, but she also didn't want to talk about a relationship. If they had a discussion about how they felt, it would make it too real, and she would never be able to leave with any part of her heart intact. She watched him get out of the bed to retrieve his phone from his pants.

Ben looked at the caller ID because if he could ignore it, he was going to, but of course, it was his mother, so he had to answer it. "Hello," Ben listened to his mom tell him the meeting was going to be a little earlier and knew he wasn't going to have time to have that discussion with Liz. He still needed to go home to shower and shave before work. "Okay Mom, I'll be there," Ben hung up and turned to see Liz had put on a robe.

He would have another busy day at work, and he was going to have to leave now if he was going to make the meeting. Ben didn't want to leave things the way they were, so he said, "I have to leave to shower and shave before work, but I want to cook for you tonight at my place. I get off at eight tonight, so it'll be a bit late, but I want you to stay with me." Ben was now getting dressed, and he stepped toward her and put his hands around her waist to pull her close. He could feel the reserve in her body from what had happened earlier. "I want you to pack an overnight bag, so you have everything you'll need, and make sure you bring your swimsuit because it's going to be a full moon tonight."

"I'm not certain that's a good idea. Maybe a break would be good." She thought maybe some self-preservation was in order as Liz looked at him to see Ben wasn't happy with her statement.

"I told you; I want to see you tonight. You're not going to be here that much longer, and I don't want to waste any time. I know you might not want to hear this, but I love being with you." Ben brushed his thumb over her cheek and could feel her starting to melt. He needed her to give him time if he was going to make her fall in love with him, as he was with her. He slid his hand into her hair and pulled her up to kiss him and knew he had to get going but needed her to agree to be with him tonight. Ben pulled back and said, "Meet me at my apartment at eight Liz, please."

She knew she couldn't say no to him, and she couldn't handle a serious discussion either. "Okay, but I don't want to do any serious relationship talking. I don't think I can manage that right now."

"I do want to talk about us at some point, Liz, but I'll agree not to bring it up tonight if you'll stay with me. Now tell me you'll be in my bed this evening," Ben gave Liz the most brilliant smile, "Please?"

"I'll be there. Where is your apartment? Do you want me to wait for you at the shop?" Liz asked as her body relaxed, knowing he postponed the conversation.

"It's on the third floor of the store, and you can park in the back lot, then you'll see the steps that go to my apartment. The key is in the planter on the steps, you can let yourself in." He cupped her face and said, "Thank you."

"You're welcome. I could start dinner if you want," but the look in Ben's eyes said it all.

"Absolutely not. I don't want you to do anything. I want you to relax. If you want, you can bring your computer and write, it could take some time to close the store if we still have customers. But I will be up as soon as I can." Ben kissed her forehead and turned to get his shoes because he really needed to go.

Ben left as Liz felt pushed, stretched, and then forced back into shape. Her emotions were all over the place. She walked into the bathroom, looked at the huge tub, and decided she would run a bath and soak. Liz started the water and knew it would take some time to get enough water to fill it. She went in search of bubble bath. If she couldn't find any, she could always use her shampoo, it would make bubbles, and it did smell good.

~ ~ ~ ~ ~ ~

Ben ran up the stairs two at a time and knew he would be late. That was so unlike him, but now that the majority of his time was spent with Liz, he would put being with her before anything else. Ben showered as fast as he could and decided not to shave to save some time. He knew his brother would have something to say about it, but he didn't care. Ben ran into his office to get his paperwork for the meeting that was supposed to have started five minutes ago. Then went to his mom's office and knocked, walking in. Jeff was sitting in one of two chairs his mom had on the other side of her desk. Ben sat in the other one.

"Hi honey, sorry the meeting had to be moved, but it couldn't be helped," Linda said to Ben.

"Yeah, so glad you could take the time out of your busy schedule," Jeff said sarcastically. "By the way, nice beard, or you just don't have time to shave anymore."

"Kiss my ass, Jeff, when I start caring about what you think, I'll be in big trouble." He took a deep breath and relaxed into the chair.

"Boys, your grown-ups, so stop, please. I'm going to call Danielle now." Linda picked up the phone and dialed her daughter. Linda put it on speaker and put down the receiver.

"Hello," It was Danielle.

"Hi honey, we have a lot to go over, so let's get started. Owen is holding down the shop, so I need to keep it short. I have Benjamin and Jeffrey here, too. First, I want to say that I have made a decision to make changes that we will be discussing. Benjamin has some suggestions that we talked about, and I agree with him, and as of right now, we divide the end-of-the-year profit checks equally. But I'm not going to do that anymore because it's just not fair."

The voice came over the speaker and asked, "What do you mean not fair. We all own an equal part of the shop. So…"

Linda cut her daughter off, "I'm going to tell you. You don't do anything for your check, and Benjamin does too much, and Jeffrey does just what he has to. If you want an equal part of the profit checks, then you have to contribute and do your part."

"Mom, you can't be serious. You know I can't do that. I have a job here and a life."

"Well then, I guess you have made the decision easier for me, and there will be more money for the rest of us." Ben and Jeff just looked at each other as if they couldn't believe that their mother was going to cut Dannie out like that. Ben glanced back to his mom, and she winked at him. "I will also be adding someone to the cut of the checks, even if it comes out of my portion. I want Owen to have a small part because he's worked for us for years now, and he cares about this shop and deserves it. Now Benjamin, you had some suggestions for changes you want to make the store run better."

"Yes, as I have discussed with you Mom, and I mentioned to Jeff yesterday, I would like to see him take over the ordering. I will show you how it's done and help in any way I can." He turned and looked at Jeff. "Until you know what you're doing, and I was hoping if Dannie came back, she would help with payroll and scheduling. But as she said, she couldn't do that, so... I have made a rotating work schedule. As of right now, I don't have Owen on it because...."

Danielle interrupted Ben when she said, "Wait. Why isn't he on the schedule?"

"He'll be attending college in August, and I'm not sure how many hours he'll have to work and get what he has to get done for school."

"So, let me get this straight, Owen is going to get money at the end of the year, but I'm not," Danielle said as everyone could hear her anger over the phone.

Linda jumped in and said, "Owen has been working all year, and he has done more for the store than you have in the last few years, so yes, you have it straight." Ben knew his mother was being hard on his sister, but he also knew Dannie wouldn't come back if his mother didn't push her too.

"Wow, I can't believe how shitty this is. I had plans for that money."

"Well, you can come home and earn it," Linda said.

Jeff kept quiet but then piped in, "You are not the only one that things are changing for, but Ben has been running this business for a long time, so we all get those bonus checks. I haven't been doing my share either, Dannie. I hadn't realized it until this weekend just how much he does around here."

Ben couldn't believe what he was hearing. Jeff had complimented him and understood how he had devoted his life to the surf shop. The difference in Jeff's attitude was remarkable. With the changes and them working together, it could make his life so much easier and free up time for him. If things worked out with Liz, it would be great, but if they didn't, what would he do with all that time? Man, he was so lame and needed to get a life. The meeting went on for a few minutes more before they said goodbye to Danielle. Mom asked Jeff to cover the floor and send in Owen.

When Jeff shut the door, Linda said, "I know I was hard on her. You know as much as I do that if I didn't put my foot down, she would be okay with just getting a check at the end of the year and not stepping a foot in this place again, and I want her back here where she belongs."

"I know you do, but I'm not sure breaking her financially is a good idea because Dannie can be stubborn, and she doesn't like to be backed into a corner." Just as Ben finished his words, a knock came on the door, and he turned to see Owen step in.

"Well, it looks like everyone made it out alive," Owen said with a smile.

"Well then, sit down, and we can see if we can change that," Linda said, grinning back at him.

Owen sat next to Ben and said, "Did I do something? Am I in trouble? I didn't do it, Jeff did." Owen tried to lighten the mood that was floating around the office.

Linda chuckled and said, "Owen, I asked you in here to tell you that at the end of the year, when the checks go out, you will get one.

You have worked very hard around here, and we appreciate your dedication to the shop. It's a bonus check."

"You're kidding me, right? Because I just do what you pay me for. I love the surf shop, and it probably kept me out of jail. So, I should be thanking you for taking me into your family. It has meant so much to me," Owen's emotions showed.

Ben put his hand on Owen's shoulder and gave it a squeeze.

~ ~ ~ ~ ~ ~

Liz's water for her bubble bath was ready, and she put on music and stepped in. The tub was so big that her body didn't even take up half of it. She could almost drown in it. Liz was going to miss all this, the shower, and the huge kitchen, when she went back home to her modest house that she shared with her daughter. After becoming a writer, she could have bought a bigger house but didn't want to change anything for Paige. She had gone on living the same way, not spending money just because she had it. Renting this house was supposed to be a treat for Paige. But it had turned out to be a treat for her, not just the house, but meeting Ben.

What was she going to do about him? When he wanted to talk about them, how could she tell him there would be "no them?" Ben was stuck in California because he had responsibilities here that she knew he took very seriously. There was no way she would leave Paige, so all they could ever have would be the three weeks she had left. Liz had a sick feeling that the minute she expressed to him that she couldn't make any kind of commitment to him, it would be finished. Knowing she didn't want to lose the little time they had left. She'd have to try to prolong the talk for as long as she could. Somewhere in the back of her mind, she knew it was being dishonest by stringing him along, and it was lying, and she didn't lie as a rule.

That didn't sit well with her, but could she risk telling him the truth and having him walk away from her? But wasn't that what she was doing to him, walking away. "Have a great day now, had fun, gotta go." Now, she knew she'd have to tell him, and the chips would have to fall as they may, and she would have to live with the consequences. It was part of taking responsibility for her actions, she got involved with him, and he deserved her honesty and respect. She needed just a little bit longer to be with him, she thought. Soon she would talk to him, soon.

She cared what he thought of her, and she didn't want to do anything that would hurt him. Ben had been straight with her about how he was looking for more for himself. He said that when they talked about wanting children. She knew then, it wasn't going to be her to give him everything he wanted. Caught up in the great sex and the feelings of him wanting her, she didn't see what she was doing to him. It was not like her to be so selfish, but she was being greedy when it came to Ben. Deep down inside, she wondered what having a life and being married to Ben would be like.

Ben was so attentive to her needs, and that alone was so different from Michael. Her marriage felt like they never had time alone to take care of each other's needs. She loved her husband, but they never seemed to have that close connection. Ben was so aware of how she felt, and he cared if he hurt her feelings. Like what happened that morning, when she thought he wanted a break from her, a major overreaction on her part. Right away, he wanted to know what had upset her and make sure she was alright. Ben never belittled her about how she overreacted and didn't make her feel stupid for her feelings. A marriage to Ben could be so comfortable and easy. Liz closed her eyes, imagining being married to Ben, loving him. She knew thinking like this was going to make leaving much harder, but the thought of being with Ben just made her happy in an extreme way.

Knowing secretly, she wanted it but couldn't have it made her chest ache. The water was turning cold, and she needed to get some writing done before she met up with Ben tonight, and she needed to call Kat and check in because she knew if she didn't, she would get a knock on her door and find a pissed off Kat standing there.

~ ~ ~ ~ ~ ~

Ben went to his office and grabbed a cup of coffee and hadn't realized just how much he needed it. A knock on his door surprised him, as Ben looked up just in time to see Jeff come in and sit, "What can I do for you?" Ben asked.

"I just wanted to say, I'm sorry for being such an asshole lately. I'm going to take a break from dating for a while to concentrate on the shop because I want to be a part of the success of this place. I never wanted it before. When I was younger, I always felt trapped here. I guess we all knew we would end up here in the end. Dannie was the only one that had the courage to do something else, and Mom wants her back here, but I'm not sure that's a good idea."

"I know, I really appreciate that you're willing to help out around here but take it from me. I learned the hard way, a life outside of the shop is important, too. I might not have wanted to run the shop when I was younger either, but I knew I didn't want Mom to sell it. I think if we all worked together, it could make everyone happier, and having Dannie here, might not be good at first because she will resent Mom for forcing her back, but I think she'll come around in time."

"Are you closing tonight?" It surprised Ben by Jeff's question.

"Yeah, then I'm making dinner for Liz at my place," He watched carefully as Jeff considered what he was going to say.

"I'll close for you," and Ben couldn't believe how Jeff was acting.

"Who are you, and what did you do with the pain in the ass, brother of mine?" Ben smiled at the expression on Jeff's face.

"Funny, I could just let you close then…" he started to get up.

"You're crazy if you think I'm going to turn that down. Thank you, I do appreciate it," Ben was going to call Liz the second Jeff left his office.

"I figured I owe you lots of weekends and nights, and I know Liz isn't going to be here long, so I can give you some time to be with her. If it ever happens to me, I'd appreciate you helping me out."

"What do you mean, if what happens?" Ben was confused.

"If I ever fall in love, you are in love with her, right?" Jeff paused and added, "I can tell by how you're acting. Taking an entire weekend off, making out in the dressing room, and being late for the meeting, and I don't think I have ever seen you not shave."

"You can tell by all that, hah… I am definitely something because I have never wanted someone like I want her," Ben sat back.

"I really never thought I wanted to be tied down to just one person, but I'm starting to see that it might have some merit."

"I have to tell you; it scares the shit out of me because how can I have such strong feelings for someone I just met a week ago? I have thoughts of forever, and I know if I even mention how I feel to her, she'll run." He knew that's why she didn't want to have that talk.

~ ~ ~ ~ ~ ~

After Liz's bath, she went right to making her call to Kat and knew that she was just concerned. At this moment, she didn't want to share her feelings for Ben with her. She really needed to talk to him first. Liz made the call anyway and found that Kat was in a meeting, so Liz just left a message with her secretary that all was well and knew Kat would call her back, but at least she didn't have to talk to her right now, she could put it off a little longer too. Liz's phone rang in her hand, and it startled her because she hadn't expected it to ring. Looking down at her caller ID, she smiled because it was Ben.

"Hello," she couldn't help the feeling that came over her just hearing his voice.

"Hey, I wanted to tell you, I don't have to close tonight. Jeff offered to do it for me. I still can't believe it, but I'm not going to look a gift horse in the mouth. So, can you be at my place, say around six, which will give me time to pull something together for dinner?" She thought even his voice over the phone sounded sexy as hell.

"I can be there any time you want. I'm just going to get some writing done today," she tried to sound just as sexy.

"Great, I can't wait because I know what I'm planning for you tonight, wanta hint?"

"If I say yes, will you think of me as a sex fiend?" She smiled at how easy it was to have fun with Ben.

"You're not a sex fiend? Well damn, I thought you were already. So, you want a hint or not?" He was teasing her.

"You know I do, so stop teasing me and tell me." Her heart started pounding in her chest with anticipation.

"Okay, you ready, outdoors, spontaneous, moonlight," Ben didn't add any more.

"That's my hint? You're going to have to give me more than that." Okay, this was going to drive her crazy all day trying to figure out what he had up his sleeve.

"Not a chance, see you later," Ben hung up.

Now, how was she going to get any writing done with that kind of hint? She went into the kitchen and set up as if she was going to write, even though she knew she wouldn't. "Okay, he said outdoors. Did that mean he wanted to have sex outside? He couldn't mean out in the open, could he?" Well, she wouldn't do that, so that was out. "Next, he said spontaneous, well if he had planned it, how could it be spontaneous? Right, maybe he meant it would be spontaneous for me." Then there was moonlight, okay that one's easy because he had already said there was going to be a full moon tonight. But what did it all mean together?" Liz found herself wanting six o'clock to come sooner rather than later.

Liz sat down at her computer and tried to get into her story but try as she might, Ben's words kept coming back to her. This was not working. She wasn't getting anything done on her book. She needed to do something else. Maybe she could turn the tables on him. She could do that research on how she could please him. Then the next time, when they were back at her house, she could drive him crazy like he was so good at doing to her.

After a few hours on the internet, she had all the information she was going to need to make Ben pay in the best way possible. Now she was going to need to do some shopping if she wanted the right outfit to pull this off. This shopping trip was going to have to be on her own because, as helpful as Tara was the last time, she didn't want to explain this. Liz grabbed her purse, keys and went out the door.

~ ~ ~ ~ ~ ~

Ben found himself again, wondering if Liz was going to go for what he had in mind. He knew she didn't like any PDA, and being out in the open was going to be a challenge. However, if he could get her in the right frame of mind, maybe he could get her to loosen up some of that control she held so tight. Ben had been watching the clock all morning, but it didn't make it move any faster. He needed to figure out what he was going to make for dinner. He knew who he had to talk to. Ben went to her office and knocked.

"Hey Mom, I need your help because I'm making dinner for Liz tonight, and I have no idea what I'm making. I want to impress her because she's a great cook, making all kinds of great food for me, and I wanted to do something special for her."

"Okay, you have no idea what you might like to make for her? I have some of my spaghetti sauce in the freezer at home, then all you'd have to do is make the noodles and maybe a salad or garlic bread," Linda smiled at Ben standing on the other side of her desk.

"Well, isn't that cheating? I'm supposed to be making the dinner."

"You will have to make the rest of the meal, so technically, you are making dinner, and if you went out and bought jar sauce and made spaghetti, wouldn't you still consider that making dinner? I'd have to kill you for serving her that, and I much prefer you didn't."

"Okay, I'll take your sauce, but I will have to tell her the sauce is yours. Now tell me how to make the rest of the meal." He knew how to cook, but he didn't want to screw anything up.

After Linda went over how he needed to make dinner, Ben ran up the stairs to make sure his apartment was clean. He knew it was, but he wanted to change his sheets, make sure his toilet was clean, and had to stop by his mothers to pick up the sauce and let it defrost. He wanted everything to be perfect for Liz tonight.

Liz packed a bag and wasn't sure what she was going to need. Her overnight bag turned into a small suitcase. She was feeling anxious and wished she was at his apartment already. "Well, he did say I could go and wait for him, or would that make me look too eager?" Liz decided to have a tall glass of lemonade out on her deck, trying not to think about what the night would bring. When her glass was empty, she couldn't stand it any longer, grabbing her bag and she started for Ben's house. She'd just drove slowly, taking her time, but that didn't work. Ben's apartment was only two minutes away.

She pulled into the back lot as he had said. She saw the stairs but stayed in her car looking up at them, because how was she going to get her suitcase up those stairs without breaking her neck? When a knock on her window startled her, Owen was standing outside. Her hand flew to her chest as she whizzed down her window.

"Hi, you okay?" Owen asked.

"Oh yeah, I… I'm meeting Ben, and I have this bag, well suitcase, and I'm not sure if I can get it up those stairs." She felt embarrassed, revealing to Owen that she was staying at Ben's apartment.

"I'll help you," Owen said with a big grin.

"Thank you, that would be so sweet of you," Liz got out of her car but didn't move.

"No biggie," Owen pulled her bag from the car and started for the stairs. He turned to say something to her and found her just standing by her car, looking at the stairs. "Hey, you coming, or do you want just the bag to go up."

"Oh, I'm coming. I was just thinking." She ran to catch up to him and knew she was just stalling.

Ben heard someone talking on the stairs and went to see who it was. It was a little early for Liz, he still hoped it was her, but when he opened the door, he found Owen standing there with a suitcase. Ben was confused because what in the hell was Owen doing at his door with a suitcase? Then, Liz stepped around him, and Ben's face lit up. Seeing that Liz had packed a suitcase made him happy in a strange way. Like, she was going to stay with him for the long hall, Ben took the bag from Owen, thanked him for his help, then pulled Liz into his apartment and shut the door. He had her back against the door, and he was kissing her as he had never before. Ben released her from the kiss and said, "I'm so glad you're here."

"I'm a little early. I hope you don't mind," she tried to reclaim her breathing.

"Not at all," Ben eased up on his hold on her to pull her to his side. "Let me show you my apartment, it's not big like your place, but I like it," he said as he moved her farther into the apartment.

Ben's apartment wasn't that small because it was the same size as the shop below. His living room had a very nice-looking couch and a chair, and the biggest television she had ever seen. Then, they went through the dining room, where Ben had set the table with candles and cloth napkins. A small bouquet of flowers sat in the middle of the table setting looked very romantic. Ben had done all this for her, and that thought made her feel all warm inside.

"This is my dining room, and over here is my very small kitchen. I'm making spaghetti for dinner, if that's okay with you, not that I have a backup plan." That made her smile.

"That sounds good. I love pasta. You have a nice apartment." Liz looked into Ben's kitchen, it was small and had older appliances, but workable. She could cook dinner for Ben in there, it was smaller than her kitchen at home, but it was cozy. Ben took her hand and guided her down a hallway that she knew would lead to the bedroom. He stopped in one of the doorways, and she could see he used this room to workout in. There were some free weights, a weight bench, and a big piece of equipment in the corner. There was a hard bag hanging from the ceiling. This was how he kept his body looking so good, and she did enjoy his body.

"This is my workout room, when I have time or need to burn off extra energy." He smiled down at her. "I haven't had either lately."

He pulled her from the room and went to the next doorway. It was his bathroom. It was also small, with beige walls and a brown shower curtain. He had a shelf built into the wall over the commode and a towel rack on the opposite wall. "It doesn't have multiple shower heads, and it's not very big like yours."

"At home, I don't have any of that either, just one shower and a regular tub." Liz didn't want Ben to feel like he was any less adequate because he lived a modest life. She lived the same way. She'd never want to make him feel like she was above him. "I rented that house as a treat for Paige, it was going to be our last summer together, and I wanted it to be special. I already had put down the deposit six months before I knew she wouldn't be joining me."

"I like my apartment, but it's just me, and I never felt I needed any more space than I have here, and the rent is great," he smiled at her.

"That's how I've always felt about my house. It's where I raised Paige. The only home she's ever known, so I never wanted anything else." Ben pulled her back into the hallway, and he looked down at her hand.

"You're wearing the bracelet I bought you." He ran his thumb over it, brushing against the pulse in her wrist. She could see how it made him happy, she hadn't put it on right away, but she did love it.

"I kinda forgot about it, someone has kept me very busy, but I love the bracelet, and I'd like to get more charms for it. I've always wanted a bracelet like this." She was looking down at it and ran her own finger over the delicate key that hung from it. Ben was smiling down at her, and she could see the deepening feelings he had for her. She found it necessary to try to move away from where this was heading. "So, show me the rest of your place."

Drawn away from the bracelet, Ben moved to the next room, which she knew would be his bedroom. She could handle the sexual part much better than the emotional part right now. They walked through his bedroom door, and the first thing she saw was his huge bed. It was made of dark wood and had a light color quilted bedspread that was a great contrast. He had light curtains on the windows as if he didn't mind the morning sun coming through. The room felt very casual, light, and a place where he went to relax. It had a calming effect on her, and she liked it.

Liz broke away from him, walking to his bed, and ran her hand down the spread. It was very soft, she turned to face him, and he was watching her as she familiarized herself with his things. "I like your bedroom. It has a very calming feeling to it," she turned away from the bed to look out the window, and he had a perfect view of the ocean. She could see surfers out on the water and wondered if one of them was Owen. Ben's hands came around her waist, and he pulled her in close.

Ben whispered in her ear, "We need to eat dinner now, or I might strip you right here," Liz turned in his arms and nodded.

They went back into his tiny kitchen, and he opened a bottle of wine and poured her a glass, then one for himself. He raised his glass to hers and said "cheers" as he clinked his glass to hers.

Ben made her go and sit at the table because he didn't want her to do anything. He brought the food to the small table that only had two chairs. It looked so nice, and the food smelled incredible. "It smells great. I can't believe you made this just for me," Liz could feel her emotions building because no one had ever done anything like this for her.

"Well, I have to confess the sauce is my mom's, but I did make everything else." He sat in the other chair.

They ate and talked about how the meeting went that morning, and Ben told her about his sister and how his mom was trying to convince her to come back. He told her how Jeff changed overnight, and he wasn't going to be dating, to devote more time to the shop, and how out of character it was for him.

At some point, Liz realized this was what it would be like to be in a real relationship because they talked so easily about his day, and he would want to know about hers. She never had that with Michael, he didn't want to burden her with what was happening in his life, and she didn't think he really cared to know how her day went. She hadn't realized that before, just how alone she felt in her marriage.

Ben pulled her out of her thoughts when he asked, "Did you get any writing done today? I bet the book will be finished in no time."

"I didn't get any writing done today. I couldn't concentrate because someone had me very distracted, trying to figure out some crazy clues," she watched as a huge smile crossed Ben's face. She couldn't believe a man as good-looking as Ben was interested in her.

"I didn't mean for you to get distracted. I just wanted to build you up for tonight." They had finished dinner, Liz was starting to clear the table, and Ben put his hand over hers to stop her, "I'll do that. You go and put your bathing suit on. I want to take a walk on the beach before it gets too dark."

Liz had gone to his room to change. He cleared the table as fast as he could. Ben loaded the dishwasher and went to change into his own suit. Liz had a loose sundress over her suit. Ben took her hand, leading her down the stairs. Neither of them put on shoes, and the sand felt warm on his feet. He loved the feeling of the sand. As they started down the beach, only a few people were still out in the water.

Ben looked down at her, "I know I agreed not to talk about us, but I want to know about your life. That first night you made me dinner, and we talked some about your husband. You told me if I wanted to know more, you would tell me. I want to know about that part of your life. Were you happy, being married, I mean?"

"Wow, I didn't see that coming," she just looked forward.

"I'm just curious if you really don't want to talk about it, I understand." Ben held onto Liz's hand.

"No, it's okay. I just don't think it's going to be very interesting. As you know, I dated my husband in high school. We dated for a year and a half, went to senior prom together, and that's when I had sex for the first time. He was going to go off to college as I had planned to do, so we wanted to show each other that going off to school wasn't going to change anything between us. I got pregnant right out of the gate. My parents had a fit, they wanted me to end my pregnancy, and I refused. I haven't seen or spoken to them since. I graduated, and that summer, I turned eighteen, Michael and I married, and we moved into his parent's house. Michael went to school, not the one he had planned to go to, but lots of things changed. I worked cleaning houses because I wanted to save some money so when the baby came, we might be able to get our own place."

Ben was very quiet, so she looked up at him. He just seemed to be taking it all in, so she went on. "So, I worked until Paige was born, and we finally got our own place. I thought it was going to be great. We could be a family. Michael still had to finish school, so he was busy with that, and I was busy with trying to be a mom. I strapped Paige to my back and went back to cleaning houses. Michael also got a part-time job, so we never saw each other. It was a hard time. I felt so alone at times. I kept thinking that it would get better once Michael graduated and he got a better job, and things would get a little easier. I still wanted to go to school. I had always wanted to teach. So, I worked during the day and went to school at night. Michael hated it because he had to babysit Paige."

Ben interrupted, "Wait, you don't babysit your own kids. That's called parenting."

She let a little laugh escape her lips. "Yeah, that was pretty much how I looked at it, but Michael didn't see it that way. I tried to understand. He had worked hard all day and then had to come home and take care of a baby."

"His child," Ben added.

"Yes well, after I got my teaching degree in English, I wanted to work in a school teaching. Michael wanted me home with Paige. So, I figured I'd wait until Paige went to school, and then, I'd work when she was in school. After a few years, I wanted to have another child. We tried even though I didn't really think he wanted any more kids, much less the one he had. When I didn't get pregnant, I started to get very emotional. Michael didn't know how to handle it. I would cry each month when I got my period, and he would just say it just wasn't meant to be. Which pissed me off. Finally, I went to my doctor and found out there was a reason why I wasn't getting pregnant."

Ben squeezed her hand to let her know he was listening and felt for her. That comforted her. "That was a very bad time for me, even though I knew it might never happen. I still had hoped only to be let down every month. Michael told me at least we had Paige and that there were people out there who couldn't have any children. After I came to terms with that fact, I would never have any more children. Michael and I lived our lives, we didn't talk much, and when we did, it was to disagree with each other."

"One day, I wanted to make a special dinner, but I didn't have all the ingredients, so I asked him to run to the store for me. He didn't want to do it, and he told me just to make something else. That made me so mad that he wouldn't do this for me. We fought over it, and he grabbed his keys off the table, and as he walked out the door, he said, "You will be the death of me yet, Elizabeth," and slammed the door. I started dinner and went as far as I could without the ingredients I needed from the store. When an hour passed, I thought he was being late on purpose. I was so mad and seeing red. My doorbell rang, and when I opened the door to two police officers, I knew it was going to be bad." Ben pulled her into a hug that she really hadn't realized she needed. Tears stung her eyes, and she rested her face on Ben's chest.

"You okay? I'm sorry I made you relive that. It must have been so hard for you." Ben pulled back some to see the tears and wiped them with his thumb. "You are an incredibly strong woman." Ben kissed her cheek and turned them to head back. It was getting dark even though there was a full moon. So, her marriage wasn't the happiest, and now he could understand why she didn't remarry. It wasn't because she had loved her husband so much that she couldn't love anyone else. It most likely was because she didn't know what real love was. "After you lost your husband, how did you go from wanting to be a teacher to being a writer?"

Liz pulled herself together, "I tried to get a teaching position, but it was in the middle of the school year, so no positions were available. I needed to have a steady income, and I loved to write in school, so I tried to do that. It was hard because it didn't happen right away, but I hung in there, and by my third book, I was making money to support Paige and myself very well. I took Paige out of school to homeschool her, so when I had to go out of town to do book signings or meetings in NY, I just took her with me. Pretty much it was her and I, before I knew it, my life was all about taking care of my daughter." Liz realized they were back to where they started their walk, and Owen was leaning against Ben's surfboard.

"I didn't think you were ever going to make it back," Owen stood there smiling.

Ben walked up to Owen and said something, and then Owen said, "Have a great night," and walked away. Ben took hold of his board and her hand and started into the water.

"What are you doing?" Liz asked him.

"We are going to take a swim in the moonlight," Ben answered.

"It's dark out there. I don't like it, wait, I still have my dress on," She pulled it over her head as Ben just kept pulling her deeper into the water.

"Hop on my board, and I'll pull you out," she climbed on but felt like shark bait in the dark, even with the moon shining on the water.

"Ben, what are you doing? I don't like it out here. It's too dark" her heart was pounding.

"You'll have to wait and see," she was watching him, and all of a sudden, it dawned on her, what he was doing, when he hopped on the other end of his board facing her.

"Oh my God, tell me we are not going to have sex on this board, out in the middle of the ocean. We don't have any condoms, and I am not taking my clothes off."

Ben smiled at her fanatic ranting as he moved closer to her, until there was no space between them. "Don't have to take off anything, and I do have protection." He reached into the small pocket in his suit, pulled out a shiny package, held it up for her to see, and loved how her eyes got so big looking at the condom in his hand. He reached out and pulled her lips to his as the waves moved the board up and down in the water. She kissed him back, so that was a good sign, deepening the kiss, running his tongue along her teeth, then along the seam of her lips and down her neck. He could tell she was getting into it. Ben pulled down his suit to put the condom on.

"Ben—I don't know about this." She was watching him push his suit down in the moonlight. Ben rolled the condom on his hard shaft, and he stroked himself as she had her eyes glued to him.

"It'll work, you'll see," he pulled her bottoms to the side, letting her climb on top. He held his dick up so she could sink herself down on him. Ben closed his eyes, letting her rest herself on him. He grabbed her hips, lifted her, and let her drop back down as she rocked her hips, the board went up and down with the waves.

Ben lay back on the board as she sat on top of him and lifted her hips harder, and she rocked them faster. "I need to see your tits move with you on top of me like that," Ben was going to blow soon, and he wanted her to come first. He was distracted when she reached up to her neck and dropped her top. Now he could see them, and he reached his hands up to squeeze her tits together and ran his fingers over her tight buds. Liz moaned her response to his teasing and rocked her hips. She leaned back and put her hands on his thighs, which sent him deeper inside her. Ben had to make her come now. His hands moved to her hips, and his fingers were over her center, spread her lips, and ran his thumb over her clit, making little circular motions over her hard nub. She broke with a shout as her body convulsed over him. Ben could hold back no longer, pumping harder into her, coming hard, throwing his head back with a roar.

Liz rested on Ben's chest to catch her breath as he had his hands wrapped around her tight. They stayed like that for so long, and it was as if the waves were rocking them into a peaceful sleep. Ben broke the silence, "That was so hot, and now you know it can be done."

All Liz could muster up was, "Yeah."

~ 13 ~

After Liz and Ben returned to the apartment, they showered, and sheer exhaustion overtook them. As Liz was drifting off to sleep, she thought she heard Ben say something but couldn't make it out, so she just moaned her responses. As she slipped into a deep slumber, she dreamed of the most delicious man.

Ben smiled as he watched her, knowing how much he wanted Liz in his life, and he couldn't help it when he told her he loved her. He wasn't even sure if she had heard him, but it didn't matter. He would have to deal with that later; he needed to let her know just how he felt because it was overwhelming him. On one hand, he knew she was the one for him, and on the other, he wondered how he could have such strong feelings in such a short time. Tonight, with Liz on his board, was something he would never have tried with anyone. What was it about her that just made everything inside of him feel so perfect? He felt comfortable in his own skin. He could be who he was with her. Ben snuggled closer, breathed her in, and relaxed.

The next morning, when Ben's alarm went off at seven a.m., he rolled out of bed to turn it off before it woke Liz. As he climbed back in, Liz turned to him, "Sorry, I didn't want it to wake you, I have to go with Owen today to get him registered for school, and since I have no clue what I'm doing, he wanted to try to get it done early. I think once it's done, we'll both feel better."

"Do you want my help? I have some idea how it's done. I just went through this with Paige." Liz smiled up at him, and he was looking at her as if she was his angel.

"You'd do that? Owen and I would totally appreciate it. He's been turned inside out for days, just thinking about going to school." Liz started to get out of bed.

"Of course, I would do whatever I could to help. Just make sure you bring your checkbook because they want their money upfront, and they're not shy about it. I don't know about Owen's school, but I don't think there's a college anywhere that you walk away and not feel like your bank account has been raked over." Liz laughed at the face Ben made. They got dressed and went to pick up Owen. On his way, Ben went through a drive-thru for some coffee.

Owen was standing outside waiting for Ben. He was so nervous. His stomach was doing flip-flops. When he got up, he couldn't eat, and he had changed his clothes twice. He had never felt so unsure of himself in his life. He had been a confident kid growing up, and when he wasn't, he faked it. He would act as if nothing or anyone ever bothered him. He was smooth and cool until now. When Ben pulled up, Owen saw Liz was sitting in the front seat. Owen wasn't sure how he felt about her being part of this. If it was just Ben, he could let his guard down, but now that Liz was here, he was going to have to act like this was nothing, and he wasn't sure he could pull it off.

Owen opened the door to the Jeep, and Liz stepped out and wrapped her arms around him. He looked over Liz's head and saw Ben smiling. "What's that for?" Owen could feel Liz's warmth and her reassurance, and it felt good. He knew she was trying to comfort him. He hadn't realized just how much he needed it. Owen returned the tight hug and let her encouragement fill him. When he released her, she looked up into his eyes. It was as if she could sense his fear. Liz put her hands on each side of his face, pulling Owen down, and kissed his cheek.

"Owen, I know just how you're feeling, and I'm here to tell you it is going to be all right. You are a very intelligent young man, and this is just the start of a new beginning for you. Appreciate this opportunity. Someone just recently told me the unknown is what makes us have fear. That's why we don't like change, but with it, we grow, and we all need to grow. It's okay to be nervous, try taking a deep breath as you keep telling yourself everything will be fine."

Owen looked down at Liz. "Thanks, am I that easy to read? Does the fear show on my face or what?"

"Not at all, I just know, call it a mother's intuition," she smiled.

Owen hugged Liz one more time just to let her support seep into him and to show how much he appreciated it.

Ben said, "Ok, now let go of my girlfriend and get in so we can get this over with." Owen pulled Liz just a bit tighter and grinned over her head just to get under Ben's skin. "Dude, are you trying to antagonize me because you will pay for it later." Owen felt better and released Liz, and they both climbed into the Jeep.

They pulled into the parking lot of the community college, and Owen took in a deep breath. "Remember to repeat it's going to be okay," Liz said to him. They went into the building, and there were kids and parents everywhere. "Make sure you have your paperwork out and ready, so when they ask for it, you aren't fumbling for it," Liz whispered to Owen. They got into a long line and waited. The line moved slowly, and the longer they waited, the more Liz could see the tension building in Owen. "So, how was surfing the other day?" Liz asked him to try to get his mind on something else.

"The waves were great. You should have come with Ben. It would have been cool having you out there with us." Owen smiled down at her and added, "I could have givin' you some pointers."

Ben just snorted at Owen's statement. The line was starting to move, and Ben could see how Liz was distracting Owen. He was so glad that she had agreed to come. He put his arm around her waist and thought how she would fit right into his life so easily.

"I didn't want to intrude. I know Ben's been spending a lot of time with me, and I thought you might want some of his time, just the two of you." She put her hand on Owen's arm.

"I wouldn't have minded. I just really wanted to talk to Ben about school. I think you're cool, Liz, and you're welcome any time as far as I'm concerned." Liz gave his arm a little squeeze and let her hand drop.

"Thanks, Owen, that's so sweet of you, I'd love to try it again, but I was so sore after the last time." Liz watched as Owen relaxed.

"That will ease up the more you surf, and all depending on the water conditions, sometimes I even get sore afterwards. But it's a good sore, yah know, like you know you just worked out hard."

They moved about halfway through the line, Liz just kept talking about surfing, and Owen didn't even realize she was distracting him. Ben smiled at how she was controlling the situation. He could tell that she was a great mom, by the way, she was nurturing and caring for a kid she just met a week ago. Didn't he know that about her already? She was the one to take care of others, and from what he was observing right now, she was good at it.

"I want to get better, but I'm still not sure what I'm doing." Liz bit her bottom lip thinking about getting out there again, and what they did last night on Ben's board came to mind.

"Maybe we could do some surfing tonight after work. I know Ben has taught you how to do your stances, and the more practice you get, the better you'll be at it, and once you master that, the rest will be easier, and it'll be more fun when you're not wiping out all the time." Liz had to smile at him. He was so cute, to be young again, to have your whole life ahead of you.

"Next," came from one of the empty booths, where one of the counselors was sitting. Owen took a big breath again as he walked up to the desk, taking a seat. Ben and Liz sat on either side of him.

"Hi, my name is Mrs. Jones, and I'm here to help you through the processes of getting registered. I'll try to make this as painless as possible." She smiled a warm and welcoming smile as if she had practiced it for hours, as she said, "Your name, and do you have all your paperwork?"

"Owen Fisher and I have everything right here," handing her the papers, he felt Liz's hand on his back, and it comforted him.

"Okay Owen, do you know what your major is going to be?" She wasn't looking at him and just kept typing.

"Business," he answered.

"Well, let's see," she looked at her computer screen, "You need to start with your core classes, Math, English, and so on. Are you going full-time or part-time?" She asked.

Ben answered that question, "He's going full-time."

"Oh, all right, Mr. Fisher," she looked up at Ben now.

"This is my boss, Mr. Jacobs, and his wife, Liz," Owen said.

Ben liked the sound of that, he looked over at Liz, but she was rubbing Owen's back and didn't look at him.

"Sorry, I just assumed you both were his parents," she hit a few more keys and printed out his schedule. "Now, you can move to the purser, hand them your paperwork, pay your fees, buy your books, and then you're done. Remember, you'll have orientation. You'll get a reminder in the mail with the date and time," then smiled that same smile as before.

"Thank you," Owen took his schedule from her, and they got up to move to the next line.

"Now, that wasn't so bad," Liz put her arm around Owen's waist and pulled him in for another hug.

"All we have to do now is pay, and we're done," Ben said as he pulled Liz back to his side. "I think we should get something to eat after we're done because I know Owen didn't have anything before, we left." Ben knew Owen was too anxious about college to eat.

"Are you kidding me? I would have barfed it up if I even tried to eat anything," Owen said as they walked into the next line, which was moving much faster. Ben wrote the check for all the fees, and then they were off to the campus bookstore. Liz took Owen's schedule and handed it to one of the workers, they helped him to get everything he was going to need, and then it was over.

"See, you made it, and you're still in one piece," Liz beamed at Owen.

They walked to the Jeep, and Owen said, "Breakfast is on me, and I want to thank both of you for helping me. Hey Liz, I'm sorry bout introducing you as Ben's wife back there. I just didn't want to explain to her who you were and make me sound any more dysfunctional than I already am. Yah know, without a parent and all. I won't let you guys down."

Ben stood next to the Jeep, put his hands on Owen's shoulders, and looked into his face. "Owen, you have never let me down. I have to ask, is this what you want to do, go to school?"

"Of course, why would you ask me that?" Owen looked surprised by Ben's question.

"I just wanted to make sure this is what you wanted and not something I was pushing on you."

"Ben, you have never pushed me. I always looked at it as guidance. You have supported me and always looked out for my best interest."

Ben nodded and said, "Ok, I just had to make sure because I didn't have that chance to go to school, and I needed to know it wasn't something I pressured you into."

Liz watched the whole exchange and decided to lighten the mood. "Well, if you did and he doesn't really want to go to school, it's too late to get your money back. So, let's go, I'm hungry."

They went to the same diner that Ben had taken her to the other morning, and this time it wasn't so busy. The waitress sat them in a booth and took their drink order. Liz was looking over her menu when she noticed Ben staring at her. She looked up, and he smiled. God, he was so handsome. He had a great smile. She smiled back at him and could see he appreciated her help today, and she was happy she could do it. She liked Owen and would do whatever she could to make this experience as easy as possible.

Ben was watching her, her movements as she looked over her menu. He knew it wasn't going to be long, and he would tell her he had very serious feelings for her. She helped Owen today in a way he knew he wouldn't have been able to do. Ben looked at Owen, smiling as he talked to the waitress.

"I have to say you are amazing, how you handled him when we were in line. You talked about something he knows and loves. Something he feels comfortable with when he felt so out of his element. I'm so glad you offered to help. I'm sure we'd have made it through, but it would have been much harder, and the way you handled the bookstore. I think we'd still be there finding what he needed."

"Ben, I didn't really do very much, I talked to him in line, and the employee at the bookstore would have asked for his schedule and helped to get everything he needed." She knew she didn't take compliments well, so she tried downplaying her roll today.

"Liz, you don't realize just how much you do for people that are around you. I bet when you care about someone, you give your all to them." Ben took her hand and kissed it. "Liz, we need to talk soon about us. I know you really don't want to, but I can't help how I feel." Owen came up to the table, sitting on the other side of them.

"I feel so much better now that's over. Liz, I appreciated your help today. I wasn't sure at first how I felt about you coming along. I usually don't feel so unsure of myself, but for some reason, I couldn't get a hold on my feelings. I didn't want you to see me like that. You know how us guys are, all macho and shit."

"Like I just told Ben, I didn't really do anything." Liz smiled at him. She couldn't help saying a silent prayer that Owen had saved her from having any further relationship talk. She knew Ben wasn't going to let her put it off much longer. The waitress came and took their order, and the conversion turned to the surf shop and the possibility of surfing that evening. She was glad for the subject change.

How much longer could she hold on to him? The time she had spent with him had been the best she'd had in a very long time. She needed more time because there were only three weeks before she left to go home, and as selfish as it was, she wanted to spend them with him.

She had this battle going on in her head over what was right and wrong and what she wanted. Liz blinked when Owen moved his hand back and forth in front of her face.

"Hello, earth, to Liz. Are you with us?" He was grinning at her expression.

"Sorry, I was just thinking. What did you say?" She tried to concentrate on what he was now saying.

"I wanted to know if you're in for surfing later." He was looking at her with wonder in his eyes.

"Yeah, I'd love to, but it will have to be before it gets dark. I don't like it when it's dark, like last night." Both Ben and Owen had huge grins. Liz wondered if Owen knew what they did on Ben's surfboard.

"The water was calm last night. I'm sure surfing sucked." He said it as if he definitely knew they weren't surfing last night, and that left her wondering. It was time to take a little of the control back.

"Besides, I have plans for later tonight," Liz said, and that wiped the smile right off Ben's face.

Ben's surprised look was priceless as he asked, "You do?"

"Yes, I do," she was the one smiling now. She was going to set her plan in motion, the one where she planned to tie Ben to her bed.

"Do I have plans too?" Ben sounded as if he sure hoped so.

"You might… if you're a good boy," she cooed in a sexy voice.

Owen just cleared his throat to remind them he was still sitting there, the waitress came with their food, and they dug in. Ben didn't know what Liz had planned for their evening, but whatever it was, as long as he was with her, it didn't matter. He wanted to have that talk, but at the same time, he wasn't sure it was in his best interest to push her. If he pushed too hard, he might not like how she reacted. What would happen if she left and went back to Jersey? Would he go after her? He wanted her in his life, and what would he give to have her there? The word "EVERYTHING" went through his mind.

After Owen put away a huge breakfast, Ben took him back to the shop, and then he drove Liz back to her house. He was wondering what was going on in her head. "So, any hints for me about the plans you have for tonight?" Ben grinned over at her.

"I'm not sure I want to give anything away," she stuck her chin up as if to say I'm not telling.

As Ben looked over at her, she looked like a little kid hiding a secret, smiling at the thought, "I gave you hints yesterday, so why can't I get at least one now?"

"Okay, turn around is fair play," that's all she was going to say.

"That's my hint. You have to give me more than that," it wasn't any kind of hint. Ben found her intriguing, and it fascinated him.

"Not a chance. You'll have to wait and see," she grinned. She liked keeping Ben guessing. "What time will we be surfing?" She had to get ready for her night with him.

"The shop closes early today, so I say around six or so," they pulled into her driveway, and Liz leaned in, kissed him on the cheek, and started to get out, saying she'd see him later. Ben grabbed her arm to stop her from trying to get out. "Hold up a minute, I want a real kiss because I've waited all morning, and I just can't go the rest of the day without it." He pulled her close, pressing his lips very softly to hers. The kiss didn't stay soft as she leaned into him and pressed her chest to his side. He wanted her, although he knew she didn't like the PDA, but having her so close, it did crazy things to him. Ben was getting hard as her tongue swiped across his bottom lip. He wanted to pull her onto his lap but knew she would never go for that in her driveway. He groaned as he said, "Liz, I need…" as he took a pull of air into his lungs.

Liz pulled back, looking up into his eyes, and could see his desire, she wanted to jump into his lap but needed to try to control herself. Ben's irresistible pull was not easy to resist, but she had to be the first to pull away. If she wanted to be in control tonight, then she would have to start it now. Liz pulled back further to break the hold Ben had on her. It would be so easy to just pull Ben into the house and have her way with him right now, but she wanted to set up a night that Ben would not soon forget. As she had already had so many, it would be his turn. "Ben, I need to get some writing done today, and you need to get back to work." Ben let out a huge growl and closed his eyes as if he was trying to get some control. "You will be here in a few hours to pick me up for surfing," she smiled up at him as she batted her eyelashes at him.

Ben let out the breath he had been holding and said, "Please tell me what you have in mind for tonight. It might hold me off, and it'll give me something to think about while I'm missing you."

"Or it could just drive you crazy instead," Liz looked down at their joined hands as her hand was playing with his fingers.

"I'm not going crazy. I think I've been there ever since I laid eyes on you at the beach a week ago." He was now getting into the finger action as he took control and pulled her hand to his mouth and kissed her, running his tongue in between her fingers.

"I have to go now," she pulled her hand free. "But tonight, I want control, can you do that, Ben? Let me be the teacher and the one to teach you?" She watched his reaction to her question.

"Well, what did you have in mind?" A big, wicked smile crossed his handsome face.

"I'm not going to tell you that, Ben. Do you trust me?"

"Of course, I do, but I need a little bit more to go on here. I'm not like you. I want to know what's coming," as he said the words, it was Liz's turn to smile.

"I guarantee there will be coming, and this time Ben, I will not be first or last. You are not going to get me to say anymore," Liz hopped down from his Jeep before he could grab her again. He watched as she walked away with a little extra sway to her hips.

Ben watched her go, and he heard that voice in his head that said, "Mine." He waited until she was inside before he put the Jeep in reverse and started back to work. He didn't want to sit in his office the rest of the day because he knew his thoughts would be of Liz. Ben didn't really care what she had in mind for them tonight because he knew he would love every minute of it.

As he pulled into the parking lot at the shop, his mother was getting into her car, and she stopped when she saw him. "Oh great, now I'm going to have to talk to her just a minute more, and I would have missed her," he pulled into his parking spot next to hers.

"Hey honey, I heard registration went well, thanks to Liz."

"Yeah, Liz was a big help. She seemed to know what she was doing after doing it with her daughter."

"I can't believe she has a daughter that age. She looks so young to have an adult child."

Ben just laughed at his mother's assessment of Liz because she was older than he was. "I hate to tell you, but Liz is older than me. Not that it matters to me because I like her just the way she is."

"Older than you, Benjamin? By how much older?" Ben could see the wheels turning, Liz's age, no grandkids. "I knew she had a daughter, but I just thought she got pregnant as a teen," Linda's brow had that big crease between them. It was something she did when she was over thinking things and didn't even realize it.

"Mom stop, I can see your wheels going, so just stop because I'm going to tell you something, and I want you to understand and know that I have given this a lot of thought. Liz can't have any more children, and I'm okay with that. I want her, not for how many children she can give me. I know you have an image in your head about having a house full of grandkids someday, but if things work out, you will get a step-granddaughter, and that will have to be good enough." Ben pulled back because he hadn't realized he was getting loud and into his mom's face. "Sorry Mom, I didn't mean to yell at you. I just want you to know I chose her. I just didn't want you to get your hopes up about babies. I have to convince her I'm the one for her," then he added, "first." Ben's voice trailed off as if he was thinking.

"I'm sorry," Linda said quietly. "I didn't mean to overstep. I just want what's best for you, Benjamin and you know I am one-hundred percent behind you. If you think she is the one for you, then I would love to have a step-granddaughter. It's a start, not that I will get any grandkids from Jeffery. I guess I can hold out hope for Danielle," Linda gave Ben a weak smile that didn't reach her eyes.

"Mom, I didn't mean to…" Ben stopped because he could see he had upset his mother. Ben never did anything to upset her, and he didn't like it now. He reached out and pulled her into a hug, "I just wanted you to know that she has become very important to me."

"I know, Benjamin." She said into his chest as she hugged him back. "Is it okay if I get to know her? I'd like to invite her to lunch sometime?" Linda pulled back to look up at him.

"Yeah, I think that would be nice, but Mom, give me some more time, maybe give it a week or so, ok? Because I don't want to freak her out," he looked down at her now.

"You know I love you. I will always be here for you, and I know if you love her, I will, too."

~ ~ ~ ~ ~ ~

Liz went into the house and shut the door, *okay, now what*? She went into her bathroom because that's where she was going to begin the transformation. Liz started the water for her huge tub and then went into her kitchen to figure out what would be for dinner. As she looked into her refrigerator, Liz pulled out anything she thought would work. Dinner was definitely going to be in bed, and the thought made Liz smile. She went back to check on her water.

She got out her shaving cream, stepped into the tub, and got busy. When she was done, there wasn't going to be a hair on her body that she didn't want there. This was so not like her, and that's what she liked the most of all. She could be anybody with him, but she was being herself.

The real Liz, she just hadn't appreciated anything like this before. How could she? She didn't know, "How could I not know? I'm a writer. I make this stuff up," but that was just it, what she wrote was made up, and this kind of relationship shouldn't be real. It felt like a dream, something she conjured up just for herself to enjoy. It was better than anything she could've made up. Getting out of the tub, putting on her bathing suit with shorts and a white T-shirt over it so she'd be ready.

Liz pulled the outfit out of her closet that she had bought for tonight and looked it over. She had tried it on at the store, but now that she was going to have to wear it for Ben, she could feel that little self-doubt creeping in. What had she told Owen that morning about fear and the unknown?

Liz took a deep breath and hung it back up. She would do this. Next, she went to her nightstand and pulled out that other little thing that Ben hadn't paid any attention to the other night, and now she was glad because she had plans for it tonight. Liz could feel more of that confidence coming back and put the item back into the nightstand and then pulled out the pages she had printed out on pleasing a man. She went over each pleasure point. Liz wanted to look like she knew what she was doing, even if she had no clue. She didn't want Ben to know that she wanted him to be impressed with what she could do to him.

Once she felt more comfortable with the articles, and she memorized all the points it said would drive him crazy, she put that away. One thing she didn't want was for him to find out how she had to look up on the internet how to pleasure a man. A small amount of doubt came over her again. What would happen if the triggers didn't work, then what? What would she do then? Would he laugh at her? No, she knew he wouldn't do anything to make her feel any more insecure. She needed to back away from this until it was time. It occurred to her how would she get into her outfit and everything in place without Ben knowing anything?

Liz went into her closet, took everything she was going to need, and then went into the bathroom. Where could she hide all this stuff? Liz opened the linen closet where the towels and washcloths were stored, and she pulled them out, putting all her stuff in and placing the towels back on top.

~ ~ ~ ~ ~ ~

Ben went into his office because he needed some time after getting upset with his mom. He had never been so stern with her before. What he was building with Liz was very important to him, but to take out his frustrations on his mother was not ok. Ben knew there were only a few hours left before the shop closed, and he'd be picking Liz up to go surfing. Ben picked up the phone and ordered his mother's favorite flowers, and then Ben called the jewelry store where he bought the bracelet for Liz. There was a little lock that he had liked the last time, and he wanted to give it to Liz because she had the key to his heart now, as he could feel his heart locking down. Ben gave the man his credit card number and set it up to be delivery the next morning.

He knew he should be holding back, but every part of him wanted to run to her and tell her just how he felt about her. He knew there was time, he kept telling himself three more weeks, and he was going to show her just how she couldn't live without him. Ben started to plan his and Liz's next night together. He wanted to show her he could take her out to a very nice dinner and then dancing.

After they returned to her place, he would make good use of that hot tub on her deck and give her the new charm. Ben smiled big, just the thought of her in that hot tub. He now wondered what she had up her sleeve for tonight. She wanted the control, which might be very thrilling to have her doing the things she wanted to him. Liz had said turn around was fair play, and now which play was she turning on him? Ben had to think of all he had done to her. He went over in his mind every minute he spent with her, and after the thought, he wouldn't mind if she turned the tables on him.

There was a knock on the door, and he looked up to see Owen standing there, "Do you want me to load up the boards? We aren't busy now, and we have less than an hour before we close."

"That would be great, Owen; you ok? I know today had you in knots," he gestured for Owen to sit.

Owen walked into the office and sat down. "I'm just so glad that part is over. It wasn't as bad as I made it out to be. I think Liz was right about fear of not knowing, and she was a big help today."

"Yeah, she did seem to have control of the situation. She offered her help, I didn't ask. Just goes to show you that having a very intelligent woman at your side is a smart thing to have," a smile filled Ben's face. "Hey, did you ask Jeff if he's going surfing?"

"I asked, he might be there for a bit, but he has a date."

Ben thought about how that vow of not dating didn't last long. He needed to take time to show Jeff how to get the ordering done if he expected him to take it over. "So, it's not busy out there. I need to start to show Jeff how to do the ordering." Ben got up from his desk, and he and Owen walked out into the store together. Ben stopped to look for Jeff, and Owen went to take care of the surfboards. He found Jeff by the man's t-shirts, and he looked like he was counting them.

"Hey Jeff, got a minute? I'd like to go over ordering with you."

"I was just trying to see if we needed any shirts but counting all this shit is going to take forever. No wonder you wanted me to take it over," Jeff was still bending down, counting.

"You don't have to do that. I can show you a much easier way. Come on into my office, and I'll show you how to print out all the merchandise we've sold in the last month. Then, all you have to do is keep track of that and order what we sell. Sometimes we get advertisements on new items and then decide if we should carry the product or not." They both went back to Ben's office, he showed Jeff how to print the spread sheet and went over how to read it, and after about forty-five minutes, Owen popped his head in and announced the store was closed for the night.

"I didn't realize how much work it is to keep track of all this stuff. I don't think I have ever really given it a thought about how the merchandise got here. I know now that you do way more than I thought." Jeff was in awe over the small bit Ben had shown him.

"I know it seems overwhelming right now, but you will get the hang of it, and you'll make some mistakes along the way, and I'll help you every step. I wish I had somebody to show me my first time. I had to make a lot of mistakes before I figured it out. Thank God, I didn't do too much damage," Ben patted his brother on the back. "Now you gonna surf with us?"

Ben left the shop feeling better than he had in days. He was on his way to pick Liz up, and that was always good. Jeff was trying to do his share at the shop, and Owen's registration for school went well, thanks to Liz, and they were all going surfing. This is just the way his life should be the way he always saw it. Everyone was out on the water, having fun. It all just felt so right. Ben drove the short distance to Liz's house with the biggest grin. He knew he probably looked like an idiot, but he didn't care because he was happy. Ben pulled into her driveway, whistling as he walked to the door. Liz opened it before he could knock. She smiled up at him.

"So, I'm just guessing here, you had a good day after you dropped me off," Ben pushed her back into the house as he had before and pinned her to the closed door.

"I did, but I still missed you," he bent his knees so he was as close to eye level as he could get. "I had the best day, and it's all because of you," he watched the expression that came across her face.

"What did I do?" She snuggled into his chest.

"You just make everything better," Ben couldn't hold back any longer and kissed her the way he had wanted to all day. He cupped her ass and picked her up, so she was his height.

Liz pulled back again, control because if she let things get out of hand now, she wouldn't have control later, and Ben let out a groan because he knew she was going to stop him.

"Liz, I want you, no, I need you," and he started kissing down her neck, trying to get better access to her collarbone. Ben slid his hands into the back of her shirt, moving them up to the bottom of her bathing suit top.

"Ben, stop. We are supposed to be surfing right now, and everyone will be looking for us," she was trying to catch her breath.

"I don't care about them. I missed you," he started to move toward the bedroom.

"Ohhh, you poor baby, you had to do without me for a couple hours. "Somehow, I think you'll live," Liz was saying it as if she was talking to a small child, and when she noticed where he was heading, she put a stop to it. "We are not going into the bedroom. That's after surfing." Now Liz was using her best mommy-in-charge voice, and Ben stopped in his tracks, looking into her face. *Stay strong, and don't waver because if he sees you falter, it'll be all over, hold your ground.*

"Man," Ben said as he put her down, pouting, he was so cute. "I promise you. I will take care of you, and you'll be very satisfied when I'm done," Liz smoothed back some hair that fell onto his face.

"Ok, I'm not happy about waiting because you've spoiled me. I don't want to ruin your plans," and they walked to the door.

"Now, we need to get out there and do some surfing. You have to make sure I don't kill myself," Liz poked her finger into Ben's chest as he backed her up against the door again.

"Yes Mommy, I promise to keep you safe, and I won't let any sharks eat you. Only I'm allowed to do that," now Liz smacked him hard in the chest. "Hey, I don't let girls hit me, don't make me restrain you," and pinned her hands above her head and kissed her.

She kissed him back, she was only human, after all, and he was a hunk. Her hunk, and he wanted her. Yes… and she broke the kiss one more time, "Hey, are you trying to distract me?"

"Is it working," Ben said with a smile.

"No," Ben made that pouty face again. "Let's go," she pulled him out the door. Owen and Jeff were already out in the water when they arrived. Liz hadn't realized that Jeff would be there too, and now she wasn't feeling so sure of herself. Would Jeff make fun of her about how bad she was? Ben looked over at her and grabbed her hand.

"What's wrong? Because I can see how your expression just changed."

"I didn't know that Jeff was going to be out here with us today. I thought it was just going to be Owen and us. I'm not sure I can keep up with everyone," she said nervously.

"You don't have to keep up with everyone. It's their job to keep up with you because you're the newbie. Don't worry, Jeff is not going to give you a hard time. I'll drown him first."

Liz took a big breath and got out of the Jeep, then noticed that they were out there in just board shorts, "No one has wetsuits on."

"No, we don't need them because the water is warmer this time of day. Like last night, we didn't wear them," he smiled down at her with the reminder of last night.

"Oh my God, what am I going to wear over my suit to keep it in place. Ben, I can't go in there and try to surf and keep my suit on. Do you want me to be flashing your brother and poor Owen?"

Ben was trying to hide his laughter because somehow, he thought both his brother and poor Owen would survive just fine if Liz's top flew off, but did he want them to see what was his? *Hell no,* he didn't want anyone ever seeing Liz naked. "Just leave your t-shirt on. It should hold everything in place, and if after a bit you don't feel comfortable, we can go." Liz nodded and went to taking off her shoes and shorts. Ben grabbed the boards from the top of his Jeep as he watched Liz bend over to take off her shorts, and he could feel his blood rush south. He took her hand and pulled her into the water before he had a full boner.

Once they were in the water, it didn't get any better because now Liz's white T-shirt molded to her body like a glove. He tried not to stare, but she was hot sitting on her board. Ben knew she was feeling self-conscious about her body and being out there. He tried to pretend that she was fully clothed as he went over the things, he had done the previous day. Ben talked Liz into taking the next wave. She laid her chest on her board and started to paddle, just as Owen and Jeff came up to where he was, they all sat watching her. Liz caught the wave just at the right time as she popped up into her stands.

Knowing they were all watching her, she took a big breath and held it. If she was going to do this, then she might as well do it the best she could. She paddled as hard as she could, and when she felt the rise in the wave, she popped up. In a matter of seconds, she was up on the board, looking at the water, and in the next, she was wiping out. She held that same breath through the whole ride, so when she came to the surface of the water, she had to gasp for air. Two seconds after her head cleared the water, she heard the cheers, and then Ben was there with his arms around her waist. They were in the water about waist deep, and she rested her head on his chest.

"That was awesome, Liz. You blow me away with how fast you are picking this up. Come on, let's do it again." Liz got back on her board to paddle back out to where Owen and Jeff were.

Owen was the first to encourage her when he said, "Liz, that was great. You're on your way to being one of us."

Jeff added, "Owen just told me that this is only your second time out here. I know guys that have been surfing for a long time, and they still can't feel the rise in the wave. But you popped up right on time, and timing that's half the battle."

"Thanks, I still don't really know what I'm doing."

"Well, I think you're doing great for someone who doesn't know," Jeff added.

"Yeah, I definitely think with a little more practice, she'll be great. Of course, I was her teacher, as a matter of fact, I taught all of you to surf," Ben said with a wide smile.

"Yeah, that's because you're an old man, and you've been around longer than the rest of us, just sayin','" Owen was laughing at the face Ben made.

"I'll have you know I'm not the oldest…" Ben stopped talking when he saw Liz's expression.

Owen asked, "What?"

Ben said, "Nothing, let's surf!" Jeff caught on that Liz was older and had to hide his smirk.

For the next hour, they each took some great waves, and even Liz got a few more great rides in. They all managed to encourage and rib each other on the great rides and on the wipeouts. Liz gave as good as she got. If she wiped out, Owen or Jeff would give her a hard time or tell her what to try the next time. When one of them wiped out, which didn't happen often, she made sure to give them hell, even though she didn't know what she was talking about when doing so.

Ben observed how Liz interacted with his family, not only did she handle Owen this morning, but she also wasn't intimidated by Jeff. She might have been at first, but he must have pushed something in her because she was sending zingers his way, and Ben loved it. Every time she hopped on her board, she gave it everything she had, and it sent a streak of pride through him. As much as he wanted her all to himself, he also loved watching her with his family. Now, if he could get her to realize how wonderful a life could be with him and his crazy family. He didn't think she realized just how incredibly sexy she was with her tough, strong side along with her oh-so-soft and fun side. How no other man had scooped her up was beyond him, but he was so happy no one had because he wanted her for his own.

Ben knew it was going to be an uphill battle, but anything worth having always was. Liz was definitely worth everything he had to do to win her over. She must have felt him watching her because she stopped talking and looked in his direction. He couldn't help the big smile that crossed his face because he loved her.

~ 14 ~

Done surfing, Ben and Liz hopped into his Jeep just as the sun was starting to go down. It was a beautiful site. The sky was filled with magnificent shades of magenta and pinks, with the last of the sun's rays sprayed through the clouds. Quiet for a minute or two, Ben reached for her hand, and that strong feeling came over him again. He needed to tell her how he was feeling before he just blurted out that he loved her again, and this time not while she was asleep.

Ben said, "I had the best time out there today surfing with you and my family, and I don't want to scare you, but I feel like I'm falling for you. I'm not sure what you're thinking, but I know I want more. I'm well aware you have to go home and get Paige off to school, but I want you to think about coming back after you get her settled." He glanced over at her and could see this was making her uncomfortable, so he rushed out the last part, "You don't have to give me an answer now. I just want you to think about it, okay?"

"Ben, you know I can't...." She tried to take a deep breath but couldn't because this was it, the conversation she didn't want to have. "I don't think I can give you more. You deserve so much more than me, to have someone that can give you children. You will make a great father someday and teach them to surf, have someone to hand the shop down to, but I don't really want to talk about this now." She took that deep breath again and continued, "You think you might have deeper feelings for me. I understand that because I also like you more, too, but I don't think getting into a serious relationship is going to be good for either of us. I can't leave Paige, and you can't leave the shop. All we have is the time I have left, and I'd understand if you don't want this," she moved her finger between them and finished, "to go any further." Liz closed her eyes and held her breath because she didn't want to see his reaction.

Ben squeezed her hand, and she opened her eyes. They were now in her driveway, and Ben turned off the Jeep. He was looking at her and then got out and came around and helped her out. He didn't say a word, and that was making her stomach do flip-flops. Was he going to walk her to the door and kiss her goodbye? Was this the end? She sure hoped not, but his face didn't give anything away. He held her hand and walked her up to her door and stood there waiting. Liz looked up into Ben's eyes, and he smiled.

Ben's heart was pounding out of his chest, but he knew he had to keep calm and breathe, "Are you going to open the door? Or are we just going to stand out here?" Liz reached for her keys, but her hands were shaking so hard she couldn't get the key in the lock. He took them from her hand and unlocked the door. They both walked inside, and Ben pulled her over to the couch and sat down.

"Liz, I need to know if you want to stop this relationship because if you don't want to spend any more time with me, then there's nothing I can do." Ben hoped like hell she wasn't going to end things because he would have to beg and plead to make her change her mind. All he knew for sure was he wasn't done with her, not by a long shot.

"Ben, I don't want to stop seeing you, and that's very selfish of me, and I know how unfair I'm being to you. I just can't give you more than what we have right now." She was looking down at her hands, afraid to look at him.

Okay, this he could work with. She wasn't ending things. He would have the rest of the time she had to convince her to come back to him, he was going to fight for what he wanted, and Liz was worth everything he had. He didn't care about children, but he knew if he tried to convince her of that right now, she would fight harder to change his mind. He could see the biggest problem was her daughter, and how was he going to work around that? He knew he couldn't ask her to leave her child. Liz was a great mom, and being a mom was very important to her. Even if Paige would be off at college most of the time.

Ben needed to figure out some way to compromise, so he could be with her. Could he leave the shop? How would his family feel about that? Could Jeff take over the everyday operation? Ben knew the answer to that question. It was going to be a big undertaking just to get Jeff to take over ordering for the store. Ben knew he couldn't just leave his family to run the surf shop, but there had to be some way to make this work.

"Why don't you let me worry about what's not fair to me? I want what time you have and more." Liz started to say something, but Ben put his finger to her lips. "But I will take whatever I can get, just know I will keep trying to change your mind. I'm going into this with my eyes wide open. I know you might leave after three weeks, and I'll never see you again, and you have to know I hope that won't happen, but if it does, I'll be ok."

"Ben, I don't know what to say. I do love spending time with you. I've had more fun in the last week than I can remember. I have enjoyed your company. You are so easy to be around, and what we have shared between us, you know, in the bedroom." Liz's face was turning bright red. "I have never ever experienced anything like it, and I'm not sure I will ever again once I leave."

It reminded Ben of just how much he liked it when she got embarrassed. He put his hand on the side of her face so he could feel the heat there. "I love it when your face gets all red like this." Ben pulled her into his lap and kissed her slow and tenderly. She wrapped her arms around his neck and tangled her fingers in his hair to hold him tight to her; he wasn't going anywhere. She pressed her chest up against his. He knew he had his work cut out for him if he was going to get her to be with him forever, but he was going to try like hell. The kiss was now getting much hotter, and he ran his hands up the back of her wet T-shirt, which reminded him that they would need to shower. They were still wet from surfing, and he pulled back, "Let's go shower," and stood with her still holding on.

Liz had to get her mind working if she wanted to have the night go as planned. "We have to shower separately, I will use my shower, and you can use the one in the hall."

Ben looked confused, "What, why?"

"Because, if we shower together, we both know there'll be sex in there, and I have plans for you tonight." Ben didn't look happy about her statement. "When you're done, I want you on my bed, naked." That put a smile on his cute face, and he looked like a little boy on Christmas morning.

"Ok, is there any specific position you want me in?" He was grinning now.

"I want you on your back, and there will be a pair of pink handcuffs on the bed. I want you to cuff yourself to my headboard."

Wow, he didn't see that coming, but he liked it just the same. Now, he knew what she meant about turn around was fair play. He thought about how he had tied her to the bed a few nights ago. They walked down the hallway, and he stopped outside the bathroom. "And while I'm handcuffed, what are you going to be doing?" He brushed a hair away from her face.

Liz just smiled up at him and said, "Wouldn't you like to know? When you're done, I want you to say the word "PLEASE.""

He looked confused again. "You want me to say Please?"

"Yes, don't you know it's the magic word," she let his hand drop and started down the hall to her bathroom. She looked over her shoulder to see him watching her and smiled.

Ben watched her go, and he was getting hard just thinking about what she might have in mind for him. He went into the bathroom and turned on the water. Maybe he should take a cold shower because if he kept thinking about her, he'd be harder than nails by the time he was done. Ben stepped under the water and tried to wash as fast as he could, so the fun could begin. He still couldn't help thinking about her running her hands over his body as he soaped up. He closed his eyes and conjured up images of her hands on his chest. He could feel her chest pressed to his back as her hands roamed farther down his body. Ben was stroking himself as if she was doing it. What would it hurt if he took the edge off? He was going faster and harder, thinking of her hands moving over him, his balls tightened, and he knew. He thought of Liz's tits pressed against him, how he loved to play with her nipples, and that was it. He came as he kept stroking and milking himself.

~ ~ ~ ~ ~ ~

Liz laid out the handcuffs on her bed and then went into her bathroom and shut the door. "Ok, that looked like you were confident and knew what you were doing." She blew out a big breath as she leaned against the closed door. She had a lot to do before she would be ready for Ben, so she went straight to the shower. Liz was a woman on a mission. She showered as fast as she could and went about drying her hair. Once her hair was dry, she styled it, so it looked a little wild. Then she did her make-up, and once she was done, went to the closet where she had stashed her outfit earlier. Liz slipped on the black corset and adjusted her breasts, so they lay in the open cups, then she pulled up the sheer fabric and tied them in place. Liz knew she had a little more boob than this outfit held but didn't think Ben would mind. Then she pulled on the tiny panties, and once they were in place, she went for the boots.

Ben had finished showering and went into Liz's bedroom. He found the pink frilly handcuffs on the bed. This was going to be fun, so he put the cuffs through the headboard and hooked one around his wrist and then laid back and hooked the other one. Now all he needed was Liz. He waited a minute and tried to listen very hard to hear anything she was doing in the bathroom. He was ready for her, so he yelled please as she told him to.

She was zipping up the stiletto heels when she heard Ben say the magic word. She took a big breath, let it out, and took another. She wrapped the black silk robe around herself and tied it. Liz opened the bathroom door, and Ben's eyes were wide as he watched her move around the room.

Ben could feel his body responding to her because she did it for him. Her red hair was teased to look like she already had rolled around in bed, and she was wearing a shiny black robe that stopped just at the top of her thighs, but it was her boots that caught his attention because they went up to above her knee with stiletto heels. He watched her as she went to the door.

"Wow, you look great, but where are you going?" He wanted her to move closer to the bed, not away from it.

"Now, what did you say to me?" She put her fingertip to her lip as if she was thinking, "Oh yeah, I have to leave you for a minute. I'll be right back." She said as she walked out the door, she could hear him calling for her, but she just ignored him. Going to the kitchen and pulling out the fruit she had prepared earlier. Liz put the chocolate in the microwave to make it good and hot. Once she had everything she wanted on a tray, she took a big breath and went back to her bedroom. Ben was watching her every move as she laid the food on the nightstand. She opened the drawer where she kept her toys, and she pulled out that little thing that Ben hadn't paid any attention to the other night and a tube of lube and put it on the bed so he could see it.

Now Ben wasn't sure what she was going to do with the little toy, but there was only one reason she would need lube. He wasn't sure he wanted to experience anything up his ass. "Hey now, what are you going to do with all that? I don't think you are going to need the lube." Ben sounded very nervous, and Liz just laughed at him.

"Oh, I see, when it was me tied up, and I wasn't sure about what you were going to do to me, you asked if I trusted you. Now, I have you tied up, and you think you can control what happens to you. Well, I guess you're just going to have to trust me now, aren't you? I promise you're going to like it, but if for some reason you don't, we'll stop." Liz said as she threw his words back at him.

Ben wasn't sure about this, but he was going to let it play out because, one, he wanted to see what was under that robe, and second, a part of him wanted to know what she had in mind for him. Ben said, "What have I created? When I met you a week ago, you were very timid and shy, and now you're standing in front of me with the sexiest boots I've ever seen. I haven't seen what you have under that robe yet, but if it matches those boots, I think I might have created a sex fiend after all." Ben watched as Liz stood at the end of the bed and pulled on the tie of her robe. He could see whatever she had on was black, too. Ben wanted to pull that robe off her and run his hands all over her body. His dick was so hard, and she hadn't even touched him yet. She was running her hands down the open robe, so he could see just a bit more. "I want to see more, Liz."

"All in good time. What's the magic word?" she said with a grin. She started to move her hips as she pulled the robe off her shoulders. Liz turned so her back was to him and let the robe drop to the floor. Then she turned around and watched his eyes devour her, and that was all she needed to pull this off. It was the confidence he gave her that made her feel so sexy.

Ben was speechless when she turned around. His eyes raked over her body and the black lingerie she was wearing. Tt was more than he could handle. He could see her nipples through the sheer top, and her tits were spilling over the fabric that held them. Ben's mouth watered because he wanted her closer. The outfit laced up the front and pulled in her waist, and then there were her little panties and those fuck-me boots. Ben needed to have his hands free because he needed to touch her now.

"Liz, I need you to undo my hands. I have to touch you now!" Ben pulled at the handcuffs. "Please." She could hear the want in his voice.

"I think you have forgotten, but this is all about me pleasing you, and I will let you touch me after I finish with you." Liz moved to the side of the bed, leaned in, and kissed him. It was time to put the first pleasure triggers to the test. The kiss was very passionate and was getting very hot fast. She kissed that slope between the outside of his lower lip and chin, and he moaned. Liz knew how extremely turned-on he was. She wasn't sure if it had anything to do with what she was doing, but she kept it up anyway. She then moved back to his lips as she sucked his bottom lip into her mouth, and she ran her tongue on the lower lip.

Liz pressed her chest to his, and Ben went crazy. He arched his back to try to get closer to her, and she sucked a bit harder on his lip and then bit down softly on it. Now she laid her entire body on top of his as she moved down his body. She was going through the triggers one after the other, and he did seem to be enjoying what she was doing. Liz kissed the front of his neck just below his Adam's apple, ran her tongue up and down the hollow of his throat, and then made circular motions over his thyroid just below his Adam's apple.

"Oh my God, Liz, I'm not sure how much more I can take." He said it as if he was in pain. She felt his hardness as she pressed her body even harder against him and was just as turned on as he was.

Liz whispered into his ear, "I'm not even close to being done with you, but if you need me to take the edge off, I will. I don't want you to surfer, at least not too much." She moved further down until her breasts pressed against his penis. Liz pressed her breast together and slid up and down his penis, so it was sandwiched in between them. He was watching her every move, so she slowly untied the bow at her neck, and this freed her breasts. Each time the head of Ben's penis came out from between them, she licked it. That was driving him wild, so the next time she sucked him as deep as she could. Then she did it over and over again. Her saliva was running down him, and it lubricated the motion of him moving between her breasts. Ben threw his head back as far as he could and let out a sound Liz had never heard, and he came unyielding as his body bucked and shook. Liz kept moving as he came, so now his come was all over her chest. Ben was breathing so hard that Liz thought he might hyperventilate and pass out. His eyes closed as he tried to catch his breath.

"Ben, are you okay?" She asked because she didn't want him to pass out on her.

"I…" He took a big breath and tried again to speak. "That was… I want to touch you now, Liz. I need…"

She slid up his body so she could kiss him again. He tried to break the kiss, so Liz pulled back just a bit so he could say what he wanted.

"I can't just lay here and not want to touch you and please you." His eyes were so intent on her.

Liz knew he would need a break before she went any farther, so she climbed even further up his body. Now she was sitting on his chest, looking down at him. "What do you have in mind?"

He smiled up at her. "I want you to slide up here and sit on my face as you hold yourself open for me to eat you up." He knew he was being so crude talking to her that way, but she had got him so worked up. He didn't care now, as she did as he asked. He noticed she was bald and smooth.

God, this woman is everything I've ever wanted. It's not just the sex because Liz is the most stimulating woman I have ever met. Her smart wit and the way she loved so deeply. I want her to love me that way. I don't care what it's going to take. She will be mine.

He wanted to show her just how much he loved her; it was all he could do because telling her would for sure make her run. But tomorrow, he was going to put his plan in motion to win her over. "Liz, you're so smooth, that's sexy as hell."

Liz scooted up so her knees were on both sides of Ben's head. She sat up so he could reach her, and she reached down with one hand and parted her lips for him, and Ben moaned. Liz closed her eyes and held onto the headboard with her other hand as she let Ben have his way with her. He made her feel so good. How was she going to be able to leave him?

Liz knew she should pull back or at least try to keep her heart out of this affair. Is that what it was? Or could it be more? No, she needed to keep herself in a place where she didn't get emotionally involved. She only had the time she had left to appreciate Ben. Her daughter still needed her, and that meant she needed to be in New Jersey, where she could be close. As Ben worked his magic, all intelligent thoughts left her. She was so very close, he did this thing with his tongue, and that was it. Liz sat back onto his chest as she gasped for air, and when she reopened her eyes and looked down at Ben, he was staring up at her.

"I just love watching you do that from the very first time I made you come, and I don't think that's ever going to change." His eyes flicked with something she couldn't read.

"Well, I have to say, I think I love it too." Liz moved to get off Ben, and he protested.

"Hey, where are you goin'?"

"I'm going to get something to clean up with, and then I'm going to feed you."

"I think you already fed me just fine. But if you want me to do it again, I will," Ben said with a huge grin.

Liz's face and neck turned pink from Ben's words. It was one thing for him to do it, but when he talked dirty like that, it still flustered her. She turned in hopes he wouldn't see the state he put her in, but of course, no such luck because he didn't miss a thing.

His voice was filled with emotion as he said, "Liz, look at me."

"I'll be right back," she tried avoiding his request.

"Come here before you get what you need. Please." At his plea, she turned around so he could see her face and walked back to the side of the bed.

"Kiss me." Liz leaned into him, kissed him, and when the kiss ended, he asked, "Why is your face all red? Did I embarrass you?"

"You know what you do when you talk that way." She ran her hand down the side of his face and rested it on his chest.

"Do you want me to stop making you blush? If you don't like it, I'll stop."

Liz smiled and said, "Don't stop, you know it embarrasses me, but I like it when you talk dirty. It's just— I'm not used to it, and when you catch me off guard, I can't help getting flustered."

"Liz, I don't want you to ever feel like you have to be on your guard with me." Now that he knew she liked it, he said, "For some reason, I don't want you to get used to my crude remarks because I love it when your face does that," he smiled up at her.

Liz started to pull away again and said, "I'll be right back," and walked into the bathroom.

Ben could hear her moving around in the bathroom, the water came on, and she was running something under it. He couldn't help feeling responsible for how much she had changed. Liz had come out of her shell, and he knew she had a passionate side to her. Also, the more self-assured she got, the more he could see her coming alive. She must have been starving for love and affection. How did she go so long without anyone, and why hasn't any guy come along and just gobbled her up? Did she push all the guys that might have shown any interest away? So, why was she letting him get so close to her? He wasn't sure why, but he was definitely going to take advantage of the fact that she wanted to spend time with him. He looked up as she walked back into the room a minute later with a washcloth in hand. She was so hot and sexy. He couldn't wait to start his plans to woo her and win her over. He watched as she came closer, and he could feel his dick getting hard again with her tits freed and her nipples hard and standing at attention. He wanted to touch her and love her.

"So, are you going to un-cuff me? I want my turn to touch you."

"Not just yet, I still have plans for you." She ran the washcloth over his chest and down his abs. "I love your chest, and how when I touch you, your ab muscles get all tight. You must work out a lot to keep a hot body like this." She continued moving down his body as she wiped his groin.

Ben closed his eyes, and he pushed his hips up against her hand. She could tell he wanted her to touch him, so she took the washcloth and moved it over his penis. Liz wrapped the cloth around him and slid it up and down as she squeezed him the way she knew now he liked. She could see him growing in her hand and then moved down and wiped his balls. As she embraced them one at a time, she massaged them. She grasped one and gave it a light squeeze and then the other. Liz went back and forth until Ben opened his eyes and looked down at her.

Ben's voice was so muted when he asked, "Liz, are you trying to drive me crazy?"

Liz almost didn't hear him, but she smiled because she knew it was pushing him to the edge. "I'm going to do something to you now that I think you're going to like, but if for some reason you don't, just say the word, and I'll stop." Liz moved on the bed as she took the little object that she had pulled out earlier and the lube off the bed. Ben's eyes went wildly big as he watched to see what she was going to do with it. Liz put the little vibrator on her finger and tapped the button to turn it on. It made a very low humming noise, and Ben gasped as she put some lube on the tip of it.

OH shit, what the hell was he in for now. If she was going to do what I think she's going to do, I'll have to stop this? Ben watched with great intent as she moved up his body. Relief swept over his face, okay, so he could wait to see what she had in mind. Ben let out the breath he was holding when she ran her finger over his nipple. The sensation sent waves of want over his whole body. He closed his eyes as he was absorbing her touch, and her finger went back and forth over his right nipple. Ben hadn't ever really enjoyed his nipples played with before, but this was something altogether different, and it was Liz doing it. He could feel the tingling all the way down to his dick. He was already hard and wasn't sure he could last. She moved over to his other nipple, she was flicking it back and forth, and he could feel it was hard, too.

"Liking it so far? I don't hear you yelling to stop or anything," Liz said with a joking tone.

"I'm not sure I can take much more," Ben said with a strain in his voice. The vibrator was small, but it was mighty.

Liz pressed her lips to his as their tongues intertwined. She pressed her chest to his. He responded by trying to press his body up to hers. Liz ran her finger down the side of his abs as she felt him suck in. She didn't break the kiss but moved even further down and reached in between them. Ben gasped when she touched the head of his penis. Liz lifted her lower body up so she could have better access to him. She took hold of him in her hand and held tight as she moved up. She knew she needed more lubrication, so she ran her finger over the tip of him again. She wiped the beads of pre-come off and broke the kiss.

"How do you like it so far?" she asked again.

"I…Liz," was all he could manage to say. She scooted down his body again, and Ben took a big breath and said, "I won't last if you do what I think you're going to do, and I want to come inside you."

"I promise you will get to do that, but I'm going to do one more thing before we get to the main event." Ben let out a sound from the back of his throat. Then she moved even further down his body and put more lube on her finger.

Now this part made Ben nervous because if she went anywhere near his ass, he'd stop her fun, but she was just pressing her big tits against him, and he liked that. Liz moved so she could put his dick in her mouth, and he was watching and waiting. As she took him into her mouth, she ran her hand with the vibrator over his balls, the sensation was nothing like he'd ever felt before. She was now pressing the vibrator just between his balls and his ass, and she sucked him in deep. He let out a roar and tried to hold onto his restraint, but he was losing the battle. He could feel his back tense and his balls pulled up so tight.

"I'm going to come! Liz, need to come!" He yelled and watched as she straddled him and sank herself down on him. He closed his eyes and tried to revel in the feeling of being inside of her. Liz laid her body on his and didn't even realize that she had reached up and unlocked the handcuffs until she pulled his hands down over her. He gripped her ass and pounded up into her.

Ben was not gentle, he was crazy with want and need. He found her mouth and kissed her hard. Ben wanted to fuck her hard, and he flipped her so fast. One minute she was on top, the next, she was under him. He pulled her legs up over his shoulders with those fuck me boots so he could get deeper. He looked down at her, and she had her head back as far as it would go against the pillows and a pained look on her face. Ben immediately slowed, *oh God, was he hurting her*? So wrapped up in how crazy she made him feel that he wasn't even thinking about her.

"Liz, you ok?" Ben asked.

"Don't stop," was all she said.

Ben reached in between her spread legs and moved his finger over her clit, because he wanted her as crazy as he was. She let out a moan, and he knew it wasn't going to take much. He wanted them both to come together and fucked her hard again as he circled her clit. She let out a scream as he felt her muscles contract around him, and he let himself go. Ben moved in and out of her until he had nothing left. He released her legs and just laid on top of her, he needed to move off her, but his body wouldn't comply, so he rolled her on top of him without breaking their bond as they both tried to catch their breath. They lay there quietly for the longest time, and all that he heard was the hum of the vibrator that was still on Liz's finger. When she regained her thoughts, she turned it off, and she rolled from him.

After a long time, Ben was the one to break the silence. "Liz, I have to know, did I hurt you? Because I got carried away, I couldn't seem to control myself." He waited for her answer as he held his breath because he would never forgive himself if he hurt her.

"Ben, I would have told you to stop if you were, but I got so wrapped up in it, too, that I'm not sure I would have stopped you. That was unlike anything I have ever felt before." Liz could hear Ben let out the breath he had been holding. She smiled at him and asked her own question. "So, on a scale of one to ten, how was it for you?" Ben didn't answer right away, and that made her feel like maybe he hadn't enjoyed it as much as she thought.

After a minute or two, he said, "Liz, I think what I'm about to say might make you pull away, but if you really want to know how you make me feel. Then I'll tell you." He waited to see what she'd do, knowing she didn't want a serious relationship, but he was in too deep.

"I—" she started but didn't finish what she was going to say.

"I know we just talked about this, and we've only known each other a short time, but I think we're very compatible and not just sexually. I want time to show you what we could have together. I also know you have responsibilities that you take very seriously, as you should. I would never ask you to make a choice between your daughter and me because I know I'd lose, as I should. But I want you, Liz. I'm falling in love with you."

Liz started to climb off him when he pulled her in close. "Please, I'm begging you to just give us a try. I want to take you out for dinner tomorrow night. I want to show you how I feel about you." He could see she was fighting with herself to pull away or stay, so he went on. "In the last couple of years, I have been just going through the motions in my life. I worked all the time because I didn't have a life outside of the shop and surfing and my family. I have never connected with anyone before, not the way I feel when I'm with you."

Now Liz had to say something before this went too far. "Ben, we can't get serious. I told you that already. I can't give you what you really want. I'm damaged goods, as much as I love spending time with you, I have to go home. I live in New Jersey. My life is there. My work is there, well, my agent is there, and I just don't see how we could ever be more. I can't let my heart get involved because I will never survive. Don't you see, I have to go home, Ben?" Her voice trailed off on that last part. She put her hands over her face to hide the tears that started to fill her eyes. Ben pulled her hands away from her face as he kissed the tears away.

"I'm sorry, I didn't mean to make you cry. I just want you to know how you make me feel. What you did for me tonight, I loved every minute of it. I am sorry. I'll try harder to keep my thoughts and feelings to myself."

What Ben just said made the tears fall faster and harder. Liz could feel how she wanted to please him, show him she was falling for him too, but she didn't dare. She would never be able to leave. She would definitely need to back off, way off.

Ben could feel her pulling away from him. He hated that he was making her upset, but he couldn't help how he felt about her. He knew it was going to be hard to convince her to stay with him but pushing her might not be the best way. He just needed to go about it differently, less talk and more showing her how he felt. He wanted to lighten the mood because it had gotten so tense. He pulled her back to him and kissed her softly and tenderly. She came willingly, and that had to be a good sign.

Tomorrow couldn't come fast enough for him. He held her until he could hear her breathing had slowed. He laid there for a long time thinking how he might have messed up big time, but in his mind, he couldn't see himself with anyone but her. He wasn't sure what it was about her that made him want to be with her so badly. She was the most genuine person he had ever met, and when he closed his eyes, he could see their lives together. Just how did he convince her that they belonged together, and how were they going to work out that she had her daughter that still needed her mother? There had to be a way, it had to work somehow because he wasn't letting her go without a fight. That was the last thought Ben had as he drifted off to sleep.

It was hours later when Ben woke as he rolled over to find the bed empty. He looked at the clock, it was four AM, and his stomach was growling. That's when he realized they hadn't eaten anything earlier. Ben rolled out of bed and went in search of Liz, and he found her in the kitchen at the breakfast bar tapping away on her computer. She didn't hear him come into the room, so he watched her write. He could see the wheels turning as she typed faster than anyone he'd ever seen. Ben moved into the room. He didn't want to scare her, so he tried to move into her sight. She must have caught his movement because she looked up and gasped.

"Sorry, I didn't want to scare you by saying anything, so I thought if you saw me, it would be less likely to freak you out. I rolled over, you weren't there, and then I realized I was hungry. So, I thought I would come and find you and get something to eat." He smiled at her because he could see she was still deep in thought.

"I know, I'm sorry I didn't feed you, I had all that fruit, and we didn't eat any of it."

He didn't want her to feel bad, so he came up beside her and kissed her temple. "I think we got a little too distracted, and I wouldn't have traded the food for what we did."

"But you're hungry now. You want me to make you some eggs or something?" She started to get up, and he stopped her.

"Nah, I can make us something if you're hungry, that is."

"I guess I could have something." She said as she watched him move about the kitchen, getting his ingredients from the refrigerator. She couldn't help herself as she checked out his perfect ass.

Ben looked over his shoulder to ask Liz what she wanted in her omelet and had to smile because he knew right away, she was checking him out because, by the way she looked away, she didn't want to get caught. "Is there anything you want special in your omelet?" He asked as he pulled out the eggs and some of the other ingredients that he was going to need.

"No, just surprise me," she said as she watched him start cooking in just his boxers and no shirt.

Ben got out the pan and a knife to cut up the meat, peppers, and onions, mixing it all together with cheese. He moved around her kitchen as if he lived there. Ben didn't seem to notice that she was watching him. He cracked the eggs like a pro and whipped them until they were light and fluffy, then added buttered the pan and went to cooking the omelets. She couldn't see what he was doing anymore because his broad body blocked the stove. She was still admiring his backside as the smell pulled her out of her admiration for his body. Her stomach growled loudly, and Ben turned.

"I guess you are hungry, too." Ben grabbed a plate, slid the omelet onto it, handed it to her, and gave her a fork. He went to whipping up his, and then he sat next to her. He noticed she seemed to be enjoying it, and that made him happy to be able to take care of her.

"This is really good. You weren't kidding when you said you make a mean omelet." Liz was just finishing when she looked over at him. He had this big grin on his face. "What?"

"I'm so glad you liked it. After all the stuff you've cooked for me, I'm happy I could make you something."

"You made me dinner at your place."

"That was cheating because it was my mother's sauce. All I had to do was cook the noodles, how hard was that? Not that making an omelet is hard either."

"But what you don't seem to understand is that, I don't have anybody cooking for me. So, you see, Ben, I really appreciate it whenever anybody makes a meal for me, whether it's just a simple meal or some big deal."

Ben couldn't stop the thought of how he wanted to take care of her for the rest of his life. He wanted to take care of her every need. Ben took her empty plate and his own and started to clean up.

"Ben, I'll do that," she said.

"No way, you keep writing, I can clean up my own mess." He put everything away and went to wash out the pan he used and then the plates. He wiped down the counters, and when he was done, he came around the bar and kissed her on the side of her face. "Are you going to stay out here and write some more?"

"I was getting a lot done, so yeah, I might work for a little longer now that my stomach is full."

Ben grinned because he liked that she let him take care of her but didn't want to pull her away from her work. "Okay, I need to get more sleep before I have to work." Even though he wanted her to come back to bed with him, he kissed her and went back to bed alone.

Liz just sat there for the longest time, thinking how she wanted to be with him, but she knew it wouldn't work because what he wanted from her was a real relationship. She did want someone to love and someone to love her. She wanted what she couldn't have and knew she'd never find anybody like Ben because no one could take his place. All she could come up with was if she was going to leave with her heart intact, she had to back up. She knew he felt so much more for her, but she couldn't allow him to get any more involved with her. She didn't want to hurt him when she left, so she had to protect him for his own good.

~ 15 ~

The next morning when Ben's alarm went off at 7 a.m., he rolled over to turn it off. He automatically reached for Liz, and she was sound asleep next to him. He didn't want to wake her because he knew she had worked until early this morning. So, he climbed out of the bed as carefully as he could. He went into the bathroom, shut the door, and put his hands on the counter, looking at his reflection in the mirror. "I hope like hell I didn't fuck up," he said to himself. Even though Liz didn't say any more about how he felt about her, he knew he'd overwhelmed her.

He couldn't seem to help himself because she brought out those feelings, the ones he knew scared her. The feelings he knew that would make her pull away. He had to bide his time, work slower. He didn't know how the hell he was supposed to do that when his heart wanted her. Ben splashed some water on his face, hoping it would help clear his mind, but it didn't. Ben used the bathroom, went to collect his clothes, and had to stop by his apartment before going to work.

He tried to be as quiet as possible as he gathered up his clothes. He went into the kitchen, started some coffee, and pulled on the clothes he had brought with him. He knew to bring a bag of clothes after the last time they went surfing, and he didn't have anything to change into and had to wear Liz's shirt home. Liz had left her computer on the counter where she was working last night and her notepad, so Ben pulled out a page to leave a note for her.

Dear Liz,

       I had to go to work, and I didn't want to wake you. I know you worked until the early hours. I want to take you for a special dinner tonight. I will call you with the details, and I want you to know, last night meant so much to me. I know it took plenty of courage for you to put on that outfit and handcuff me to your bed. I want you to know, I loved every minute of it.

Love, Ben

Ben went over in his mind the note he had left her. Maybe he shouldn't have signed it with love. He didn't want to make matters any worse, but he couldn't change it now because he had signed it and left. Ben went to his apartment, showered, and was downstairs before anyone else showed up. It was nice and quiet. Usually, he liked it this way, but not today. He knew it was going to be another hard day, and it hadn't started. He would be thinking about her and what happened last night. Dinner tonight had to be different, he needed to convince her.

Ben went into his office and sat behind his desk, a place that was like a second home to him. He had spent almost as much time here as he did in his apartment. But today, he didn't find comfort, instead, he felt like his skin was too tight. "Okay, I had planned to take her to dinner and go back to her place and make good use of that hot tub. That's not going to work. I need to woo her, make her feel very special." Ben heard a knock on the doorframe, and he looked up to see Owen standing there.

"Talking to yourself again. I thought you didn't do that anymore now that you have Liz to talk to." He walked in and sat down in the chair. "You don't look so good. You okay?" Owen asked.

"I just might have fucked up big time, that's all." Ben was rubbing the back of his neck where he could feel the tension headache coming on.

"You fuck up, not likely. You're the one who always does things on the straight and narrow. What are we talking about anyway?" Ben made a sound in the back of his throat as if he couldn't believe it either, and he shook his head.

"You know, Liz had a special night planned for me, right?"

"Hey, I don't want to know any of that stuff," Owen said as he waved his hands in the air.

"I wasn't going to go into any details, and you couldn't be so lucky, anyway. It was more than I ever could imagine, and then I had to go and run my mouth. I think I might have scared her off. I couldn't help myself because she just brings out these crazy feelings in me," he rested his face in his hands and let out a strained breath.

"If you don't mind me asking, what did you say that has you so upset?"

"I couldn't hold back any longer, I told her I was falling in love with her, and I knew the minute it was out, I had fucked up. She had already told me she didn't want anything serious, and I know she has to go home and take care of getting her daughter settled in school, but I had hoped I could convince her to come back. I just know she's going to pull away from me, and it's my own damn fault." Ben wanted to smack himself because he knew better, and yet he did it anyway.

Owen was very quiet for a few minutes, and then he said, "Ben, you shouldn't have to hide how you feel, and she has a right to feel the way she does, but so do you."

"Okay, so what now? I wanted to take it slow and win her over, and then she sends me into overdrive, and then all my plans of going slow gets thrown right out the window." Ben tried to take a deep breath, but it wasn't helping.

"So, you know she needs time, so give it to her." That sounded so easy, but it was going to be the hardest thing to follow through on because he was afraid if he gave her time to think, she would not want to continue their relationship.

"I wanted to take her to dinner tonight, somewhere special," Ben's mind was racing.

"You need to let her control what goes on from here, so ask her to dinner, but be prepared for her to say no, and you definitely need to go back to going slow and remember what it is you want." Owen sounded so mature and grown up, now if he could just follow his advice.

"Owen, how did you get to be so smart?" Ben asked, shaking his head.

Owen just smiled big when he said, "That's easy, I had the best teacher, and you'll see, it'll all work out. Just be patient, and she will be yours." Owen got up and added, "Oh yeah, by the way, I have orientation on Tuesday afternoon, that's what I came in to tell you."

"Do you need me to go with you?" Ben asked and added, "I know this has been confusing for you, so if you need me, I'm there." Ben put his troubles aside to reassure Owen.

"If you don't mind, I don't think it's going to take long, they're having lunch and going over everything, and then I can walk the campus and find my classes."

"Just let me know what time, so I can make sure Jeff will be here to cover the floor."

"It's at eleven-thirty," Owen started for the door.

"Hey," Owen turned around.

"I want to thank you for listening to me. I'm going to try my best to follow your advice." Owen just smiled again and walked out, shutting the door on his way out.

~ ~ ~ ~ ~ ~

Liz woke up, and right away, she knew she was alone. Ben was gone. How fast the loneliness came back to her. This is how she woke up every morning ever since Michael's death. She hadn't really realized just how much she hated it, until now. She had no choice before because that's just the way it was, but here Ben was giving her a choice now, and it scared the hell out of her. What he wanted was a real partnership. What would it be like to have someone to depend on, or someone to support her emotionally? She would have him to share her life with, and Liz wanted it more than she wanted her next breath. But she knew it wasn't going to happen, and thinking this way was dangerous. Liz pulled herself out of bed and went to take a shower and get her day started.

When Liz went into the kitchen and found Ben had made coffee. It wasn't anything big, but no one made her coffee and felt herself tearing up. What the hell was wrong with her? It was just coffee. She wondered why she was crying, as big tears streamed down her cheeks. She went to get a tissue and found Ben's note on the counter and read it twice, how he didn't want to wake her. If he only knew, she was up half the night thinking about him. Even though she did get some writing done, it was only because her book and her characters were sounding a lot like her real life right now.

She never wrote about her own life before. It might have been because she didn't really have a life. No one wanted to hear about how great of a mother she was because, after that, there wasn't much more to her life. She loved being Paige's mother, and now Liz was crying harder because Paige had grown up and was going to have her own life and wouldn't need her anymore. Why was she so emotional? Did it have to do with Ben wanting more from her? Maybe she needed to take a walk to clear her head. She had the best view right outside her door, so she grabbed a sweater and her phone and went out the door.

Liz knew she needed to talk to someone, and Kat and Paige were all she had. But somehow, she didn't want to share her feelings with Kat, and she would never involve Paige in this mess. But if she didn't talk to someone soon, she might just explode. Her head was spinning, one minute, she wanted to stay and see where this would lead her, and in the next, she felt like she needed to go home as soon as possible.

Liz walked down the beach, and she tried to settle herself by taking deep breaths and letting them out again. She sat down because black dots blurred her vision, and the dizziness threatened her standing. She put her head down between her legs and tried to relax and get her breathing under control. What was going on with her? She had never been so indecisive in her life. There was only one thing she could do, and it was to call Kat. Liz dialed her number and waited, her stomach was in turmoil, and she felt like she could throw up.

Kat answered on the third ring, "Hello there, stranger. You were supposed to call me every day." Kat sounded half-annoyed, and the other half was relieved.

"Sorry, I know, but I got busy, and you know," Liz's voice broke from crying.

"What's wrong?" Kat knew her well, so once she made the call, there was no way to get out of telling her everything.

"I need to talk to you. Do you have time because this is going to take a while?" Liz ran her hand through her hair and tried to get her thoughts together.

"For you, I have all the time in the world, but before we get into why you called me. Let me have my secretary hold all my calls and make sure I'm not disturbed." Kat put her on hold, and Liz wanted to just hang up and pretend she never called, but she knew Kat would be here faster than she could blink her eyes.

"Okay, now tell me everything. What's going on?"

Liz didn't know where to begin, but when she started to cry yet again, that made Kat very concerned.

"I'll kill him. Damn it, did he hurt you, Liz? You tell me, now?"

"No," she started to laugh at the way Kat had jumped to the wrong conclusions, "He hasn't hurt me in any way. He told me he's falling in love with me. What the hell am I supposed to do with that? I can't do this. I can't even think straight. I have been crying all morning, and I have no idea why. I want to be with him, but…" She closed her eyes because once she said it out loud, it made it too real.

Kat cut her off, "But what? What's wrong with him?"

Liz was even more confused, "Wrong with him, what do you mean? There's nothing wrong with him, he's wonderful, and he made me coffee this morning before he left for work, and he left me a note because he didn't want to wake me. It was so sweet." Liz could feel the tears again running down her face, and she knew she needed to pull herself together because she was losing it fast.

"So, if he's wonderful, what's the problem?"

"You already know I can't fall for him because I live all the way across the country, just in case you've forgotten." Liz couldn't believe Kat didn't recognize the magnitude of her problem.

"Liz, you don't have to stay all the way across the country if you don't want to." This statement shocked Liz.

"I can't leave Paige," Liz said as if that was the craziest thing Kat had ever said to her.

"Liz, breathe. I didn't say or even imply that you would leave Paige. But she will be at school, and you will be doing what, waiting around just in case she needs you?" Kat didn't say anything for a minute because she knew what she said had hurt Liz's feelings. "I didn't mean it the way it came out."

"Yes, you did, I know what you're saying, but I don't know how to stop being Paige's mother. That's how I have defined myself for so long, and I don't know anything different."

"I never said you would stop being her mother because we both know that would never happen, but you need to find a life of your own, and I'm sure Paige wants you to live your own life. She would want you happy."

"I need time to think, but Ben wants to take me for a special dinner tonight, and I don't think I can handle him pressuring me. I wanted to spend as much time with him knowing I was leaving, but I thought I would get my fill of him, be free to experience new things, and then go home. Now, he wants more, and I don't think I can give him anymore, but I don't really want to hurt him either."

"Liz, you have always been one to think things through, so take what you need for yourself. Tell Ben you can't see him tonight. Make up an excuse. Tell him you're tired or you need to work and take one night to get your head straight."

Liz had to do it, and she knew Ben wasn't going to like it, but she had to know where to go from here. "Kat, I have to go. I'm sitting out on the beach in wet sand." She hadn't realized until now that her butt was wet, *great now, I'll have to walk back to my house with a huge wet spot on my ass*. This day just kept getting better and better. She said goodbye and promised to call tomorrow.

Liz pulled her sweater as far over her butt as she could and walked home. She climbed her steps and went inside to try to get her head straight, as Kat had put it. Liz decided to take a bath, it might make her relax a bit and let her think, plus she was cold from having her ass wet. She went into the bathroom and started the water. "Boy, I'm going to miss this tub when I have to go home," she said to no one. Liz went and made her bed, she hadn't made it earlier, as she always did, and got out new clothes to wear after her bath. She was trying to keep herself busy waiting for the water to fill the tub.

~ ~ ~ ~ ~ ~

Ben worked on the books and checked his e-mail, sending out responses to the vendors he thought had products they could sell. This would be part of Jeff's job soon, but Ben knew it would take a while for him to learn the ropes, but as long as Jeff was trying, he wouldn't push. Ben checked the clock because he wanted to call Liz, but he didn't want to call too early. When he heard a knock on his door again, he looked up to see Jeff walk through the door.

"This came for you. I saw it was from the jewelry store, so I thought you would want it right away," he handed it to Ben.

"Yeah thanks, I got Liz another charm for the bracelet," he looked at the small envelope.

"So, she liked it?" Jeff sat down.

"She was wearing it and said she loved it, thanks to you." Ben opened the package and pulled out a little box.

"What did I do? I just told you where you could get something like what you were looking for." Jeff watched as Ben opened the small box leaning in to see what was inside. Jeff asked, "What is it?"

"It's a lock," Ben didn't add anything else but ran his finger over the small charm.

"So, you gave her a key first, right, and now a lock. Is it supposed to mean something? I don't get it. Why a lock?"

"I know this is going to sound corny, but I gave her the key, because from the first time I saw her, I knew there was something there. The key to my heart and all that, but she's the key to my life. The lock is for how my heart feels because it's locked onto her, and once a lock is locked, you can't open it without the key."

"And she's the key. Okay, I think I get it," Jeff said, still looking a bit confused.

"Yes, I think the next one is going to be a flower."

"So, how many are you planning to give her? I never gave a bracelet that much thought before, but I guess you could kinda tell a story with it by what charms you give her."

Ben hadn't either, but he liked the sound of the bracelet telling their story. Liz was the writer, but Ben was going to try writing his and Liz's story to have a happily ever after. "I'm not sure at the moment, but I'm going to try to lead Liz on my journey to happily ever after." That tiny thought made him smile for the first time.

Jeff just smiled because, as corny as it sounded, he knew Ben deserved to be happy. He could see the changes in his brother, like how work was taking a back seat to the time he wanted to spend with Liz. In a way, he felt a little envious of his brother to know he wanted someone more than anything, knowing that someone was the one for him.

"I plan to give this one to her tonight at dinner," Ben said as he put the box in his pocket.

"Do you have time to show me more about ordering? It's slow on the floor right now."

"Yeah, I can do that. Oh, by the way, Owen has orientation on Tuesday at eleven-thirty. Can you handle the shop by yourself? Owen said they're having lunch, and then he's going to walk around and find his classes. We might be gone about two hours."

"No problem, besides Mom will be here, too. You know what you're doing for Owen is really a great thing."

"Owen is family, he has grown up here, and I want him to have the opportunity we didn't have. He is a great kid, and I want to see him succeed in life."

"You know Ben, ever since Dad died, you really have been taking care of this family. I'm not sure if I've ever thanked you for that, you know, like when we were kids, and you would get me out of trouble."

"Well, trouble did seem to find you, didn't it?"

"Still does sometimes," they both laughed at how true that statement was.

Ben pulled up his e-mails to show Jeff how most of the vendors sent information about new products. He told him that they would go over them together and figure out what they could sell or pass on. For the next hour, Ben showed Jeff more about keeping the store running.

Liz's water was ready, and she climbed in and sank deep into the tub. The hot water felt so good, and she just laid back and closed her eyes. Ben's image cuffed to her bed came to mind, and it made her smile because he was so hot laying there waiting for her and looking at her as if she was a sex Goddess. As Liz relived every little detail of last night, and how Ben had made her feel free to be so daring. She knew in her old life she would never had the courage to try anything like that. Michael would have thought her crazy. Besides, she just wasn't comfortable with her own sexuality. Ben had shown her there's no shame in what gives someone pleasure. It wasn't plain sex in the missionary position, like how Michael liked it. Maybe he was afraid to ask for something different, but last night felt so good to have Ben at her mercy and to know that it was all her that got him so worked up that he lost control and went a little crazy.

Liz pulled out of her thoughts when she heard her phone ringing. With everything going through her head, she forgot to bring her phone into the bathroom. She would have to let it go to voicemail, and whomever it was, she'd call them back. Ben did say in his note that he would call, but it could also be Paige.

Liz realized she hadn't talked to her daughter in a few days. She wondered to herself how she had managed that. Paige had always been the biggest part of her life. When she left for this trip without her daughter, she thought the loneliness would overwhelm her, but this time away from Paige had proven to be a learning experience. What would happen when she did go home? Would she fall back into that old life? Or would she have the courage to keep trying new things?

Liz realized that the water had gone cold and let it out. She climbed out and wrapped up in a big plush towel and went to see who had called. If it was Paige, she would need to call her back right away, but if it was Ben calling, what should she do? What was she going to say to him? She hadn't figured out anything while sitting in the tub, and she knew she needed more time before she talked to him. Did she give

Ben an excuse or tell him the truth? Giving him some made-up excuse to her that was lying, so she had to tell him the truth. Liz picked up her phone to see whom she would be calling back, Ben or Paige. When Liz looked at her phone, she didn't recognize the number, but she did have a voicemail. It could be a wrong number, yet as she listened to the message, she wasn't prepared for the voice that came on.

"Hi Liz, this is Linda, Benjamin's mother. I wanted to talk to you. If you could call me back, I would really appreciate it. Thanks, hope to hear from you soon, bye."

Liz dropped her phone so fast as if Ben's mother had just burned her. "Oh...shit, what the hell could she want? As if I don't have enough to worry about right now, do I call her back? Did Ben tell his mother about what happened last night, and now she's going to try to talk me into...what?" Liz was hyperventilating and getting lightheaded. She sat on the floor and put her head between her legs. *Breathe...just breathe...breathe.* As she gained her composure, she thought Ben would never tell his mother what happened, so what did she want? It might not have anything to do with what was going on between her and Ben. There was only one way to find out, so she called Linda back. Liz dialed Linda's number and tried her best to relax.

"Hello, this is Linda."

"Hi Linda, this is Liz."

"Oh Liz, I'm so glad you called me back. I have a big favor to ask of you, and if you can't do it, I'll understand." A small amount of relief came over her.

"What can I do for you, Linda?" Liz held her breath waiting.

"I was wondering if you could come and talk to my book club. I told them how you were here in town doing research for your next book, and I might have bragged a bit about how you came into the shop, and now they all want to meet you." Liz thought, now a book club she could do.

"Oh…I can do that. When would you like me to talk to them?" She always tried to remember that without people reading her books, she would not be an author.

"We meet on Monday nights at seven. Will that work for you?"

"Sure, that will be fine. I wish I knew because I could have given your book club signed copies of one of my books. Well, I could call Kat and get her to send some if you'd like?"

"Oh Liz, that would be wonderful, that's so nice of you to do," Linda sounded pleased, and in a way, it pleased her, too.

"Do you have any preference as to what book you'd like to have and how many women are in your club?" Liz thought she was going to have to call Kat back and have her overnight the books.

"Any book you want to give us, I'm sure they'll love whatever you choose. There are nine of us, and I really do appreciate you doing this for me. I know you have been very busy."

Liz could feel herself stiffen. Was Linda about to mention Ben? God, she hoped not. "I have gotten some writing done. The new book is moving along," Liz wanted to steer the conversation to her work and away from how she was getting busy with her son.

"Has Benjamin been helping you with your research? He knows everything there is to know about surfing. Benjamin has been surfing for as long as he could stand, and his dad had him on a board just as soon as I'd let him." Linda let out a little laugh. "Benjamin taught Jeffery and Danielle to surf, too." Linda sounded like a proud mother. "Oh, and Owen, too. Has he gotten you out there yet?"

Oh, she was good, Liz thought to herself. If Liz didn't know better, Linda was trying to get information about what was going on between them. "Actually, he has. I surfed with him, Jeff, and Owen the other night. They say that I'm pretty good, even though I have no idea what I'm doing, but I do get to stand for a few seconds before wiping out." Liz decided she would have to be very general in the information she gave to Linda.

"I knew he would get you out there. He just loves teaching people to surf, he likes helping the underprivileged kids around here, and he says it's for the business, but I know he does it because he likes giving them something to keep them out of trouble, as a matter of fact, that's how Owen started."

"I got to watch Ben teach his clinic. I enjoyed watching it. It's nice that Ben takes the time to give back to his community." Liz found it easy to compliment how Ben helped the kids.

"Yes, Benjamin does give a lot of himself, but sometimes he gives too much and can be taken advantage of." Liz didn't like where this was heading then Linda went on. "Like at the store, Benjamin has been running it for so long and doing more than his share, while Jeffery, I love my kids all the same, but Jeffery and his sister have never had to pull their weight. I tried to get Benjamin to make them be more responsible, but he just took it all on, until recently anyway."

Oh man, Linda is letting me know she knows something was up. Would she come right out and ask what was going on? I couldn't give her an answer because I have no clue either. I need to get off this phone before I have to answer questions I don't really want to.

"Oh Linda, my phone is beeping. I have to go, but I will be there for your book club."

"Okay, see you on Monday, bye."

"I can't believe I just lied to Ben's mother, but I do need to call Paige." Liz ran her hand through her half-dried hair. She called her daughter and got her voicemail. Liz left a message for Paige to call when she had time and went back into the bathroom to put her hair in a ponytail. Then she grabbed her computer and went out on the deck to get some writing done.

~ ~ ~ ~ ~ ~

Ben had wanted to call Liz all morning, but he was afraid of what she was going to say. He hoped to God, she wouldn't tell him she didn't want to see him. Tonight, had to be different, he needed to go slow. Ben went into his desk and pulled out the list he had written to himself after their lunch that first day. As he looked over it, he knew he hadn't followed his own advice. The first thing on the list was to pull back and not to come on too strong. Well, he had blown that one. Next was more talking and less touching. Talking about how he felt about her is what got him into this mess, and less touching didn't happen either because once he had his hands on her, there was no stopping him. As for the third thing on the list, try not to look at her like he wanted to eat her or jump her bones. That wasn't happening either.

Ben thought about when she came out of the bathroom in that black outfit, he couldn't help himself. So okay, he might have accomplished the fourth thing on his list. They had been having fun and enjoying being with each other, and the last thing on his list was to let her control their relationship. Well, he kinda took that over, too. Now the only way he was going to know what she was thinking was to call her. Ben dialed her number and held his breath as the phone rang.

Liz's phone rang, and she picked it up to see it was Ben and took a big breath, then let it out before answering. "Hi, Ben."

"Hey," he said, not sure how he should proceed. "Did you find the note I left you this morning?"

"Yes, I did. It was very nice of you to make coffee for me." Liz was dreading telling him she wouldn't be seeing him tonight.

"I didn't want to wake you. I knew you were up until late last night." Ben didn't like how this was feeling to him, like both of them didn't want to broach the subject of what happened last night. "I want to take you for dinner, and I know we need to talk about what happened last night."

"Ben, I'm going to need some time, I need to think, and I can't do that with you here with me." She closed her eyes and held the phone so tight to her ear as if Ben could know how hard this was for her.

"Please don't pull away from me, Liz. I'm sorry… I didn't mean to put any kind of pressure on you, and I know you have other, more important responsibilities, and I don't want to push you." She hated the desperation in his voice.

"Ben, you're not making this easy for me. Please. Before we spend any more time together, I know we do need to talk, but I need tonight to think… so please, don't put me on the spot because I don't want to make a decision here that neither of us will like."

That stopped Ben in his tracks because he was definitely pushing too hard. He didn't like it, but he would have to live with her decision not to see him tonight. If he forced her into making a decision about them now, he didn't think he would like the outcome. So, he had to give her tonight, and as long as she needed to realize she loved him because that would be the only outcome he could accept. "I don't like it, but I understand. I'll give you all the time you need. Will you call me tomorrow?"

"Yes, I will. I don't want to stop seeing you, Ben, but I can't let this get out of hand. I don't want to hurt you, but I can't give you more. I just can't." As she said the last part, something in her broke in two, it was her heart.

"Okay, fair enough, have a good night, and I'll talk to you tomorrow." Ben hung up and could feel an awful pain in his chest. He should have kept his big fat mouth shut because he needed, this time, what he had left to make her see they belonged together. What was he going to do with himself all night? He knew he'd torture himself with thoughts of how to stay away. Ben called Owen and Jeff into his office. Maybe they could keep his mind off Liz.

"Hey, you guys want to surf tonight?" He asked when they walked into his office. Owen and Jeff both looked at each other, and Jeff said, "I thought you had plans with Liz tonight?"

"Yeah well, there's been an unexpected change. Liz needs the night to think, and I need a distraction." Ben let out a frustrated breath. He was mad at himself and disappointed.

"I see," Jeff said. "If you need a distraction, we could surf and then get some drinks. I'm sure I could introduce you to someone that could make you forget Liz's name."

Owen shoved him, "You're an idiot, Jeff. He doesn't want to forget her. He needs to give her time and needs our help to keep him from going crazy, right?" Owen gave Jeff a duh look.

~ ~ ~ ~ ~ ~

After hanging up with Ben, Liz went back out onto the deck and called Kat. Now that she had told Ben she couldn't see him tonight, she felt awful. Liz could hear his disappointment, and it was just not in her nature to disappoint people. But she disappointed her parents by not going to college and having Paige against their wishes and always felt like she had disappointed Michael in some way or another. It was probably why she was now a people pleaser.

"Hello, if you're calling so soon, things didn't go well with Ben." That pulled Liz out of her thoughts.

"I told him I needed time. Now I want to call him back and tell him I don't care about any of it. I just want to say screw it. I want to be selfish." Liz could hear Kat laughing. "What's so funny? I'm here losing it, and you think it's funny? What kinda friend are you?" Liz didn't find anything in her situation funny.

"I just know you, that's all, and you are the most unselfish person I know. And to hear you say you want to be selfish is like me saying I personally want to be nice to every person in N.Y., and we both know that's not going to happen, so it's not being selfish for wanting something for yourself."

"It is because what I want is going to hurt Ben in the end and knowing that I still want him." Who was she to cause pain to someone like Ben?

"Does he know you're leaving at the end of the month, Liz?"

"Yes," Liz whispered as she closed her eyes.

"Then he's going into this with full disclosure. You are not responsible for him getting hurt."

"How can you say that? I can't intentionally hurt him," but that's exactly what she was going to do.

"Liz, you have to know, it doesn't matter when you leave. He's going to get hurt because he thinks he has feelings for you. He's a big boy and will get over it."

That just made Liz mad. How could she have gotten herself into this? It was a no-win situation. Her life before might have been safe and boring, but she didn't have to worry about anyone else's feelings, and now she's pulled Ben into this.

"Obviously, I need to do more thinking because now I've involved someone who doesn't deserve what I'm doing to him. Ben has been nothing but really great to me. He's helped me get over the fear of being with a man and taught me so much about myself," and this is how she was going to return the favor.

"Liz, you sound like your developing strong feelings for him, too."

"Kat, I can't...I have to go." Then she added as an afterthought, "Oh yeah, before I forget, I need you to overnight me nine copies of my newest book."

"Liz..."

"Don't, I have to go. I'll call you tomorrow." Liz hung up as tears started to pool in her eyes. She looked over the water, and there wasn't anyone out surfing on the water, and the tears fell.

~ ~ ~ ~ ~ ~

After work, Ben went upstairs to get ready to go surfing, although he really didn't feel like it, but if he didn't keep his mind occupied, he knew he would end up at Liz's house. He went into the kitchen, looked for something to eat, and then realized he wasn't hungry. He had some time to kill before he'd meet up with the guys, so Ben went into his weight room. Ben had so much pent-up energy, so he put on his boxing gloves and started pounding away on the hard bag. He hated that he had no control over what Liz decided. What was he going to do? Maybe he should be the one to pull back and protect his own heart, but he knew he wouldn't. It was all or nothing. She needed time, so that's what he'd give her, even if it killed him to do so. Ben worked the bag for twenty minutes, and when he could hardly move his arms anymore, he heard Jeff's voice.

"What did that bag ever do to you?" Jeff was standing in the doorway. Ben had been so deep in thought. He hadn't heard Jeff come in.

"Don't you knock?" Ben pulled off his wet gloves and shirt.

"I did, but you didn't answer, so I used the key in the flowerpot."

"Remind me to take it out of there," Ben said as he walked pasted him and went into his bedroom. He needed a shower, but he was only going surfing anyway. Jeff followed him, and Ben said, "Do you mind? I'm going to change." Jeff went back into the living room to wait. When Ben came out and asked, "Did Owen load all the boards already?"

"Yeah, Ben, you okay? I know you're in deep here. Is there anything I can do?"

"Nah, I just have to let it play out, that's all." Ben started for the door, and Jeff stopped him.

"You know, if you need anything, I'm here for you."

Owen was waiting downstairs, and they all hopped into the jeep to head to the beach. This is what Ben liked to do when he needed to think or clear his head, but he felt like he was just going through the motions. He had wanted to put his plans to win Liz over in action tonight, but now he wasn't sure if he would ever get the chance.

Owen was in the back and said, "It will work out, just have some faith." Ben looked into the rearview mirror. "She cares for you, Ben. I can see it when she looks at you, but she needs to realize it. It's hard right now for you because you know how you feel but think how confused she must feel not knowing." The kid seemed to make so much sense.

"Thanks Owen, I'll try to keep that in mind." Ben pulled up to where they liked to surf. Owen and Jeff got the boards down. Ben was just looking down the beach at the house Liz rented.

Ben felt a hand grab him, and Owen pulled him toward the water. "Come on, it'll look better after a few hours of surfing. Let's go old man."

After an hour, Ben knew his heart wasn't in it, and he just couldn't get her off his mind. If he wasn't wondering what she was doing, he was hoping she was thinking of him. What would she do? Ben sat on his board, the same board they had sex on a couple days ago.

"Ben, you wanna leave? You don't seem to be gettin' into it?" Owen was right next to him, and he hadn't even known it.

"Yeah, you guys can take the jeep. I'm going to walk. I have to do some thinking." Ben paddled in and put his board on the rack. He knew he shouldn't head in the direction of her house, but knowing and stopping himself were two different things. He wouldn't bother her, but he wanted to feel close to her.

~ ~ ~ ~ ~ ~

Liz didn't know what was wrong with her. She had been crying all day, and she needed to relax because if she kept this up, she would go crazy. It was getting dark, so she poured herself a large glass of wine and changed into her bathing suit. She went out onto the deck and uncovered the hot tub. Liz turned on the bubbles and the lights that lit the water. It was dark except for the light coming from the water. Liz put on the most calming music she could find and climbed into the tub. The hot tub had contoured seats, and the jets hit all in the right spots. She laid her head back and closed her eyes.

Yes, this is just what I needed. Now what am I going to do about Ben? Her inner voice said, *You know you want him, so don't even try to say you don't.* Liz asked herself, *how do I really feel about him? I know he makes me feel comfortable and secure. I feel like I could talk to him about anything, and that was something I didn't have with Michael. Also, I could ask for anything sexually, and he wouldn't turn me down. He makes me feel content in my own skin, and okay, those are all good reasons to stay.* Her inner voice asked, *So what's the problem?* She told herself, *I have Paige to consider. I can't possibly leave her. I have to go home, and he has to stay here. How could I ever ask him to give up his life here for me when I'm not willing to do the same for him?*

There just didn't seem to be any answers that would work for them to have a relationship. "It's so weird because it's as if I can feel him, almost as if he's here. I know he isn't, but it must be that I want him to be here with me. I miss being with him. Maybe I should call."

Ben sat on the beach watching her. He knew it was a bit stalker-ish to sit in the dark, knowing she couldn't see him, but because of the lights from the hot tub, he could see her, and every part of him wanted to walk up those steps and join her. Knowing if he did that, he would definitely ruin any chance he'd have with her. She moved to climb in, and now he couldn't see her anymore, but it didn't matter because he knew she was there.

~ 16 ~

Ben sat there on the beach long after Liz had gotten out and gone inside. He felt close to her here and didn't want to go home to his empty apartment. It was getting cold, but Ben didn't care. He watched as she moved around inside. Ben had to come up with some way to force her to realize they belonged together, but at the same time, he couldn't drive her away from him for good. Liz had to know there was so much more here than just great sex.

Liz wanted no strings attached, and he'd known that from the beginning, but he wanted more from her. At first, he couldn't see past getting his hands on her, but now that didn't seem to be as important as keeping her. Ben knew he would need to dig deep inside and use every ounce of strength to control his emotions. He knew she didn't have anyone taking care of her, so that was exactly what he was going to do. Once Ben had this new plan, he could feel some relief come over him and a calming sense as the lights in Liz's house went out.

Liz thought about sitting in the hot tub and how she couldn't shake the feeling that Ben was there. She looked over the water but didn't see anything because there was no moon tonight. She showered, wrapping herself tight in a towel. Thinking about what she should do, but she still hadn't come up with any answers. If she kept seeing Ben, it would only be harder to leave, and if she let him get any closer, it would hurt him even more. That would all be on her. In her mind, she knew she had to stop seeing him, but in her heart and soul, she couldn't stop.

Liz went to get her laptop to try to write. At least the characters in her book could have a happily ever after. Liz picked up everything she needed and turned out the lights in the house. As Liz walked past the doors that went out onto the deck, she could now see out onto the beach. There was something out there. As she stood there looking and her eyes adjusted to the darkness, she could make out a figure sitting on the sand, looking up at her house.

At first, it creeped her out, thinking that someone was watching her, but as she watched the figure stand and start to walk away, she knew who it was. Ben, he had been out there watching her, and in a way, she felt relief because at least she wasn't losing it when she thought she felt him close by. However, how did she feel about him sitting out there? A part of her wanted to go to him and pull him inside with her so she didn't have to be alone. She knew it wasn't just about being alone, but she didn't want to admit it was more. Liz took a big breath and watched him until he was gone.

~ ~ ~ ~ ~ ~

Ben woke and reached for her, then his mind cleared, he knew she wasn't there. He pulled the pillow she had slept on when she stayed with him close to his face. He could smell her, and Ben thought about how he was going to approach the major process of changing Liz's mind. He would start with the charm bracelet, the lock he bought yesterday. He'd put it away for a different time because he needed to go with fun charms. When Ben got up, he wanted to call her. He wanted to know where her head was because if she decided not to see him anymore, his plan would be in trouble before it even started. *No, I can't think that way there's always a chance. I have to have a chance.* Ben went to get ready for work, but the minute the jewelry store opened, he was going to be there.

~ ~ ~ ~ ~ ~

Liz had tossed and turned all night, and the bed was just entirely too big. She rolled over, pulled off the covers, got up, and went into the kitchen to make coffee. Today, there was no one making her coffee. She looked out her door at the beach, where she saw Ben last night. She still didn't have any answers. All she knew, she didn't want to hurt him any more than she already had. But she wanted to be with him; it was as if she had this deep aching need for Ben. He was teaching her so much about herself, and she knew she wasn't done yet. How could she intentionally mislead him and knowingly hurt someone she cared for. This was a part of herself she didn't like. Things changed because, in her old life, she always put others first, but now she wanted something for herself, no matter the consequences.

The doorbell rang, and because she was still dressed in her nightclothes, she went to the door but only opened it a crack. A man stood there with a package in his hands, and right away, Liz thought it was the books she had asked Kat to send her.

The man asked, "Miss Liz McGreary?"

"Yes, that's me," she said as she opened the door wider, and the man handed her a clipboard to sign her name and a brown envelope.

"Oh, thank you." As she took the package, it dawned on her this couldn't possibly be the books because it wasn't big enough or heavy enough to be nine books. Liz took it back to the kitchen, looking to see if it had a return address, but there wasn't one. Now she was intrigued. She ripped the flap off, reaching inside. She pulled out a small box. There was a handwritten note with the box, so Liz read it aloud.

Dear Liz,

I know we have hit a bump in the road, but I wanted you to know, that I have thought all night about how we could work this out. I didn't come up with anything that would get us both what we wanted. I don't want to lose any more time with you. I told you I want to be with you, and I know this scares you, but if all I have is until the end of the month, then I choose to spend it with you. I hope you like the new charm I picked out for you.

Love,

Ben

P.S. I still want to take you to dinner tonight. I'll be waiting for you to call me to let me know if you still want to go.

Liz could feel the tears again as she opened the box. A small flower charm sat in the center. It reminded her of their first dinner together when he brought her flowers. She wanted to call him this very instant, but what was she going to say. I want to be with you, too, but I'm still going to leave.

Liz went to get her bracelet to put the new charm on. As she was putting the flower on, she looked at the charm that Ben had picked out first for her. The workmanship on the key was so delicate. As she ran her finger over it, she wondered why he had picked this one for her. Keys have so many meanings. If you looked it up in the dictionary, the word key could mean how you open a lock or the keys on a computer, as if writing something. It also could be a code to solve a mystery, or it could be essential to a person or thing. On the other hand, it could mean music, but if he wanted it to mean that, then he would have given her a musical note.

Liz went back to where she left his note and read it again. He had said he wanted to be with her, and she wanted to be with him. So, what was the problem? She knew what it was, but didn't want to think about it anymore, so she did what she wanted to do all night. She picked up her phone to call him.

~ ~ ~ ~ ~ ~

Ben was sitting in his office, fidgeting because he couldn't sit still. He knew she must have gotten the charm by now, but why didn't she call? Ben got up and went out into the store. He needed to change his surroundings because he was going to go crazy in his office if she didn't call soon. He saw Jeff by the boards talking to some guys and went over to listen in on the conversation. It might take his mind off her. Jeff was selling these guys on some expensive boards and telling them why they were worth the extra money. Jeff turned, saw Ben standing there, and put his finger up to the one guy, "I'll give you a minute. I'll be right back," Jeff walked over to Ben, "Did you need something?"

"No, I didn't mean to pull you away from the customers. I just couldn't sit in my office any longer," Ben said as he let out a big breath, "The walls were closing in on me."

"Alright, let me finish here with these guys, and we'll get some lunch or something."

Ben watched Jeff as he walked to the guys. Then he heard Owen calling his name. He turned to see Owen holding up the phone.

"Ben, you have a call," Owen just smiled at him. God, he hoped it was Liz.

"I'll take it in my office," Ben told Owen as he practically ran.

He took a deep breath as he picked up the receiver because this call hadn't come through his cell, so he couldn't be sure if it was her. "Hello, this is Ben Jacobs."

"Ben, I tried your cell, but you didn't answer, so I hope it's okay that I called the store?" Ben let out the breath he was holding because she was calling him, but he wasn't sure what she was going to say. Ben was pulled from his thoughts when she said, "Ben, you there?"

"Yes, I'm here. I…" he didn't finish because he wasn't sure what he was going to say. It was quiet for a moment before she said anything.

"I got the charm, and it's beautiful. It reminded me of that first night I cooked for you, and you brought me flowers." He took some comfort in the fact that she was talking about a time they shared and not saying goodbye.

"I thought you'd like it, so Liz, are we still on for dinner, or are you just calling to thank me for the charm?" He had to know what she was thinking.

"I called to do both, thank you, and tell you I will have dinner with you, BUT we need to talk."

Ben didn't like that she had added a "but" in there. At least she was going to dinner, and he could work with that, "I know we do, but really, isn't that what got us in this trouble in the first place?"

"Ben, I don't want to hurt you," she said in a small voice.

"Liz, I'm a big boy. Can we just talk tonight?" Ben didn't want her talking herself out of going to dinner with him.

"Yes…what time are you going to pick me up?" She could feel a strange vibe between them.

"I want to have dinner before we get into what's going on with us. Can we just enjoy the night with each other before…" Ben didn't want to finish that sentence.

"Okay, we can do that. What time?" Liz wanted to be ready when he picked her up.

"I'll be there at seven, and I'll make reservations for seven-thirty. I wanted to take you somewhere special."

"Ben, you know I don't need anything like that," Liz thought a crowded restaurant might be a good thing right now.

"I know, but this is something I want to do for you, so just go with it, ok," he was starting to feel some hope.

"Okay Ben, I'll see you at seven then."

"See you then," Ben hung up and jumped up out of his seat so fast it knocked his chair over, hitting the wall, making a big bang. He bent to pick it up, as a smile spread across his face, he was so happy.

"Benjamin, you alright?" Linda came rushing into the room as she caught sight of him, and he had the biggest smile on his face.

"I'm so much better than okay," Ben said.

"Oh, when I heard the noise, I thought… Well, I'm not sure what I thought." Ben came around his desk and kissed his mom, as she just looked at him as if he was crazy, "What's that for?"

"I just love you. Can't I kiss you?" He felt the adrenaline running through him from anticipation.

"Of course, you can, but when you have that look on your face, I'm not sure what's going on." Ben's mother pulled back to look up into his face, "What is going on, Benjamin?"

"Liz and I hit a bump in the road, and she has agreed to have dinner with me. That makes me really happy."

"What kind of bump, did you fight?" Linda asked with a concerned look.

"No, it was nothing like that, I just…" Ben stopped talking because he realized whom he was speaking to, and he knew she'd try to get right in the middle of him and Liz.

"What Benjamin, what did you do?"

"I didn't do anything, Mom. We just had a disagreement, that's all." Ben pulled back and turned, so his mother couldn't see his face anymore because if she caught on, he was hiding something she wouldn't stop until she knew everything.

"She didn't sound upset when I talked to her." That stopped Ben, and he turned back to her.

"You talked to Liz? Why… no, wait, how did you get her number?" Ben wasn't looking so happy anymore, "Mom?"

"I called Liz to ask a favor. She agreed to talk to my book club. She is going to give everyone a signed copy of one of her books. Why are you looking at me like I just killed someone?"

It figured that Liz would do this for his mother. She would probably do anything someone asked of her. *Except stay with me*, Ben shook that thought out of his head. "Okay, Mom, how'd you get her number?" Ben stepped closer.

Linda put her chin in the air when she said, "I got it off of your phone because I knew you wouldn't have given it to me if I asked.

You'd give me some reason you didn't want me to talk to her. I'll have you know, we had a very nice conversation. You act as if I'm going to scare her away." Ben's face softened.

"Mom, I'm sorry, I didn't mean to sound like you wouldn't be anything but loving and caring towards Liz. But sometimes you love too much, and I just didn't want you to push her, that's all."

"We just talked about her speaking to the girls and how her book was going. I asked her if you were helpful and if you had gotten her out on a surfboard yet. I didn't ask anything personal, Benjamin. I can handle a conversation." Now Ben wanted to know what Liz had said about him to his mother.

"So, what did she say about me helping her?" He had hoped he sounded casual.

"Oh now, Benjamin, I don't gossip. If you want to know what she said about you, you'll have to ask her yourself," Linda smiled.

"I just want to know if she said that I was helpful. I'm not asking if she told you anything in confidence." Oh, but he did, even though he knew Liz wouldn't have talked to his mother about what was going on between them. But his mother could be swift when it came to getting the information she wanted.

"We didn't talk that long. Her phone beeped, and she had to go."

In some way, Ben was relieved and pleased that his mother and Liz seemed to get along. "I'll let it go for now that you went into my phone, but don't do it again. Mom, what happens between Liz, and I is just that, it's between us. I don't need you to help my case, okay, because I want to make myself very clear on this," Ben thought he was putting enough pressure on Liz all by himself.

"Okay Benjamin, I understand. I won't interfere," Ben knew his mother couldn't help herself when it came to her kids. She wanted the best for them. Jeff walked in just as Linda was walking out.

"Hey, everything okay in here?" Jeff looked at his mom and back to Ben as he shut the door.

"I just had to give Mom a stern warning about interfering," Ben sat on the edge of his desk.

"You still want to get out of here for a while? Mom can help Owen for an hour or so." It was lunchtime, and Ben wasn't hungry, but getting out of the office for a while did sound good.

"Yeah, that sounds good," he turned to grab his phone. Ben let Jeff lead the way. Ben had no idea where Jeff was taking him but anywhere was better than staying in the shop. They hopped into Jeff's truck and drove out of the lot onto the main drag. Jeff pulled into a burger joint, went through the drive-thru line, ordered for the both of them and pulled back into traffic. They didn't say a word, and Ben was okay with that. It gave him time to think. Jeff drove to the highest point that overlooked the ocean, a place where the kids liked to come and make out. It was a beautiful view during the day, and Ben thought how he'd like to bring Liz up here as Jeff handed him his burger and fries.

"So, you want to talk or just eat?" Jeff asked as he started to eat.

"I'm just not sure. I feel just so out of sorts. I was up half the night, trying to figure out how to keep Liz here. She has a daughter in Jersey, I can't ask her to leave her life there, and I'm stuck here. No offense, I love living here and the shop. I don't want to give it up either, but I want her more. She just fits. I can't explain why. Liz just does it for me. I just can't see a way to make it work. On one hand, I should be pulling away and letting her go home, saving myself from a whole lot of hurt in the end, but I can't." Ben just looked down at his burger and said, "I don't know if this makes any sense because all I do know, is I want her. I can see us together."

"You know, I'm a bit jealous of you right now, not the situation, of course, but the fact that you know how you feel about Liz. She's great, by the way, I like her, and I think she's good for you. I haven't seen anything that has been able to pull you away from the shop. To see you have a life outside the store. At first, I didn't like it because it meant I had to do more work. Over the years, you've done your share, and it's time I stepped up and did mine. I'm spoiled. I didn't even appreciate it. I'm selfish." This was nothing Ben ever expected to hear from his brother.

"Why would you be jealous of me? You have a different girl every night. Besides, I let you get away with an awful lot, so it's partly my fault that you didn't do your share," Ben bit into his burger and took a big sip of his drink.

"I don't want to have a different girl anymore. I want to find the one. The one that makes me want to drop everything and makes my mind go crazy, along with my body," Jeff raised his brows up and down. "I want what you have with Liz. When I saw how you looked at her that first day on the beach, I knew, but I didn't think I'd ever see you fall in love before me. You didn't even date, so how could you find someone? She just showed up here, and you knew. I want that, I've dated so many women, but none have ever been the one."

This was really great. Ben never really took the time to talk to his brother and find out what was going on with him. He just always thought Jeff was a playboy and liked being with someone new. "It'll happen for you, too, but be prepared because it's never easy. Just look at what I'm going through."

"But I don't think you'd change it. You'd still want to fall for her, the fact that you're working for it makes it even better. If it came easily, you wouldn't appreciate it, take it from me."

"It's still so hard because I can't see any way for this to work out," Ben could feel a pain in his chest, and he ran his hand over it.

"You have to have faith that you belong together. Ben, you like to know where you're going and to be in charge of everything. That's why you've controlled the store for so long. You like to be the one running things. This way, you could control where it went, and now you have no control over Liz or what happens next, and you don't like it."

Wow, Ben didn't give Jeff enough credit. He knew exactly how Ben felt. "I didn't think you paid much attention, but I can see you do," Jeff just gave him a big smile.

"You ready to head back? Mom is probably driving Owen crazy by now," they wrapped up the trash, and Jeff started the truck.

"Thank you, it was nice talking. I don't think we spend enough time like this. It really helped to talk and get away from the store."

"We never had time because you were always working, and I always was on a date," Jeff said as he was laughing.

~ ~ ~ ~ ~ ~

Liz tried to get some writing done, and all she wrote in the last five hours was three pages, which for her, was nothing. When the words came, she could write a chapter in a few hours. Today, it was like pulling teeth, the words didn't want to come. She knew why because she couldn't get into her character's heads. Liz was too busy in her own head. Her thoughts ran around like a squirrel trying to cross the street. Stay, no go, stay, and each time she contemplated leaving, her heart would pound out of her chest. When she considered staying, she felt like she was betraying Paige. Why couldn't she have everything she wanted? Didn't she deserve to be happy?

She lived many years with Michael, not truly happy, and after his death, she struggled to make a good life for Paige. Why couldn't she put herself first, her wants, and needs? "Enough, I can't sit here any longer. I have to get ready for tonight. I wonder what Ben is going to do. Is he going to try to get me to stay? He said he didn't want to talk about what was happening between us at dinner. I need to try to do what's best for everyone. I'm not sure what that is right now. I just need to get through dinner first and see what happens next. As if you can do that when you know you can't control what's happening to you." That thought just pissed her off, she shook her head to clear it, and it didn't help.

Liz went into her bedroom, and right away, she could feel Ben's presence in the room. Why did she feel so connected to him? She went to her closet to look over what she could wear for tonight; she wanted Ben to want her, but at the same time, she wasn't sure if that was such a good idea.

She picked a modest black heel to match the dress she wanted to wear and included her bracelet. The one Ben had given her. Liz went into the shower and finished getting ready. Something in her wanted Ben to want her, to want her as much as she wanted him. Liz knew it wasn't fair, but she couldn't help herself. She dabbed some perfume on the backs of her ears, on each of her wrists, and a little down her chest. Liz looked at the clock on the nightstand and knew she didn't have much time.

She was dressed and waiting for Ben when he rang her doorbell, but Liz was not prepared for what she saw. Ben stood there, with his haircut shorter and styled. He was clean-shaven, wearing a suit and tie. Liz couldn't help herself as she looked him over from top to bottom. He was gorgeous as a beach bum, but this, wow, he cleaned up really well, and when her eyes finally came back to his face, he was smiling. She didn't know what to say, so she just stared.

"Liz, you look beautiful. Are we ready to go?" Ben said as his heart was pounding.

All she could do was nod, and once she regained her composure, she said, "I just have to get my bag, and we can go." She went back inside to get it and noticed that Ben waited at the door. She tried not to make anything of it.

Ben waited at the door because he knew if he followed her, he wouldn't be able to control the want in him. Seeing her in that dress, she was sexier than hell, and he could feel his suit pants getting tighter by the minute. She came to the door, and he stepped aside so she could go first. He rested his hand on her lower back, feeling her warmth. This was going to be so hard, not touching her, but he had to do this right. She stopped short, and he almost ran into her.

"Where's your Jeep?" She looked surprised to see the classic Mustang in her driveway.

"What did you think I would pick up my date in a beat-up Jeep? I have more class than that. Give me some credit here," she turned and looked up at him.

"I just didn't know you had any other vehicles, not that I cared if you had picked me up in the Jeep. Although, I thought my hair wouldn't look the same once we made it to the restaurant." She smiled up at him, and he could feel that pull again in his groin. He had to get this date started because he really wanted to drag her back inside. Rule number three came to mind, stop looking at her as if you want to rip her dress off, even though that's exactly what he wanted to do. "Ben, did you hear me?"

Ben hadn't heard a word she said, "I'm sorry, what did you say?"

"I said this is a very nice car. I didn't see it in the lot."

"Oh yeah, that's because I keep it at my mom's house. I restored it a few years back. It was my dad's car." He opened the passenger door for her, helping her in, before coming around to get in himself.

"I can see why you don't drive it all the time." The restaurant wasn't far, so when he pulled into the parking lot, she looked around to see the lot was full.

"We're a little early, but I wanted to get here so we could have some time together before we go in for dinner. I see you're wearing the charm bracelet," he watched her as she looked down at it and ran her fingers over the two charms on it. "I have something for you. I don't think I want to wait until later like I had planned," he reached into his pocket to pull out the same box she'd opened that morning.

"Ben, you don't need…" Ben put his finger to her lip to stop her protest.

"I know that. This is something, I want you to have." He handed her the box and watched her open it.

"Oh my, how cute, it's a little surfboard. I've never seen anything like it." She reached for her bracelet, and Ben took over as he held her wrist in his hand, so he could remove her bracelet and add the charm. He could feel her pulse quicken as his fingers ran over her skin when he returned it to her wrist.

"I'm really glad you like it." It made him happy to see she was wearing it.

"I love it, Ben. It's something I have always wanted, but when I would have to buy all the charms for it, it kind of takes the pleasure out of having it. I like how you take the time to pick out the one that would mean something to me." She was running her finger over the key. Ben was wondering when she would ask about it, why he had picked it, and what it might mean. "Ben, can I ask why you gave me a key? It's so beautiful and very delicate. Keys have so many meanings. I just wanted to know what you were thinking. Does it mean something to you?"

Ben wondered how he was going to explain what he was thinking when he bought it for her. This kind of talk is what got him into trouble. "I think we should go inside. We can talk about it later." Ben got out and came around to open her door, helping her out. He took her hand, and once she was out, he didn't drop it. He needed to touch her, have his hands on her in some way. Ben could smell her as he pulled her close to him when they went inside. It was busy, but Ben went up to the maître d and gave his name. The man gave Liz a once over, and Ben could see he liked what he saw. Ben pulled Liz closer to his side as his other hand balled into a fist. A streak of jealousy went through his body because Liz was his.

Liz must have felt his distress she looked up at him, whispering, "You, okay?"

He leaned down so he was next to her ear and whispered back, "Yeah, I just don't like how he was looking at you." He could feel a shiver run through her body. He didn't know if it was because of what he said or because he was close to her, but either way, he liked it. It was a good thing he had a jacket on that covered his crotch. They came to their table, and the maître d tried to pull Liz's chair out for her, but Ben wasn't going to have it. He stepped in front and sat Liz. The closer he was to her, the more his body reacted, and this was him trying to control himself. What Jeff said earlier came to mind, how he needed to control everything. He took a cleansing breath and sat on the other side of the table from her. The maître d opened the menu for Liz and then looked at Ben, opening his. Ben wanted him to go away and stop regarding Liz the way he was. If the man wanted to lose his teeth, all he had to do was keep it up. Then the man finally left their table after he told them the specials, but not after giving Ben a smirk.

"Ben, what's going on? You look like you want to kill someone?" If she only knew, Ben thought to himself.

"I told you. I didn't like how he was looking at you. He should know better than to be checking out someone's girlfriend. I don't appreciate it at all." Ben knew he was sounding like a possessive jerk, but he couldn't seem to help it.

Liz just laughed and not just a giggle. She was enjoying his anger, and he could feel the anger dissipating as the sound of her laughter moved through him. "I know…I sound like an idiot, but you are my date, and I didn't like the guy undressing you with his eyes."

"Ben, I'm with you, he can look, but you know what I look like under my clothes, and he never will." That made Ben smile, she could make him feel so good in a heartbeat, and the image of her naked under him came to mind. Now his dick was at full attention.

"You know what you do to me when you talk about you being naked. It's probably a really good thing we're sitting down."

The waiter came over to take their drink order, Liz ordered wine, and he had the same. The waiter left, and Liz said, "Ben, I didn't say how great you looked in that suit, but when you came to the door, I was speechless." She took a sip of her water, and he could see she was nervous. He didn't want this dinner to be uncomfortable.

He needed to make her laugh again, he liked it when she laughed. She had these small lines around her mouth when she smiled, they were so cute. They were like dimples and only showed when she smiled. "So, I guess I made an ass out of myself with the maître d.'" She smiled at him. He could see the little lines as her smile reached her eyes. She covered his hand with hers, and he intertwined them together. The waiter was back with their drinks, and they hadn't even looked over the menu. He said he would give them a minute and then was gone.

"Ben, I don't think you made an ass out of yourself. I think it was sweet. I've never had anyone act jealous over me before."

"I just want you for myself. I'm selfish that way."

"Ben," she said his name as if she wanted to scold a child, and he knew he had stepped over the invisible line they had drawn for tonight. It was his idea not to talk about what was going on between them until after dinner.

"I'm sorry, I shouldn't have said that. We should figure out what we want for dinner before our waiter gets pissed at us." Ben tried his best to smooth over the awkward moment, and he noticed how she released his hand. He watched her as she looked over the menu and thought, *Shit. This is not how I wanted dinner to go. Maybe if you stopped trying to control the evening, it might go better*. The waiter came back, and they ordered their meal. "After dinner, I have a surprise for you," Ben said to try to lighten the mood.

"Ben, I think you already have given me so many surprises. You gave me two charms today, not that I don't love them, but…."

"It's not anything like that kinda surprise. I know of this place on the top of the world. I wanted to show it to you, it overlooks the ocean, and you can hear the waves crashing against the cliff. I thought it might be a nice spot where we could talk." He could see her whole expression change, and he knew he shouldn't have mentioned the conversation they still needed to have.

"That sounds so nice. I'd love to see it, Ben."

Their dinner came, and it was more food than either of them could eat. After they did their best to finish, the waiter wrapped their leftovers in tin foil that looked like swans. Ben paid the bill, took her hand, and wrapped it around his arm as they walked out. He couldn't help but give the maître-d the same smirk as he walked out with Liz on his arm. She looked up at him and was on to him. He helped her into the car. He knew this was going to be the hard part of the evening. Ben climbed in, reached over, and pulled Liz in for a kiss. He made sure it was soft and light. He had to have that contact with her, she pulled him closer, and the kiss started to be so much more. Ben had to pull back if he planned to regain control because his dick was so hard that he wanted to pull her into the back seat and do her right there. Liz protested, but he couldn't let her have the control right there. They needed to talk first before they went any further.

"Liz, we need to stop," she pulled back too, and he was sorry for the loss of her body.

"I know, I'm sorry, I shouldn't have…" Ben stopped her again.

"Liz, don't be sorry. We just need to get everything out in the open first. I have to have some kind of control if I'm going to make it through tonight." Ben started the car pulling out to take her to the spot where he'd had lunch today. It was a perfect place to talk, it was quiet, and no one would bother them. Liz reached to take his hand, and he let her intertwine their fingers together. He pulled the car right up to the spot and looked over at her.

"Do you want to talk here, or we could get out of the car?" He looked out the windshield.

"I would like to look out over the ocean, so let's get out." She didn't wait for him to come around, so he met her at the front of the car, and they sat on the hood. "It's so beautiful here. I love the sound of the ocean and the smell of the salt water." She looked so happy and content, but Ben knew it wasn't going to last. Something in him wanted it to stay just like this.

Ben took her hand in his and said, "Liz, we need to get this over with. I have to tell you just how I feel." He took a big breath and went on. "I love you, and I want to be with you," and watched her as she looked at the ground. He reached for her chin to pull up her face to look at him. She pulled away from him as he knew she would, and he took another breath. "I know you feel you can't love me back and you're needed somewhere else. But I need you, too. I want to be one of those people in your life that you give everything to because I want to give everything that I am to you." Ben could see the tears starting to run down the side of her face, but he couldn't stop once he started.

"You wanted to know why I bought you the key. I knew from the first time I saw you on the beach the minute you touched my hand, and a shock ran through my fingers. I was going to fall hard, even if I kept telling myself there was no way I could be falling in love with you because I didn't even really know you, but everything in me wanted to know more. You are the key to my happiness, the key to my life." Now she was sobbing, and Ben tried to pull her to him. She hadn't said anything, but she allowed him to hold her. Ben rested his head on the top of hers. "I'm so sorry I've upset you, Liz. I'm really sorry," Ben said into her hair.

Liz's voice was so small he almost missed what she said, "Ben, I think I love you, too, but I can't... I can't because I need to go home. I have a daughter who depends on me, and I can't just move my whole life here. No matter, how much I wish I could. I wasn't looking for love, Ben." It was getting hard to understand what she was saying between her sobs. "I didn't even know I wanted this... because I don't ever put myself first. I have been trying to think of ways this could work, and, and there aren't any. I don't want to hurt you, Ben, but I can't stay away, either. I can't believe how selfish I'm being." She was starting to hyperventilate, and Ben could see this was tearing her apart.

"Liz, please breath, try to calm down because you're going to faint on me."

"I can't... I can't..." was all she kept saying.

"I know, sweetheart, please stop crying. I can't stand it, you're breaking my heart. It'll work out, you'll see. I'm not sure how, but it will," Ben pulled her into his lap, and she curled up into a ball and held onto him. Ben rocked her, as he rubbed her back, and he kept saying, "It's going to be ok," over, and over. He didn't know how, but at this very moment, he would give up everything for her.

She had gotten so upset and was breathing with gasping breaths. He held her until her cries had turned calm, where she would gasp for air only every so often. Her body had gone slack. Ben knew she had cried herself to sleep. He held her tight to his body, and he laid them both on the hood. He told her again he loved her, and it had to work out. He cuddled into her and closed his own eyes. Ben wanted to take her home, where he could tuck her into bed, but didn't want to wake her. He would love to be climbing into that bed next to her, even though he knew it wasn't going to happen.

After an hour or so, Ben picked her up. She was like a small rag doll, putting her into the seat and strapping her in. She didn't wake, she was still out. Ben drove her home. He took her keys, opened the door, and turned down her bed. Then he went for her, and she never even made a sound. He scooped her up again and carried her inside. Ben laid her on the bed, took off her shoes, and covered her. He sat in the chair, watching her sleep. Ben knew there was only one way they could be together. He was going to have to leave his life here and go with her. Ben wrote her a note, put it on the pillow next to her, and went home. He had a lot of thinking to do.

~ 17 ~

Liz woke to the doorbell ringing repeatedly. She got up half asleep, went to the door and flung it open, not really caring who was on the other side, and said, "What do you want?"

"Wow, I didn't think I'd ever see you still wearing clothes you must have worn last night because I can't see you wearing that to bed." Kat nodded toward Liz and added, "Late night, or did you actually get drunk for once in your life, and if you did, I'm going to be so pissed because I missed it."

Liz looked down, and sure enough, she still wore the clothing she was wearing when she had dinner with Ben. She tried to clear the fog from her brain. What the hell was Kat doing here? Her mind just couldn't catch up with what was going on. "What the hell are you doing here, Kat? Did something happen with Paige?"

Kat shook her out of her stupor, "Nothing has happened to Paige. She's fine, just the way you left her." Liz let out the breath she was holding as Kat walked past her pulling a small suitcase behind her. Liz was still looking at Kat as if she was imagining her being there, "Kat, not that I don't love you, but what are you doing here?" She said it again as she followed Kat into the house.

"I wanted to make sure you were okay, and I thought it would be cool for us to have a long weekend."

"Kat, I'm fine," Liz said, even though she knew she wasn't, and had no idea how she got home last night, or into bed. The last thing she could remember was crying all over Ben's jacket. She didn't know what happened after that, now Kat was here, and she had no clue how she left things with Ben. Liz's head was spinning. She couldn't make it stop. Kat just looked as if she knew better.

Liz showed her the house and put Kat's belongings in one of the bedrooms. She needed some time to clear her head and figure out what was going on. "I need to shower and change. Then I'll be right back." Liz disappeared into her bedroom and sat on the bed. "How'd I get here? It had to be Ben, but why isn't he here?" She looked over at the top of the bed, then she spotted a note. She reached for it as if it was her lifeline. Ben said how he didn't want to wake her and that he'd call her today. Relief fluttered over her because he would call. She hadn't ended it, and neither had he? But how did they leave things between them? Liz wanted to call him, but she was afraid, so she decided to wait for his call and went to shower in hopes it would help clear her head.

When she came out, she found Kat on the deck sitting on one of the lounge chairs. She had rolled up her pants legs and took off her jacket. Liz went out to join her, "Getting a little sun? You know, you can get skin cancer sitting out here without sunscreen." Liz sat next to her on the other chase.

"Yeah, I'm not going to be out here long. I just wanted to get a little color, so when I go back home, I look like I went somewhere." She pushed her face up to the sun and made a relaxing sound.

Liz laid back, closed her eyes, and wished she knew what happened last night. Kat's voice broke through her thoughts, "So, are you going to tell me what's going on? Or am I going to have to beat it out of you because I have to say, you already looked like crap when you answered the door." Kat didn't even open her eyes when she said, "Don't try to bullshit me, Liz."

"Okay so, I'm not really sure what happened last night, and all I remember is going for dinner with Ben, and he took me to a place that overlooked the ocean, and it was beautiful. We were supposed to talk about what was going on between us. I remember crying all over his suit jacket and then nothing. I have no idea how we left things, and I really want to call him, but I'm afraid." Liz's voice was strained and edgy.

Kat's answer to Liz's dilemma was to go shopping because she thought Liz was under too much stress. Liz thought getting out might help her think, so she agreed. Kat tried to say it would be fun. She had asked Liz if she was sleeping and eating right, because Kat was so big into taking care of her body, she always tried to get her to do the same. Liz went with sleeping and eating when she could get it.

"I have been sleeping, and I try to eat the best I can." Liz knew she was lying through her teeth.

"Didn't I tell you not to bullshit me? I know you better than anyone." Well, Kat had her there.

"Okay, I haven't been taking care of myself. Is that what you want to hear?" Liz ran her hand through her hair. "I don't know what's going on with me." Her whole world had felt like someone had flipped it upside down.

~ ~ ~ ~ ~ ~

Ben woke in his own bed, alone again. He hated leaving her last night, but he had to think how he was going to tell his family he would be leaving with Liz when she went home. He knew his mother would take it the hardest, and he had no idea how they would manage the shop without him. He'd have to teach Jeff more than doing the ordering, and he'd have to really step up, but in the back of his mind, he knew Jeff couldn't do the job. Couldn't or just not the way he, did it? Ben didn't really want to leave his family or the business his dad had started, but he couldn't see any other way. He would work it out, but he wouldn't tell her until he told his family.

Liz had told him last night she thought she loved him too. Even though she was crying, he couldn't help feeling relieved. She did have feelings for him, and that's all he needed to make up his mind. Ben got up, jumped into the shower, and when he was done, he was going to call her. He showered as fast as he could because he wanted to hear her say she loved him again. Ben went right to his phone and dialed her number, and it rang, then went to voicemail. Ben figured it was too early, and she wasn't up yet, so he left a message for her to call him when she got up. Ben went into the kitchen to start some coffee; he looked out the small window over his sink and thought how he would miss not seeing the ocean every day. He told himself she was worth it. He turned away and went to get dressed for work.

~ ~ ~ ~ ~ ~

Liz and Kat went to the mall that she had gone to with Tara. They had shopped for hours, and Liz's feet were hurting her, so they stopped for some lunch. Picking a place where Kat would actually eat the food wasn't easy. Liz decided to let Kat eat where she wanted, and she would have a sub sandwich. After Liz and Kat got their food, they sat at a table, and Liz's feet thanked her, and that's when she realized she had forgotten her phone at home. How would she know if Ben called? Well, they'd finished shopping soon if her feet had anything to say about it. After they finished eating, Kat wanted to do more shopping, and Liz complained the whole way.

"Would you stop whining? It's like I have Paige when she was a kid. Suck it up. I'm only here for the weekend. Besides, if you exercised more, you'd have more stamina. When we get home, I'm going to make it my new mission to get you into shape." Kat never seemed to get tired. She was like the freaking energizer bunny, she just kept going and going.

"I am in shape, round is a shape," Liz tossed back. "And, I've been surfing. If you don't consider that a workout, then I should get Ben to get you out there, and then you might leave me alone about being out of shape. Just because I don't go to the gym like you do, to torture the shit out of my body, so I can say I'm in shape." Kat turned and looked at Liz with surprise. "What?" Liz added.

"I can't believe you just defended yourself. Is this the new Liz because I like her?" Liz stuck her tongue out at her, and Kat just laughed, "Now, you are really acting like Paige." All Liz wanted to do right now was to return home and call Ben or at least see if he had called her. Liz also realized she hadn't talked to Paige because she hadn't called back. Liz made a note to make sure she talked to Paige today. After a few more shops, Kat said, "I can see you're not into it, sometimes you're just no fun."

"I'm sorry, I just can't help thinking about Ben, and the fact I haven't heard from Paige in days. I'm starting to get that feeling that something is wrong." Liz was starting to get concerned.

"What did she say the last time you talked?" Kat's voice sounded a little concerned also. They were walking to the car.

"I called the other day and left a message, and she hadn't called back. Paige sounded fine the last time we talked, she had made friends and was going out with them, doing stuff."

"What kinds of stuff?" Kat asked with a sharp tone to her voice.

"She had said they were going to the movies and bowling as a group. I guess with some of the other kids that were there for the summer." That got Liz thinking, she hoped Paige hadn't gotten herself in trouble with these friends.

~ ~ ~ ~ ~ ~

Ben waited an hour, but she hadn't returned his call. She should be up by now, so he tried again, and he got the same thing. Her phone rang and then went to voicemail, so he left another message for her to call him. Ben got a strange feeling and tried to push it aside. He hoped she wasn't avoiding him. There had to be some other explanation why she couldn't pick up her phone. Maybe she was working, her phone went dead, and she hadn't realized it. "Yeah, that could be it," Ben said to himself. He would just go over there after work, and it would be fine. Too bad he didn't have the landline number to the house. He could call her on that and see if she answered.

Ben pulled out the telephone book, but he didn't know who owned the house, so whose name would he look under? He went to his computer and did a search by the address when the number came up. Ben dialed and waited. The phone just rang and rang, and that feeling was back. He pushed it away again, saying maybe she went for a walk on the beach and forgot to bring her phone. Yeah, that could be it, and he'd wait a while longer to try again.

Ben got up from his desk and paced his small office space, but the feeling as if something was wrong just wouldn't leave him, so he had to get out of his office, or he was going to go crazy. Ben walked right past his mother because he didn't want to talk to her right now.

"Benjamin, where are you going?" she asked him. Ben didn't answer her, just kept moving up the stairs that led to his apartment. He took the stairs two at a time, and when he finally reached his door, he could feel his anxiety levels were higher than he had ever felt. He went inside and straight to his workout room and put on his boxing gloves, hitting the bag harder and harder. "She wouldn't just leave me and not say a word," as he let his mind go there and hit the bag with all his pent-up frustrations. Ben was breathing hard, and tears in his eyes blurred his vision, but he didn't stop; he kept hitting it harder. Ben knew what he had to do, see for himself. If she was still there, he hoped there was a good explanation for why she hadn't called him back. One he hoped he could accept, but if she was gone, what was he going to do then?

Ben pulled off his gloves and went into the bathroom to clean up. He looked into the mirror at his reflection, and realized he looked like shit. Ben took the washcloth and wiped his face and then his arms and chest. He put on a clean shirt, went down the back stairs, jumped into his Jeep, and was on his way to her house. He kept telling himself it was going to be okay. She was going to be there. He said it over, and over in his mind. When he pulled into her driveway, he didn't even notice her car and just ran to the door and rang the bell. Ben could hear someone moving inside, and relief came over him. She was in there, but when the door opened, and a blonde woman stood in the doorway that Ben didn't recognize, his heart dropped. "Who the hell are you?" He asked in a very rude voice.

"Who the hell are you?" She asked back in an even ruder voice.

"Where is the lady who rented this house?" He asked as he tried to look inside the house.

"I don't have to tell you anything until you tell me who you are, and I will slam this door right in your face." She said back, and this woman was starting to piss him off because he was in no mood. Why wouldn't she just tell him where Liz was?

"I'm Ben Jacobs, and I want to know where Liz McGreary is right now," Ben demanded.

The woman just smiled at him and said, "She left."

Ben's heart just stopped, and he didn't believe what the spikey blonde was saying because Liz had left him without a word. He couldn't breathe.

"Kat, who's at the door?" A very familiar voice came from inside.

When Ben heard her voice, he thought he was imagining it. He forced himself inside right past the twig of a woman who was attempting to block the doorway. "Liz," Ben yelled, and then he saw her, wrapping his arms tightly around her, and picked her up as he spun her around.

"Ben, what's going on? Why are you acting like this?" Ben just held his face to her hair and breathed her in. She could feel the intense anxiety in his body.

"It might have something to do with something I said," the voice came from the bitch that had been guarding the door.

Liz looked over to the woman, "Kat, what did you do?" Liz couldn't imagine what would make Ben this upset and distraught.

Kat said, not sounding apologetic for doing it, "I might have told him you left."

Now Liz was catching on to what transpired, and she said, "Ben, I didn't leave. I just went shopping with Kat and forgot my phone." Then she turned to Kat and said, "I don't think this is funny, Kat, not at all." Liz grabbed Ben's hand, walked him into her bedroom, and slammed the door. She would deal with Kat later. She sat Ben on the bed and put both her hands on his face looking into his eyes to see he was deeply hurt. "Ben, I'm not going to leave without talking to you first." He didn't say anything, so she went on, "Didn't you see my car in the driveway?"

He cleared his throat because he could hardly speak, "I just had this feeling you left when I couldn't get a hold of you, and that woman opened your door and said you left. I…I didn't even look for your car. I just ran to your door and..." Liz pulled him into her chest and rested his head there. She ran her fingers through his hair, trying to soothe him. He put his arm around her waist.

How was it going to be when she really did leave? This was just a preview of what was to come, and she hated it. She knew he loved her, and she loved him, but she had to go home. She felt the burning in her eyes as the tears threatened to spill. She was doing this to him, and it was only going to get far worse before it was over. "I need to talk to Kat. Can you give me a minute with her?" Ben nodded and let her go. "I'll be right back, okay?" She stepped away from him and went out the door.

When the door shut, Ben let out the breath that he felt like he had been holding forever. She was still here, but for how long? She said she wouldn't leave without talking to him first. Ben had the nagging feeling this wasn't going to work out for him. He tried again to push it away, but what happened today was just the tip of the iceberg on how insecure he was feeling. How could this be happening to him? He finally finds someone, and he can't have her.

Liz was beyond mad. She was downright furious with Kat. This threatened the calm she always worked so hard to keep. But now, she went out to where Kat was sitting on the deck, and before she could say a word, she heard Kat say, "I know you're mad, but what I did was for you."

"What!" Liz took a deep breath, and said, "Kat, I know you can be mean, but what you just did to Ben is over the top, even for you. For you to say you're doing it for me. I'm beside myself, I'm so angry with you, and all I can come up with, is why you'd do something like this is, you're jealous of Ben. All these years, you've had me to yourself, and now you might have to share me."

Kat laughed aloud, "I'm not jealous, Liz. I wanted to see his reaction. It might have been mean, but now I know that he really cares for you, and by your reaction, that tells me a lot, too. I do want to see you happy, you deserve that, and I think Ben just might be the right guy for you."

What Kat was saying totally confused her and defused her anger, "No Kat, I can't, and you know why. I have to go home. I have other responsibilities." Liz could feel herself losing any control over her life that she felt she had.

"Don't you have a responsibility to yourself, too?" Liz fell quiet as she looked at her feet and tried to steady her breathing. This was all getting to be more than she could handle.

"Kat, I can't do this right now, not while I still have Ben in the bedroom. I just wanted to tell you, IF you plan to stay, then I will not put up with any more interference from you, where Ben and I are concerned. Do you understand, because if you can't help yourself, then you need to go home?" Liz was using her stern voice, at the moment, it was all the conviction she had.

"Wow, you've changed, talking back, threatening to send me home."

"It's not a threat. If you can't play nice, you will be on the next plane home, I swear to God, Kat."

"All I want to know is, are these changes because of him?" She sat up to look at Liz.

"I don't know, but this is important to me, he's important." As Liz finished her words, she looked up to see Ben standing there. Liz took another deep breath and introduced Kat. "Ben, I want you to meet my agent and best friend, although I'm not sure about the last part after the stunt she pulled." Kat just huffed and turned to Ben.

"Hi," she reached out her hand. "I might need to apologize for what I said at the door." Ben just looked at her outreached hand and didn't move.

"Might need to, you know you do, IF you plan on staying," Liz shot back.

"Okay then, I'm sorry," She looked to her outreached hand and realized he wasn't going to shake it.

Ben said as he looked straight into her eyes, "I'm not usually this rude to someone I just met, but I have to tell you, I don't like you. I know you're someone that's important to Liz, so I'll attempt to be cordial for her sake, but I can't guarantee it if you keep pulling any more shit."

Kat stepped closer as if his words didn't intimidate her in the least bit. "Ben, at some point, I'd like to sit down and have a conversation with you. Just so you know, I love Liz, like my sister, and I don't give a damn how you feel about me. I can be rude to people I know and some I don't, but I am a no-bullshit kind of person, and if you didn't like how I analyzed you, well, that's too damn bad," she stared right back at him.

Liz's voice broke through as she tried to step in between them, and Ben was just giving Kat a look of contempt. "Kat, I mean it. You will be on the next plane."

Kat looked from Liz back to Ben and stated, "He should know how I am, Liz."

Ben stepped in front of Liz and pointed his finger in Kat's face. "That's fine, just so you know, I happen to love Liz, too. I will not stand by and let you or anything else get in between us." Now Ben was right in Kat's face, and Liz grabbed his arm to pull him back.

"Ben, Kat, you both need to step back. Kat, I don't need you protecting me. I can take care of myself, and Ben, we need to talk." Liz turned to Kat and said, "I will be back in a little while, so keep you're self-entertained." Liz took Ben's hand, pulling him from the deck. "Let's go for a drive, so we can talk without being interrupted."

That was the best thing Ben had heard all day, and he let her pull him toward the door. She still held his hand, so he intertwined his fingers with hers. Ben helped Liz into the Jeep, but he didn't want to let go of her. He kissed her hand as he let it drop and climbed into the driver's side. He backed out and wasn't sure where he was going, anywhere alone as long as he was with Liz, it was all good.

"I should apologize," he said.

"Ben, why are you apologizing? You didn't do anything to be sorry for."

"I should've controlled myself better. I should've known you didn't leave." Ben ran his hand through his hair and made Liz look over at him, and she started laughing. "What's so funny?" He asked because, at that moment, he didn't find anything funny.

"When you just did that, it made your hair stand straight up. You're so cute, you know that?" Ben smiled over at her, and the tension on his face seemed to disappear.

Ben pulled the Jeep onto an unoccupied part of the beach and just looked out the front windshield as he said, "Liz, I feel so confused right now, my head is spinning because one minute, I think we're getting somewhere, and the next, I think you've left. When I went to your door and that bit—ch..., your friend answered and said you left,

I…" Ben rested his head on the steering wheel because he felt like he could hyperventilate, he needed to calm down, but he was worked up.

"I don't want to discuss Kat at the moment. I need to know what happened last night because all I remember is us having dinner and you taking me to the cliff to talk and me crying into your jacket, but after that, nothing," Ben now looked at her.

"You don't remember because you fell asleep from sheer exhaustion. I took you home, tucked you in, and then I left." He needed to touch her but didn't think this was the time to pull her into his lap and bury himself deep inside her.

"Ben, I don't know how we left things between us." She stared down at her hands because she hated to admit it.

"Do you remember telling me you loved me? Or that I told you the same." He was watching her expression to see if she would try to back away and deny her feelings for him.

"I did what! I said it to you, aloud? You heard me say it?" The look on her face told him, she really didn't recall saying she loved him, and he wasn't sure how he felt about that.

"Yes, you said it. Are you taking it back, Liz?" He waited with labored breath for her answer.

"No," She whispered, but she still couldn't believe she admitted that she loved him aloud, when she had a hard time acknowledging it.

"No, you don't believe you said it, or no, you're not taking it back?" He needed the clarification.

"Both, I can't," she didn't say anymore.

"What can't you do Liz?" He still needed to know what she was thinking.

"I can't fall for you, Ben. I can't stay here or come back." There was sheer distress in her voice.

"Liz, I know you don't want to have feelings for me, because it makes your life feel impossible, but it doesn't change that you do have feelings for me. You're a mother who loves her daughter with every part of your being, but I also know that the feelings you have for me makes you feel as if you're choosing one or the other, and I would never ask that of you. You put everyone else first at your own expense. What I want from you right now, is to try to keep an open mind. You said, we have the time you have left, right?" Liz nodded. "So please, give me that, and when it's time for you to go home, we agree to talk about what we could do about us then."

"Ben, I just don't know where avoiding talking will change the facts. There just can't be an "us," and if we wait and then both of us have stronger feelings, then what? I can't figure a way this can work out. I wish I could." Liz's voice dropped off as she said the last part.

"Please," Ben's pleading tone broke her heart. She could see he wanted so much more than she could give, but she couldn't hurt him by telling him no.

"Ben, I don't want either of us to get hurt, and with us spending so much time together getting more involved, it will only end badly. We can't just escape what will happen at the conclusion, just because we don't like it. I crave this time with you, I really do. Being with you has been the absolute best thing for me, I won't deny that." She could hear her own heart beating in her chest and felt the ache there.

"Liz, when I close my eyes, I can see us together. For me, it's something I can't seem to control. I'm so drawn to you, I'm not even sure why. I mean… I know that I'm sexually attracted to you, but it doesn't stop there for me. You intrigue and fascinate me, you just fit. I don't know how else to explain. I just feel it." He was wearing all his emotions on his sleeve, but he didn't care because if it made her realize they belonged together, then so be it.

"But…" Liz started to protest, but Ben kissed her words away.

"Please, give us the time we need and deserve." His voice was filled with hope.

Liz couldn't fight him anymore, she wasn't emotionally strong enough, "Okay Ben, but I am not promising you anything and that things will be any different at the end of the month."

The relief that swept over Ben's body was overwhelming. It was still going to be an uphill battle, he knew, but it was a start, and that's what he needed. She was going to keep an open mind. Ben looked over at her and asked, "So, you won't freak out if I tell you I love you?" He smiled at her expression.

"Don't push your luck, mister. All I'm agreeing to is the same thing we started with. We will have the time I have left, and anything else, I'm not making any decision on."

Ben liked how she was trying to sidestep the fact that they both had deeper feelings for each other. A small amount of satisfaction came over him. He would win her over with love, support, and compassion. All the things she didn't have but so deserved. He was going to be different from her husband because he wanted Liz with every fiber in him. What would she say if I told her right now?

"I love you, Liz McGreary, so get used to it."

"Ben."

"No, no, your response is, I love you, too, Ben." Liz just shook her head and started to smile. "Now, I think we need to talk about Twiggy."

That statement pulled Liz from her emotional stupor, and she looked confused and asked, "Twiggy?"

"You know that woman at your house. Your friend, what's her face?"

"Her name is Kat, and where did you get Twiggy from?" He was referring to her height and how thin she was, and it was somewhat funny how he saw her.

"Well, you don't want to know what I really wanted to call her." Ben didn't like his first impression of Kat. If he had his way, she would be on the next plane home, and if she never showed her face again, that would be too soon.

"Ben, I'm going to ask you to try to understand where Kat is coming from." Liz was going to try to defend Kat's actions, when she was still mad at her for acting the way, she did.

When Ben said, "Oh, I know where she came from, Hell," it made Liz start to laugh so hard because Ben had nailed Kat. She could be someone's worst nightmare, no doubt. Kat had a very protective streak, and if you were someone she cared about, then she would do anything for you. Kat was a great person to have on your side.

"Okay, I know she wasn't very nice to you, and how you feel about her isn't unwarranted, but she is my best friend. She wants the best for me, and you know I haven't had anybody in my life. I never let anyone get as close to me as I have let you."

"You know, I've asked myself a couple of times why that is. Not that I'm not really glad you did, but why hasn't some guy come along and snatched you up?"

"I guess, I never showed any interest in anyone, and the guys never tried to get to know me before." Liz looked over at him, and there was disbelief in his face.

"Well, I, for one, have to say, they're all idiots. I'm glad they were because then I never would have had my chance with you."

"Let's get back to discussing Kat. She's going to decide whether she approves of you or not. Some of that is going be by how much shit you'll take from her, but she does have my best interest at heart, and she wants to know if you're good enough for me." Liz put up her hand when Ben started to protest, "Let me finish. When I was trying to get my first book published, I had my work cut out for me until I met Kat. When I told her my story about how Michael died and I was raising Paige alone, she became my rock, fought for me with the publishers, and got me the money or anything she thought I deserved. At that time in my life, I needed someone like her, and we hit it off. When Kat cares for you, you get all she has, and if she doesn't like you, she can be the biggest bitch you've ever seen. For most people, she is a bad enemy to have, so they give her what she wants. So, when she is fighting for you, you like that she's such a hard ass, but at the same time, most people give her own way, so she's like a spoiled kid."

"Liz, I meant what I said on the deck. I'm not going to just stand by and let her interfere when it comes to us, and I don't give a shit if she approves of me or not. I am not going to kiss her ass to prove I am good enough. There's only one person I care about what they think of me, and that's you. I can see she is a big part of your life, and I am glad you had someone like her in your corner when you needed the support. I know it would make my life easier if she likes me, but I won't win her respect by taking any shit from her."

Liz could see this was going to be a very stressful weekend. Ben was right, he shouldn't have to take crap from Kat. Yet Kat would be dishing it out just the same, it's just how she was. "Kat is family to me. She is all I have and Michael's parents. Paige calls her Aunt Kat, and you know the story with my own parents. So, when you have so few family members to count on, you really appreciate the ones you do have."

Ben had his family, as much as they could be a big pain in the ass, he wouldn't trade them. He knew his mother sounded a lot like Kat, except she might not be a bitch. She would kill you with kindness as she was stabbing you with a knife for messing with her kids. He could understand where Liz was coming from, and he would do his best to coexist with the twiggy bitch, if it got him, Liz. He thought he would do anything for her, even take some shit from her friend. "So, my question is, am I going to see you while she's here? How long is she staying anyway?"

Liz knew she could send Ben into a tailspin and tell him she was going to be here for the rest of her trip, but she knew that would be cruel, as a matter of fact, it was something Kat would do.

"Well, that's going to depend."

Ben didn't like the sound of that and asked, "Depends on what?" He lost enough time with her and didn't want to waste anymore.

"I can't just leave her while we go off, and I'm pretty sure you don't want to hang around with her." Liz made a face at him as if she knew how he felt.

"Can't you just guide her back on a plane, and we can go back to what we were doing?" Ben pulled Liz in close as he ran his fingers through her fiery red hair and kissed her.

"Ben," she said, his name so sexy, his dick started to come alive because it had been days since they had sex, and he wanted her extremely bad.

"Can we please go back to my place? I need to touch you." His hands wanted to rip her clothes off.

"I can't," she said. Ben made a frustrated sound, and then she added, "She's only going to be here for the weekend, and then she goes home on Monday morning," Ben groaned even louder it was going to be at least two more days before he would be able to be alone with her. Somewhere in the back of his mind, he reminded himself that he was supposed to be pulling back when it came to sexual contact. He wanted her to realize there was more to their relationship than just sex. This is how his willpower would be seriously tested. He was going to have to keep his eye on the prize and this prize he was going to win. Ben pulled back.

"I guess I need to return you, or she might summon the National Guard. I have to figure out how I'm going to see you with her around. I want you to know you already promised this time to me." Ben looked over to see how she reacted to his words and then went on. "Maybe we need to find a date for her." As the words came out of his mouth, he got a wicked idea. "What if we went on a double date tomorrow night?"

"Ben, whoever you get for her date, she'll chew up and spit him out. I don't think this is a good idea, and whoever the guy is, he is not going to be your friend after tomorrow night."

"Don't you worry about the dude, he can handle himself, and if she's giving him a hard time, then I might be left alone." Ben liked the plan that was brewing in his mind, *oh yeah, I have the perfect person in mind, too.*

He heard her say, "What do you have in mind?" He told her of a nightclub, "I thought we could meet up at The Surf Shack. It's a club on Main Street. I might not be able to do what I want, but at least we could dance, and that's better than not seeing you at all." Liz blushed, and that made him smile because he loved that about her.

"You dance? I didn't think you would be that kind of guy." She sounded surprised, and Ben looked insulted.

"What you think, I have two left feet? I'll have you know, I can hold my own. You ladies meet us around nine out front because it's a place if you don't know someone, you'll have to wait in line. Then I'll show you. I have the moves."

Liz started laughing, and Ben loved the sound of her laugh. He started the Jeep, pulled off the beach, and headed back to her house. He didn't really want to drop her off, but he knew it was what he had to do. Then he was going to have to convince his brother to go with him on this date. If anyone could get Twiggy distracted, it would be Jeff, and if she did chew him up, Ben wanted to be there to see it happen. Ben kissed Liz goodbye with a very soft press of his lips, because he knew if they did anything more, he would be taking her back to his place for sure.

Ben pulled out his phone to call Jeff, the sooner he got this over with, the better. When Jeff answered, Ben said, "Hey, where are you? I need to talk to you." He heard his brother say, "What's up?" He could hear noise in the background and knew Jeff was out, "Like I said, I need to talk to you in person. Where are you?"

"I'm at that small bar on Fourth Street, everything all right?" Ben headed in that direction.

He said, "I need a really big favor, but I'll tell you when I get there." Ben pulled into a parking place on the street. "I'm here," Ben said and hung up. He hadn't gone to a bar in ages, but when he walked in, he found Jeff sitting at the bar. It was busy for a Friday night, not that he would really know. It was a small place, and they had music playing from somewhere.

Ben walked up to where Jeff sat, and Jeff said, "Let's go in the back, where we can talk about this big favor you need from me." Ben followed him through the people dancing, and a blonde reached out to grab him as she said, "Why don't you dance with me?" She was looking him over as she pressed her tits on his arm.

Ben looked down at her as he untangled her hold on him and stepped back, "Sorry, I don't think so, sweetie." He kept walking even though he could hear her protesting. He didn't give a shit. He had no interest in any other woman, he knew whom he wanted, and no one else would do. When he made it to the booth, Jeff was sitting, and he slid into the opposite side.

"So, what's my big brother need from me?" Jeff's eyes looked bright and a little surprised.

"Okay, I'm going to give it to you straight. I need you to go on a double date tomorrow night."

"Why would you need me on a date with you and Liz?" Jeff looked confused.

"It won't be just Liz and I and a date of your choosing. Liz's agent appeared this morning, which means I can't spend any time with her, without her best friend tagging along. I thought you might be able to help me out." Ben was hopeful that Jeff didn't already have plans for the evening.

"Why, is she disgusting or something? You know, homely or obese?" Ben had to consider what Kat really looked like because he hadn't really paid her much attention besides the fact that he disliked her.

"No, why would you think that? I just need someone to keep her occupied, so I can spend time with Liz."

Jeff asked, "So what does she look like?" Ben noticed that he hadn't refused or said he was busy, so this was going to largely depend on how exceptional he makes Kat sound to Jeff.

"She's taller than Liz, and she has spiky blonde hair." Ben was trying to contemplate something else he could say about her that was enticing. "And she's thin and in great shape."

"What about her tits, big or small?" Jeff was pushing his luck, and he knew it.

"I don't know. I wasn't checking her out. Will you do it or not?" Ben was losing his patience with his brother.

"Where is this date going to take place? If it's dinner, you're paying." Ben took a deep breath because if he could pull this off, it was going to be a miracle.

"I made arrangements for the girls to meet us outside of The Surf Shack at nine o'clock tomorrow night." This was it, Jeff would either do it or renege.

"Okay, I'll do it, but you owe me big time." Jeff had no idea how much he was going to owe him once he actually met her and found out just how nasty and rude, she could be. Jeff just might have met his match, especially if this woman isn't taken by his charm. Ben smiled at the thought.

~ ~ ~ ~ ~ ~

When Liz walked through the door, Kat was still out on the deck and sipping her water when Liz went out to talk to her. This was going to be a fun conversation. "I have no idea where to start, what you did to Ben, or why you're here."

Kat sat up and looked at Liz, "I didn't mean to cause such a big deal. I guess I didn't realize he had such strong feelings for you, but the look on his face said it all. I'm sorry Liz, I know I overstepped, and I'm guessing the fact that he was someone you let in, you feel the same about him. I had to be sure he was the real deal."

Liz couldn't believe what she was hearing. This was the closest thing Liz had ever heard to Kat admitting she was wrong or giving an apology. She blew out a breath, "I don't want to talk about Ben at the moment. I want to know why you're here."

"When we talked, you seemed to be in distress. I just thought you needed me. We have always talked about everything, so I thought a girl's weekend was a good idea."

"And you wanted to check Ben out for yourself. What am I, too naïve, I can't make a decision for myself?" A small part of her wished for her quiet and simple life back.

"Liz, I have more faith in you than that, and you know it, but I know you better than anybody. You do things to please other people, and sometimes, you put your needs last. I know this because I've watched you do things, even when it was detrimental to yourself."

She knew Kat was talking about putting Paige first and putting her own life on hold. "Kat, that's what mothers do. They take care of their children. I did what I had to do."

"So, not going out on a date, was taking care of Paige? Liz, come on, I know at first you didn't want to bring anyone into Paige's life. But there are many women who lose their husbands and date or even remarry. You never did. Why do you think that is?"

Liz didn't have an answer. She didn't know why, it just was. "I don't know, Kat. Why don't you tell me because you seem to have all the answers."

"You told yourself it was for her for so long that you were afraid to step out of the safe life you made for the both of you. Losing Michael made you scared, to love, and to take any chances. How you let me in, a pushy, bossy, rude person, is beyond me." Kat reached out and took Liz's hand. "But you did, and I have been trying to get you out of your safe bubble for years. Now something has changed, you changed.

I'm not sure if it's about him or if it is because you finally wanted something for yourself bad enough to push out and take a chance. It could be that you don't have the excuse that it's best for Paige. She is an adult and making decisions for herself. In some ways, you have done a disservice to Paige by trying to protect her." Kat could see Liz was getting pissed off. Even though Liz didn't like what she said, she still needed to hear it. "What I'm saying is, after losing Michael, Paige was all you had, so you couldn't lose her too, and I totally understand why you did what you did, but now Paige has to decide what's best for her and what you taught her is to make only safe choices."

Liz tried to absorb Kat's words and, at the same time, wanted to pretend they weren't true. "You're crazy," Liz started to get up, and Kat held her hand tighter.

"I don't think you understand what I'm trying to say. I am not saying you are or have ever purposely done anything that wasn't in Paige's best interest. I'm not saying you were a bad mother, just safe, overprotective."

"Kat, you don't have children, so you don't understand what it's like. A child grows inside of you, and from the moment you know you're pregnant, you love this child. There isn't a parent on this earth that would ever allow anything to happen to their children." Tears stung her eyes, but she fought them back.

"I don't have to have a child to understand that, but you have to let your kids make mistakes to learn what's right and wrong for them. All parents hope the mistakes are small and not life-threatening, but this isn't just about you being overprotective with Paige. It's also about you being too protective of yourself. I never brought it up with you before because you weren't ready to hear it."

"If I recall, you have given me shit a time or two about not letting Paige do stuff." All of this was making her head spin, and what Kat was saying did hit a nerve. Did she always play it safe? Did she not take any chances? She became a writer. That was a big chance, but she knew that wasn't what Kat was talking about because what she was saying was about love and loss. Liz knew some of what she was saying was true. "Okay, my head is now spinning more than it was before. I don't agree with everything you said, but I get what you're saying. I need to change the subject. Ben has set up a double date for us tomorrow night. I need you to be on your best behavior toward Ben and whoever he's bringing as your date."

Kat just rolled her eyes and said, "Why do I have to go on this date anyway? I don't need Bubba to get me a date." Then she said in a little sex kitten voice, "I'm sure I could find my own beach bum around here, besides, how hard could it be to find a guy with a long, thick board I could ride?"

Now that made Liz roll her eyes, "Why do you have to be so crude? We're just going to a club to dance and have a few drinks."

"You are going to be like really drinking and not some wimpy glass of wine either, because if that's the case, then I'll have to go just to see that." She paused and then added, "I don't have to dance with the guy right because if he gets all handsy on me, I'll have to hurt him. Just so you know ahead of time." Liz hoped whoever Ben brought was big and tough because Kat would kick a wimpy guy's ass in a heartbeat, maybe a tough guy, too.

~ 18 ~

When Liz went to bed, she lay awake in the dark, thinking about the day's events. Ben told her he loved her, and she confessed her love for him, too. She picked up her phone, wanting to hear his voice, should she call him? Liz bit her lip as she contemplated it, and before she could change her mind, she dialed his number.

"Hello gorgeous," Ben's voice was warm and soothing to Liz's ears. All the comfort that surrounded Ben was in his voice. It made her feel an amazing amount of security.

"Were you sleeping? I shouldn't have called so late. I was just laying here in the dark, thinking about you." Liz could hear Ben moving around, as if he was sitting up in bed. She wished he were there with her, lying next to her, holding her, loving her.

"I was thinking about you, too, and you can call me whenever you want. I wasn't sleeping anyway; I'm used to having you beside me, so falling asleep has been tough." She knew just how he felt because she hadn't been sleeping well either without him.

"I know this bed is so freaking big, I get lost in it." Liz rolled to her side and tried to imagine he was there with her as she held tight to the phone like a lifeline.

"I wish I could help you with that. You don't know how badly." It destroyed her to hear the want and need in his voice.

"Ben I…" Liz wished she could invite him to, "come right now." She couldn't deny the strong pull she felt toward him and her own wants and needs.

"I know, but are you certain I can't just sneak in and spend the night and slip out in the morning?" Ben wanted to be there holding her, but this was the next best thing.

"I wish you could, too, because you can't understand just how having you hold me has made me feel." She wanted him to know even with all they'd been through in the last couple of days, he was very important to her.

"Liz, you don't realize how you've made me feel, and having you in my arms, holding you, is where I want to be." She knew how unfair all this was to Ben, and it killed her to know she was going to hurt him.

Liz needed to change the subject. "When I spoke to Kat tonight, she expressed her opinion on some things, and at the time, it just pissed me off, but I've been thinking.…" Liz went quiet a moment as she thought over whether or not she wanted to tell Ben what Kat had said.

"Ah shit, that doesn't sound good. What's Twiggy giving you a hard time about now?"

Liz let out a little laugh at the sound of Ben's voice and the way he was annoyed on her behalf. "No, she didn't give me a hard time. She just pointed out some things to me, and like I said at the time, I didn't want to listen." She hesitated, and Ben picked up on her reluctance.

"You want to talk about it? Because I have all night, I don't think I was going to get any sleep anyway." He was letting her know he was there for her.

"Well, she said lots of things, but at the heart of it, it was her pointing out that I have lived my life safe. That after Michael died, I didn't take any chances, and apparently, I did the same with Paige because I would never let her do anything where she could get hurt." It still made her a bit angry thinking about Kat's words.

"Liz, all parents try their best not to have anything happen to their kids," and she knew that.

"I know, I said the same thing, but did the fear of losing her, too, make me overprotective? What Kat was trying to say is that, I taught my daughter to do the same, not take any chances. In life, you have to take some chances to learn what's right and wrong and what you like and don't like."

"Okay, I can see what she was saying, but we live our lives by our own experiences. Like take me, for instance, I lost my dad, but I wasn't old enough to understand it totally. So, I didn't worry, I could lose, say, like my mom or one of my siblings. When we were kids, Jeff and I did all kinds of crazy stuff, and I never, not once, worried we'd get hurt. That's how kids are they don't think of safety."

"See Ben, that's just it, I only had Paige, and she only had me. I didn't let her do horseback riding lessons because she could get hurt. I didn't let her go off without me. I mean, I did let her go with friends, but I had to know the parents. I tried to protect her, to control what happened, so nothing bad could ever happen to her. I would have never survived it." The tears started rolling down Liz's face, and her heart just pounded thinking of anything happening to Paige.

Ben could hear the anguish in her voice, and it was tearing him apart. "I wish I was next to you, so I could hold you. I would pull you in so close, so you could feel the warmth of my body."

"Just having you to talk to helps," Liz said as she sniffed and wiped her tears on her sheet. "I lived my life safe, Ben and this is why Kat thinks I never let a man into my life. I can't lose what I didn't have to begin with, and in some ways, I know she's right, but it scares me, Ben. What if I put myself out there, take a chance, only to lose again?" She was opening up to him, trusting him.

Now it dawned on Ben what he was up against. She wouldn't allow herself emotional attachment because she couldn't handle a loss again. What he had to demonstrate to her was he wasn't going anywhere. How could he do that? He couldn't promise nothing would ever happen to him, so how could he get her past this? If anyone knew how to help Liz through this, it would be Twiggy. Ben was aware of what he would have to do, suck it up, and make nice with Kat. Because it looked like she would be the key to how to unlock Liz's fears. But Liz was taking chances. She let him in as much as she could.

"Ben, are you still there?" Liz asked because Ben had gotten so quiet, she thought they might have lost their connection.

"I'm here, I was just thinking. You've been here what a week and a half, almost two, right?"

"Yes," she answered him but didn't really know where he was going with this.

"I can't speak to your life before you came here, but what I've seen while you've been here, you are taking chances. Like you let me into your safe life for one. You didn't really know me from Adam, and yet it wasn't but three days before we were ripping each other's clothes off. I'd like to think it was that you just couldn't resist my massive manly magnetism." Ben could hear her laugh through the phone, and it made his heart ease a bit. "It must mean something, and two, you let me talk you into surfing." He wanted to show her she didn't always live life safe.

"This was Kat's point, I guess, that's why she brought it up now. She thinks I wasn't ready to hear it before, although she did try to get me to do all kinds of crazy things for years. She would try to set me up on blind dates and try to get me to go out to clubs with her. I would always tell her no, I couldn't go because I had Paige and no one to watch her." As Liz said the words aloud, she realized it was all true, everything Kat had said about how she hid behind Paige to stay in her safe life. Liz knew she wouldn't let anyone babysit her daughter because she felt they couldn't keep her safe. Wow, this was a huge epiphany. Now that she was aware of it, could she change? She had told Ben she couldn't stay because Paige needed her. Again, she was using her daughter as an excuse not to take a chance on Ben, love, and a life she couldn't control.

Ben pulled her out of her thoughts when he said, "Liz, you did what you had to do to survive and what you thought was best for your daughter. No one can fault you for that. You knew, even subconsciously, what you could handle and couldn't. Knowing why you did what you did, is a big part of understanding it, but what you might want to think about is where you want to go from here. What do you want to do about your life now?"

That was the million-dollar question. She had no clue, and if she didn't know, how could she drag Ben through it with her. "I have no clue, Ben. When I met you, it was the first time I wanted to be with a man. I didn't have Paige here, and I told myself, I could have a fling, and no one would know. Have sex and then go back to my safe life. I just didn't expect it to get so complicated. I could have fun, let myself go for once." Liz paused a moment to gather her thoughts. "When I left home to come here, I really thought I would be dreading this time being alone. I wasn't even sure I would stay the entire month. Sending

Paige off to school was going to be truly hard for me. To release control, I told myself over and over, this is where I wanted her to be. Going to college, I homeschooled her, too..."

Liz laughed again and didn't finish what she was going to say because this was another example of what gave her control over what happened to Paige and keeping her safe. "See, I just realized, by homeschooling her, I could make sure she was safe and with me. At the time, I told myself it was so I could write and go out of town and take her with me. I told myself, I could educate her better and prepare her for college. The only reason she's not here with me right now is that when this internship came up, she pleaded with me. Paige wanted to do this so badly, I didn't have the heart to say no, and a part of me said, she's eighteen and she could do it without my consent. I would have canceled this trip, but I had already paid for the house, and she wouldn't let me. She told me it was what I needed to do." Liz was crying again. "It took everything in me every time I let her go, and when she went on a vacation with one of her friends. I called to check on her. I had to tell myself repeatedly she would be okay. She had to be. Wow, I've never seen myself as so controlling before. I always saw myself as easygoing."

Liz was talking so much about how she had been existing when she thought Ben hadn't said a word, maybe he'd fallen asleep. Maybe she bored him into la-la land. She said his name just to reassure herself he was still with her.

"I'm here, Liz. I'm just listening to you. I've just recently been told that I'm very controlling." Ben snickered, as they both were control freaks.

"I'm so drained, Ben, all this is making my head spin, and I can't even think anymore." All these revelations were making her exhausted, and her mind couldn't deliberate anymore. She needed to relax her mind and soothe her body.

"Do you want me to let you go?" He didn't really want to hang up with her but knew she needed to rest.

"No," She didn't want to be alone right now, and having Ben to lean on was comforting and so foreign to her at the same time.

"Okay, how about I stay on the line until you fall asleep?" He couldn't be there for her physically, but he sure as hell could be there for her emotionally.

"How will you know?" She asked, as her voice got softer.

"I'll just listen to you breathe. I won't hang up. I got you, Liz. Just relax and let sleep take you. I'm here." She was letting him support her, and that alone was a big deal. Liz was allowing someone to comfort her.

Liz whispered, "Thank you," she felt so content and relaxed and closed her eyes.

"You got it, honey," The line went silent, all but her breathing. Ben closed his own eyes and let the sound of her soothe him. After a long time, he whispered, "I love you," he didn't expect a response.

"I know," she whispered back. That made Ben smile. She must have been listening to him breathing, too. Ben allowed sleep to overtake him, but he never disconnected with her.

The next morning, Liz woke to the aroma of something mouth-watering, and at first, she thought it was Ben making her one of his fantastic omelets. Then she knew, he wasn't here, Kat was. It all was coming back to her, the conversations she had had with Kat and Ben last night. How she had been living her life safe and trying to control things, so nothing life-threatening could happen ever again. And yet, she let Kat into her and Paige's life. Of all people, Kat liked to live on the edge and pushed the envelope whenever she could. Did she live through Kat, watching from the sidelines, just close enough not to get hurt but still make it so her life didn't seem boring? Liz heard a knock on her door, and Kat came in.

"You conscious, I made a peace offering, but it's a healthy one. I'm only willing to go so far." Kat sat on the edge of the bed, putting the tray on the nightstand.

"Peace bribe, huh? Now what have you done?" Liz moved up in the bed and looked at her.

"Well, I think I might have been a bit too aggressive yesterday. I wasn't trying to make you feel bad. I just wanted you to see…" Liz put up her hand to stop Kat.

"You were one hundred percent right." The look on Kat's face was priceless. "I have lived just the way you said, but I know at the time, I did the best I could. Around the time I lost Michael, we didn't have the greatest marriage, and I think we might have even ended up divorcing, but at the same time, I depended on him. I never had to worry about paying the bills or if we were going to eat. There was always a roof over my head, and after I couldn't conceive more children, our marriage changed. I realized I couldn't depend on him for emotional support. I shut down that part of me, and when he died, the safety net ripped away like a Band-Aid. It hurt, and I was furious with him for making me feel so out of control. Now, I had to worry about money, feeding my child, keeping the roof over both our heads. So, when I finally regained control over our lives, I never wanted to feel like that again."

Kat climbed up next to her and took her hand. "I'm sorry. I know that had to be a very hard time."

"You don't need to be because you were right. I needed to hear it, but when you said those things, I just shut down. I guess it's how I protect myself from getting hurt, and as far as Paige is concerned, I couldn't lose her, so I tried to control what happened in her life to keep her safe. She was all I had."

"Liz, you have come a long way, and this trip has been the best thing for you. You needed to be away from Paige, and I'm sure she needed it, too. The fact you let her do this, while you came here was remarkable. I never thought you would leave and travel all the way across the country and let her do her own thing."

"Kat, it was something she wanted, and she wouldn't let me back out. It was her, not me. In some ways, she knew what we both needed." Liz felt calmer this morning about what was going on in her life, and she knew Ben had a lot to do with that.

Kat asked, "Now, what are you going to do?" Liz just shook her head.

"I have no clue, and as for Ben, I don't need any pressure. Okay? I need to try to figure things out on my own. I have to determine if I can open up and let someone in to love me."

~ ~ ~ ~ ~ ~

It was Saturday morning, so Ben was in his office early because he knew he would be working all day. His chances of seeing Liz today were slim and none, and Slim left town. He knew it would be important to keep busy until they closed because he would be seeing her tonight. Ben could hold her then, and he leaned back in his chair, thinking about how the night might go. It put a huge smile on his face when he thought of the situation concerning Kat and Jeff. That's going to be very entertaining to watch. In a way, he wanted to see how Jeff would survive her. The way Kat might rip Jeff a new one if she didn't like him, and from what he saw of her, she didn't like anybody. Well, that wasn't entirely true because she loved and cared for Liz. It would be an interesting evening, to say the least, but at some point, he was going to need to have a conversation with Kat about Liz.

Ben went back to looking over spreadsheets and taking care of his emails. When his thoughts returned to Liz, he tried to push them away. His phone rang, and right away, he hoped it was Liz. He looked at the caller ID, and relief filled him. Ben felt the joy come over him right away. "Hi there," he said in a happy tone.

"Hi, are you working?" She sounded so much better today, and he wondered if she slept well last night.

"I'm trying, but this gorgeous redhead won't get out of my head." He liked to tease her, and the reward was her saying his name with a warning tone to her voice. "I know, but it's true. I just can't seem to help myself," and he truly couldn't, she was always there in his thoughts.

Liz went on and ignored what he said. "We still on for tonight, and who'd you bribe to be Kat's date?" She heard Ben's loud laughter, and it took him a minute to stop and answer her.

"That's so funny, Liz, oh God," he said as he caught his breath. "I didn't bribe anybody, but I did get some unsuspecting soul, a well-deserving guy of Kat, just the same." If he wasn't able to touch Liz tonight, at least Kat and Jeff would entertain him.

"What's that supposed to mean?" Ben thought, *wait until he told her who Kat's date was.*

"It's going to be funny to watch, the main event of the evening," he paused to add to the anticipation. "The Survival of the Fittest," Ben paused again, "Kat vs. Jeff."

"Oh my God, you asked Jeff. Kat eats guys like him for a snack," and that was going to be the best part of the evening.

"I know, why do you think this is going to be so much fun to watch? Jeff hasn't met a woman he couldn't totally woo, and Kat, well, you are already aware of how she's going to react to him."

"Ben Jacobs, I can't believe you would do such a horrible thing to your own brother."

"You can't tell me it's not going to be entertaining, and it will definitely mean she won't be giving me a hard time."

"Oh, now I see your motive, self-preservation." She laughed and thought how Kat was going to react to Jeff and whether she would need to be apologizing to Jeff in the morning for her behavior.

"You bet your cute little ass I did." He didn't want to spend all night fending off Kat. He would much rather be a spectator than a participant in the evening events.

"I'll see you tonight. Any suggestion on what to wear?" He liked that she was asking his advice.

"I could say that black outfit you had on the other night, but that would have to be under your clothes. So that I could undress you after we dance, and I can rub my dick on your ass, until you want me as bad as I want you." He heard her gasp, and he smiled because he knew her face was red.

"Ben," she said in a huff. "Never mind, I'll figure it out." She hung up.

Ben was ready for tonight to be here, and now all that teasing about rubbing his dick on her made him hard. Even though his mind knew he wouldn't have her, his body didn't want to acknowledge it. He might need to go upstairs and take care of a few things. He tried forgetting it, and it wasn't easy. A few hours later, Jeff knocked on his doorframe. Ben said, "What's up?"

"I was looking over the spreadsheets, and I think I have the order for next month, but I wanted you to look it over." Ben took the papers from him and went line by line with Jeff, and Ben was impressed by how Jeff did everything right.

"Jeff, you did a great job here. I didn't think you'd catch on so quickly." Ben put the paperwork on his desk.

"You showed me exactly how Ben. I just followed your instructions. It's not hard when somebody shows you correctly how to get it done. You had to figure this out on your own, and I bet you're the one who made up this system to keep track of what we sold." Jeff sat and leaned on Ben's desk.

Ben had converted the store from keeping paper records to putting everything on computers. He invested in cash registers that barcode-scanned items, so there was a record of every item they sold. The store had transformed with the advances since he took it over. Now how well would Jeff do when he had to take responsibility for the store? That thought hit Ben hard, and he had to shake his head to clear it.

"I still think you did really well here for your first time. We can review some of the new merchandise that I think we could sell."

"There's a new line of boards I found, and I wanted to discuss it with you. They sound good, but I'm not sure how the company works. You know whether they make you buy into being a dealer or if they work on commission. I'm still researching how they work all that."

"We could look into it if you think you could sell the boards. What makes them different from what we sell now?" Ben liked that Jeff was taking the initiative to discover new products.

Ben listened to Jeff's opinions about not only the new boards but also other products. He had some great new ideas about how to change some of the store displays. As Ben listened to Jeff's ideas, he realized that by not making Jeff take on more responsibility earlier, it was not only a disservice to him but to the whole store.

That evening, Liz and Kat were waiting outside the club. This was making Liz very nervous because this wasn't her scene, but Kat appeared not bothered by all the people. She was just swaying to the music they could hear coming from inside when Liz spotted Ben walking toward them, and it took everything in her not to run to him. She could do this, she told herself over, and over again.

They were about ten feet away when Kat spotted them, and she stopped dancing. "Look what the dog dragged in." She stepped up to Ben and gave him a glance up and down.

"Kat, remember what I said, be nice." Liz had just finished what she was saying when Ben was right in front of her, and she smiled.

Kat said, "Hey Bubba, who's your friend?" Liz thought I'm going to murder her.

Ben just smiled at her over Liz's head, "Well, lookie here, you brought Twiggy with you. You'd bring her muzzle, so she doesn't maul someone?" Ben shot back, and Liz stepped back and looked up into Ben's face. She couldn't believe this was her Ben.

"Touché, I like that one because you never know, do you?" Kat liked that Ben was going to stand up to her and not let her intimidate him because he had to prove he cared for Liz.

Jeff had a confused look as he watched his brother, who he had never seen insult a woman before, and a woman who looked like she took no prisoners. This was going to be his date, well, it was going to be one fun night. He did notice how hot she was, and maybe it would get interesting.

"Okay, you two, that's enough." Liz pointed her finger at Kat first, then at Ben. She looked back and forth between them, she felt like a referee. Then she went on to introduce Jeff. "Kat, this is Ben's brother, Jeff, and Jeff this is my BEST friend on her BEST behavior Kat."

Kat stepped closer to Ben and said, "Your brother, huh, that's the best you could do?" Ben just smiled down at her, she had heels on, but Ben was still taller.

"Yeah, at such short notice, they weren't letting any inmates out of the prisons today. Maybe next time," he threw the jab right back without missing a beat.

Kat just smiled at Ben because she could do this all night, but then she caught sight of Liz giving her an unhappy look. So, she glanced in this guy's direction and said, "Nice to meet you." As nice as she could and gave Liz a look as if to say, "look, I'm playing nice."

"Let's go inside," Ben said as he took Liz's hand, leading them past the line that was waiting.

The guy at the door just nodded and stamped their hands. Jeff put his hand out so Kat could go first, and she looked at his outreached hand and rolled her eyes. Once they were inside, Jeff went to the bar to talk to someone, and Ben found a table. Jeff was back a minute later and relaxed in the empty chair next to Kat, she just scrutinized him and sent the vibe of, don't even consider touching her. Jeff pushed his chair a bit closer just to see what she would do.

The music was so deafening you couldn't really talk, so Ben squeezed Liz's hand and pulled her from the table. He wanted to get his hands on her, and she went willingly but turned and pointed her finger at Kat. Once Ben pulled Liz far enough from the table, he leaned down, so his mouth was right next to her ear and said, "I've missed you." Ben could feel the shiver run through her body, and his dick jumped.

She turned her head, so they were face to face, and she mouthed, "me too," then leaned in and kissed him. His body reacted to her being so close he pressed his body up against hers. Ben walked her backwards until she knocked into the wall. Ben's body prevented anyone from seeing her. It wasn't hard because she was so small, he spread his arms above her head, and she just disappeared. He knew how she felt about PDA, but he needed to have some part of her. She was rubbing her body against his, so he knew she needed it, too. Ben slid his thigh between her legs, and now she was riding it. Ben broke the kiss, kissed down her neck to her ear, and asked, "Do you need to come?" He bit her collarbone and then swiped his tongue over the sting, and he knew she was aroused.

Ben moved his hand between them and was now stroking his thumb over her jean-covered heat. He pulled back just enough to appreciate her face as the pleasure of what he was doing came over her expression, and she came. He felt her shuttering against him, and he held her tight as he continued flicking his finger back and forth over her. Ben had to muster all the control he had not to press his dick on her because he was so close himself.

When she reopened her eyes, he could see right away, she was embarrassed, and he couldn't let that happen. "No one could see you. I made sure." Ben pulled her away from the wall and tucked her under his arm, and they moved back toward the table.

When they reached the table, they could see there was something currently happening between Jeff and Kat. The main event was underway as Ben and Liz sat down to watch. Ben noticed right away there were definitely some strong sparks and some sexual tension in and around them. Oh yeah, his brother was in for it now because they were yelling at each other.

"I don't need you to ask me to dance," Kat gave him a dirty look as she yelled over the music.

"I was just trying to be polite, that's all." Jeff shot back as he leaned into her so she could hear.

"If I want to dance, I'll dance." Kat gave him a disgusted look.

Ben just had the biggest smile on his face because he was with Liz, and he was watching his brother fight for his life, and Kat was leaving him alone. This was just a great night all the way around for him. The only way it could be better was if he took Liz home and spent the night.

"I just didn't want you to feel like a flat-tire," Jeff yelled back.

"You mean a third wheel," then she realized that wasn't what he meant at all. It was a metaphor because he was saying that her personality was flat and unpleasant. Well, he hadn't seen anything yet if he thought she was being hostile toward him, not that she cared what he thought of her.

"Ya know, I can dance with any woman I want to in this place?" Jeff had a smug look on his face. He didn't know why he wanted her to know that fact, and he knew he was being arrogant.

"Yeah, well, all you have to do is ask. I can dance with anyone in here, and I don't have to do the asking." She was as smug as he was, and a guy like him wasn't going to shake her self-confidence.

"Have at it lady, don't let me stop you." He moved his hand to say she was free to do what she wanted. This woman was so infuriating. She could rub a smooth edge rough. Jeff could feel her getting under his skin. He couldn't allow her to get the best of him, so he rested his arm on the back of her chair. He could see how having his arm there was making her feel uncomfortable, and that made him happy.

Liz looked up at Ben and then back to Kat and Jeff. This was going to get ugly fast, and she didn't like it. "Ben, we should interfere because this is going to get dangerous." She looked very concerned.

Ben leaned in and spoke in her ear, "Not a chance." He was enjoying the hell out of himself.

"Ben, we have to. They're going to kill each other." Liz had a worried expression on her face.

Ben smoothed the lines wrinkling on her forehead with his finger. "It will be alright. I won't let anyone get hurt too badly," he said with a sinister smile.

Kat reclined in her chair, so she was now touching his arm. She wouldn't allow him to push her emotional buttons because this guy was irritating the hell out of her. "I need a drink. They do serve alcohol in this place, right?" She started to get up, and Jeff put a hand on her to stop her and smiled.

"What can I get you?" He asked, knowing it was going to get her even more pissed at him.

"I'll get my own damn drink." She pulled away and got up and walked to the bar. It was crowded, this was going to take forever, and she really needed a drink.

Jeff got up also and asked Liz, "What does she drink?" He didn't know why he even considered going out of his way for a woman that was such a bitch.

"She likes apple martinis," and watched him walk away. Ben and Liz turned in their seats to see what was going to happen next. This confrontation was a battle of wills, and you couldn't look away. It was like driving by a seriously bad accident and afraid of what you might see, but you still couldn't help looking anyway.

Jeff strolled up to the side of the bar and got the bartender's attention, and he came right over.

"Hey Jeff, what can I get you?" The guy was a good friend of his.

"I need an apple martini and a beer." He glanced over to make sure Kat was still waiting in line to be served.

She looked in his direction and then turned away as the bartender came back with his drinks. He paid and headed straight for her. He was not going to allow her to have the last word. Jeff stood right behind her, and he leaned into her ear and said, "We could fight each other if that's what you want, or we could dance and have a drink." He reached around her arm and positioned the drink in front of her. She took it, and he took that as a good sign.

Kat turned slowly and was now face to face with him. Her breath hitched when she said, "I told you I could get my own drink." Now that she was so close, she caught sight of the golden flakes in his brown eyes. He was taller than she was, and she was wearing her highest heels which usually made her tower over men. She wanted to throw the drink right in his face for making her notice him, but she needed to consume the alcoholic beverage more than it would have satisfied her to watch it run down his face. Then he smiled, and her heart did a thud. *What the hell?* Kat's breath hitched, and she stepped back, so she could bring her much-desired drink to her lips. The drink was so satisfying. She downed half of it and licked her lips to get every drop as she closed her eyes to enjoy it.

He was so close to her, he could smell her and watched as she brought her drink to her lips. Something down south stirred when her tongue came out and swiped her lips. He watched as her blue eyes closed, and she dragged in a ragged breath. She was hot as hell when she was silent. If he could just Duct tape her mouth shut, then her eyes reopened, and she was now looking straight at him like he was disgusting and revolting. He took a step back.

She closed the space between them. "Don't think just because you bought me the best martini I have ever had, that I owe you, because like I told you before, when and if I want to dance, I'll find my own partner. You got it?" She was so close. She could kiss him. Why did her mind go there?

Jeff could feel her breath on him as she spoke. He leaned in just a bit closer, so their lip was just an inch away. "So, you've picked fighting, fine by me." Then turned and walked away from her and went back to the table and sat down.

Kat had to get herself under control, she took another sip of her drink and walked away from the bar, but she didn't want to return to the table, so she headed to the lady's room. That's where Liz found her, sitting on the counter with her back against the mirror, sipping her drink.

"Hiding out in here?" Liz walked up to her checking her makeup in the mirror.

"Hiding from whom? Certainly not from Bubba's brother. I just didn't want to disfigure him. I thought you might seriously frown upon that."

"Would you stop calling Ben Bubba? You know it just annoys the hell out of me, and what's up with you and Jeff?" Liz realized there was something a little off with Kat. She seemed flustered and off her game.

"Okay fine, but he's calling me Twiggy, even though I do like that he's attempting to fight back. It shows he has some balls. No match for me, just sayin,' at least he's trying." She hopped down from the counter and considered her own reflection in the mirror.

"You guys need to stop, you and Ben, and you and Jeff. This was supposed to be a fun night, and you have my stomach all in knots," she turned to face Kat.

"Sorry, I didn't mean for you to get in the middle, but guys like Jeff just piss me off," she took another sip of her martini.

"What kind of guy, ones that are trying to be pleasant to you. I think you have a thing for him, and that's why he's pissing you off, because if you didn't care, it wouldn't be getting under your skin." Liz watched Kat's reaction, and she tried to conceal her irritation and annoyance.

"Don't try to shrink me, Liz. You're not any good at it. I just don't like it when guys think they have the upper hand. They think by smiling at a woman, it'll make them fall under their spell."

"Jeff does have a great smile." Kat just made a noise and rolled her eyes. Liz thought, *yep, there was definitely something there.*

Back at the table, Ben was watching Jeff. He had his arms folded over his chest and could see that Jeff was deep in thought. Ben wondered if something more was happening between Jeff and Kat. Jeff looked over at him and asked, "What?"

"Nothing. I'm just waiting for Liz to come back." Ben turned toward the bathrooms, not looking at Jeff, and smiled.

Jeff asked, "Did she go after Kat? I guess I scared her," he smiled as the thought brought him delight.

"Not likely. I think it takes someone bigger and badder than you to scare Twiggy." Ben knew better than to think anyone could scare Kat.

"Why do you keep calling her that?" Jeff asked as he was now glancing toward the restrooms.

"You wouldn't believe what she did to me yesterday when I went to see Liz. When I couldn't get in contact with her all day, I had a horrible feeling, and when she opened the door, I just knew Liz was gone. I asked where Liz was, and she told me she had left. She was trying to guard the door, so I couldn't check for myself. That bitch had my heart in my damn shoes." Just the thought shook him, and it wasn't anything he wanted to relive.

Jeff had to laugh at Ben's expression. "Why did she tell you that?"

"Because, I told you she's a bitch that enjoys watching other people suffer. I still can't see how sweet Liz ever managed to hook up with her. She was testing me, to see if I cared for Liz, and from what Liz told me about her, when Kat cares for someone, she can be very protective. I know Liz loves her, and her daughter even calls her aunt. Unfortunately, it means for me that I have to get on the good side of the wench, if I can find the good side." He still needed to talk to Kat about Liz.

"Well, good luck with that. I'm just glad all I have to do is make it through tonight. Then I don't have to deal with her anymore."

"Finally, a woman you can't woo. I see how it is, you don't want to bring down your average." Ben liked the look his brother shot him.

"If I wanted to woo her, I could, but I don't. She is so not my type," but she seemed to do something to him, well, at least to his dick.

"Yeah, that's because she has your number, and she's not impressed with your techniques." Ben had a smug look on his face, and he appreciated his brother's situation.

"You're enjoying this, aren't you? This is why you asked me to do this for you, isn't it?" Ben could see Jeff was figuring out why he was here, and he was having a great time watching it going down.

"And I knew, if she was giving you a hard time, she'd be leaving me alone. So, you see, it's a win-win situation for me." Ben could see Liz and Kat were on their way back to the table.

The ladies came back, and Liz took Ben's hand and said, "I want to see those moves you said you have." She pulled him from his chair.

He smiled down at his brother as they left Jeff and Kat at the table alone. Liz led him out onto the dance floor, he slid his hands around her, and he bent his knees to line up their bodies. The music was loud and fast. Ben and Liz danced to a rhythm all their own while everyone else around them danced to the music. Ben's hands started to move down over her ass, and he pulled her in close. Her arms were around his neck, as she played with his hair. Ben leaned down and kissed her. He ran his tongue over her bottom lip, and she opened for him. Liz pressed her chest against him, and he almost lost his mind. His body was electrically charged, and he wanted her. Now her hands were on his face, her thumbs rubbing back and forth over his jaw. Ben broke the kiss and moved to her ear.

"Liz," his voice strained. "I want you so badly. I feel like if I don't have you, I'm going to explode." He was so hard, and the jeans he decided to wear didn't leave any room for his hard-on.

Jeff and Kat sat at the table without talking, but they both watched Ben and Liz on the dance floor. This was the first time Jeff saw them together like this, and he could see how his brother was getting hot under the collar. As a matter of fact, it was hot to watch. It was like watching live porn with all your clothes still on. The chemistry between them was undeniable. Jeff could feel his pants get a little tight, and he knew the way they moved together shouldn't be turning him on. A little pang of jealousy hit him because he wanted that. He wanted to feel what Ben was feeling for Liz. She was good for him. Jeff was pulled literally from his thoughts and his chair. When he realized what was happening, Kat had his shirt clustered in her hand and dragged him toward the dance floor, so he allowed her to lead the way. Jeff thought, *this should be interesting.*

Once they were on the dance floor, she rotated to face him. They were again face-to-face, and she said, "Don't get all cocky on me. I just wanted to dance, and don't think you're going to place your hands all over me." Jeff just smiled because when she made the statement for him not to go all cocky on her, an image came to mind, a very indecent image of him fucking her hard against the wall. Jeff blinked when she moved her hand back and forth in front of his face. "That's exactly what I'm talking about. Get that expression off your face." Jeff held up his hands as to say, "Easy does it."

"I'll follow your lead, and I won't touch you, I promise." She started dancing, and he just watched her as her hips moved, swaying back and forth to the music as she turned away from him. He was now checking out her ass, and Kat was a great dancer. Her ass had just the right amount of jiggle to it. As she moved, Jeff noticed the muscle tone in her arms. When she turned back around to face him, she realized he wasn't dancing but staring at her. He let his eyes move down over her body and then back up. *Oh yeah, she had a great body.*

"What are you doing?" She asked as she still moved her hips.

"I'm watching you," he answered. His body was stimulated and aroused by her.

"I see that, why?" She stopped dancing and stepped closer.

"I was seeing how you move, so I could move with you without touching you." He stepped right up to her body but didn't touch her. Jeff started to move with her, and he was anticipating her every move. He was so close you might not be able to slide a piece of paper between them. Jeff could smell her, feel her heat. He could tell she was trying to get him to touch her. She would move and change direction just to make him move to not touch her. It was a dance of wills, who was going to get the better of the other. Then, she reached out and grabbed hold of his shirt again, and he held up his hands again, but they were so close he had to hold his breath.

"I know what you're doing. You think I'm going to touch you and open the door." She was right in his face.

Jeff just looked down at where she had his shirt and said, "I wasn't touching you, but I think you wanted me to." They had been evading the fact that they both wanted to be touching each other. So, Jeff took a chance, put his hand on her hips, and pulled her into him. The look on her face made him smile, and he started moving again. She still had an angry look on her face, but she started dancing again, too. He leaned his face into the side of hers so he could close in on her ear. "Now, isn't this better?" She just ignored him, but he felt the shiver that ran through her body, and it gave Jeff some satisfaction to know he softened her up just a bit. They moved with each other like that for some time.

Ben pulled Liz from the dance floor because if he stayed any longer, he would blow in his jeans. He directed her out the side exit, and when the music wasn't so loud, she asked him where they were going, but he didn't answer her. Once they moved through the alley, Ben turned to face her. "I had to get out of there, Liz. I have to know what you're wanting right now." She just looked up at him with confusion on her face. He started again, "I need to know... shit, this isn't coming out right." He pulled her in close, "I need you, and I want to take you to my place, but if it's not what you want, I have to know." Liz looked down the alley where they just came from and back to him. He could see her debating on what she should do. "Liz, look at me, what do you want? Not anyone else. Jeff will keep her busy because I have to know." Ben could hear his own heart beating in his ears as he waited for her answer.

"Ben, I can't just leave Kat." The look of disappointment spread over his face, and then he dropped his head into his hands. She knew he was frustrated by the way his breathing accelerated. Ben leaned against the building as he slid down, so he was almost sitting on the ground and put his head down. "Ben, I'm sorry." She said it knowing her apology didn't comfort him.

"Give me a minute," he said in a strained voice.

Liz crouched down in front of him, running her hands across his shoulders and back, as she heard him say, "I'm such a fucking idiot, God, I can't even control myself," he said with a little laugh.

"What do you mean? You are no such thing," she sat next to him.

"I had a plan, and the minute I get close to you, I forget everything." He was running his fingers through his hair.

"What kind of plan? What are you talking about?" She didn't understand what he was trying to say.

He laughed again, "I wasn't going to have sex with you." He heard her gasp and turned to face her. "What I meant was to show you we have more than sex. I want to show you that you mean more to me, but once our bodies started rubbing all up on each other, the blood goes south, and I can't think straight because I wanted to take you to my place and rip your clothes off. I'm so sorry Liz, you just drive me crazy," he sounded truly pained.

Now it was her turn to laugh. "You know, I don't think you're looking at this the right way."

"Okay, and what way should I be looking at it?" He faced her.

"Well, when we entered the club, you did something for me, and you got nothing. We danced, and you still didn't have any release. So, if you're looking at it correctly, there's not a man on earth that could withstand that without going a whole lot of crazy. I know you said no sex right now, so does that mean all sex or just intercourse. Because if no sex at all was what you were going for, then you broke your own rule within ten minutes of going into the club. So, here's how I see it, no intercourse is still on the table, but you got me off, so it's only fair that I take care of your little problem." It was not like her, but she considered taking care of Ben in the alley.

Ben laughed because he liked the way she was thinking. "Just so you know, never use the word little when referring to my dick, and I'm good. Sitting here talking, I've gotten myself under control." Liz pouted when Ben kissed her and pulled her off the ground. "I think we need to go back inside. Let's hope Kat hasn't skinned Jeff yet, because I don't want to miss anything."

Look for Part Two!

Find me on the Web.

Facebook ♥ Trish Collins – Author

Instagram ♥ trish_collins_author

X ♥ Trish Collins – Author @collins_author

Website ♥ https://TrishCollinsAuthor.net

Email ♥ TrishCollins.Author@gmail.com

Facebook Store ♥ https://www.facebook.com/TrishCollinsAuthor/shop

♥ Amazon.com/Trish Collins

www.ingramcontent.com/pod-product-compliance
Lightning Source LLC
Chambersburg PA
CBHW060349260626
47160CB00006B/2247